**Clare Connelly** ......... nong a family of avid ............ ... ... her childhood up a tree, Mills & Boon book in hand. She is married to her own real-life hero in a bungalow near the sea with their two children. She is frequently found staring into space – a surefire sign she is in the world of her characters. Writing for Mills & Boon Modern is a long-held dream. Clare can be contacted via clareconnelly.com or on her Facebook page.

**Faye Avalon** lives in the UK with her super-ace husband and one beloved, ridiculously spoiled Golden Retriever. She worked as cabin crew, detoured into property development, public relations, court reporting, and education before finally finding her passion: writing steamy romance. Between writing, practising yoga, and keeping the keyboard free of dog hair, Faye can be found checking out Pinterest for hero inspiration. Visit her at fayeavalon.com

**Jennie Lucas'** parents owned a bookstore and she grew up surrounded by books, dreaming about faraway lands. At twenty-two she met her future husband and after their marriage, she graduated from university with a degree in English. She started writing books a year later. Jennie won the Romance Writers of America's Golden Heart contest in 2005 and hasn't looked back since. Visit Jennie's website at: jennielucas.com

# A Dark Romance Series

June 2025
**Veil of Deception**

August 2025
**Surrendered to Him**

July 2025
**Thorns of Revenge**

September 2025
**Bound by Vows**

# VEIL OF DECEPTION:

## A Dark Romance Series

CLARE CONNELLY

FAYE AVALON

JENNIE LUCAS

MILLS & BOON

First Published in Great Britain 2025
by Mills & Boon, an imprint of HarperCollins*Publishers* Ltd
1 London Bridge Street, London, SE1 9GF

www.harpercollins.co.uk

HarperCollins*Publishers*
Macken House, 39/40 Mayor Street Upper,
Dublin 1, D01 C9W8, Ireland

ISBN: 978-0-263-41739-5

MIX
Paper | Supporting
responsible forestry
FSC
www.fsc.org
FSC™ C007454

# THEIR IMPOSSIBLE DESERT MATCH

**CLARE CONNELLY**

# PROLOGUE

*Nineteen years ago. The Royal Palace of Ishkana,
on the edge of the Al'amanï ranges.*

'TELL ME IMMEDIATELY.' It didn't matter to His Royal Highness Prince Amir Haddad that he was just twelve and the advisors in his bedroom were all at least three times that in age. From birth he had been raised to know his place in the kingdom, the duty that would one day be his.

Having six men sweep into his private quarters at four in the morning might have caused a ripple of anxiety deep in his gut, but he revealed nothing. His dark eyes fixed on advisor Ahmed, one of his father's most trusted servants, and he waited quietly, with an unintended look of steel in his eyes.

Ahmed took a step forward, deeper into Amir's bedroom. Ancient tapestries adorned the walls and a blade of moonlight caught one, drawing Amir's attention for a moment to the silver and blue threads that formed an image of the country's ancient western aqueducts. He felt that he should stand up, face whatever was coming with his eyes open, and so he did, pushing back sheets made of the finest linen, pressing his feet to the mosaics—gold and blue and green, they swirled like water and flame beneath him. At twelve, he was almost as tall as any of the men present.

'Tell me,' he repeated, the quality of steel shifting from his eyes to his voice.

Ahmed nodded slowly, swallowing so his Adam's apple shifted visibly. 'There was an attack, Your Highness.'

Amir waited.

'Your parents' convoy was targeted.'

Amir's only response was to straighten his spine; he continued to stare at Ahmed, his young face symmetrical and intent. Inside, his stomach was in knots and ice was flooding his veins.

'They were hurt?'

He heard one of the other servants groan, but he didn't take his eyes off Ahmed. With Ahmed he felt a degree of comfort; he trusted him.

'Yes. They were badly hurt.' Ahmed cleared his throat, his gentle features showing anguish. He put a hand on Amir's shoulder—a contact that was unprecedented. 'Amir, they were killed.'

The words were delivered with compassion and a pain all of his own—Ahmed had served Amir's father for a very long time, since he himself was a boy. The pain he felt must have run deep.

Amir nodded, understanding, knowing he would need to deal with his grief later, when he was alone. Only then he would allow his pain to run through his body, felling him to his knees for what he had lost. He wouldn't mourn publicly; that was not his way, and it was not what his country required of him. How long had that message been instilled in his heart? He was now his country's King, his people's servant.

'By whom?'

One of the other servants stood forward. Amir recognised the military medals he wore across the breast of his white uniform. He had a thick moustache, black and long. 'A band of renegades from Taquul.'

Amir's eyes closed for a moment. The country directly to the east, with whom Ishkana had been embroiled in bitter unrest for over a century. How many lives had been lost because of it? And now his parents were gone.

He, Amir, was Sheikh of Ishkana.

'A band of renegades,' Ahmed continued gently, 'led by His Highness Johar Qadir.'

Amir dug his hands into his hips, rocked on his heels, and nodded slowly. The King of Taquul's brother was a well-documented troublemaker. It was known that he sympathised with the people who inhabited the borders of their two lands, a people who had benefited for years from the ongoing conflict and wanted it to continue, at all costs. But this?

This was a step further. This was a new twist in the century-old war, one that was unforgivable. And for as long as he lived, Amir would make the Qadirs pay. He hated them with a vengeance that nothing—and no one—could ever quell.

# CHAPTER ONE

Princess Johara Qadir cut through the room with an innate elegance, pleased the evening was a masquerade for the anonymity it afforded her. The delicately constructed mask she'd been given to wear was made of onyx and pearl, with diamonds around the eyes and ostrich feathers on one side, which rose at least two feet above her head. The mask concealed everything but her eyes and lips, meaning she could pass unrecognised on this evening to all but those who knew her very, very well and could recognise the sparkle that lit the depths of her golden brown eyes.

*'You have no choice, Johara. The whole family must appear to be united behind this decision. For our people...'*

Yes, for their people. The prospect of peace with neighbouring Ishkana meant too much, would save lives, improve safety and lifestyle—of course she must support her brother's decision to enter a treaty with the neighbouring Sheikh.

It wasn't that that bothered her.

It was being summoned to return to the kingdom—for good. To leave behind her life in New York, the important work she was doing to support childhood literacy; it was leaving behind the identity she'd carved out for herself there. And for what? To come home to Taquul where her future was all mapped out for her? A ceremonial title and marriage to the man her brother deemed most suitable,

Paris Alkad'r? A role in this kingdom as ornamental but useless and ineffective?

It felt like a form of suffocation to even contemplate that kind of life and yet she understood her over-protective brother's thinking. He'd seen the way she'd been after Matthew—the American she'd fallen in love with and who had broken her heart. The newspaper articles had been relentless, the tabloids delighting in her pain. Malik wanted to spare her that—but an arranged marriage was about ten steps too far. Besides, the kind of marriage he and Paris envisaged—a political alliance—was the last thing she wanted!

A spirit of rebellion fired inside her.

Her brother was the Sheikh. He was older, true, but, more importantly, he had been raised to rule a country. Johara's importance—compared to his—had never been considered as particularly great—at least, not by their parents. Even Malik seemed, at times, to forget that she was a person with her own free will, simply snapping his fingers and expecting her to jump. Her closest friend in New York had commiserated and said that it was the same with her and her older sister—'older siblings are always bossy as hell'—but Johara doubted anyone could match the arrogance of Malik. She adored him, but that didn't mean she wasn't capable of feeling enraged by his choices, at times.

She expelled a sigh, took a glass of champagne from a passing waitress and had a small sip, then replaced it on another waitress's tray. Every detail of the party was exquisite. The National Ballet were serving as wait staff, each ballerina dressed in a pale pink and silver tutu, dancing as they moved through the crowd, mesmerising, beautiful, enchanting. The enormous marble hall had been opened for the occasion—showcasing the wealth and ancient prestige of the country, the windows displaying views of the desert in one direction and the Al'amanï ranges in the other. Large white marble steps led to an enormous lagoon; man-made, centuries ago, it had a free-form shape and was lit with small fires all around it. Glass had been carefully laid over the edges, allowing guests to hover over the water. Gymnasts danced in the water, their synchronised routines drawing gasps from those who stood outside. Fairy lights were strung overhead, casting a beautiful, 'midsummer night's dream' feeling.

Nothing had been missed.

Another sigh escaped Johara's lips. In New York, she had still been a princess, and the trappings of home had, of course, followed her. She'd had bodyguards who accom-panied her discreetly wherever she went, she'd stayed at a royal apartment, and from time to time had taken part in official functions. However, she had been, by and large, free to live her own life.

Could she really give that up to come home and be, simply, ornamental? What about her burning desire to be of use?

Her eyes flicked across the room. Dignitaries from all corners of the globe had travelled to Taquul for this mo-mentous occasion—an occasion most said would never happen. Peace between Ishkana and Taquul was almost an oxymoron, despite the fact the war had raged for so long that it had become a habit rather than anything else. A foreign diplomat was strutting proudly, evidently con-gratulating himself on bringing about this tentative peace accord. Johara's lips twisted into an enigmatic smile. Little did the diplomat know, no one could force her brother into anything that was not his desire.

He wanted this peace. He knew it was time. The ancient enmity had been a part of their life for generations, but it didn't serve the people. The hatred was dangerous and it was purposeless. How many more people had to die?

Perhaps in the beginning it served its purpose. The landscapes of Ishkana and Taquul were inhospitable. True, there was beauty and there was plenty in parts, but not enough, and the regions that had been in dispute a hundred years ago were those most plentiful with water, most arable and productive. Though a property accord had been reached, the war had continued and the accord had always seemed dangerously close to falling through. Add to that a group of tribes in the mountains who wanted independence from both countries, who worked to ensure the mistrust and violence continued, and Johara could only feel surprise that this peace had finally been wrought. Detailed negotiations between both countries and an agreement to impose strict laws on both sides of the mountains had led to this historic, hopeful event.

She hoped, more than anything, the peace would last.

'You are bored.' A voice cut through her thoughts, drawing her gaze sideways. A man had moved to stand at her side. He wore a mask over the top half of his face— soft velvet, it hugged the contours of his features, so she could still discern the strength and symmetry that lay beneath. A jaw that was squared, a nose that was strong and angular, and lips that were masculine yet full. His hair was dark as the depths of the ocean might be, and just as mesmerising—thick with a natural wave, it was cut to the collar of his robe and, though it was neat, she had the strangest feeling it was suppressed wildness, that it wanted to be long and loose, free of restraint. His eyes were dark like flint, and his body was broad, muscular, tall, as though cast in the image of an ancient idol. The thought came to her out of nowhere and sent a shiver pulsing down her spine. He wore an immaculate robe, black with gold at the cuffs and collar, complementing the mask on his face. He looked...mysterious and fascinating.

*Dangerous.*

He looked temptingly like the rebellion she wanted to stage, so she forced herself to look away while she still could.

'Not at all.' She was unrecognisable as the Princess of Taquul, but that didn't mean she could speak as freely as she wanted. And not to a stranger.

But she felt his eyes on her, watching her, and an inexplicable heat began to simmer inside her veins. She kept looking forward. 'There is somewhere else you'd rather be though?' he prompted, apparently not letting his curiosity subside.

She felt a burst of something shake her, willing her to speak to him, to be honest.

'I—' She swallowed, tilting her gaze towards him. The mask emboldened her. She was hidden, secret. He didn't know who she was, and she had no idea who he was. They were simply two strangers at a state function. No rank, no names. A smile curved slowly over her lips. 'Up until twenty hours ago, I was in Manhattan.' She lifted her shoulders, conscious of the way the delicate gown moved with her.

'And you would prefer to be there.'

'It is a momentous occasion.' She gestured around the room, then turned back to face him fully. 'Everyone in Taquul will be rejoicing at the prospect of peace with Ishkana after so long.'

His eyes gave little away; they were stony and cool. 'Not everyone.'

'No?'

'There are many who will harbour hatred and resentment for their lifetimes. Peace does not come about because two men snap their fingers and decide it should.'

Fascination fluttered inside her. 'You don't think people see the sense in peace?'

His lips curved in an approximation of a smile. There was something about its innate cynicism that sparked a fire in her blood. 'Ah, then we are talking about sense and not feeling. What one feels often has very little to do with what one thinks.'

Surprise hitched in her throat. It was an interesting and perceptive observation; she found herself more interested in him than she'd expected to be by anyone at this event. She took a small step without realising it, then another, leading them around the edges of the space.

'Nonetheless, I believe the people of Taquul will feel enormous relief, particularly those in the border regions. What's needed is a unified front to quell the unease in the mountain ranges.'

His eyes burned her with their intensity—strange when a moment ago she'd been thinking how like cool stone they were.

'Perhaps.'

'You don't agree?'

His lips curved in another mocking smile. 'I do not think peace can be so easily achieved.'

'I hope you're wrong.'

'I doubt it.'

She laughed; she couldn't help it. His cynicism was so completely natural, as though he barely realised he was doing it.

'I believe people can obey a peace treaty,' he said quietly, his voice dark. 'But that hatred dies a long, slow death. Many lives have been lost on both sides. How many deaths have there been in this war? Would you not wish to retaliate against a man who murdered someone you loved?'

Sadness brushed through her at his words and she

couldn't help wondering if he'd lost someone to the awful unrest of their people. 'I think vigilantism is bad for that very reason. It's why victims should never get to enact retribution—how easy it would be to answer death with death, pain with pain, instead of finding the restorative properties of forgiveness.'

He was silent; she couldn't tell if he agreed or not, only that he was thinking. They reached the edge of the enormous marble room and by unspoken agreement proceeded down the stairs. They were not steep, but his hand reached out, pressing into the small of her back in a small gesture of support.

It was meaningless. Absolutely nothing—yet it was the sort of thing that would never have been allowed to happen if he knew who she was. The Royal Princess of Taquul could never be simply touched by a commoner! But no one knew her identity except the few servants who'd helped her get ready. She moved down the steps and unconsciously her body shifted with each step so that they were pressed together at the side, touching in a way that sent arrows of heat darting through her body.

At the bottom of the stairs, he gestured to the edge of the pool. 'Stand with me a while.' He said it like a command and she suppressed a smile. People didn't dare speak to her like that in Taquul—or anywhere.

She nodded her agreement. Not because he'd commanded her to do so but because there was nowhere else she wanted to be. His hand stayed pressed to her back, guiding her to the edge of the pool. There was a tall table they could have stood at, with ballerina waitresses circulating deftly through the crowds. It was everything they needed, so Johara wasn't sure why she found herself saying, 'Would you like to see something special?'

He turned to face her, his eyes narrowing in assessment before he moved his head in one short nod of agreement.

Relief burst through her. It should have signalled danger, but she was incapable of feeling anything except adrenalin. No, that wasn't true. She felt excitement too, and in the pit of her stomach, spinning non-stop, she also felt a burst of desire.

The man strode beside her, completely relaxed, his natural authority impossible to miss. She wondered if he was a delegate from a foreign country, or perhaps one of the powerful industry leaders often included in palace occasions. A wealthy investor in the country's infrastructure? He certainly moved with that indefinable air of wealth and power.

Steps led away from the pool—these older and less finessed than the marble—giving way to a sweeping path. She walked down it, and his hand stayed at the small of her back the whole way, spreading warmth through her body, turning her breath to fire inside her and deep in the pit of her stomach she had the strangest sense of destiny, as though something about him, this night, her choice to walk with him had been written in the stars a long, long time ago.

He couldn't have said why he was walking with her. From the moment he'd seen her across the crowded ballroom he'd felt a lash of something like urgency; a *need* to speak to her. The room had been filled with beautiful women in stunning couture, dripping in gemstones with ornate face masks. While her black gown clung to her body like a second skin, showcasing her generous curves to perfection, it had been a long time since Amir had allowed physical attraction to control his responses.

Desire wasn't enough.

So why was he allowing her to lead him away from the party—knowing he had to stand beside Sheikh Malik

Qadir within the hour and showcase their newly formed 'friendship'? At least, for the sake of those in attendance, they had to pretend.

Nothing had changed for Amir though. He still hated the Qadirs with a passion. Nineteen years ago, with the death of his parents, he had sworn he would always hate them, and he intended to keep that promise.

'Where are you taking me?'

'Patience. We're almost there.' She spoke with a slight American accent and her voice was smooth and melodious, almost musical.

'Are you in the habit of taking men you don't know into the wilderness?'

She laughed, the sound as delicate as a bell. 'First of all, this is hardly a wilderness. The gardens are immaculately tended here, don't you think?'

He dipped his head in silent concession.

'And as for dragging men I don't know anywhere...' She paused mid-sentence, and stopped walking as well, her eyes latching to his in a way that communicated so much more than words ever could. He felt the pulse of response from her to him, the rushing of need. Her breathing was laboured, each exhalation audible in the quiet night air. Overhead, the stars shone against the desert sky, silver against velvet black, but there was no one and nothing more brilliant than the woman before him. His hands lifted to her mask; he needed to see her face. He wanted to see all of her. But her hands caught his, stilling them, and she shook her head a little.

'No. I like it like this.'

It was a strange thing to say—as though she liked the anonymity the mask provided. He dropped his hands lower, but instead of bringing them to her side he placed them at hers. His touch was light at first, as though asking a question. In response, she swayed forward a little, so her body brushed his and he was no longer able to deny the onslaught of needs that were assaulting him. He felt like a teenager again, driven by hormones and lust. How long had it been since he'd allowed himself to act on something so base?

'Come with me,' she murmured, hunger in the words, desperation in the speed with which she spoke. She reached down and grabbed his hand, linking her fingers through his, pulling him beside her. The night was dark and here they were far from the revellers, but as an enormous shrub came out of nowhere he was grateful for the privacy it created. She reached for the loose branches and brushed them aside, offering him a mysterious look over her shoulder before disappearing through a wall made of trees. Her hand continued to hold his, but he stood on the other side a moment, looking in one direction and then another before stepping forward. Large, fragrant trees surrounded them, the foliage thick to the ground.

The sky overhead was the only recognisable feature, but even that was unable to cast sufficient light over the structure. It was black inside, almost completely, a sliver of moonlight offering the faintest silver glow.

'This way.' She pulled him a little deeper, her other hand on the leaves as if by memory, turning a corner and then another, and as they turned once more he could hear water, faint at first but becoming louder with each step. She didn't stop until they reached a fountain in the centre of this garden, this maze.

'It's beautiful, isn't it?' she asked, turning to face him. He didn't spare a glance for the space in which they stood. He was certain she was right, but he couldn't look away from her. He ached to remove her mask; even if he did so, he would barely be able to see her face, given how dark it was this deep in the maze.

'Yes.' The word was guttural and deep.

He lifted a hand to her chin, taking it between his thumb and forefinger and holding her steady, scrutinising her as though if he looked hard enough and long enough he could make sense of this incredible attraction.

'It's famous, you know. The Palace Maze.'

He nodded. 'I've heard of it.'

'Of course. Everyone in Taquul has.' She smiled, a flash of dark red lips. He didn't correct her; she didn't need to know he was from Ishkana—nor that he was the Sheikh of that country.

He continued to stare at her and her lips parted, her eyes sweeping shut so beyond the veil of her mask he could see two crescent-shaped sets of lashes, long and thick.

He should leave. This wasn't appropriate. But leaving was anathema to him; it was as though he were standing in quicksand, completely in her thrall.

'How long are you in Taquul for?'

Something shifted in her expression, in the little he could see of it, anyway. 'I don't know.'

'You don't like it here?'

She expelled a soft sigh. 'I have mixed feelings.'

It made more sense than such a vague statement should have. 'What do you do in New York?'

Her smile now was natural. 'I started the Early Intervention Literacy Association. I work on childhood literacy initiatives, particularly for children aged four to seven.'

It surprised him; he hadn't been expecting her to say anything like that. She looked every inch the socialite, the heiress, rather than someone who rolled up her sleeves and worked on something so important.

'What drew you to that?'

Her eyes shuttered him out even as she continued to look at him, as though there was something she wanted to keep secret, to keep from him. He instantly hated that. 'It's a worthwhile cause.'

He wanted to challenge her, to dig deeper, but he felt he was already balancing on a precipice, and that the more he knew was somehow dangerous.

'Yes.' Silence wrapped around them, but it was a silence that spoke volumes. His dark eyes bore into hers—a lighter shade of brown, like oak, sunshine and sand. He stared at her for as long as he could before dropping his eyes to her lips, then lower still to the curve of her breasts. The dress was black but so glossy it shimmered in the gentle moonlight.

'This is incredible,' he muttered, shaking his head as he ran his hand along her side, his fingertips brushing the flesh at her hips, then higher, tantalising the sweet spot beneath her arms, so close to her breasts he could see her awareness and desire, the plea in her eyes begging him to touch her there. His arousal hardened; he wanted to make love to her right here, beneath the stars, with the trees as their witness to whatever this madness was.

'How long are you in Taquul for?'

*Only as long as he absolutely needed to be.*

Every moment in this kingdom felt like a betrayal to his parents and their memory. 'Just this event. I leave immediately afterwards.'

Her eyes glittered with something like determination and she nodded. 'Good.' It was a purr. A noise that was half invitation, half dare. The latter made no sense but the former was an utter relief.

'In answer to your earlier question, I don't ever do this.'

He was quiet, waiting for her to say something else, to explain.

'I don't ever drag men I don't know into the maze, or anywhere.'

Her breath snagged in her throat, her lips parted and her head tilted back, her eyes holding his even as she swayed forward, totally surrendering to the madness of this moment.

'But you're different.'

His smile was barely a shift of his lips.

'Am I?'

'For starters, you're the only man here wearing black robes.'

He nodded slowly. There was a reason for that. Robes just like these had been worn at an ancient meeting between these two people, an event to mark their peace and friendship. His choice of attire was ceremonial but yes, she was right. All the other men wore either western-style suits or traditional white robes.

'Except, it's not what you're wearing.'

She lifted a hand, pressing her fingers to his chest. The touch surprised them both, but she didn't pull away.

'Have you ever met someone and felt…?' She frowned, searching for the right word.

But it was unnecessary. She didn't need to explain further. He shook his head. 'No. I've never felt this in my life.'

And before either of them could say another word, he dropped his mouth to hers and claimed her lips with all the desire that was humming inside his body.

# CHAPTER TWO

THE DRESS WAS impossibly soft and, at its back, small pearls ran the length of her spine, so he had to undo each one in order to free her from the stunning creation. He was impatient and wanted to rip the dress—but the material was seemingly unbreakable. Besides, he had just enough sense left to realise he'd be doing this woman a great wrong if he left her to emerge from the maze with a snagged dress.

What they were doing was mad on every level. He knew nothing about her—he could only be grateful she knew nothing about him either. The last thing he needed was a complication that would detract from the peace accord.

She'd been right about the masks. Anonymity was perfect. He removed the dress as quickly as he could, stripping it from her body with reverence, a husky groan impossible to contain when he saw the underwear she wore. Flimsy white lace, it barely covered her generous breasts and bottom. The effect of the silk and her face mask had his cock growing so hard it was painful.

He swore under his breath, dispensing with his own robes with far less reverence, stripping out of them as he'd done hundreds of time before, unable to take his eyes off her as he moved. He was half afraid she'd change her mind, that she'd tell him they had to stop this. And she'd be right to do so! This was utter madness, a whim of desire and pleasure and hedonism, a whim he should deny himself, just as he'd denied himself so many things in his time for the sake of his country.

He knew that his kingdom required him to marry—he was the sole heir to the throne and without a wife the necessary children were impossible to beget. Yet he had only ever engaged in careful, meaningless affairs, and only when he'd felt the conditions were right—the right woman, who would understand he could give her nothing in the way of commitment, because he had an obligation to marry for the good of his kingdom. Did this woman understand that?

She reached around behind her back, as if to unclasp her bra, drawing his mind away from his thoughts and back to the present. He watched as she unhooked the lace, her breath hissing between her teeth, her eyes on his as the garment dropped to the ground beside her, revealing two perfect, pale orbs with dark, engorged nipples.

He swore again, and when her eyes dropped to his very visible arousal, he felt a little of his seed spill from his crown. Her eyes looked as though they wanted to devour him.

*Aljahim*, he wanted this. He wanted to feel her, to taste her, to touch her all over, but time was against them. This would be so much faster than he wanted.

'I cannot stay long,' he said quietly; it was only fair to forewarn her of that before they began.

'Nor can I.' She reached for the elastic of her tiny scrap of underwear but he shook his head.

'Allow me.'

Her eyes widened and she dropped her hands to the side, nodding once.

He closed the distance between them, pausing right in front of her, his pulse slamming through his body.

'This is what you want?'

She nodded.

'You're on the pill?'

Another nod, wide-eyed, as though the reality was just dawning on her.

'I don't have any protection—'

'I'm safe.'

He nodded. 'As am I.'

She bit down on her lip, a perfect cherry red against the dark hue of her skin. He ached to remove the mask and see her face, and yet it also served to draw attention to her lips and eyes, both of which were so incredibly distracting.

'Please.'

The single word was his undoing. He groaned, kissing her once more, dragging her lower lip into his mouth and moving his tongue so that it duelled with hers, teasing her at first before dominating her completely, so her head dropped backwards in surrender and he pillaged her mouth, each movement designed to demand compliance—yet it was he that was complying too, with the current of need firing between them a most superior force.

His hands cupped her naked breasts, feeling their weight, their roundedness, pushing his arousal forward against the silk of her underpants so she whimpered with need—a need he understood.

Her fingers dug into his shoulders, her body weak against his. He understood. It was overwhelming. He broke the kiss simply so he could drag his mouth lower, over her décolletage, conscious of the way his facial hair left marks as he went, his teeth adding nips, something primal and ancient firing inside him at the sight of his proof of possession. If he were less fired by desire he might have felt ashamed by such an ancient thrill, but he didn't.

He took one of her ample breasts into his mouth, seeking her nipple with his tongue, rolling the sweet flesh until she was whimpering loudly into the night sky. Only then did he transfer his attention to the other breast, lifting his thumb and forefinger to continue the pleasurable torment on the other. She bucked her hips forward; he knew how she was feeling, for his own body was racked with the same sense of desperation.

He wanted her but he didn't want to stop this yet. He could feel her pleasure tightening, her body responding to his instantly, and he wanted to indulge that responsiveness, to show her how perfectly they were suited. With his teeth clamping down against her nipple and his fingers teasing the other, he wedged her legs apart with his knee then brought his spare hand to rest there, parting the elastic from her with ease to allow a finger to slide into her warm, feminine core.

She groaned, a sound of complete pleasure and surrender and delight. He didn't stop. He pushed another finger into her depths and then used his thumb to stroke her, pleasuring her breasts as he paid homage to her.

She crumpled against him; his arms, his mouth, were holding her body in place. He felt her stiffen then, and begin to shake; she was exploding, gripping him hard as her body was racked with an intense, blinding release. He didn't relinquish his touch; he held her close, the squeezing of her muscles against his fingers eliciting an answering response from him.

He needed her; there was nothing else for it. Before her breath could calm he let her go, moving his hands to her hips instead, holding her steady as he knelt in front of her. His teeth caught the elastic of her underpants, pulling them loose and lower, low enough for her to step out of, and then he kissed her feminine core, his tongue flicking her until she was crying again, moaning, and, for lack of a name, she could only say 'please', again, and again, and again.

He smiled against her. Yes, he'd give her what she wanted—and what he wanted—and he'd do it soon. He stood, scooping her up and kissing her lips, unspeakably aroused by the idea that she might taste herself in his kiss, carrying her to a soft patch of grass to the right of the fountain. He laid her down, then took a moment to simply marvel at the view she made. Her body was curvy and slim all at once, her hair dark and tumbled around her shoulders, her mask adding an element of mystery and allure—not that she needed it.

This woman was the definition of alluring—distracting and perfect. What other explanation could there be for the instant attraction he'd felt for her? It was as though the very heavens had demanded this of him—of them. This was so out of character and yet it didn't feel wrong.

He brought his body over hers, feeling her softness beneath the hard planes of his frame, his mouth seeking to reassure her with kisses as his knee parted her legs, making way for him. He hovered at her entrance, the moment one he wanted to frame in time, caught like one of the butterflies he'd chased as a child and occasionally held in the palms of his hand for a precious instant before releasing it back into the forest. He caught her wrists in his, pinning them above her head, holding her still, and as he pushed up to watch her face as he entered her, he committed every instant of their coming together to his memory. Her eyes widened before sweeping shut as her lips parted on a husky moan, her hips lifting instinctively to welcome him to her body.

She was so tight, her muscles squeezing him almost painfully, so he moved more slowly than his instincts wanted, taking her bit by bit until he was buried inside then pausing, allowing her to grow used to this feeling before he moved, pulling back a little then driving forward, his hips moving slowly and then, as her cries grew more fervent, taking her harder, faster. His grip on her wrists loosened, his fingers moving instead to entwine with hers, squeezing her hands before releasing her so she wrapped her arms around his back, her nails scoring his flesh with each thrust. Her cries grew louder and her muscles tightened then fell into spasm and he felt the moment she lost her grip on reality and tumbled off the side of the world in an intense orgasm. She writhed beneath him and a moment later he joined her in that ecstasy, allowing his body the total surrender to hers and this moment, releasing himself to her with a hoarse cry that filled the heart of this maze with their pleasure.

She should have felt regret but she couldn't. She watched as he dressed, covering his body with the black robes—a body that she had somehow committed to memory. It was a honed frame, all muscle and strength, and on his left pectoral muscle, he had words tattooed in Latin in a cursive font: *amor fati*. His back bore signs of her passion all over it. Her fingernails had marked his smooth, bronzed skin, leaving a maze of their own in bright red lines, frantic and energised. A smile played about her lips, her body still naked beneath the glorious night sky, the sound of the water fountain adding an air of magic to what they'd just done. Or perhaps it wasn't the fountain, it was just the act.

Pleasure exploded through her. Relief. As though what she'd done was a connection to her true self, a timely reminder that she was an autonomous being, not controlled by this kingdom and her brother, by the expectations upon her. And it was more than that—it was as though the heavens themselves had conspired to bring them together. It had all happened so quickly, so completely, his possession of her so absolute. She'd only been with one other man before,

Matthew, and she'd thought herself to be in love with him. She'd presumed that was a prerequisite to enjoying sex.

*Enjoying* sex!

What a bland way to express what she'd just felt! Her soul had changed orientation. North was now south, the world had altered shape, everything was different. She hadn't known what her body was capable of until a master such as this man had taught her how to truly feel. Wonderment filled her.

She knew only one regret then—that this wasn't the beginning of something more. It was impossible to hope for that. She wasn't utterly deluded as to her position in the royal family to think she could shun her obligations so completely and pursue a sexual fling with some random man—even one of obvious wealth and importance.

A sigh left her lips; she reached for a blade of grass, the dew on its tip delicate and glistening in the moonlight. The man turned to face her, and she smiled at him as though it were the most natural thing in the world. He smiled back; there were no barriers between them.

'Let me help you.' His voice was deep and husky, tinged with a slight accent. She couldn't quite pick it. She'd presumed he was from Taquul but perhaps he was from a neighbouring state, here to mark the new peace in the region.

Her brain was beginning to work again, after the fog of desire had made thinking impossible. He reached for her underwear, holding it out to her, the smile still on his face so something shifted in the pit of her stomach. He was so handsome, but it was more than that. She'd met plenty of handsome men before, and never felt like this. Powerful men, too. Handsome, strong, wealthy, sophisticated. After Matthew, she'd been difficult to impress. *Once bitten, twice shy* had become somewhat of a mantra for Johara without her realising it.

Perhaps it came down to the fact she knew nothing about him—he hadn't lied to her, he couldn't have, because they hadn't spoken. They'd let their bodies and mutual desire do all the communicating. Pleasure had been paramount.

Her nipples tingled as she slipped the bra into place, and he expelled a harsh breath as her underpants covered her femininity, so she knew he too regretted the necessity of ending this. Beyond the walls of this maze a party raged, a party at which she was expected to stand at her brother's side. Soon, the masks would come off, for the members of royal family at least, so that they could stand before the Sheikh of Ishkana as their true selves, and see his true self, pledging a better future for their two countries. And just for a moment, a blade of something like worry punctured the perfection of this moment. She pushed it away; she couldn't let it ruin this wonderful thing she'd just done.

Yet she had always hated everything the Haddad family was—that hate had been taught to her from a young age and even now, as a twenty-five-year-old woman, when she could acknowledge it was an ancient prejudice she'd been brought up to bear, she couldn't free herself from those feelings.

The idea of standing beside Malik and pretending she welcomed the Sheikh of Ishkana filled her with abhorrence. But she must do it. This encounter had been her act of rebellion, a last, secret giving-in to her own needs. Now she must be what her country needed.

'This dress is unlike anything I've ever seen.' He ran his fingers over it then held it open for her to step into. She moved closer, lifting one foot and placing it in the middle of the dress, putting a hand on his shoulder to steady herself. She'd marked him there too; little fingernail crescents were woven over his skin like a pattern that told of her impatience and need. She stroked the marks absent-mindedly as she moved her other foot into the dress.

'It's made of spider silk.'

The jerk of his head towards hers showed surprise.

'It was my mother's,' she added. 'Made a long time ago, and over the course of many years. A tribe to the west spent a long time harvesting the silk of spiders and spinning it using a special loom.' She ran her hands over it then turned, so he could fasten the buttons at the back. 'It's virtually un-breakable. It's supposed to signify strength and courage.'

His hands stilled a little at the small of her back before continuing with her buttons. 'Do you need these things?'

She thought of what was ahead and nodded. 'We all do, don't we?'

He reached the top button and pressed it into place, then let his hands move over her shoulders without answering. She turned to face him, looked up into his face and smiled.

'Thank you.' It was a strange thing to say but she felt gratitude. They'd never see each other again but what they'd just done had been incredibly important to her.

He dipped his head in silent concession. 'I have to go back.'

Her brow furrowed behind her mask as she looked to the entrance of the heart of the maze. 'Me too.'

He took her hand in his. 'Lead the way, *inti qamar*.'

My moon. She smiled at the casual term of endearment, pushing through the maze effortlessly.

'You know the way well.'

'Yes.' She could have elaborated on that. She could have said that she used to come here to hide as a child, that the maze was hers alone. The gardeners who tended it had brought her treats for the days when she would come with a book and lie on the grass for hours on end. Not the kind of food that was served in the palace, all perfect and delicate and with the expectation that she sit with her back ramrod straight and make polite conversation with the children her parents had deemed suitable companions. No, here in the maze she'd feasted on food from beyond the palace walls, street food and market delicacies that the gardeners had brought in for her. Sticky pastries, figs that were sun-dried and exploding with flavour, spiced meatballs, marinated cheese, rice stuffed into vegetables and packed with spices. It was messy and organic, each mouthful a tribute to life and goodness. She could have told him that in this maze she'd spent some of her happiest times—and that tonight had simply added to that.

But instead, she simply nodded, already feeling as though the woman who'd just done such a daring and spontaneous thing was disappearing, being pushed deep inside Johara. The closer they moved to the start of the maze, the more she was reminded of the life that was ahead of her.

Rebellion aside, she couldn't keep hiding in mazes for ever. She was a princess of Taquul and that brought with it obligations and expectations. She would do as her brother said. She would stand at his side tonight and welcome the peace accord and then, if he insisted on it, she would consider the marriage to Paris, even though the idea turned her blood to ice.

At the entrance to the maze, she paused, pulling her hand from his and rubbing her fingers together.

'You go ahead of me,' she said, simply. 'It's not worth the trouble of being seen coming out of the maze together.'

He seemed to consider that a moment and then nodded. She had no idea what else she could say.

'If things were different,' he murmured, lifting a hand to her chin, holding her steady beneath him, 'I would have liked to see you again.'

Her answering smile was lopsided with wistfulness.

'If things were different,' she agreed, 'I would have liked that too.'

Neither said what their commitments were and why it wasn't possible. They didn't need to.

'Goodnight.' He bowed his head low in a mark of deference and respect, something she was used to, so for a moment she wondered if perhaps he'd guessed at her identity. But, no. He was simply showing her what their assignation had meant to him; how he viewed her. Her heart felt as though it had exploded to three times its size. She kept a polite smile in place, used to maintaining an expression of polite calm when she felt anything but.

'Goodnight...sir.'

# CHAPTER THREE

'Goodnight, sir.'

Her words hummed through his brain, flooding him with memories. His body felt as though it was infused with a special kind of energy. He emerged from the maze, stalking past the pool, deliberately evading anyone who might try to catch his eye. At the entrance to the ballroom though, he could no longer ignore his reason for coming to this place he'd always despised.

Ahmed, his long-time servant, stepped from the shadows. 'Your Highness.' He bowed low, and Amir stilled, pushing aside thoughts of the beautiful woman and what they'd just shared. The entire encounter had been like a dream and already the threads of it were drifting away, impossible to catch.

'It's time.'

Amir nodded once, scanning the ballroom. 'Where is he?'

'In the stateroom.'

Amir's eyes narrowed with determination. 'Take me there.'

'Yes, sir.'

Amir paused as her words filled his brain once more. He walked beside his servant, using every ounce of willpower not to look over his shoulder to see the woman return to the ballroom. He wouldn't look for her again; he couldn't.

At the doors to the stateroom, Ahmed said something low and quiet to one of the guards. Both bowed low then opened the doors inwards.

There were only three men in the room, though the space was opulent and large enough to house two hundred easily. Marble, like the ballroom, with pillars to the vaulted ceilings, and tapestries on the walls—burgundy and gold with threads of navy blue to add detail.

Amir strode through the room as though he belonged. These men had removed their masks; he identified Malik Qadir easily enough.

'Your Majesty.' Malik silenced the other two with the address, extending a hand to Amir's. Amir hesitated a moment, his veins pounding with hatred and enmity. Only a love for his kingdom had him lifting up to remove his own mask before taking the outstretched hand and meeting Malik's eyes.

'Your Majesty,' he returned. But it felt like a betrayal of everything he knew in the world; he felt as though he was defacing the memory of his parents by treating this man— the nephew of his parents' murderer!—with such civility. He had always sworn to hate this family, and that included the Sheikh and Princess of Taquul.

'My chief aide, Tariq.' Malik indicated the man to his left. Amir nodded and introduced Ahmed with the same title.

'And Paris—my friend, and the man my sister is to marry.'

Amir nodded. He didn't say that it was a pleasure. He was honest to a fault and always had been. But he forced his lips into something approximating a smile. 'Let's get this over with, then.'

Malik's eyes glittered, showing a matching sense of antipathy. They were both putting aside their personal hatred for the sake of their kingdoms. For peace and prosperity and in the hope that more senseless deaths could be avoided.

'One moment,' Malik murmured, turning to Tariq and speaking low and soft. They shared the same language but he swapped to an ancient dialect that Amir only passingly understood.

A moment later, Malik looked at Amir. 'My sister is expected.'

Paris's smile was indulgent. 'She is often late.'

It was clear from Malik's expression that he disapproved of that quality. It was a sentiment Amir shared. Punctuality was not difficult to master and was, at its base, a sign of respect.

'Would you care for some wine?' Malik gestured to the wall, where a tray had been placed with several drinks.

Amir shook his head.

'Then we shall simply wait.'

The silence was tense. It was not natural. To be in the depths of this palace, surrounded by men who a year ago might have wished him dead? Hell, who probably still did. The peace talks had been ongoing, difficult and driven by emotion on both sides. It had taken Amir and Malik's intervention with their aides to achieve what they had.

And now, there was simply this. To stand in front of the assembled guests and speak to the importance of what they hoped to achieve, the ancient bonds that had, at one time, held these countries together. The mountain ranges separated them but that had, generations ago, been a passage alive with trade. The cooler climates there had created villages full of people from both countries. Only in recent times had the mountain range come to serve as a barrier.

He must focus on their past, on the closeness that had once been natural to their peoples, and on the future they intended to forge.

* * *

'I know, I know.' Johara ran a hand over her hair, meeting her servant's eyes in the gold-framed mirror. 'I'm late.'

'Very,' Athena agreed, pursing her lips into a small smile. 'Your brother was expecting you in the staterooms fifteen minutes ago.'

Another flicker of rebellion dashed through her soul. So she was keeping her brother waiting. It was juvenile and silly, particularly given the importance of the evening, and yet there was pleasure in the perversity of running behind schedule.

'Send word that I'm on my way,' she murmured to another servant, reaching up to remove the thick black ribbons that held the mask in place. Her hair was loose; it tumbled over her shoulders, but for this meeting, she wanted it styled more severely, more formally. That felt like an armour she would need.

Her hands worked deftly, catching the lustrous brown waves low at her nape and swirling them into a bun. 'Pins?'

Athena reached into her pockets—from which she seemed capable of removing all sorts of implements at will—and handed several to Johara. 'I can call a stylist?'

'Is it necessary?' Johara returned archly, pressing several pins into place to secure an elegant chignon.

'No. It's perfect. Neat and ordered.'

The opposite of how she presently felt. When she lifted her hands to her cheeks to pinch them for a hint of colour, her nipples strained against the lace of her bra and she felt a hum of memory, a reminder of what she'd shared with the stranger. A *frisson* ran the length of her spine—had it really happened? It was the most uncharacteristic thing she'd ever done in her life and yet she didn't regret it. Not even a little.

'Lipstick.' Athena passed a black tube over and Johara coloured her full lips and then nodded.

'Fine. Let's go.'

She didn't portray a hint of the turmoil she was feeling. Her country stood on a precipice. Everything was new. The old ways must be forgotten. He had been wrong to say hatred would persist. The possibility of peace and safety was too alluring. Surely their people would force themselves to forget the anger and bigotry and come to see the people of Ishkana as their brothers and sisters?

She was barely conscious of the way servants bowed to her as she walked. It hadn't been like this in New York but, despite the fact she'd lived there for several years, she had grown up here in Taquul, for the most part, and this sort of respect came part and parcel with her position.

At the doors of the stateroom, she paused, turning to Athena. 'You'll come with me.'

'Of course.' Athena's eyes dropped to the marble floor a moment, as though she too was fortifying herself for the night ahead. And that was natural—Athena had served the Taquul royal family since she was a teenager, her sentiments matched theirs.

Beyond that, she was a friend to Johara. Johara reached out and squeezed Athena's hand for comfort. 'Let's just get it over with.' She unknowingly echoed Amir's earlier sentiments. The doors swept open, the noise of their intrusion drawing the attention of all in the room.

Her eyes naturally gravitated towards her brother's. His gaze held a warning, as though he expected her to make trouble in some way. From him, she turned to Paris. His smile was kind; she returned it. She might not find him at all attractive but he was sweet and they'd been friends for a long time.

Someone moved at the side of the room, catching her attention. She turned that way naturally, and missed her step, stumbling a little awkwardly as her eyes tried to make sense of it.

The man across the room was…unmistakably…the same man she'd made love to in the heart of the maze. His dark robes were instantly recognisable, but it was more than that. Though he'd worn a mask his face was…she'd seen it as they'd kissed. She'd *known* what he looked like.

Had he known who she was? Had it been some kind of vile revenge?

No. Shock registered on his features too, though he covered that response much more swiftly than she was able, assuming a mask of cool civility while her blood was threatening to burn her body to pieces.

'Jo.' Malik crossed to her but she couldn't look away from Amir. She saw the way he flinched at her name and wondered why. The world was spinning, and not in a good way. Malik put his hand under her elbow, guiding her deeper into the room, and she was glad for his support. She could hardly breathe. What were the chances?

He *had* to have known. He had come to speak to her out of nowhere—why else had he approached her like that? It couldn't have been random happenstance.

Except he hadn't known; she was sure of it. They'd both sought anonymity. It had been a transaction between two people: faceless, nationless, without identity. It had been about him and her, their bodies and souls, and nothing more.

She dropped her head, almost unable to walk for a moment as the reality of what had happened unravelled inside her.

He'd use this to destroy her. To destroy her brother. If Malik knew what she'd done… Oh, heck.

Panic seized her.

'Calm down,' Malik muttered from the side of his lips.

'This is to commemorate a peace treaty, remember? He is no longer the enemy yet you look as though you would like to kill him.'

Startled, she jerked her eyes away from Sheikh Amir of Ishkana and looked at her brother instead. 'I would.'

Malik's expression showed amusement and then he shook his head, leaned closer and whispered, 'Me too, but my advisors tell me it would be a bad idea.'

She forced a smile she didn't feel. Paris moved to them, putting a familiar hand on hers and pressing a kiss to her cheek. It was a simple greeting, one that was appropriate for old friends, but in front of Amir, after what they'd just shared, she felt as though she should distance herself. She needed space. From him, from everyone. But it wasn't possible. There were far greater concerns than her personal life.

'Amir.' Malik addressed him by his first name, and it didn't occur to Amir to mind. In that moment, all of his brain power was absorbed in making sense of what the hell had just happened.

She was… Johara? The Princess of Taquul? The woman he'd made love to, been so blindsided by that he'd given into physical temptation against all common sense was…a Qadir?

He wanted to shout: *It can't be!* Surely it wasn't possible. And yet…there was no refuting it. Her dress…she moved and he remembered how she'd felt in his hands, how her body had writhed beneath his. He could close his eyes and picture her naked, her voluptuous curves calling to him, even as she now walked elegantly towards him, her hair neat, her make-up flawless, and he saw only a Qadir princess. Her parents had hated his. Her uncle Johar had killed his parents. Johar… Johara. She'd been named for that murderous son of a bitch.

Something like nausea burst through him. Hatred bubbled beneath his skin. As she came close, he inhaled and caught a hint of her fragrance, so familiar to him that his body couldn't help but respond, despite the fact he now knew who she was.

'This is my younger sister, Princess Johara of Taquul.'

Their eyes met and locked. It was impossible to look away. He saw fear there. Panic. But why? Because of what they'd done? Or because of what she thought he might do next? Did she believe he was going to announce their prior relationship? That he'd do something so foolish as confess what they'd shared? To what end?

His eyes narrowed imperceptibly and he extended a hand. 'A pleasure to meet you.'

He saw the moment relief lit her eyes. Her smile was barely there—a terrible facsimile of the vibrant smiles she'd offered in the maze. She hadn't known who he was. Neither of them had understood.

How had he failed to notice the signs though? Her familiarity with the maze. A dress made of spiders' silk. Both such obvious signs of her place within this family. Yet he'd been blinded by her, and by the attraction he felt. It was the only answer.

'Likewise.' Her accent. It was so American—naturally he'd assumed she was a foreigner, here in Taquul just for the ball. But now he recalled the biographical details he'd been furnished with prior to this treaty: that her mother had been American, that she'd gone to school in America for some time, and had lived there for several years.

'You look flushed. Do you feel well?' It was Paris, to her left. Something else flared in Amir's mind.

*The man my sister is to marry.*

'I'm fine.' At least she had the grace to look ashamed.

'Your Highness? They're ready.'

\* \* \*

It was a blur. Johara stood between her brother and Paris as the peace accord was announced. Fireworks burst overhead to celebrate the occasion, and answering displays were seen across the countries. Peace had come—she could only hope that it would hold.

And all the while, those in attendance smiled and nodded with rapt faces, and finally cheered, so Johara smiled along with them and nodded as her brother spoke. But it was when Amir began to address the crowd that everything inside her dissolved into a kind of never-ending tumult.

'For too long we have seen our people die. We have fought over nothing more significant than on which side of the mountains we were born; this war has been a plague on both our countries. Our people were once unified and great, strong in this region, capable of anything. Our prosperity was shared, our might universally known. It is time to set aside the last one hundred years. It is time to forge a peace between our people, a lasting peace—not into the next century, but the next millenium.' She was captivated, staring at his deep, dark eyes as he scanned the crowd.

'It will take work. It will require us to actively forget how we have been taught to feel. We will need to look behind the masks of what we believe our peoples stand for, to see the truth of what is there. A baker in Ishkana is no different from a baker in Taquul. We see the same stars, worship the same god, dance to the same songs, have learned all the same tales. We can be unified once more.' He turned to look at Malik, but his eyes glanced over Johara, so she was sure he must have seen the effect his rousing speech had on her.

She couldn't hide her admiration, she was sure of it.

'Tonight begins a new way of life for us, a life of peace.'

Silence lasted for several seconds and then applause broke out, loud and joyous. If Johara had been in any doubt as to how desperately the people wished for peace, the proof was right before her now. And for Amir to take what was largely a crowd of Taquul dignitaries and have them eating out of his hand—it showed the magnetism he had.

Not that she needed any further indication of that.

The official requirements of the evening were at an end. She left the makeshift stage gratefully, giving a brief farewell to Paris before slipping through thick gold curtains that hung along the edge of the ballroom. She moved quickly, desperately needing air, space, a way to breathe. She found her way to a long marble corridor and moved through it until she reached glass doors at the end.

The cool desert air glanced across her skin as she pushed them open, onto a small Juliet balcony that overlooked the Sheikh's aviary, where his prized falcons were kept. In the evening, the stark outline of trees was striking. Beyond it, the desert lay, and the light breeze stirred the sand, so when she breathed in she could smell that acrid clay that was so reminiscent of her childhood. How she'd loved to carry bottles of water into the desert and pour it over the sand to make little streams, turning the sand into a malleable substance from which she could build great structures.

For a child who could barely read, making things with her hands had been her own source of satisfaction.

'Your Highness.'

She stiffened, curving her hands over the railing of the balcony as his voice reached her ears. Had she known he would follow? No. And yet, she was hardly surprised.

She turned slowly, bracing for this—or at least attempting to. Nothing could prepare her for what was to come. Without his mask, alone on the balcony, so close she could touch him. And more than that, the coldness in his face. The anger. Oh, he was trying to control it but she felt it emanating from him in waves so she rushed to say, 'I didn't know who you were. I had no idea.'

She knew, even as she spoke the words, that it wasn't completely true. Their connection had defied logic and sense. Perhaps she might have been able to resist him, but not if he'd set his mind on seducing her.

'So you simply took the chance to sleep with another man behind your fiancé's back?'

'I…' She frowned. 'I don't have a fiancé.'

That surprised him.

'There is a man my brother wishes me to marry,' she stressed, 'but that's not quite the same thing. Last time I checked, I still have some say in the matter, so no, I didn't "cheat" on anyone.'

He dipped his head forward. 'I apologise. I was misinformed.'

She was surprised by the instant apology, and more so how he could deliver it in a way that was both genuine and infused with icy coldness. If she turned to the right, she'd see the edge of the maze. She couldn't look that way. She'd likely never look at it again, certainly never walk within its verdant walls.

'You're named for him.'

She frowned, but only for a second. She should have remembered sooner, the awful, bloody death in her family's—and his family's—history. 'My uncle Johar? Yes.'

'You're named as a tribute.'

'I was born before he…'

Amir's shoulders squared. 'Murdered my parents?'

Her eyes swept shut in anguish. 'Yes.'

'And yet he had knowingly hated them for a long time.'

'You said yourself, hate has been felt by all our people for a very long time.'

'True.' He crossed his arms over his broad chest. She

wished he hadn't done that. It drew her focus in a way that was dangerous, flooding her body and brain with too many feelings.

'A moment ago, I listened to you implore us to move on from those feelings. To remember that we were once allies.' She swallowed, not realising until that instant how badly she wanted that to be the case. 'Let's not speak of Johar. Not when a new period of peace is upon us.'

His lips curled into what she could only describe as a grimace of derision. 'Publicly I must advocate and encourage peace. Privately I am allowed to feel whatever the damned hell I please.'

His anger and vehemence were palpable forces, rushing towards her. 'And what do you feel?'

He stared at her for several seconds and then looked beyond her, beyond the aviary, to the desert planes in the distance, made silver by the moonlight. 'It's better not to discuss it with you.'

'If you'd known who I was…' She let the question hang between them unfinished.

'Would I have allowed it to happen?' He compressed his lips. 'No.'

'You think you could have stopped it?'

His eyes shifted back to hers and she saw it—what she'd been conscious of and yet not fully understood before. He was a king. Born all-powerful to a mighty people. Born to rule and fully cognisant of what the world required of him. His natural authority was exactly that. She'd perceived it from the outset and she felt it now. She shivered involuntarily, a whisper of cold seizing her core.

'Absolutely.'

Courage was failing her, but she wouldn't allow what they'd shared to be lost completely. 'You're wrong.' She moved forward, putting a hand on his chest, but he flinched away from her, his eyes holding a warning. Pain lashed her. She had to be brave; he couldn't deny that what had happened between them was real. That it held meaning. 'There was something about you, and me, that needed us to do that.'

He made a noise of disagreement. 'It was a mistake.'

Hurt pounded her insides. She shook her head in disagreement.

'Let me be clear.' His voice was deep and authoritative. She stayed where she was, but her body was reverberating with a need to reach for him, to touch him. 'If I had known you were a Qadir I would not have touched you. I would not have spoken to you. I will always regret what happened between us, Johara.' And her spat her name as though it were the worst insult he could conjure. 'Tonight, I betrayed myself, my parents, and everything I have always believed.'

Pain exploded in her chest. She blinked at him, uncertain of how to respond, surprised by how badly his words had cut her. 'I'm not my uncle. I'm not my parents and I'm not my brother.' She spoke with a quiet dignity, her voice only shaking a little. 'You cannot seriously mean to hate me just because of the family I was born into?'

His eyes pierced her. 'I'm afraid that's exactly what I mean, Your Highness.'

# CHAPTER FOUR

'IT'S IMPORTANT.'

'It's dangerous.' Paris spoke over Malik in a rare sign of anger. Johara watched the two of them discussing her fate with an overarching sense of frustration. As though where she went and why came down to what they said.

'The peace is already fraying, and only eight weeks after the accord was signed. We need to do something more to underscore our intent that this be meaningful.' He turned to Johara, frowning. 'I hate to ask it of you, Johara, but you know that it's time.'

She said nothing, simply lifting a brow in a silent invitation for him to continue. 'You've avoided your obligations for years, and I've allowed it.' Inwardly she bristled. Malik crouched before her. 'Because you're my sister and I love you; I want you to be happy. But I *need* you now. Someone has to go and do the sorts of visible politicking I don't have time for.'

She ignored the way her brother so easily relegated the responsibilities he was trying to foist on her as though it were just glad-handing and smiling for cameras, rather than wading into enemy territory and attempting to win the hearts of the Ishkana people.

'You should go.' Paris spoke quietly, addressing Malik, his eyes intense. 'For a short visit.'

'It's not possible.' Malik sighed. 'You know there are matters here that require my urgent attention.'

Paris expelled a breath. 'Then send someone. A diplomat. A cousin.'

'No. It can't be a snub, nor a regular visit. This has to have meaning to his people, the way his visit did for ours.'

'It can't have meant that much,' Paris pointed out, 'for the skirmishes to be continuing.'

'Sheikh Amir is right. We have to be unified in this.' Johara spoke above both of them, standing with innate elegance and striding towards one of the windows that framed a view of the citrus gardens. Their formal layout was designed as a tribute to a French palace, each tree surrounded by bursts of lavender, white gravel demarcating the various plantings.

Paris and Malik were silent; waiting.

'I hate the idea of going to Ishkana.' She did, but not for reasons she could ever share with either man. She had tried to forget everything about Sheikh Amir and his hateful kingdom since they'd spoken on the balcony; to be sent there now as a guest of the palace? She trembled at the idea, and with outrage, nothing more!

'So don't go,' Paris murmured.

'I have to.' She turned to face him, her smile dismissive. He was a good friend but the more time she'd spent back in Taquul, the more certain she'd become that she could never marry him. There was no doubt in her mind that he had her brother's best interests at heart, and yet that wasn't enough. She would speak to him about it, put the idea from his mind once and for all. His concern was worrying because it suggested he cared for her in a way that went beyond duty to the Sheikh, and the last thing she wanted to do was hurt Paris.

'Malik is right. We have to show the people of Ishkana

that we value this peace accord,' she said with quiet resolve. 'For our people, we must appear to be moving forward. We have to lead the way. How can we expect them to find peace in their hearts if we don't demonstrate it? I will go to Ishkana as a guest of the palace. I will attend state dinners and speak to the parliament. I will tour their ancient ruins and libraries and smile for the cameras. Is that what you want, Mal?'

He made a small noise of agreement. 'You know how I hate to ask it of you.'

She waved a hand through the air. 'If you hadn't asked, I would have suggested it. It's the best thing for everyone.'

'No, Johara. You will be exposed—'

'I'll be a guest of their King, will I not?'

Malik dipped his head forward in silent agreement.

'And staying in the palace?'

Another nod.

'So I presume His Majesty will vouch for my safety?'

'For what it's worth,' Paris responded dubiously.

At that, Malik held up a hand. 'I believe Amir is a man of honour.' The words were dark, troubled. 'He is a Haddad, so naturally I mistrust him, but I believe that, having invited you to the palace, he will go out of his way to ensure your safety.'

Johara's heart skipped a beat. 'Sheikh Amir invited me?'

Malik's smile was dismissive. 'A figure of speech. The suggestion came through diplomatic channels and no specific guest was mentioned. It was my idea that you should attend.'

'Of course.' She turned away again quickly, hoping she'd hid the look of disappointment she knew must be on her face. What had she expected? That he'd roll out the red carpet for her eight weeks after they'd last seen each other? He'd made his feelings perfectly clear that night.

*It was a mistake.* Her heart skipped another beat. It wasn't a mistake. It was the single greatest moment of her life and she wouldn't let him take that away from her. Oh, she desperately wished that they weren't who they were—the Haddads and Qadirs had hated each other for too long to allow it to be forgotten. But in that moment, it had been too perfect so even now she struggled to care.

'So you'll go?'

What would it be like to enter his kingdom? His palace? She'd never been to Ishkana. It wouldn't have been safe until recently. She'd seen photographs and knew much of its history, but to see it for herself? Curiosity sparked inside her, and she told herself the rushing of her pulse was owing to that alone.

'Yes, Mal. I'll go to Ishkana.'

In many ways, it was just like Taquul. The sand was the same colour, the heat was the same, the trees innately familiar. But as the limousine approached the palace she felt a flash of anticipation warm her skin. The approach to the palace was lined with palm trees, and on one side, a colourful market had been set up. The limousine was obliged to slow down as pedestrians meandered across the road, in no hurry to clear the way for the car. It gave her time to observe. An old woman sat in the shade cast from her brightly coloured market tent, an ancient spinning wheel before her. She moved effortlessly, each shift of the wheel an act she'd obviously repeated millions of times in her long lifetime. A vibrant red wool was being formed at one side. Another woman sat beside her, talking and cackling with laughter. The next stall showed spices, piled high in pyramids, just as vendors did at home, the next sold sweets—she recognised many of the same illicit delicacies she'd been introduced to by the gardening staff who'd tended the maze.

As the car neared the palace gates, she saw something that broke her heart. Several people stood in a cluster, shaded by a large, old umbrella. Their clothes were poor, their faces grubby and bodies frail. She turned to the driver, leaning forward. 'Stop the car.'

He pressed the brakes, looking over his shoulder. 'Madam?'

'A moment.' She spoke with all the authority she could conjure, unlocking her door and stepping out. The sun beat down on her relentlessly, causing a bead of perspiration to break out on her brow. She wiped at it but continued to walk to the group. There were perhaps eighteen people. She was conscious of one of the palace guards stepping out of the car and following behind her—she resented his intrusion, and the suggestion that these people must be dangerous because they happened to be poor.

Fixing him with a cool stare, she turned back to the people at the gate and smiled. 'It's warm,' she said to a woman in perhaps her early thirties, nursing an infant on her hip. The child looked at Johara with enormous brown eyes.

'Very hot, yes.'

'You need some lemonade from the markets,' Johara said with a smile. The mother's eyes widened but she shook her head almost instantly.

'It's not possible.'

'Here.' Johara reached into the folds of her linen dress, removing enough bank notes to pay rent for a month. She handed them to the mother, who shook her head.

'Please, take it. Buy some food and drink.' She gestured to the group behind her. 'For all of you.'

'But…it's very generous…'

Johara's heart turned over, and simultaneously she felt a blade of anger pierce her. How could Amir sit in his palace and allow this kind of poverty to exist on his doorstep? True, Taquul wasn't perfect but this was so blatant! So heart-wrenching.

'I insist.' She leaned out and tousled the little boy's hair. He didn't react at first but then he giggled, so Johara did it again.

'He likes you,' the woman said wistfully. 'It's the first time he's smiled in days.'

'I'm sorry to hear it,' Johara murmured truthfully. 'He has a beautiful smile.'

She turned to leave but before she'd gone three steps, the woman arrested her. 'What is your name, miss?'

Johara paused, aware that it was a turning point. She'd come to this country to spread word of the alliance and reverse people's opinions; now was as good a time to start as any.

'Johara Qadir,' she said without inflection—not anger, not cynicism, not apology.

A rippled murmur travelled the group but the woman spoke over it. 'Thank you, Your Highness.' And she bowed low, but with a smile on her face, so Johara was glad the people knew who she was.

The security guard followed her back to the car, and as he opened the door he said firmly, 'You should not have done that, madam.'

Johara's surprise was obvious. In Taquul, a servant would never speak to a guest in such a manner! 'I beg your pardon, why exactly not?'

'Because it is dangerous and the Sheikh gave your brother his word you would be safe here. That means he will want to control every aspect of your safety. If you display a tendency to make such poor decisions he'll likely confine you to the palace.'

She stared at him in disbelief. 'Confine me...*me*...to the palace?'

The guard lifted his shoulders. 'We should go. He will be waiting.'

Emotions flooded Johara's body. *He will be waiting.* The idea of Amir waiting for her did unreasonable things to her pulse.

She slid into the car, waving at her newfound friend as the car drove through the palace gates, trying to work out why her nerves wouldn't settle.

This wasn't about him. He'd made it very clear that he regretted what had happened between them and she had no choice but to accept that, to feel as he did.

Johara held her breath, marvelling at all the many ways in which the palace differed from the photographs she'd seen. Oh, it was enormous and impossibly grand, she knew parts of it had been constructed in the fifth century—the old stone foundations and underground tunnels and caverns rumoured to run all the way to the mountains—but the rest had been completed in the sixteen hundreds; enormous white stone walls with gold details formed an impressive façade. The windows were arched, the roofs shaped to match with colours of gold, turquoise and copper. Around the entire palace there was a moat of the most iridescent water, such a glorious pale blue it reminded her of the clearest seas of the Mediterranean.

She peered at it as they drove over the moat, then fixed her attention on the palace. The car stopped at a large golden door. Servants and guards stood to the ready and at the top of the stairs, him.

Amir.

His Majesty, Sheikh of Ishkana. Nerves fired through her but she refused to let them show, especially to the bossy security agent who'd told her she shouldn't have stopped to speak to the poor people at the gate. Since when was compassion forbidden?

The security agent opened the door without meeting her eyes and she stepped from the car, conscious of everything in that moment. Her dress, her hair, the fact *he* was staring at her and that everyone was watching them. Conscious of the photographer who stood poised to take an official photograph that would be printed in all the newspapers in both countries and around the world the following morning.

Most conscious of all though of Amir as he moved down the stairs towards her, his eyes not leaving her face, his face so familiar, so achingly familiar, that she could barely remember to act impassive.

It took all her self-control to stay where she was, a look of polite calm on her face. He extended a hand in greeting; she placed hers in it. The world stopped spinning all over again. Arrows drove through her skin. Her mouth was dry, breathing painful. She stared at him in bewilderment—she hadn't thought he'd still be able to affect her like that. She'd thought knowing who he was and how he felt about her might have changed…something.

She pulled her hand away as though he'd burned her, with no idea if the photographer had succeeded in capturing a suitably friendly photograph—and not particularly caring.

'Welcome, Princess,' he murmured, and, though it was a perfectly acceptable thing to say, she felt her skin crawl, as though he were condemning her title just as he had her name on that last night. 'Johara.' He'd spat it at her and she felt that again now.

'Thank you.' She didn't flinch.

'Smile for the camera,' he said quietly, leaning down so only she caught the words. She looked in the direction he'd nodded, eyeing off the photographer and lifting her lips in a practised smile. They stood there for a moment before the Sheikh put his hand to the small of her back, to guide her to the palace. It was too much. She wanted to jerk herself away from the simple contact, or she wanted to throw herself at his feet and beg him to do so much more.

She did neither.

Her upbringing and training kicked in; she put one foot in front of the other until she reached the top of the steps and then beyond them, into the cool corridor of the palace. Then, and only then, when out of sight of photographers, did she casually step beyond his reach.

If he noticed, or cared, he didn't show it. 'How was your flight?'

*Like you care.* The acerbic rejoinder died on the tip of her tongue. This would never work if she went out of her way to spar with him. 'Fine. Easy.'

'Easier still when we can repair and reopen the mountain roads; the drive will take a matter of hours.'

Johara looked towards him. 'That's what you intend?'

He began to move deeper into the palace and she followed after him. 'Why not? There were always easy links between our people. It's only as a result of the conflict that these have been shut down.'

'And trade?' she prompted.

'Naturally.'

She nodded, considering this. 'Even as the peace seems so tenuous?'

'I expected it would.' He shrugged. 'Surely you didn't truly believe it would be smooth sailing simply because Malik and I signed an accord?'

Her brow furrowed as she considered that. 'I…had hoped.'

'Yes.' The word was delivered enigmatically. 'You had hoped.'

'You're still cynical about this?'

They reached a pair of thick, dark wood doors, at which four guards stood sentinel. He gestured for her to precede him. She did so, without looking where she was going, so when she stepped into the space she was completely unprepared for what awaited her. She drew in a sharp breath, wonderment filling her gaze. She hadn't been paying attention; it had felt as though they were moving deeper into the palace, yet this room was a sanctuary of green. A stream ran in front of them, covered by dark timber bridges. The walls were dark wood, but filled with greenery. Vines had tentacles that reached across everything. Johara reached out and ran her fingers over the velvety surface of one of the plants.

Amir watched Johara.

'What is this?' She turned to face him, a smile unknowingly lifting her lips. It was impossible to feel anything but uplifted in this room.

'A private hall, now just for my use. It's one of the oldest spaces in the palace.'

She nodded, looking upwards, where several openings showed views of the sky. She could only imagine how stunning it would be in the evening.

'I'd never heard of it. It's not in any of the information we have.' Her cheeks grew hot. 'The texts, I mean.'

He lifted a brow. 'You've been studying my country?'

'As children, my brother and I were taught much about Ishkana.'

'And how to hate us?'

Her eyes flashed. 'As you were taught to hate us.'

'A lesson that I never really understood until I was twelve years old.'

She stared at him blankly.

Amir moved deeper into the room. 'The age I was when my parents were assassinated.'

Her heart squeezed for the boy he'd been. She wanted to offer condolences, to tell him how sorry she was, but both sentiments seemed disingenuous, given the strained nature of their relationship. So instead, she said, 'That must have been very difficult.'

He didn't respond. His profile was autocratic, his features tight. Where was the man she'd made love to in the maze? It felt like such a long time ago. Then, she'd had no inhibitions, no barriers. To him she would have known exactly what to say, without second-guessing herself.

'This room is completely private—for my use only, and for those guests I choose to invite here with me.' He tilted a gaze at her. 'I'm sure you are aware of how difficult it is to have true privacy in a palace.'

'Yes,' she agreed, looking around. The more she looked, the more she saw and loved. In the far corner, an old rug had been spread, gold and burgundy in colour, and against it, sumptuous pillows were spread. 'Thank you for showing it to me.'

He turned to face her, his eyes glittering like onyx in his handsome face.

'I wanted to speak to you. Alone.'

Her body went into overdrive. Blood hummed just beneath her skin, her heart slammed into her ribs and her knees began to feel as though they were two distinct magnetic poles. She walked slowly and deliberately towards the centre of the room, where an enormous fiddle leaf fig was the centrepiece. 'Did you, Amir?'

Using his name felt like both a rebellion and a comfort. She didn't look at him to see his reaction.

'It's been two and a half months since the masquerade.'

She studied the detailed, intricate veins in the leaves of the fig tree, her eyes tracing their patterns, every fibre of her being focussing on not reacting visibly to his statement.

'So you would know by now.'

'Know?'

'If there were any consequences to that night.'

Consequences? Her brain was sluggish. The heat, and having seen him again, made her feel a thousand things and none of them was mentally acute, so it took a few seconds for his meaning to make sense. Her breath snagged in her throat as she contemplated what he meant—something which hadn't, until that moment, even occurred to her. 'You mean to ask if I'm pregnant?'

The room seemed to hush. The gentle vines no longer whispered, the water beneath them ceased to flow, even the sun overhead felt as though it grew dim.

'Are you?'

Something painful shifted in her belly. She swallowed past a lump in her throat, turning to face him slowly. 'And if I were, Amir?' This time, when she said his name, she was conscious of the way he reacted, heat simmering in his eyes.

'I will not speak in hypotheticals.'

It was so like him. She felt a ridiculous burst of anger at his refusal to enter into a 'what if?'. 'No, that's not fair. You asked the question, I'm entitled to ask mine back. What would you do if I were pregnant?'

His face became shuttered, impossible to read, unfamiliar and intimidating. 'What would you have me do?'

She should have expected that. 'No, I'm asking what you would *want* to do.'

'Are you hoping I'll say something romantic, Johara? Do you wish me to tell you that I would put aside our ancient feud and marry you, for the sake of our child's future?'

Her lips parted. The image he painted was painful and somehow impossible to ignore. She shook her head even when she wasn't sure what she felt or wanted.

'Even for the sake of our child, I would not marry you. I couldn't. As much as I hate your family, you deserve better than that.'

Curiosity barbed inside her. 'You think marriage to you would be a punishment?'

'Yes. For both of us.'

'Why, Amir?'

He moved closer, and she held her breath, waiting, wanting, needing. 'Because I would never forgive you, Johara.' It was just like the first time he'd said her name. An invocation, a curse, a whip lashing the air in the room and crashing finally against the base of her spine.

'For what? What exactly have I done that requires forgiveness?'

'It is not what you've done.'

'But who I am? Born to the Qadir royal family?'

The compression of his lips was all the confirmation she needed.

'And what we shared changes nothing?'

'What we shared was wrong. It should never have happened.'

'How can you say that when it felt so right?'

His eyes closed for a moment then lanced her with their intensity. 'It was just sex.'

She stared at him in surprise. It was such a crude thing to say, and so wrong. She hadn't expected it of him.

'You weren't a virgin. You knew what sex was about.'

Her eyes hurt. It took her a second to comprehend that it was the sting of tears. She blinked furiously, refusing to give in to such a childish response.

'So that night meant nothing to you?'

He stared at her without responding. Every second that stretched between them was like a fresh pain in her heart.

'I'm not here to discuss anything besides the possibility that you conceived our child.'

Her heart lurched. She couldn't help it—out of nowhere an image of what their baby might look like filled her eyes, all chubby with dark hair and fierce dark eyes. She turned away from him, everything wonky and unsteady.

'I'm not pregnant, Amir. You're off the hook completely.'

She heard his hiss of relief, a sharp exhalation, as though he hadn't been breathing properly until then. She wanted to hurt him back, to make him feel as she did, but she feared she wasn't properly armed. How could one hurt a stone wall? And whatever she'd perceived in him on the night of the masquerade, she could see now that he was impenetrable. All unfeeling and strong, unyielding and determined to stay that way.

'If that's all, I'd like to be shown to my suite now.'

# CHAPTER FIVE

'IT IS CALLED *albaqan raghif*,' he said quietly, his eyes on her as she fingered the delicate piece of bread, his words murmured so they breathed across her cheek. She resisted the impulse to lean closer. This was the first she'd seen of him since their discussion earlier that day. For most of the day, she'd been given a tour of the palace by a senior advisor, shown the ancient rooms—the library, the art galleries, the corridors lined with tapestries so like those that hung in the palaces of Taquul. Looking at them had filled her with both melancholy and hope. A sadness that two people so alike and with such a richly shared history could have been so combative for so long, and hope that their shared history would lay the foundations for a meaningful future peace.

Now, sitting at the head of the room with him, various government ministers in attendance, she concentrated on what she'd come here for—this was a state visit and she the representative of Taquul—how she felt about the man to her right was not important. 'We have something similar in Taquul.' She reached for a piece of the pecan bread and bit into it. She concentrated on the flavours and after she'd finished her mouthful said, 'Except ours generally has different spices. Nutmeg and cardamom.'

'My mother made it like that,' Amir said with obvious surprise.

She took another bite and smiled at him politely. 'This is very good too.'

His eyes narrowed. 'But you prefer it the way you're used to.'

'I didn't say that.'

Silence stretched between them, all the more noticeable for how much conversation was swirling around the room. The mood was, for the most part, festive. Some ministers had treated her with suspicion, a few even with open dislike, but generally, people had been welcoming. It saddened her to realise how right Amir had been—the peace would not come easily. Prejudices died hard.

'I'm sorry your brother sent you.'

She was surprised by the words. She squared her shoulders, careful not to react visibly. 'You'd prefer I hadn't come?'

He angled his face to hers. 'As I'm sure you would have wished to avoid it.'

'On the contrary—' she reached for her wine glass '—I relished the opportunity.'

His eyes held hers curiously.

'I've heard a lot about Ishkana. All my life, stories have been told of your people, your ways, your ancient cities. To be here now is an exercise in satisfying my curiosity.'

He lifted his brows. 'What are you curious about?'

'Oh, everything.' She sipped her wine. 'The ruins of *wasat*, the wall that spans the *sarieun sea*, the theatres in the capital.' She shook her head, a smile playing about her full red lips. 'I know there won't be a chance on this visit, but in time, with continued peace between our people, these landmarks could open up.'

He appeared to consider that for a moment. 'Yes. In time.'

'And our historical sites will be open to your people as well.'

He regarded her for several long moments, then sighed. 'You are an optimist.'

She laughed softly, spontaneously. 'Am I?'

Photographers were not permitted at royal banquets. It was a long-established protocol and even in this day of cell phones no cameras were used during meals. If anyone had taken a photo in that second though it would have captured two royals with their faces close together, their eyes latched, a look of something very like intimacy in their position. To a few of those present, the idea of the powerful, feared and adored Sheikh Amir Haddad sharing a meal with the Princess of Taquul was likely a bitter pill to swallow.

'If I am,' she murmured, after several seconds, 'then you must be too.'

His expression was unchanged. 'I don't think I've ever been accused of that.'

'It's not an accusation so much as an observation,' she corrected.

'Fine. That has never been…observed…of me before.'

'Doesn't it take a degree of optimism to proceed with a peace treaty? You must believe it will succeed or why bother with all this?' She gestured around the room, as if rousing them both, reminding them of where they were and how many people were watching.

Both separated a little, straightening in their seats. 'Acknowledging the necessity of something has no bearing on its likely success.'

'I take it back. I think I was right the first time we met. You're a cynic.'

'*That* I have been called frequently.'

The air between them seemed to spark. Awareness flooded Johara's body. Sitting close to him, speaking like this, she found the tension almost unbearable. She felt as though her skin was alive with an itch that she wanted to scratch and scratch and scratch.

The evening was long. After the dinner—which spanned six courses—there were speeches. The trade minister, the foreign minister, the culture minister. Johara sat beside Amir and listened, a polite smile on her face even when many small, barbed insults were laid at her country's feet. She wanted to respond to each that it took two to tango— a war couldn't be continued at only one country's insistence. Wrongs had been perpetrated on both sides. But all the while, the knowledge of what the man beside her had lost at her uncle's hand kept her silent.

She nodded politely, reminding herself again and again that her place in all this was not to inflame tensions so much as to soothe them. A necessary part of the peace process would involve humility—from both sides. The thought made her smile. Imagining Sheikh Amir Haddad humbling himself was not the easiest thing to do.

Finally, when all the speeches had been made, Johara stood. She ignored the small insults she'd heard and focussed on the bigger picture, and the fact Amir had invited her here.

'I'm gratified to sit here with you as a representative of my brother, Sheikh Malik Qadir, and the people of Taquul. I hope this is the first of many such events enjoyed by our people in this new age of peace and understanding.' She paused and smiled, her eyes skimming the room before coming to rest on Amir. He didn't return her smile and the expression on his chiselled face made her pulse rush through her body. 'I'm grateful for the hospitality of your kingdom, your people, and your Sheikh.' She wrenched her eyes away from him with difficulty. 'I look forward to getting to know the ways of your people better.'

When she sat down, it was to the sound of muted applause. Even that earned a wry smile from her, though she dipped her head forward to hide it. Only Amir caught the look, his eyes still trained on her face.

As was the custom, he led her from the room, the official engagement at an end. It would be ordinary for him to hand her off as soon as they'd left the palace hall, and yet he didn't. He continued to walk with her. On either side, they were flanked by enormous flower arrangements—filled with natives of the region, blooms, foliage, pomegranate, citrus, all in their infancy so the fruit was miniature and fragrant. There were security personnel too, carefully watchful, discreet and respectful, but Amir felt their presence with a growing sense of frustration.

At the bottom of the stairs that led to the wing of the palace reserved for visiting dignitaries, he paused, wondering at the sense of hesitation that gripped him.

'You must be tired.' His voice was gruff. He made an effort to soften it.

'Must I be?' She lifted both brows, her lips pursed.

'You arrived early this morning. It's been a big day.'

'Yes,' she agreed, looking sideways with a small sigh. 'But I'm not tired.'

Neither said anything. He could only look at her, the face held in profile, so beautiful, so achingly beautiful, but so full of the Qadir features that even as he yearned to reach for her he stayed where he was, his body taut, old hatreds deep inside his soul refusing to be quelled.

'In truth, I'm restless,' she said after a moment. 'I feel as though I've spent all day saying and doing what's expected of me and what I'd really like is just a few minutes of being my actual self.'

The confession surprised him.

'I don't suppose you have a maze I could go and get lost in for a bit?'

It was said light-heartedly, as a joke, but he couldn't fail to feel jolted by the reminder of that damned maze.

'No.' Too gruff again. He shook his head. This was no good. How could she be so effortlessly charming despite their long, bitter past? 'We have something even better.'

She put a hand on her hip, drawing his attention downwards, to her waist and the curves that had driven him crazy long before he'd known who she was. 'I doubt that.'

His laugh was deep and throaty. 'Want to bet?'

'Sure. Show me.'

What was he doing? He should tell her to go to bed; in the morning, she'd have another busy day. But a thousand fireworks seemed to be bursting beneath his skin. He wanted to be alone with her, even when he knew every reason he should fight that desire.

'May I go and change first?'

His lips tugged downwards. 'Your Highness, you're here as my guest. You do not need to ask my permission for anything.'

He'd surprised her. She bit down on her lip and he had to look away, before impulses overtook him and he dropped his head to kiss her. It would have felt so natural and easy.

'I'll wait here.'

She nodded once then turned, walking up the wide, sweeping staircase. He couldn't help but watch her departure.

Fifteen minutes later, Johara was ready. Having played the part of dutiful princess all day, she had found it a sheer, blissful relief to slip out of the couture dress she'd worn to the state dinner and pull on a pair of simple black trousers and an emerald-green blouse, teamed with simple black leather ballet flats. It was the kind of outfit she would wear in New York—dressy enough to escape criticism but comfortable and relatable. Her hair had been styled into an elegant braid that wrapped around her head like a crown to secure the actual crown she'd worn—enormous diamonds forming a crescent above her head. She deftly removed the two dozen pins that had been used to secure it, laying the tiara on the dressing table, then letting her hair fall around her shoulders in loose voluminous waves.

With more time, she might have washed her face clean of the make-up she wore, but impatience was guiding her, making her work fast. As she walked back down the staircase, she only had eyes for Amir. He was standing exactly where she'd left him, dressed in the formal robes he'd worn to dinner, his swarthy complexion and the jet black of his hair forming a striking contrast to the snowy white robes.

All night he'd been businesslike, treating her as though they had no history beyond that of their countries, but now, there was more. He was incapable of shielding his response to her—the way his eyes travelled her body with a slow, possessive heat, starting with her face, which he studied with an intensity that took her breath away, then shifting lower, moving over the curves of her breasts, the indent of her waist, the generous swell of her hips, all the way down to her feet as she walked, one step at a time, holding the handrail for fear she might stumble. And as his eyes moved, heat travelled the same path, setting fire to her bloodstream so by the time she reached him she felt as though she were smouldering.

'Well?' Her voice shook a little; she didn't care. 'What do you have to rival the maze?'

His eyes lifted to her lips and she didn't breathe—she couldn't—for several long seconds. Her lungs burned.

He was going to kiss her. His eyes were so intent on her lips, his body so close—when had that even happened?—

his expression so loaded with sensuality that memories weaved through her, reminding her of what they'd shared.

She waited, her face upturned, her lips parted, her blood firing so hard and fast that she could barely think, let alone hear. She knew she should step backwards, move away from him—this was all too complicated—but she couldn't. She wouldn't. Just as the hand of fate seemed to guide them in the maze, a far greater force was at work now.

She expelled a shuddering breath simply because her lungs needed to work, and with the exhalation her body swayed forward a little, not intentionally and not by much, but it brought her to him, her breasts brushing to his chest lightly, so that her nipples hummed at the all too brief contact.

'Johara.' He said her name with intent, with surrender, and with pain. It was all too hard. Where she could push the difficulties aside, at least temporarily, he appeared unable to. He swallowed so his Adam's apple moved visibly, then stepped backwards, his face a mask of discipline, his smile a gash in his handsome face.

Disappointment made her want to howl *No!* into the corridor. She did nothing.

'Your Highness.' He addressed her formally, gesturing with the upturned palm of his hand that she should precede him down the corridor. Her legs felt wobbly and moist heat pooled between her thighs, leaving her in little doubt of just how desperately she wanted him.

She moved in the direction he'd indicated, and when he fell into step beside her he walked closely, close enough that their arms brushed with each stride, so heat and tension began to arrow through her, spreading butterflies of desire and hope in her gut. But why hope? What did she want? He was—or had been until recently—the enemy.

*Not my enemy.*

No, not her enemy. Though she'd accepted the war between their countries and the family feud that had defined the Qadirs and Haddads for generations, she had felt no personal hatred for him, nor his parents. The fact their countries had been at war until recently wasn't enough of a reason to ignore her instincts and her desires.

But for Amir, their history was so much worse. Where she had no personal wrong to resent him for, he'd lost his parents because of her uncle's malicious cruelty. His hatred for her family was understandable. But did he have to include her in that?

What did she want? The question kept circling around and around and around her mind, with no answer in sight. After several minutes, they reached a wide-set doorway, thrown open to the desert evening. He stood, waiting for her to move through it first, his manners innate and old-fashioned.

She stepped into the cool night air as Amir spoke to the servants. 'We are not to be followed.'

There was a pause and then a deferential nod of agreement. Johara turned away, amused to imagine what they must think—their Sheikh going out of the palace with a Qadir? Did they suspect Johara, all five and a half feet of her, posed a threat to the man?

Her lips curved in a smile at the notion, a smile that still hovered on her lips when he joined her. 'Care to share the joke?'

'I was just thinking how suspicious your guards looked,' she murmured, nudging him with her elbow, so his eyes fell to hers. Heat passed between them.

'You are from Taquul,' he said simply.

She ignored the implication. 'As though I might have a three-foot scabbard buried in here somewhere.' She ran her hands over her hips, shaking her head at the preposterous idea.

'I take it you don't?'

Her laugh was soft. 'You're welcome to check, Amir.'

As soon as she said the words she wished she could unsay them. She lifted a hand to her lips and stopped walking, staring at him with eyes that offered a silent apology. 'I didn't mean for you to…'

But he stared at her with a look that was impossible to read, his breath audible in the stillness of the night.

'It wasn't an invitation?'

Her heart was beating way too fast. How could it continue at that pace?

'We agreed that night was a mistake,' she reminded him.

'No, *I* said it was a mistake. *You* said it felt right.'

Her lips parted at the reminder. 'Yes, I did say that.'

He turned to look back to the palace. They'd moved down the steps and into a garden fragrant with night-flowering jasmine and citrus blossoms, out of sight of the guards. But he turned, moving them further, into an area overgrown with trees. It was unlike the maze in Taquul. Where that was all manicured and enchanting for its formal shape—like a perfect outdoor room—this was more akin to something from a fairy tale. Ancient trees with trunks as wide as six of Amir's chests grew gnarled and knotted towards a sky she knew to be there only because it *must* be there, not because she could see it. The foliage of each tree formed a thick canopy, creating an atmosphere of darkness. Were it not for Amir's hand, which he extended to take hers, she might have lost her footing and fallen. But he guided her expertly, leading her along a narrow path as if by memory. Deeper in the forest, the beautiful fragrance grew thicker and here there was a mesmerising birdcall, like a bell and a whip, falling at once. She paused to listen to it.

'The *juniya*.' He said the word as most people said her name, with a soft inflection on the 'j', so it was more like 'sh'.

'*Juniya*,' she repeated, listening as at least two of them began to sing back and forth.

'They're native to this forest. In our most ancient texts they are spoken of, depicted in some of the first scrolls of the land. But they exist only here, in the trees that surround the palace.'

'I can't believe how verdant the land is here.' She shook her head. 'It's like the foot of the mountains.'

'That's where the water comes from.'

'The moat around the palace?'

'And in my private hall,' he agreed, reminding her of the little stream that flowed through that magical place he'd taken her to when first she'd arrived at the palace— had that only been earlier on this same day? 'There's an underground cavern that reaches the whole way; the river travels through it. In ancient times, it was used to send spies into Taquul,' he said with a tight smile she could just make out. They continued to walk once more, and eventually the canopy grew less apparent, light from the stars and moon reaching them, so she could see his face more clearly.

'But not any more?'

'It's more closely guarded on the other side.' He laughed. 'And our own guards do the same,' he added, perhaps wondering if she might take the information back to her brother, to use it as a tactical strength against him. The thought brought a soft sigh to her lips.

'Even now in peace?' she prompted him.

'Always.' The words vibrated with the depth of his seriousness. 'The water runs underground to the palace, the heart of our government. We will protect it with our lives.'

A shiver ran down her spine, his passion igniting something inside her.

'The war went on for a long time. It's only natural to think like that.'

'You consider yourself immune from the effects of it?'

She lifted her slender shoulders. 'I've spent a lot of time in New York. In truth, I've always felt I straddled two worlds, with one foot in my Taquul heritage and another in my mother's America. That isn't to say I feel the connection to my people any less, nor that I don't see the seriousness of the war, but I see it—at times—with something akin to an outsider's perspective.'

He reached out and grabbed an overhanging leaf, running his fingertips over it before handing it to Johara. She took it, lifting it her nose and inhaling gratefully. The smell was sweet and intoxicating. 'With an outsider's clarity, perhaps,' he said darkly.

It jolted her gaze to his face. 'You think I have greater clarity than you in this matter?'

He stopped walking, his expression tight. 'I think war has become a way of life,' he said with a nod. 'Like you said. Those habits will die hard.'

'It's ironic,' she murmured softly, 'that you remind me of him, in many ways.'

He braced. 'Who?'

'My brother.'

His expression was forbidding. 'I'm not sure I appreciate that.'

'I didn't expect you would, but it's true. I think it's probably an important thing to remember in war. You were the one who said that—we're more alike than we are different.'

'I was speaking generally.'

She shrugged once more. 'And I'm speaking specifically.'

'Don't.' He shook his head, his eyes locked to hers. 'Don't compare me to him.'

'He's my brother,' she reminded him. 'You can stand here with me, showing me this incredible place—' she gestured beyond her '—but you can't even speak his name?'

Amir stiffened. 'Believe me, Johara, I am conscious, every minute we're together, of who you are and what my being here with you means. You think I don't feel that I am, right this second, betraying my parents' memory?'

She sucked in a jagged breath, pain lancing her at the fact he could perceive anything to do with her as a betrayal of his parents. She spun away from him, looking back towards the palace. It was too far to see. She knew it would be there, beyond the enormous trees, glowing like a golden beacon. But it was no beacon, really. Not for her. The pain would be impossible to escape so long as she was here in Ishkana.

Her voice wobbled. 'I think you're honouring their memory by striving for peace. I think they'd be proud of you.'

His breath was ragged, filling the air behind her. His hand curved around her wrist, spinning her gently back to face him. 'Perhaps,' he agreed. 'But that doesn't make this any easier.'

His face showed the burden of his thoughts, the weight of his grief. She looked at him for several seconds and then went to pull her wrist away. He didn't release her.

'You are a Qadir,' he said darkly, as if reminding himself.

She lifted her chin, fixing him with a determined glance. 'And you are a Haddad. What's your point?'

'When my parents died, I could not show how I felt. I was twelve years old—still a child—but, here in Ishkana, old enough to become Sheikh. My life changed in a thousand ways. There was no time to grieve, to mourn, to process the loss of my parents. We were at war.' His thumb began to pad the flesh of her inner wrist, rhythmically, softly, but almost as though he didn't realise he was doing it.

'I used to fall asleep at night with only one thought to comfort me.'

A lump had formed in her throat, making it difficult to swallow. 'What was that?'

'That I would hate the Qadirs and what they had done for the rest of my life.' His eyes seemed to probe hers, his expression tense—his whole body, in fact, radiated with tension.

'You were twelve.' The words came out as a whisper. She cleared her throat and tried again. 'Of course you were angry.'

'Not angry,' he corrected. 'I was calm. Resolute. Determined.' When he breathed, his chest moved, brushing her.

'And yet you've signed a peace treaty.'

'For as much as I hate your family, I love my country and its people. For them I will always do what is best.'

Her heart felt as though it were bursting into a thousand pieces. Her stomach hurt. 'I don't know what to say.' She dropped her gaze to his chest, unable to bear his scrutiny for a moment longer. 'My uncle was imprisoned by my family after his despicable action—where he still languishes, at my brother's behest. He had no support from my parents, my brother, and certainly not from me. Our war was an economic one, a war of sanctions rather than violence.' She tilted her head, willing his defiance. 'Oh, there are the renegades on the borders and of course the military posturing that seems to go hand in hand with war, but to stoop to something so violent and…and…wrong as assassinating your parents? That was my uncle's madness, Amir. If you are to hate anyone—and I cannot stress enough how futile and damaging that kind of hatred is—but if you insist on hating anyone, have it be Johar. Not every single person who shares his surname. Not me.'

He groaned, low and deep in his throat. 'What you say makes perfect sense.'

'And yet you don't agree?' Her words sounded bleak.

'I don't *want* to agree.'

She lifted her eyes back to his. 'Why not?'

'Because this ancient hatred I feel is the only thing that's been stopping me from doing what I wanted to do the second you arrived at the palace this morning.'

Her heart stopped racing. It thudded to a slow stop. 'Which is?'

His eyes dropped to her lips. 'I want to kiss you, Johara.'

Her heart stammered.

'I want to claim your mouth with mine. I want to lace my fingers through your hair and hold your head still so I can taste every piece of you, bit by bit, until you are moaning and begging me, surrendering to me completely as you did in the maze.'

Her knees were knocking together wildly, her stomach filled with a kaleidoscope of butterflies.

'I want to strip these clothes from your body and make love to you right here, with only this ancient forest to bear witness to whatever madness this is.'

She could barely breathe, let alone form words. 'Would that be so bad?'

His eyes closed, as if it were the worst thing she could have said. 'The first time was a mistake, but I didn't know who you were then.'

'Now you do, and you still want me,' she challenged softly, aware she was walking on the edge of a precipice, so close to tumbling over.

He swore softly in one of the dialects of his people. 'You deserve better than this. Better than for a man who can offer you nothing, wanting you for your body.'

She didn't—couldn't—respond to that.

'I can offer you nothing,' he reiterated. 'No future, no friendship beyond what is expected of us in our position. I cannot—will not—form any relationship that might jeopardise what I owe my people.'

'Damn it, Amir, I have no intention of doing anything to hurt your people...'

'Caring for you would compromise my ability to rule. There are lines here we cannot cross.'

She swallowed, the words he spoke so difficult to comprehend and yet, at the same time, on an instinctive level, they made an awful kind of sense. Amir had been running this country since he was twelve years old. His life was impossible for Johara to understand. But she knew about duty and sacrifice; she had seen both these traits ingrained into her brother, she understood how his country would always come first.

And it wasn't that he perceived *her* as a threat to the country. Not Johara, as a woman. Johara as a Qadir, as a member of the Taquul royal family. It was symbolic. The peace was new. His people would take time to accept it, to trust it, and if news of an affair between Amir and Johara were to break, it could threaten everything by stirring up strong negative feelings in response. Retaliation could occur.

The war had been too costly, especially on the border.

She closed her eyes and nodded, a sad shift of her head, because the futility of it all felt onerous and cumbersome.

'I don't hate you, Amir.' She pulled her hand out of his and this time he let her. Her flesh screamed in agony, begging to be back in his grip. Her stomach looped again and again. 'But you're right. I deserve better than to be the scapegoat for all the pain you've suffered in your life.' She straightened her spine and looked beyond him. 'Shall we go back to the palace now? I think I've seen enough for tonight.'

# CHAPTER SIX

THE SUN WAS UNRELENTING, the sands from the deserts stirred into a frenzy and reaching them even here, on the outskirts of the city where one of the oldest libraries stood in existence. He'd had this added to the itinerary days before she arrived. Memories of the maze had been running thick and fast through his mind. The pride with which she'd spoken of her work with childhood literacy had been impossible to forget—her eyes had sparkled like diamonds when she'd discussed the initiative she'd put together.

He knew she'd find the library itself beautiful—the building was very old, the books, parchments, scrolls, tapestries and stone walls contained within dated back thousands of years, but more than that, there were the spaces that had been built in the last fifteen years, during his reign, specifically to make books and reading more accessible to the youth of Ishkana.

This was the last stop on what had been a day filled with formal events. So much polite meeting and greeting, smiling, posing for photographs, and all the while Johara's features had never shown a hint of strain or discomfort. Not at the proximity to a man who had been, as she claimed, using her as a 'scapegoat'. Nor in exhaustion from the heat, nor after hours on her feet in dainty high heels that must surely pinch.

Even now, she listened with a rapt expression on her face as his Minister for the Arts explained how the library spaces worked.

Impatience coursed through Amir's veins. He no longer wanted to stand to the side as she was shown through the library. He wished everyone to leave, so that it was just Johara and him, so that Amir could tell her what he'd hoped when he'd had the rooms built, so that he could tell her his favourite memories of being here in this building. Even when he was a boy, it had been one of his most delighted-in haunts.

'What an incredible programme,' she said, almost wistfully, running a finger over the bottom of a windowsill. Beyond them, the classroom was full of children—some of the poorest of Ishkana. Buses were sent each morning to various districts, a bell loudly proclaiming its arrival, giving all children who wished it a chance to get on board.

'We are working towards universal education,' Amir found himself saying, moving closer, half closing the Minister for the Arts from the conversation and drawing Johara's eyes to his. It was only then that a sense of reserve entered her expression—just a hint of caution in the depths of her eyes but enough for him to see it and recognise it. 'It was a passion of my father's.' He took a step down the marble corridor, urging her to follow him. It was impossible not to remember the group that followed them—staff, servants, media—and yet he found himself tuning them out, thinking only of Johara as they walked.

'Education?' she prompted, falling into step beside him.

'Yes. The benefits to the whole country can't be underestimated.'

'I agree,' she said, almost wistfully.

'This is the state library,' he continued. 'So we were limited in the scope of what we could achieve. Naturally

there is much here that is protected from too much public access—the oldest texts are stored on the second and
third floors and kept out of the way of children.' His smile
was genuine.

She nodded. 'Naturally.'

'This is just an example of what we're prioritising, and
serves only the inner-city children. Beyond this, we've built
twenty-seven libraries in the last decade, starting in the
poorest regional communities and working our way up.
The libraries aren't just for books, though. There are com-
puters and tablets, lessons in how to use both, and for the
children, six days per week, classes are offered. Book hiring is incentivised, with small tax breaks offered to regular borrowers.'

She gasped. 'Really?'

'Oh, yes. Really.'

'What an incredible initiative.'

He lifted his shoulders. 'Reading is a habit that brings
with it many benefits.'

She seemed to miss her step a little. He reached out and
put a hand under her elbow, purely to steady her, but the
sparks that shot through him warned him from making
such a stupid mistake—particularly in public.

'You must feel likewise to have established your childhood literacy initiative?'

'Yes.' Her smile was more natural. She casually pulled
her arm away, putting a little more distance between them.

'You enjoy reading?'

She kept her eyes straight ahead, and didn't answer. Instead, after a moment, they came to the opening of a large
room, this one filled with straight desks at which students
could study during term time, and dark wooden walls filled
with reference texts.

'What a lovely room.'

He wondered if she was changing the subject intentionally, but let it go. There would be time later to ask her again—he wasn't sure why it mattered, only it felt as if she was hiding something from him and he didn't want that. He wanted to know...everything.

The thought almost made *him* miss a step, for how unwelcome it was.

Why? What was the point? He didn't want to analyse it, he knew only that his instincts were pushing him towards her, not away, and he could no longer tell what was right or wrong.

The rest of the library tour took forty-five minutes. At the end of it, he paused, with one look keeping the rest of their contingent at a distance, leading her away separately. 'Would you like to see what's upstairs?'

'The ancient texts?'

He dipped his head.

'I...would have thought they were too precious to share with someone like me.'

His stomach tightened. Because she was a Qadir? Why wouldn't she feel like that, particularly after the things he'd said the night before? 'They are not something we routinely display to foreign guests.' He deliberately appeared to misunderstand her. 'But would you like to see them?'

Her breath grew louder, her eyes uncertain. He could feel a battle raging within her, the same kind of battle that was being fought inside him. 'I would,' she said, finally, not meeting his eyes.

Without a response to her, he spun on his heel and stalked to the group. He addressed only Ahmed, giving brief instructions that the motorcade should wait twenty minutes—that he and the Princess were not to be disturbed.

It was a break from protocol, but nothing he couldn't explain later.

Before he could see the look of disapproval on Ahmed's face, Amir walked Johara towards a bank of elevators, pressing a button that immediately summoned a carriage. The doors swished open and he waited for her to step inside before joining her and pressing a gold button. Even the elevators were very old, built at the turn of the nineteenth and twentieth centuries. It chugged slowly, and he tried not to pay attention to how close they stood in the confines of the infrastructure.

The doors opened and he felt relief—relief to be able to step further away from her, to stop breathing in her scent, to be able to resist the impulse to touch her, just because she happened to be standing right in front of him.

'Many of these are relevant to your country,' he said, indicating one tapestry that hung opposite the elevator, dimly lit with overhead lights to preserve its beautiful threads.

She studied the pictures, a look of fascination on her features. He led her through the area, showing some of his favourite pieces.

'You sound as though you know this place like the back of your hand,' she said after ten minutes.

He smiled. 'I do. I came here often as a child. I loved to sit up here and read while my parents attended to business at parliament. I was fortunate that they indulged my every whim.' He laughed.

Her tone was teasing. 'Are you saying you were spoiled?'

'Actually, I wasn't.' He grinned. 'Only in this aspect— my mother found my love of books amusing.'

'Why?'

'Because for the most part, I preferred to be out of doors. I hated restriction. I liked to run and ride and swim and climb. In that way, I was cast in my father's image. But then, here at the library, I saw the opening to all these other worlds and found a different way to run and be free.'

She was transfixed by his words, her expression completely engaged by what he was saying. 'It was a catalyst for them. Seeing how I loved these texts, how they opened my eyes and mind—I still remember the conversation between them, travelling back to the palace one night, when my father remarked that every child should be able to lose themselves in a library as I seemed to want to.'

Johara paused, looking at a small book with a golden spine and beautiful cursive script.

'They were right.' Her voice was small.

'Was this similar to your own childhood?'

A beat passed, a pause which seemed somehow unnatural. 'I...spent my childhood undertaking ceremonial duties on behalf of the palace,' she said calmly. But too calm, as though her voice was carefully neutralised to hide any real feeling. He didn't speak, sensing that she would continue only if he stayed silent.

He was right. 'My mother died when I was six. I have vague memories of attending events with her. But after she passed, I was expected to take on her role.' Her smile was laced with mockery. 'Something you know about.'

'At such a young age?'

'I didn't question it at the time. My *amalä* had focussed a lot of my education on etiquette, socialising, on how to speak and be spoken to.' She shrugged as though it didn't matter. 'It was second nature to me.'

'But you were still a baby.'

She laughed. 'I was old enough.' Her brow furrowed. 'There wasn't much time for libraries and reading, nor even for studying. None of which was deemed particularly important for me anyway.'

Amir stopped walking, something like anger firing through him. 'So your education was sacrificed in order for you to cut ribbons and make speeches?'

'I sit on the board of many important charities and foundations,' she contradicted defensively, then dropped her head in a silent sign of concession. 'But yes. Essentially, you're correct.'

'And your brother?' He couldn't conceal his anger then. It whipped them both, drawing them closer without their knowledge.

'Mal had an education similar to yours, I imagine. Well rounded, with the best tutors in various subjects being flown in to instruct him. He was taught to be a statesman, a philosopher, to govern and preside over the country from when he was a very young boy.'

Amir wanted to punch something! 'That's grossly unfair.'

Johara's eyes flashed to his; he felt her agreement and surprise. 'It's the way of my people.'

'It's as though nothing has changed for *your people* in the last one hundred years.'

She lifted her shoulders. 'And Ishkana is so different?'

He stared at her as though she had lost her mind. 'Yes, Ishkana is different. You've seen the facilities we've created. You've heard me talk about the importance of books and education for children. Have you heard me say, at any point, "for boys", as opposed to "children"?'

She didn't speak. Her eyes held his, and something sparked between them.

'My grandfather made inroads to gender equality, but he was hampered—if you can believe it—by public opinions. By the time my father was Sheikh, the Internet had been born, and a homogenisation of attitudes was—I would have thought—inevitable. My mother was progressive, and fiercely intelligent. The idea of her skill set languishing simply because women weren't seen as having the same rights to education as men...'

'I am not languishing,' she interrupted. 'I get to represent causes that matter a great deal to me.'

He stared at her, not wanting to say what he was thinking, knowing his assessment would hurt her.

'What?' she demanded. 'Say what you're thinking.'

Surprise made him cough. How could she read him so well? What was this magic that burst around them, making him feel as though they were connected in a way that transcended everything he knew he *should* feel about her?

'Only that it sounds to me as though your representation is more about your position and recognisability than anything else.'

She jerked her head back as though he'd slapped her and he instantly wish he hadn't said such a cruel thing. He shook his head, moving a step closer, his lips pressed together.

'I'm sorry.'

'Don't.' She lifted a hand to his chest, her own breathing ragged. 'Don't apologise.'

They stood like that, so close, bodies melded, breath mingling, eyes latched, until Johara made a sort of strangled noise and stepped backwards, her spine connected with the firmness of a white marble wall.

'Don't apologise,' she said again, this time quieter, more pained. He echoed her movement, stepping towards her, his body trapping hers where it was, his own responding with a jerk of awareness he wished he could quell.

'You're right.' She bit down on her full lower lip, reminding her of the way she'd done that in the maze, and the way he'd sought it with his own teeth. 'I'm ornamental. Unlike your mother, I'm not fiercely intelligent. I can't even read properly, Amir. Educating me in a traditional way would have been a waste of effort. So my parents focussed on what I was good at, at my strengths—which is people. I serve my country in this way.'

He could hardly breathe, let alone speak. 'You were not even taught to read?'

'I was taught,' she corrected. 'But not well, and it didn't seem to matter until I was much older. At twelve, I sat some tests—and was diagnosed with severe dyslexia.' A crease formed between her brows. 'It wouldn't have made any difference if they'd discovered it earlier. It's not curable. My brain is wired differently from yours. I can read—passably—but it takes me longer than you can imagine and it will never be what I do for pleasure.' Her eyes tangled with his and she shook her head. 'Don't look at me like that.'

'How am I looking at you?' he interrogated gently.

'As though you pity me.' She pressed her teeth into her lip once more. 'I still love books—I listen to recordings whenever I can—and let me assure you, I derive the same pleasure from their pages as you do.'

He listened, but something was flaring inside him, something he hadn't felt in such a raw and violent form for a very long time. Admiration. Respect.

'This is why you founded the literacy initiative in New York?'

'Yes.' Her smile, as he focussed conversation on something that brought her joy, almost stole his breath. 'To help children. Even children like I was—if a diagnosis can be made early enough—will be spared years of feeling that they're not good enough, or smart enough.'

'And you felt these things.'

Her smile dropped. His anger was back—anger at her parents, and, because they were dead and no longer able to account for their terrible, neglectful parenting, anger at the brother who hadn't troubled himself to notice Johara's struggles.

'Yes.' Her eyes held defiance. 'I *used* to feel that way. But then I moved to America and I came to understand that the skills I have cannot be taught. I'm great with people. I'm great at fundraising. I can work a room and secure millions of dollars in donations in the space of a couple of hours. I can make a real difference in the world, Amir, so please, for the love of everything you hold dear, stop looking at me as though I'm an object of pity or—'

Something in the region of his chest tightened. 'Or?'

'Or I'll… I don't know. Stamp my foot. Or scream.' She shook her head. 'Just don't you dare pity me.'

He gently took her chin between his finger and thumb. 'I don't pity you, Johara.' His eyes roamed her face and, in the distance, he could hear the beating of a drum, low and solid, the tempo rhythmic and urgent all at once. It took him moments to realise there was no drum, just the beating of his heart, the torrent of his pulse slamming through his body.

'You don't?'

'I admire you,' he admitted gruffly. 'I admire the hell out of you and damn it if I don't want to kiss you more than ever right now.'

Her knees could barely hold her. If he weren't standing so close, pinning her to the wall, she wasn't sure she would have trusted her legs to keep her upright. His face was so close, his lips just an inch from hers. She tilted her face, her own lips parting in an unspoken invitation, and she stared at him, hoping, wanting, every fibre of her being reverberating with need.

'How do you make me forget so easily?'

'Forget what?' Closer. Did she lift onto the tips of her toes or did he lower his face? Either way, her mouth could almost brush his now. Adrenalin surged through her veins, fierce and loud.

'Who you are.' He threw the words aside as though they were inconsequential, and then finally he kissed her, a kiss that was for him exultant and for her drugging. Her need for him obliterated every shred of rational thought, every ability to process what was happening. But even as his tongue slid between her lips, tangling with hers, and his knee nudged her legs apart, propping her up, her sluggish brain threaded his simple statement together. *Who you are.*

Who she was. It was so fundamental—her parentage, her lineage, her place in the Taquul royal family.

His hands gripped her hips, holding her possessively and almost fearfully, as though she might move away from him; he held her as though his life depended on her nearness. His kiss stole her breath and gave her life. She lifted her hands, tangling them behind his neck, her fingers running into the nape of his hair, pressing her breasts against his chest, her nipples tingling with remembered sensations.

*How do you make me forget so easily?*

But they couldn't forget. It wasn't that easy. He was a Haddad and she a Qadir and somewhere over the last one hundred years it had been written in stone that they should hate each other. Yet she didn't. She couldn't hate him. He'd done her no wrong and, more than that, she'd seen qualities that made her feel the opposite of hate. She *liked* him. She enjoyed spending time with him. She found talking to him hypnotic and addictive. And kissing him like this lit a thousand fires in the fabric of her soul.

But Amir would never accept her. He would always resent her, and possibly hate her. And that hatred would destroy her if she wasn't very, very careful. And what of her brother if he learned of this? Even her defiant streak didn't run that deep.

With every single scrap of willpower she possessed, Johara drew her hands between them and pushed at his chest, just enough to separate them, to give her breathing space.

'Your Majesty.' She intentionally used his title, needing

to remind him of what he claimed she made him forget. 'Nothing has changed since last night.' She waited, her eyes trying to read his face, to understand him better. 'Has it?'

His eyes widened, as though her reminder had caught him completely unawares. She could feel the power of his arousal between her legs, and knew how badly he wanted her. Yet he stepped backwards immediately, rubbing his palm over his chin.

'You're right, Princess.' His smile was self-mocking. 'That won't happen again.'

# CHAPTER SEVEN

'IT'S ONLY THREE more days.' Malik's voice came down the phone line, in an attempt to offer comfort. He could have no way of knowing that, far from placating her, the reminder that the week she'd been invited to Ishkana for was half-way over would spark something a little like depression inside her belly.

She looked out of her magnificent bedroom window over an aviary very like the one in Taquul, and again felt how alike these two countries were—just as Amir had said.

'I know.' It was the end of a busy day, filled with commitments and engagements. She'd seen so much of the city, met so many politicians and leaders, and the more she saw of this country, the less contented she felt.

The war had been so futile.

This was a beautiful country, a beautiful people. They'd been hurt by the past, just as the people in Taquul had been. Not for the first time, frustration with her parents and grandparents gnawed at her. Why hadn't they been able to find a peaceful resolution sooner? Why had it rested on two men, one hundred years after the first shot was fired?

'What's it like?'

'It's…' A movement below caught her attention. She swept her gaze downwards, trying to catch it again. Something white in amongst the olive and pomegranate trees below. Another movement. Her heart recognised before her mind did.

Amir.

He moved purposefully towards one of the aviaries, his frame powerful, his movements everything that was masculine and primal. He opened the door, and made a gesture with his hand. A large bird, with a wingspan half the height of Amir, flew from the cage and did a circle above his head, above Johara, its eyes surveying what they could, before neatly returning and hooking its claws around Amir's outstretched arm. Its feathers were a pale, pearlescent cream with small flecks of light brown, its beak tipped in grey.

'What?' Malik was impatient. 'Terrible? Awful? Are you hating it?'

'No!' She had forgotten all about her brother, on the other end of the phone. She shook her head despite the fact he wasn't there to see her. 'It's…wonderful.'

Amir's lips moved; he was speaking to the bird. She wished, more than anything, that she could hear what he was saying.

'Wonderful?' Malik's surprise was obvious. She ignored it.

'Yes. I have to go now.'

'But—'

'I'll call you another time, okay?' She pressed the red button on her screen, her eyes fixed on Amir. She could not look away. The dusk sky created a dramatic backdrop to an already overpoweringly dramatic scene. With the falcon perched on his forearm, he looked every bit the powerful Emir. She held her breath as he began to move towards the palace, her eyes following every athletic step he took, her mind silently willing him to look towards her, to see her. And do what? She stared at him as though with her eyes alone she could summon him.

When he was almost beneath her, he looked up, his eyes sweeping the windows of her suite before locking to her. He stopped walking, and he stared at her as she had been staring at him.

Hungrily.

Urgently.

As though seeing one another were their sole means of survival.

He dipped his head a moment later, a bow of respect, and her heart stammered; he was going to go away again. She wanted to scream. Impatience and frustration were driving her mad. Since their kiss in the library, she'd barely seen him. Brief photo opportunities and nothing more. And at these interludes he was polite but went out of his way to keep a distance, not touching her, his smile barely reaching his eyes before he replaced it with a businesslike look.

But here, now, the same fire that had burned between them in the library arced through the sky, threatening to singe her nerve endings.

'I...' She said it so quietly she wasn't sure he'd hear. And she had no idea what she even wanted to say. Only that she didn't want him to walk away from her.

His eyes lifted, held hers a moment, and then he grimaced, as though he was fighting a war within himself. A moment later, he began to walk, disappearing from her view completely. She stamped her foot on the balcony and squeezed her eyes shut, gripping the railing tightly. Her heart was frantic and, ridiculously, stupid tears filled her throat with salt, threatening to douse her eyes. She blinked rapidly to ward them off, hating how he could affect her, hating how futile their situation was. Of all the men she had to meet, of all the men who had the ability to make her crazy with desire, why did it have to be a king who saw himself as her sworn enemy? A man who had every reason in the world to hate her family?

With a growling sound of impatience she stalked back into the beautiful suite of rooms she'd been appointed, deciding she'd take a cool shower. Three more days. She could get through this. And then what? Forget about Amir?

Her skin lifted with goosebumps. Unbidden, memories of the maze flooded her mind, filling her eyes with visions of him over her, his handsome, symmetrical face, she felt the movements of his body in hers, and she groaned, the shower forgotten. She closed her eyes, allowing the memories to overtake her, reliving that experience breath by breath until her skin was flushed and her blood boiling in her veins.

She would never forget about him. She would return to Taquul and he would return with her—a part of him would anyway. What they'd shared had been so brief yet in some vital way he'd become a part of her soul.

A knock drew her from her reverie. She turned her attention to the door, wondering what she must look like—a quick glance in the mirror confirmed her cheeks were flushed and her eyes sparkling. She pressed the backs of her hands to her cheeks, sucked in a breath and then opened the door.

If she'd been hoping for Amir—and of course, on some level, she had been—she was to be disappointed. A guard stood there, his impressive military medals on one shoulder catching her eye. Medals that had been won in the service of his army—against her country. Another blip of frustration. The war was over now, but the hurts went deep on both sides. Did this soldier hate her because of who she was and where she came from? It was impossible to tell. His face was impassive as he held a piece of cream paper towards her, folded into quarters.

'Thank you,' she murmured, offering him a smile—perhaps enough smiles given genuinely and freely could turn hatred to acceptance, and eventually fondness.

She waited until the door was clicked shut again, then unfolded the note.

*Come to the West Gate. A*

Owing to her dyslexia and his hastily scrawled handwriting, it took her several moments to read it and when she finished, her fingertips were unsteady, her breathing even more so. She flicked another glance to the mirror, running her hands across the simple outfit she wore—loose pants and a tunic—then over her hair, which was loose around her shoulders. She reached for some pins and secured it in a low bun, added a hint of lipstick and then moved to the door.

Athena was coming in as Johara opened the door.

'Your Highness? You're going somewhere?'

'I— For a walk,' she said with a small nod.

'Shall I accompany you?'

'No.' Johara's smile was reassuring, when inside she was panicking. The company of her servant—even one she considered a friend, like Athena—was the last thing Johara wanted! 'I'd like to be alone,' she softened the rebuke, reaching out and touching Athena's forearm. 'Goodnight.'

The West Gate was not difficult to find. She had a vague recollection of it having been pointed out to her on her first day, when she'd been given a thorough tour of the palace. She retraced the steps she remembered, until she reached a wall of white marble that stretched almost impenetrably towards the sky, creating a strong barrier to the outside world. Halfway along the wall there was a gate made of gold and bronze, solid and beautiful, with ancient calligraphy inscribed in its centre.

As she approached it she slowed, scanning for Amir. She couldn't see him. But to the right of the enormous gates there was a doorway, made to blend in completely with the wall. It was ajar. She moved towards it, then pushed at it. Amir stood waiting for her.

Her breath hitched in her throat. She'd come so quickly she hadn't paused to consider what she might say to him when she arrived.

Neither smiled.

'Thank you for coming.'

A frown quirked her brows. Had he thought she might not?

'You mentioned that you wanted to see the ruins of *wasat*. They're at their best at sunset.'

It was then that she became aware of a magnificent stallion behind him. Beneath the saddle there was a blanket over its back, gold and black, and a roll of fabric hung to one side. She could only imagine it contained the sorts of necessities one might need when riding horses in this harsh climate—water, a satellite phone.

'Are they—far from here?'

'No.' He gestured to the horse. 'Ride with me.'

It was a command. A shiver ran down her spine, and a whisper of anticipation. She eyed the horse, trying to remember the last time she'd been on the back of one—years. Many, many years. Her gaze flicked uncertainly to his.

'It's like riding a bike,' he said, a smile lifting his lips now, a smile that sent little bubbles popping inside her belly.

She walked towards the horse. It was magnificent. A shimmering black, it reminded her of a George Stubbs painting—all rippling muscles and intelligent eyes. She lifted a hand and ran it over his nose. The horse made a breathy noise of approval then dipped his head.

Amir watched, transfixed.

'He's beautiful.'

'He likes you,' Amir murmured, moving closer, pressing his own hand to the horse's mane, running his fingers over the coarse hair. 'Let me help you up.'

She was tempted to demur, but, looking at the sheer size of the horse, she knew it wouldn't be wise. Or possible.

'Thank you.'

He came to her side, his eyes probing hers. 'Ready?'

She nodded wordlessly.

He caught her around the waist easily, lifting her towards the horse so she could push one leg over and straddle it. Amir's hands lingered on her hips a moment longer than was necessary and still she resented the necessity of their removal.

A moment later, he'd pressed his foot into a stirrup and swung his leg over, nestling in behind her, reaching around and taking the reins, his body framing hers completely. She closed her eyes, praying for strength, because sitting this close to him was its own form of torment. She could smell him, feel him, his touch confident and reassuring as he moved his leg to start the horse in motion.

'We'll go fast,' he said into her ear, the words warm against her flesh. Her heart turned over. She nodded, incapable of speaking.

They sped. The horse galloped north, towards the Al'amanï ranges before tacking east. The sun was low in the sky, the colours spectacular as day blurred towards night. They rode for twenty minutes, each step of the horse jolting Johara against Amir, so after a while she surrendered to the sheer physicality of this, and allowed herself to enjoy it. The feeling of his chest against her back. His thighs against hers. His arms around her, flexing the reins. Every jolt bumped her against him and by the time he brought the horse to a stop, she was so overcome by the sensations that were flooding her body she barely realised they were at an ancient site.

'These are the ruins,' he said, his face forward, beside hers, so if she turned her head just a little her lips would press against his. She could hardly breathe. Her eyes traced the outlines of the ancient building, barely registering the details. She saw the pillars and columns, one of the ornate rooftops remained, the windows carved into arches. Yes, she could imagine this would have been a resting point in the desert, thousands of years earlier. A lodging as a mid-way point across the landscape. It was beautiful but she was so overwhelmed, it was impossible to react. A noise overhead caught her attention. She glanced up to see the enormous wingspan of a bird—his falcon. As she watched, it came down to land atop the ruins, its eyes surveying the desert.

'They're…' She searched for the word and instinctively looked towards Amir. It was a mistake. Just as she'd imagined, he was so close, and in turning her head towards him she almost brushed his cheek with her lips. He shifted a little, so that he was facing her, their eyes only an inch apart. The air around them crackled with a heat that had nothing to do with the desert.

'The ruins are…'

She still couldn't find the words. Every cell of her DNA was absorbed by this man. He was too close. Too much. He was…perfect. Superlatives were something she had in abundance, when it came to Amir. The ruins just couldn't compete with him.

'Would you like to see inside?'

No. She wanted to stay right where she was. She bit

down on her lip, sure what she was feeling must be obvious in her expression.

'I—' She frowned, her brows drawing together.

'The view from the top is worth seeing.'

Was he oblivious to the tension that was wrapping around her? Did he not feel it?

She nodded slowly, awkwardly, but when he climbed down from the horse she had to tilt her face away from him because of the disappointment she was sure must show in her features. He held his hands out. 'May I?'

He was asking to touch her, again. The small sign of respect came naturally to him.

'Please.' She nodded.

He reached out and took hold of her curved hips, guiding her off the horse. The act brought her body to his, sliding down his length, so a heat that was impossible to ignore began to burn between her legs. She stood there, staring up at him, the sky bathing them in shades of violet and orange, the first stars beginning to twinkle overhead.

'Why did you bring me here?'

A muscle jerked low in his jaw. She dropped her eyes to it, fascinated. Her fingertips itched to reach up and touch, to explore the planes of his face, to feel him with her eyes closed and see him as he'd been in the maze.

'You wanted to see it.'

Her lips twisted in a half-smile. 'There are many things I want to see.'

'This was easy to arrange.'

The answer disappointed her. He was right. This had been easy—a short ride across the desert. He'd undoubtedly wanted to give the bird an outing—bringing Johara was just an afterthought.

It meant nothing to him. She was embarrassing herself by making it into more.

His voice rumbled through her doubts. 'And I wanted to see it with you. Through your eyes.' And then, with a frown, he lifted his hand to lightly caress her cheek. 'I wanted to see your wonderment as you looked upon the ruins. I wanted to be here with you.'

Disappointment evaporated; pleasure soared in its place.

He dropped his hand and took a step backwards. She wanted to scream. He stalked away from her, pulling the blanket from the side of the horse and removing a silver bottle. 'Would you like some water?'

She took it gratefully, taking a drink before handing it back to him. A drop of water escaped from the corner of her lips and before she could catch it, he'd reached out, his fingertip chasing it away then lingering beside her mouth.

She was in a world of trouble.

He took the bottle, had a drink then replaced it. 'Come on.' The words were gruff but she knew why. He wasn't impatient or annoyed. He was fighting himself, trying to get control of how he felt about her and what he wanted. He was fighting the same war he'd been fighting since the night of the masquerade, when they'd learned who they truly were.

It was a war, she realised in a blinding moment of clarity, that they were both destined to lose. Just as passion had overpowered them on that first night, without reason or sense, it would triumph again.

'Do you—?'

Another sentence she didn't—couldn't—finish.

'Do I?'

'Need to tie him up?' She jerked her thumb towards the horse without looking away from Amir. His eyes briefly flicked to the animal, his lips curling when he returned the full force of his attention to Johara.

'No. He will stay nearby.'

A *frisson* of awareness shifted across her spine. 'Because you're the Sheikh and everyone and everything in this kingdom must obey you?'

His brows lifted, amusement and something far more dangerous flickering in the depths of his eyes. 'Because he is well trained.' He shifted his body weight from one foot to the other, the act bringing him infinitesimally closer. 'And yes, because he obeys me.'

Every feminist bone in her body despaired at the pleasure she took in that—the idea of submitting to this man was sensual and pleasing and answered some archaic desire deep within her. She revolted against it, blinking to clear those desperately unworthy thoughts and forcing herself to step away from him, pretending fascination with the ruins. It was a fascination she shouldn't have needed to pretend. The ruins were beautiful, ancient, endlessly steeped in history and folklore; Johara had longed to see them since she'd first heard about them as a teenager.

Amir clearly knew them well. He guided her through the buildings, or what was left of them, describing what each would have housed. The accommodations, the stables, the hall for dining and the communal courtyard from which announcements were made.

With his words and his knowledge, he brought the ruins to life for Johara. As he spoke, she could see the colours, the people, she could imagine the noise—horses snorting and stomping, people talking, laughing. It was all so vivid.

'I never thought they would be this beautiful,' she said, shaking her head as he led her across the courtyard and through a narrow opening. A tower stood sentinel over the ruins.

'For security,' he murmured. 'This gave a vantage point in all directions.' The stairs were time-worn, carved into low depressions at the centre of each courtesy of footsteps and sandstorms.

'It's perfectly safe,' he assured her as they reached the top and he pushed open another door to reveal a small opening. The balcony was not large—with the two of them standing there, it left about a metre's space, and there were no guard rails, which meant Johara instinctively stayed close to Amir.

'Do you come out here often?'

'I used to.' The sun was so close to the bottom of the horizon, and the sky was now at its finest. Vibrant pink streaks flew towards them, spectacular against a mauve sky with diamond-like stars beginning to shine.

'Not any more?' She looked towards him.

'I have less time now.'

'Right. The whole sheikh thing.' She banged her palm to her forehead, feigning forgetfulness. 'If I were you, I think I'd come here every day, regardless.'

Her sigh made him smile. 'What do you like about it so much?'

'The history.' She answered automatically. 'The tangible connection to the past. When you described the purpose of each of the buildings I felt generations of people come back to life.'

'And you like history?'

'I like the lessons it can teach us,' she said without missing a beat. 'Nothing we do is new. It's important to remember the way things have played out in the past, otherwise humanity will keep making the same mistakes over and over again.'

He studied her face thoughtfully. 'Such as war?' he prompted.

'Well, yes. Such as war.'

'And yet, regardless of the fact we know what war entails and how badly it always ends, we keep finding ourselves in that state. Perhaps it's simply inherent to human nature to want to fight?'

'And assert our dominance?' She pulled a face. 'I'd like to think we can evolve beyond that.'

'There is a lot of evidence to the contrary.'

'We're in a state of evolution,' she retorted, a smile on her lips.

'And you are a hopeless optimist,' he remembered, and just like that, the first night they'd met was a binding, wrapping around them, making it impossible to forget a similar exchange they'd once shared.

'I'm not really. I think I'm a realist who looks on the bright side wherever possible.'

'Ah.' He made a sound of having been corrected. 'And I'm a realist who doesn't look on the bright side?'

'You're just a hyper-realist.' She smiled at him, an easy smile that morphed into something like a grin and then slowly began to fade from her face as the sun began to drop towards the horizon, so close to disappearing. She angled her face towards it, wondering why she felt as though she'd run a marathon, why her breath felt so tight in her lungs.

'From here, you can see all the way to the mountains in this direction.' He lifted his arm towards the north. She followed and nodded, her throat thick with feeling. 'And in this direction, the palace—though it wasn't there when this was built.'

'No,' she agreed, the words just a croak. The sun was a fireball in the sky, burning close to the horizon. The colours emanating from it were magnificent. Amir's falcon circled overhead and Johara's eyes followed its stately progress, each span of its wings spreading something before her. Magic. Destiny. A sense of fate.

She wrenched her gaze back to Amir's. 'Thank you for bringing me here.'

That same muscle throbbed low in his jaw. 'Don't thank me. My reasons were purely selfish.'

'Oh?' It was just a breathy sound. 'You're not planning on throwing me off the tower, are you?' She strove for lightness, something to alleviate the suffocating tension that was tightening around her.

He shook his head slowly. His hand lifted to her hair, touching it so gently, so reverently, that she pressed her head towards him, craving a deeper touch.

'I wanted to be alone with you, as we were in the maze.'

Her stomach swooped and dropped.

'You were right the other night.'

She didn't say anything.

'I intended to use you as—how did you put it?'

'A scapegoat,' she murmured quickly.

'Yes, a scapegoat.' His smile was laced with self-mockery. 'You were right.'

'I know.' She looked away from him but he lifted his fingers to her chin, gently tilting her face back to his. His fingers moved lower, tracing the pulse point at the base of her neck. He must have been able to feel the frantic racing of it.

'I do want you.'

She didn't say anything.

'But the boundaries of what this is—of what it can be—are something I have no power to affect.'

Her head felt dizzy. She swayed a little. He put a hand out, wrapping it around her waist, holding her against him. They were bound like that, drawn together, unable to be apart. At least for now.

'The peace is tenuous. And making it last is the most important thing I will ever do in my life. I must make this work—my people deserve my absolute dedication to this cause. If news were to break that something personal was happening between us, you a Qadir and me a Haddad...'

She swallowed. 'We slept together once. No one needs to know.'

His brow creased, his eyes grew serious. 'I'm not talking about then. Right now, this day, standing here with you, I want you, Johara. I want more of you. All of you. While you're here in this country, I want you in my life, my bed, I want you to myself whenever we can manage it. I can offer you nothing beyond this—the decision is yours. Is this enough?'

# CHAPTER EIGHT

'Is THIS ENOUGH?'

The sun slipped beyond the horizon, bathing the sky in the most magical, iridescent colours. The beating of the falcon's wings was slow and rhythmic, lulling her even as she felt the urgency of what he was asking. She tried to swallow; her mouth was drier than the desert sands.

There was a small part of her capable of rational thought and it was telling her that no, what he was offering wasn't enough. But it had to be. A little time with Amir was better than nothing; she knew it was temporary but she couldn't muster the strength to object to that—not if the alternative was that they close the door on whatever this was once and for all.

She blinked up at him, the inevitability of this completely breathtaking, and swayed closer. He inhaled deeply, as though breathing her in, and she smiled.

'Yes.' Relief flooded her. It was the right decision.

He made a groaning sound as he dropped his mouth to hers, kissing her even as his hands reached for the bottom of her tunic and pushed at it, lifting it just high enough to expose an inch of midriff. It was like breaking a seal; the moment his fingertips connected with her naked flesh she ached for him in a way that wouldn't be repressed. Her hands pushed at his robes, impatient and hungry, stripping them from his body as he did the same to her, revealing their nakedness simultaneously.

The sun dropped down completely; darkness began to curl through the sky. He drew her to her knees, kneeling opposite, kissing her, his hands wrapping around her as he eased her backwards: carefully, gently. The rooftop wasn't large, there was just space for them to lie together, and little more. He brought his body over hers, his eyes scanning her features, searching for something she couldn't fathom. Or perhaps she could, because she smiled and nodded, in response to his unanswered question, and then pushed up and kissed him, her mouth teasing him, her fingertips playing with the hair at his nape.

He drew his mouth from her lips to her collarbone, lighting little fires beneath her skin everywhere he kissed, his tongue lashing her to the edge of her sanity. She was tipped over the brink when he flicked one of her nipples; she arched her spine in a silent invitation, her fingernails dragging down his back. It reminded her of the way she'd marked him in the maze, making her smile—she lifted up and bit his shoulder, sinking her teeth into the flesh there and laughing as he straightened to fix her with a look that was equal parts smouldering and surprised.

His hands trapped hers, holding them over her head; she was no longer laughing. She couldn't. The power of what they both wanted was almost terrifying. He pushed her legs apart with his knee then kissed her, hard, her body completely trapped by his, her needs driven by him.

'No turning back,' he said into her mouth, pushing the words deep into her soul, where they took hold and filled her with relief. She didn't want to turn back. From the moment she'd discovered who he was, she'd wanted this—come hell or high water.

'No turning back,' she agreed, breaking the kiss just so

she could meet his eyes, in the hope he would see the seriousness of her response.

He claimed her mouth as he drove his arousal between her legs and into her feminine core. The relief of welcoming him back brought tears to her eyes. She kissed him with all the fierceness of her desire, lifting her legs and wrapping them around his back, holding him deep inside, allowing her body to glory in his possession. He began to move, hard and fast, as though driven by an ancient tempo that only they could hear.

His body was her master, and hers was his. Beneath the darkening sky, Amir made her his, watching as pleasure exploded through her again and again before giving into his own heady release, filling her with all that he was, holding her to him, their breath racked, their pleasure beyond compare.

Amir lay atop Johara for several minutes after, but it could have been days or months; there on the roof of a tower in the middle of the desert, time had no meaning. They were particles of life in amongst the sand and the history, as utterly a part of the earth as the elements that made this striking, barren landscape what it was.

Johara felt every bit a desert princess, overcome with a sense of her own power. Seeing the effect she had on him—that they had on each other—made her wonder at how they'd been able to resist doing this for as many days as they had!

Her eyes found the stars overhead—the sky had darkened to an inky black now—and she smiled at the thought that the celestial bodies alone had witnessed this coming together. It made it feel all the more powerful and important; all the more predestined.

Eventually, he pushed up onto one elbow, his gaze roaming her face possessively, as if looking for a sign of how she felt. So she smiled, and lifted a hand to cup his cheek, drawing his attention to her eyes. 'That was perfect.'

His features bore a mask of tightness but then he relaxed, smiling, rolling off Johara but simultaneously catching her and bringing her to lie with her head on his chest, his arm wrapped around her. She curled her body to his side, and his hand stroked her hip, his fingers moving with a slowness that could have induced drowsiness. Except Johara wasn't tired; far from it. She felt alive in a thousand and one ways. Her body had caught fire and she wasn't sure those fires would ever be extinguished.

'This is…complicated,' he said with a shake of his head, and then laughed, turning to face her. She saw the same thing in his expression that she felt in her heart. Surrender. This was bigger than them, bigger than the war. It was something neither could fight.

'No.' She shook her head and smiled, pushing up to press her chin to his chest. 'It's the opposite of that—it's so simple.'

He reached out, lacing his fingers through hers, stroking the back of her hand with his thumb. 'Yes.' He sighed. 'It is also simple.'

She put her head back down, listening to the strong, steady hammering of his heart. All her life she'd been told that the Haddads were the worst of the worst—not to be trusted, not to be seen as anything but the enemy. Yet here she lay listening to Amir Haddad's heart and she knew the truth—it was a good heart. A kind heart. A heart that lived to serve his people.

A heart that would never belong to anyone but his people.

Especially not her—a Qadir.

She pushed those thoughts away. They both knew what

they were doing, and what the limitations of this were. That didn't mean she couldn't enjoy it in the moment.

Her fingertips traced the inked words that ran across his chest. 'What does this mean?'

He shifted a little, flicking a glance at his chest, then focussing his attention back on the stars overhead. *'Amor fati,'* he said the words quietly.

'Yes. I love…' she translated with a small frown.

'It's Nietzsche,' he said. 'It means to love one's fate.' He turned towards her, scanning her face as if to read her reaction.

She was contemplative. 'Your fate, as in your role as Sheikh?'

His smile was dismissive. 'Partly, yes. All of it. My parents' death, the duty that put upon me. There was a time when I felt that what was required of me might cripple me. I was only young—fifteen, or sixteen—and I remember riding out here and lying just like this. Well…' a smile lifted his lips at the corners '…not quite like this—there was no woman.'

She smiled back, but didn't say anything; she didn't want him to stop speaking.

'I lay here and looked at the stars and felt as though the sky was falling down on me, suffocating me with its vastness. How could I—a boy completely alone in the world, with no parents, no siblings, only paid advisors—possibly be what was best for the country?'

'It was an enormous responsibility to bear at such a young age,' she said quietly.

'I felt that way *then*,' he responded quietly. 'I now realise that this responsibility was a gift. What a great thing, to be able to lead my people, to rule a country such as this.' He waved his hands towards the sand dunes that rolled away from these ruins.

*'Amor fati,'* she said simply.

'Yes. I lay here and realised that I was being self-indulgent. There was no sense wondering if I could be Sheikh. I was. And so I had to be.'

'If it makes any difference, you strike me as a natural at this.'

'Oh?'

She nodded. 'The night we met, before I knew who you were, I knew, somehow, *what* you were.'

'And what is that?'

'A ruler.' Her smile was slow to form. 'You have a natural authority that can't help but convey itself.'

He laughed gruffly. 'I'm used to being obeyed.'

'It's more than that. It's the way you move, the way you speak. I think that your fate chose you.'

'We could also say your uncle chose my fate.'

Her eyes flashed to his and pain sliced through her—brief and sharp. He saw it and shook his head by way of apology. 'I shouldn't have said that.'

'No.' She bit down on her lip. 'But you're right.' Her fingers chased the tattoo, running over the inky black lines. 'He was—is—an extremist. He always has been. He felt my parents were too moderate, that an all-out offensive was called for. He believed that only by destroying Ishkana could Taquul truly prosper. He wanted the war brought to an end once and for all—by any means necessary.'

'He wanted genocide,' Amir said quietly, but with a ruthless undercurrent to the words. 'And it is best if we do not discuss Johar.' The name was said with disgust.

She nodded. He was right. There was nothing she could ever say that would pardon her uncle's sins; nor did she want to. She judged him as harshly as Amir did.

'I am sorry,' she said quietly.

That drew his gaze, and the look in the depths of his

obsidian eyes did something funny to her tummy—tying it in a bundle of knots.

'It was not your fault, Johara.'

He said her name quietly, without a hint of the anger he felt for Johar.

She expelled a soft breath. 'I mean that I'm sorry you had to go through that. The grief…'

He pressed a finger to her nipple and drew an imaginary circle around it. She could barely concentrate. His touch was sending little arrows of need darting beneath her skin.

'Why did you send for me tonight?'

He lowered his mouth, pressing a kiss to the flesh just above her nipple. She shivered.

'I shouldn't have.' He lifted his head to smile. 'I told myself—after the library—that I would stay away from you. But then I saw you looking at me and I knew you felt the inevitability of this.' He lifted a finger, tracing her cheek. 'I knew that if I sent for you and you came, it would be because you didn't care about how forbidden and impossible this is.' He brought his mouth to hers. 'I sent for you because I found myself unable to resist.'

She moaned as he kissed her, her hands seeking his body once more, a new hunger growing inside her. She gave herself to the power of that, falling back against the cool granite of the tower as their bodies became one once more.

'It's best if I leave you at the West Gate.'

They hadn't spoken since leaving the ruins. It was as though each step of the powerful horse brought them closer and closer to the palace and the reality that awaited them. Out there, in the wildness of the desert, nothing had seemed impossible, but the constraints of who they were grew more apparent as the palace loomed into sight.

'Where will you go?'

'I'll take him to the stable yard.'

'You're afraid of being seen with me?'

She felt his harsh intake of breath. 'We discussed this. What we just did has to be kept secret.'

'I know.' She swept her eyes downwards, studying the horse's thick mane, wondering at the cloying sense of tears.

'There are a thousand reasons we cannot let anyone know what we're doing.' He brought the horse to a step and leaned forward, pressing a hand to the side of her face, drawing her to look at him.

His teeth clenched as he saw the raw emotion on her features.

'Johara…'

'I know. The war. The peace treaty. I'm a Qadir, you're a Haddad.'

'Yes,' he said, gently though, leaning forward and pressing his forehead to hers. 'But it's so much more than that. You are supposed to be marrying Paris. What would the press make of an affair with me while you are all but engaged?'

'I'm not engaged,' she said stiffly.

'In the media's eyes—and I believe your brother's eyes— you are. Your reputation would be damaged beyond repair.'

'This isn't the eighteen hundreds, Amir. No one expects a sacrificial virgin at the altar.'

'No, but you are a princess and people expect *you* to be perfect.'

She pulled away from him, jerking her face in the opposite direction.

'And I suppose you have similar concerns,' she said darkly.

Amir didn't pretend to misunderstand. 'One day I will marry. At present, my kingdom has no heir. But there is no one who would be hurt by our affair.'

'Paris and I are *not* a couple.'

Amir compressed his lips. 'As I said, I believe, in the eyes of your brother, your union is a *fait accompli.*'

'So what I want doesn't matter?'

'It matters. To me, it matters a great deal. I cannot speak on your brother's behalf.'

So measured! So reasonable! She wanted to scream.

And yet, he was right—she'd already felt the pain of being the press's latest object of fascination. For months she'd been hounded after her break up with Matthew. Anyone who'd known either of them had been pressed to give a 'tell all' interview. Private photographs had been found and shared in the articles. The invasion had been unbearable. It had been the catalyst for her departure to America.

Regardless of Paris, having an affair with the Sheikh of Ishkana would be huge news. Her people would hate it. Her brother might never forgive her.

She turned back to face him, regretting the concern she saw on his features, because she'd put it there with her silly reactions.

'You're right.' She nodded firmly. 'I'll go in the West Gate.'

His eyes lingered on her face a moment longer, as if he was reassuring himself before pulling on the reins, starting the horse back on the path.

At the gate, he paused in the midst of a row of pomegranate trees.

'Your schedule is busy tomorrow.'

'I know.'

'I won't see you until the afternoon.'

'At the tour of the *masjid*?'

'Yes, I'll be there too. But we won't be alone.' He cupped her face. 'Tomorrow night, meet me in the forest. Do you remember the way?'

She nodded. 'I think so.'

'Good. Just come to the edges of it. I'll be waiting.'

'What time?'

He thought of his own schedule, and knew he would clear whatever he needed to be available. 'I'll be there from seven. Come when you can.'

Her heart was speeding. Seven o'clock felt like a life-time away.

He climbed off the horse then reached up and took her hips in his powerful hands, lifting her easily off the back of the stallion. He held her close, and everything that was primal and instinctive stirred to life inside her.

'As soon as you can,' he said with a smile, but there was a darkness to that—the overpowering need shifting through them.

'I will.'

He kissed her—a light touch of his lips to hers—but it wasn't enough for Johara. She needed more—she didn't want to leave him. She lifted up, wrapping her arms around his neck, deepening the kiss, her body melded to his, and he made a thick noise in his throat as he held her tight to his body, kissing her back with the same hunger before pulling apart, wrenching himself free, breaking what was already becoming something neither could easily control.

They stared at one another for several seconds before a noise had her breaking away from him, moving quickly to the palace wall and pressing against it. He watched her for several beats before swinging onto his horse, pressing himself low to the neck and riding away.

Johara watched him go, her heart racing, her cheeks hurting from the ridiculous smile she couldn't shake.

# CHAPTER NINE

IT WAS AN hour into the tour of the *masjid* that Amir began to suspect Johara was a far better actor than he.

She was listening with all of her attention as the *allamah* showed them through the historic place of worship. It was Amir who was struggling to concentrate. He found his eyes straying to Johara when he too should have been listening. He found that he sought her out every few moments, trying to get her to look at him, wanting to see something in her eyes.

What?

Why did he need to look at her so badly?

To know that she didn't regret it.

He compressed his lips and looked away, turning his attention to a piece of art he knew well—a seven-hundred-year-old tapestry weaved from bright and beautiful threads. He moved towards it, as if fascinated by the detail, when in fact he just needed some breathing space.

There was no denying their chemistry; that was clear and mutual. But the danger for them both was real and undeniable. Shouldn't he be protecting her from that by fighting what he felt? For her sake, shouldn't he be stronger?

He closed his eyes, knowing he couldn't. They'd started on this path now and it wasn't in his power to stop.

And yet he could see danger on both sides. He had to

at least protect her from discovery. If they could keep this thing secret then when the time came for her to leave, she could continue with her life with no ramifications.

*That* was what he owed her.

And what about your people? a voice in his head demanded. What would they feel if they knew he'd been intimate with the Princess of Taquul?

He glanced towards her and something in his chest tightened. Yes, she was the Princess of Taquul, but she was so much more. To him, she was simply Johara, but to his people, was it possible she would continue to represent a threat? A reminder of past hatred and violence?

The peace was too important to risk.

Secrecy had to be ensured.

He vowed not to look at her again.

'You're cross with me?' Johara murmured, flicking him an inquiring glance as they walked side by side through the enormous room that led to the large timber doors. It was just the four of them and the *allamah* and Ahmed had moved further ahead.

He jerked his attention to her. 'No.' He looked away again. 'Why would you say that?'

'You're so serious. And trying so hard not to look at me.'

He kept his focus directly ahead. 'To avoid suspicion.'

Her laugh was soft. 'Where's the fun in that?'

And before he could know what she intended, she moved a step closer, her hand brushing against his.

He glared at her. 'Johara.' His voice held a warning.

Her smile was pure teasing. 'Relax. I'm not going to give the game away.' She brushed his hand again. 'But remember, it *is* a game. Try to have a little fun.'

Ahmed turned a moment later. Johara kept walking, no

sign of their conversation on her face. 'A crowd has gathered outside. Would you prefer a back entrance?'

Johara looked towards Amir. 'The purpose of my being here is to be seen,' she reminded him. 'We should show a united front.'

He hesitated for some unknown reason, and then nodded. 'Yes. Fine.'

Johara was effortless. He watched as she moved down the stairs, a smile on her face that disguised how she might have felt at being in the heartland of Ishkana so soon after the war had ended. If she held any anger towards his people, she hid it completely.

A woman was calling to her. He watched as she moved closer, but too close! Why didn't she stay back a little? He made a motion to Ahmed, who caught it and signalled to a security guard to intervene, to put some more space between the Princess and the crowd.

But it was too late.

A projectile left the hand of a man near the front of the group. Amir stood frozen to the spot as whatever it was sailed through the air, heading straight for Johara. He swore, began to run, but there wasn't time.

When he reached her, it had hit her square in the chest. The smell was unmistakable. Coffee. Warm, dark coffee was spreading over her white clothing, soaking the fabric, revealing the outline of her breasts. Fury slashed him.

The man was already running but Amir was quick. He reached into the crowd and grabbed him by the collar, pulling him towards through the rope line.

'Your Highness.' Johara's voice was urgent. 'I'm fine. It doesn't matter.'

But Amir barely heard her. He was not a violent man but as he held this person in his grip, he found his other hand forming a fist, and he badly wanted to use it.

'We will take him away,' Ahmed said, moving between Amir and the culprit. The man, to his credit, had the sense to look terrified.

'If you are going to act in this manner, at least stand and face your consequences. Coward,' Amir said angrily, but Ahmed was already pulling the man away, and two security guards had intervened to move Johara into the back of a waiting car.

He followed behind, sliding into the empty seat. Only once they started moving did he turn to her. Her skin was pale, her fingertips were shaking slightly but she was otherwise unharmed.

If there weren't two guards sitting opposite them in the limousine he would have reached across and put a hand over hers. Hell, he would have pulled her onto his lap and kissed her until she forgot anything about such an assault.

'I apologise, Your Highness.'

Her eyes met and held his. 'It wasn't your fault.' She reminded him of what he'd said the night before.

'I assure you, the man will be punished—'

'Don't do that either.' She sighed. 'You said it yourself. You can tell people we are at peace but you can't make them feel it in their hearts. Why should he be punished for doing something that six months ago he would have been lauded for?'

Amir ground his teeth. 'For the simple reason I have said it is wrong.'

She laughed. 'You are powerful, but not that powerful.'

'You are here as my guest,' he muttered. 'And your safety is my complete responsibility.'

'And?' She fixed him with a level gaze. 'I'm safe, aren't I?'

'It could have been—'

She shook her head. 'It wasn't.' She looked down her front. 'At worst, I'm embarrassed.'

Her phone began to vibrate. She reached into her pocket and pulled it out. Her brother's face stared back at her. She looked at Amir; it was obvious that he'd seen the screen.

She angled away from him a little.

'Mal? This isn't a good...' She frowned. 'That was quick. Yes, I'm fine.'

She was conscious of Amir stiffening in the car beside her.

'As I was just saying to His Majesty Sheikh Amir, it was only a cup of coffee.'

'I don't care.' Malik's voice showed the strength of his feelings. 'What the hell were you doing standing so close to a crowd of wild Ishkani—?'

She glowered at the window. 'How do you know where I was standing?'

'It's already on YouTube.'

'Geez,' she said again, with the shake of her head. 'Thank you, Internet.'

'I want you to come back here.'

Her heart stammered. She looked at Amir unconsciously. 'Nonsense. Because of a bit of coffee?'

'It could have been a bomb. A gun.'

'It wasn't. That wasn't the point the man wanted to make. He's angry. There's anger on both sides. We can't deny people their right to feel those things.'

'Nor should you suffer because of it,' Malik said firmly.

'I'm not suffering.'

'But it—'

'Stop!' She looked at Amir but addressed Malik. 'An inch is as good as a mile, right? It was a coffee. I believe it was a spontaneous act from a man who's suffered through the war. That's all. There's no sense making a mountain out of it.' Her PR mind was spinning over what had happened. 'In fact, if anything, we should make light—include a visit to a coffee house in tomorrow's schedule or something. Show that we have a sense of humour. And under no circumstances will I accept there being any consequences for this man.' She glared at Amir.

'But he—'

She interrupted Malik, waving a hand through the air so the collection of delicate bracelets she wore jangled prettily. 'Yes, yes, he threw a warm coffee cup at me. My clothes will be ruined, and an embarrassing clip is now on the Internet, but so what? Do you know what will happen if we respond too strongly to this?'

Amir was leaning forward a little, captivated by her, wanting to hear what she said—aware that her perspective was one he needed to have.

'We will make the thousands of people who feel that same anger in their hearts want to rise in defence of this poor man. Let's treat his actions with kindness and compassion. No one will expect that, and it will make the forgiveness all the more powerful.'

Amir's eyes drifted to the security guards. They were well trained, not looking at Johara or Amir, but he could see the shift in their faces, the obvious surprise and admiration.

'Now calm down.' She was speaking to her brother but her eyes were on Amir again, and he knew the words were meant for him, too. 'Put your feelings aside, and your concerns for me. I'm fine. Let's speak no more of this.'

'It is unforgivable.'

Ahmed nodded. 'I'm aware of this. I'll have the police bring charges immediately; he should pay for this.'

Amir was tempted. So tempted. But Johara's words and wisdom were impossible to ignore. He expelled a breath.

'No.' He frowned. 'Have him brought to me here.' Amir thought a moment longer. 'I want to speak to him.'

'To...speak to him?'

Amir flicked his gaze to Ahmed. 'Her Highness has advocated mercy. I'm interested to see if the man deserves such kindness. Bring him here.'

'Your parents were right.'

It was the first thing he said to her when she arrived at the forest, several hours later, a little after seven. They were the words he'd been aching to speak but couldn't until they were alone. Instead, he'd gone back to ignoring her in the limousine, as befitted their perceived relationship.

He drew her towards him, clasping his hands behind her back, his eyes running over her features possessively.

'About what?' The question was breathless. He held her tight.

'You have a gift with people.'

She lowered her lashes, as if embarrassed by the praise.

'I mean it.' He caught her chin, lifting her eyes to his. Something shifted through him, something powerful and elemental. He kissed her; he couldn't help it. 'Were you hurt?'

She shook her head. 'It was just coffee.'

'Hot coffee, and a plastic cup.'

'Yes,' she said, lifting her shoulders. And then, because it was just the two of them, and they were alone, he saw her mask drop, just a fraction. 'I was surprised, and I suppose my feelings were hurt. I was too confident. Everything on this trip has been so easy to date. Your people have been overwhelmingly welcoming, given the circumstances...'

'They've also been accusatory and frosty,' he remarked, pulling away from her, taking her hand and guiding her deeper into the forest.

Her smile was enigmatic. 'Well, yes, at times. But of course they see things from their perspective. Here, I'm the bad guy. In Taquul, that's you.' She lifted her shoulders. 'It's just a matter of perspective.'

'More wisdom.' He squeezed her hand. They moved quickly, both impatient to get to wherever they were going, to be alone.

'I thought you were going to hit him.'

'I wanted to.' He looked down at her.

'I'm glad you didn't.'

'I saw him this afternoon.'

'The man who threw the coffee?' Her brows lifted.

'Yes. Ahmed brought him here, at my request.'

He could feel concern emanating from her in waves. 'Why?'

'To see if you were right.'

'And was I?'

'Yes.'

She expelled a breath. 'People don't generally lash out without cause.'

'No.' He held a vine aloft, waiting for Johara to walk ahead of him. 'His twin brother died in the war. Right at the end.'

Johara's eyes closed in sympathy. 'So recently?'

'Yes.'

'And if peace had been agreed months earlier…'

'He wouldn't have died.' Amir nodded crisply. 'That's why this matters so much. We have to make this work.'

'You will.' She stopped walking to look at him. 'I know Mal is as committed to this as you are. How can peace efforts fail if you're both determined to have this succeed?'

He didn't need to answer. They both knew there were many things that could unravel the fragile accord. Their relationship was at the top of that list for him. If today had shown him anything it was how close to the surface his people's hostility was.

But he'd looked into the eyes of a man who'd lost so much, who was grieving, and instead of bringing the wrath of his position down on him, he'd spent thirty minutes talking with him. Amir understood grief; he knew it first-hand. He'd listened to the other man and when it became apparent that there had been difficulties accessing his brother's estate—a task he had undertaken for the widow and children—Amir had personally called the parliamentarian who oversaw such matters to ensure it moved smoothly going forward.

Johara had been, in every way, correct. Her wisdom was enviable, so too her grace under literal fire. She would have made an excellent queen.

The thought rocked him to the core. He stopped walking for a second, his eyes fixed straight ahead. They were nearing the edge of the forest, where it gave way to the end of the river. Here, there was a small lake, surrounded on all sides by rock. It was private, held by the palace, the last watercourse between here and the desert.

'What is it, Amir?'

He shook his head, clearing the thought. Johara was intelligent and worldly, but she was certainly not a candidate for the position of his wife. The very idea sent panic along his spine. Anything approaching that would certainly lead to all-out war. Besides, she was the opposite of what he wanted in a wife. When he married, it would be to a woman who was…what? Why couldn't he see that future now? He frowned. Because he was here with Johara—it would be the epitome of rudeness to be thinking of some hypothetical future wife when his lover was at his side.

'I was thinking of Paris,' he substituted, for lack of anything else to say.

'Really?' She frowned. 'Why?'

He began to walk again, forcing a smile to his face. 'I was wondering why your brother is so keen for you to marry him.'

'They've been friends a long time,' she said simply.

'And?'

She laughed. 'Yes, I suppose that's not really an answer.' She tilted her head to the side, considering the question. 'He's a nice guy.'

'The only nice guy in Taquul?'

She flashed him a withering look; he lifted her hand and pressed a kiss to her fingertips.

'Neither of those responses is particularly enlightening.'

'I know,' she sighed. 'Mal is very protective of me.'

Amir didn't want to answer that. He knew that if he said what he felt—that he was glad—she would become defensive. *I don't need him to protect me!* Yet an ancient fibre that ran through Amir liked the idea of someone playing that role in Johara's life, even though he knew she was right—she didn't need it.

'For any reason?' he said instead, and as soon as he'd asked the question, he knew there was more to it.

Her lips pursed, her eyes skittered away. 'You've probably read about it.'

'About what?'

Another sigh. 'Come on, Amir. It was a long time ago.'

'I'm not protecting your feelings, *inti qamar.* I have no idea what you mean.' She looked at him, the term of endearment slipping easily into the sentence. It was what he'd called her in the maze. My moon. Appropriate tonight, when it was glowing overhead, beautiful and enchanting.

'Oh.' She frowned. 'I was with someone before. I was younger, and completely unguarded. I thought I'd fallen head over heels in love with the guy—so why hide how I felt, right?'

He ignored the prickle of something like jealousy shifting through him. 'Go on.'

Johara nodded. 'We dated for just over a year. It ended badly. The papers got a *lot* of mileage out of it.'

Another burst of emotion, this time one of darkness. 'Newspapers will do that.'

But her expression showed she was lost in thought. 'It was truly terrible. I was twenty-one, and I'd been so sheltered. Worse than that, I honestly thought I loved him. I trusted him.'

Amir's chest tightened. 'He wasn't trustworthy?'

Her laugh lacked humour. 'Not even a little.'

He waited, but not patiently.

'Oh, he didn't cheat on me or anything. But I found out, about six months after our break up, that he'd been selling stories to the gutter press. So many little lies and falsehoods: that we'd had a threesome in Rome—a lie—that I'd secretly fallen pregnant—another lie! All for money!' She shook her head bitterly. 'I would have paid him off, if I'd known money was his motivation.'

Amir reached above them and snapped a twig with more force than was necessary.

'Except I think he also wanted to hurt me, and, honestly, I think he liked the limelight. When he was my boyfriend, he was followed around by paparazzi, blogs did articles on him.' She shook her head. 'Italian *Vogue* used him as a cover model. But once we broke up, he must have begun to feel irrelevant.'

Amir swore under his breath. 'What a poor excuse for a man.'

She laughed. 'That's pretty much what Mal said.'

'Your brother knew about this?'

'He's the one who discovered the truth.' Her brow furrowed. 'He had the stories investigated.'

'How did he act?'

'He paid Matthew to shut him up.' She grimaced. 'Last I heard, he's living in Australia somewhere.'

'Good riddance.'

'Yeah.' She pressed her teeth to her lower lip. 'So for Malik, he doesn't ever want me to get hurt like that again. And Paris is a great guy, and a good friend of his. Malik trusts him implicitly.'

Something inside Amir bristled. 'But that doesn't mean you should marry him.'

'No,' she agreed softly. 'And yet…'

Amir held his breath.

'This is something we shouldn't discuss.'

He forced himself to sound normal. 'Why not?'

'Because we're sleeping together.'

'And we're both aware that's where this ends. I'm not harbouring a secret desire to marry you,' he said, trying to make it sound as though the very idea was ridiculous.

'I know.' Her voice was quiet. Wounded? Now he felt like a jackass. 'I guess I feel like there's the whole duty thing. Paris is from a great family. Our marriage makes sense. I like him. I don't know if I'd ever trust my own judgement again, when it comes to men, let alone trusting someone *else* after Matthew. Maybe Paris isn't…'

Amir had changed his mind. He couldn't listen to her talk about the prospect of marrying someone else without wanting to burn the world down. He hadn't expected to feel so possessive of her, but he did. He couldn't fight that, or deny it.

'You are a passionate woman, Johara. If you marry, it should be because your passions are aroused, because your heart is caught, and because you know—beyond a doubt—

that the man deserves you. Not because he's nice and your brother thinks he's suitable.'

Her lips parted, her eyes lifting to his. 'And is that how you'll choose a wife?'

He shook his head. 'It's different.'

'Why?'

'Because I'm Sheikh. I don't have the luxury of marrying a woman I choose for any reason other than her suitability to rule at my side.'

They stood there on the edge of the forest, so close, eyes locked, hearts beating in unison, the conversation troubling to both for reasons they couldn't fathom.

Distraction came in the form of one of the *juniya* birds. It flew close to Johara's head, drawing her attention, and she followed it beyond the last tree, her eyes catching the water for the first time. She gasped, shaking her head. Stars shone overhead, bathing the still water in little dots of silver.

'What is this place?'

He saw it through her eyes—the large stones that formed walls, creating the feeling of a fortress, the calm water on the edge of the desert, enormous trees that decorated the circumference but left space for the stars to shine.

'My swimming pool.' He grinned, willingly pushing their conversation aside as he pulled on her hand. 'Are you game?'

She flicked a nervous look at him. 'I don't have a bathing costume…'

He drew her closer, pressing his nose to hers. 'Didn't you hear me? This is private…'

Awareness dawned and she laughed, reaching for the bottom of her shirt. 'I see.'

He stepped back as she discarded her clothes, stripping down to her underwear, then removing that scrap of lace, so she was completely naked. He made a growling noise low in his throat, possession firing through him. She took a step forward, her eyes asking a question he answered with a nod. Her fingers caught the fabric of his clothes, lifting them from his body, more slowly than she had her own, so that he wanted to take over, to strip himself naked and pull her against him.

He didn't.

He stood and he waited, his body being stirred to a fever pitch of desire he could barely handle.

Slowly, painstakingly slowly, she undressed him, her fingers grazing his flesh as she went. Her eyes were huge in the moonlight, dark pools every bit as mesmerising as the water beyond them.

'It's beautiful here.' Her voice was thick; he could only jerk his head in agreement.

Her lips moved forward, pressing against his tattoo, and as she did so she whispered the words, *'Amor fati'.* They reached inside him, wrapping around his heart, his soul, the essence of his being.

He loved his fate. He'd worked to love it, when it had been, at times, the last thing he wanted. His fate was not this woman; she was an aberration, a temporary pleasure— a guilty pleasure. One he found himself utterly powerless to resist.

# CHAPTER TEN

'How LONG DID you live in New York?'

Johara ran her fingertips over the water. It was sublime. She'd lost track of how long they'd been here. An hour? Less? More?

'Almost four years.'

His brows drew together.

'You're surprised?'

He laughed. 'Are you a mind-reader now?'

She pressed her face closer to his. 'Yours is easy to read.'

'Oh?'

'For me, at least.'

'Ah.' His grin sparked butterflies in her bloodstream.

'I should have thought your brother would object.'

She smiled indulgently. 'Mal didn't like the idea at first.'

She felt Amir stiffen at Johara's use of the diminutive of Malik's name. 'But you changed his mind?'

'We came to a compromise.'

Her smile became harder to keep in place. Her eyes shifted away from Amir's.

'And it was?'

'That I should go. For a time.'

Amir's features darkened. 'For a time? You mean until it suited him to have you come back?'

She wanted to defend Malik but, in truth, the terms

they'd struck—terms which had, at the time, seemed reasonable—now infuriated her. 'More or less.' She lifted her shoulders. 'I'm a princess of Taquul. My place is in my country.'

'Where do you want to be?'

Her eyes widened. No one had asked her that before.

'Let's pretend you're not a princess,' he said quietly. 'Where would you choose to make your life?'

Johara's heart turned over in her chest. The first answer that sprang to her mind was ludicrous. Too fanciful to say, much less give credit to. She'd spent five days in Ishkana, and it was a country that would never accept or welcome her. Why should she feel such an immense bond to this place? Her eyes ran over Amir's face without her meaning them to. The answer was right in front of her. *Wherever you are.*

Stricken, she tried to smile and pulled away from him in the water, swimming towards the edge. He came after her.

'You can't answer?'

Oh, she could answer, but the answer would terrify both of them. She bit down on her lip, and strove for a light tone of voice.

'I am what I am, Amir. I'm Johara Qadir, Princess of Taquul, and while I loved everything about New York, I always knew it was temporary. I knew that, one day, he'd ask me to return home and assume the responsibilities that have been mine since birth.'

But Amir was frustrated by that; she could read it in the terse lines of his face.

'Don't pretend that if you had a sister it would be any different,' she teased, surprised she could sound so light when her heart was splintering and cracking.

He frowned. 'I cannot say what it would be like,' he

agreed. 'I understand that he wants you back in Taquul. But marrying Paris is part of the agreement, isn't it?'

She dropped her gaze to the water. Tiny ripples moved from her fingertips towards the water's edge. She watched their progress, thinking of how like life that was—a small action could have such far-reaching consequences. 'Yes.' Her eyes swept shut. 'It's what my brother intends for me to do.'

'And what you want? Does it matter?'

'I can say no,' she murmured, meeting his eyes and wishing she hadn't when a feeling of pain and betrayal lanced her. 'He won't force me. If he tried, I'd leave, and I'd leave for good,' she promised. 'The decision is mine.'

Amir pulled her closer, into his arms, staring down at her for several long beats. The sky was silent; even the juniya were quiet in that moment.

'And there was no one in New York?'

Her breath snagged in her throat. 'On the contrary, Manhattan is heavily populated.'

He didn't laugh. His thumb smudged her lower lip, his eyes probing hers. 'You didn't meet anyone that made you want to stay?'

She shook her head. 'There were children. The most beautiful children. I fell in love with each and every one I worked with. I had friends—have friends. But no, there was no man.'

'I find that impossible to believe.'

'Why?'

'Because you're—'

She held her breath, waiting, needing him to finish the sentence.

But he shook his head, a tight smile gripping his lips. 'Four years is a long time.'

She exhaled slowly. 'It is,' she agreed. 'But Matthew

messed me up pretty good.' She lay backwards in the water, and he caught her legs, wrapping them around his waist, holding her there as she floated, staring up at the sky. There was such safety in his hold on her. She felt—whole. Complete. Content. But not for long, because the realisation of those sentiments brought with it a crippling wave of concern.

'Part of what I loved about meeting you was the anonymity. I felt such a connection with you, and all the better because you had no idea I was Johara Qadir.'

'No.' For a moment his voice broke through the serenity of the moment. She remembered his reaction that night, his assurance that if he'd known he would never have acted on those feelings. And none of this would have happened.

'You couldn't sell the story of what we'd done. You couldn't hurt me.'

Silence followed those words, so she began to regret them, and wish she hadn't revealed so much of herself.

But slowly, his hands curled around her back and lifted her from the water, bringing her body against his. His eyes latched to hers.

'I never want to hurt you.'

She swallowed, her throat thick with emotions. 'I know.'

Staring at him, bathed in moonlight, Johara felt as though every moment of her soul were shifting into alignment. Everything she'd ever been and whatever she was to become were resonating right there; she was her truest, purest form of self in his arms.

'I hate that a man treated you like that.'

'Yes.' She tried to sound crisp and businesslike, but the truth was it still hurt. Not Matthew's deeds so much as her own naivety and quickness to trust. She'd gone against her brother's wishes, she'd ignored his warnings, and she'd paid the price.

'I want to show you something tomorrow.'

The change of subject surprised her. She lifted a single brow, waiting for him to continue.

'The gallery, here in the palace. Will you come and see it with me?'

Her stomach looped. 'I'd like to,' she said, truthfully. 'But my schedule is already jam-packed.'

'Your schedule has been revised.'

She stared at him in surprise. 'Revised why?'

'In light of the security concerns today…'

'That was an angry man with a coffee,' she corrected, shaking her head. 'You had no business interfering with the arrangements my state department made.'

'Your safety is my priority.' He lowered his voice. 'As it is theirs—they were also anxious we limit your exposure to uncontrollable elements.'

'You mean people?'

He smiled, but she wasn't amused. Frustration shifted through her.

'Amir, I'm here to do a job. I want to do it.'

'And you can,' he promised. 'The higher profile events are still there. Your schedule has been curtailed, that is all.' He ran his eyes over her face slowly. 'But if you disagree, then have it reinstated.' He lifted his broad shoulders, but he might as well have been pulling on a string that ran right to her heart. She felt it ping and twinge. 'I trust your judgement.'

The string pulled again. Her heart hurt.

*I trust your judgement.* No one had ever said that to her before.

She lifted a palm to his cheek. 'Thank you for caring.'

His eyes widened and she saw something like shock in the depths of his eyes before he muted it, assuming an expression that was ironic. 'You're my guest in Ishkana. It's my job to care.'

Boundaries. How insistent he'd been on those boundaries, right from the start. He was insisting on them now, just not in so many words.

'I'll defer to you,' she said. 'On this matter only.'

He laughed, shaking his head. 'Heaven forbid you defer on anything else.'

Her own smile came naturally, but she knew what was at the root of her capitulation. A lighter schedule meant she could sneak more time with him. Her time in Taquul was almost at an end. They had to make the most of the days they had left.

'Your Majesty.' Ahmed's expression showed worry. 'It's four in the morning. Where have you been?'

Amir hadn't expected to be discovered returning to the palace. He stared at Ahmed, a frown on his face, wondering for a moment what he should say before realising he didn't have to say anything. He answered to no one.

'Did you want something?'

Ahmed continued to stare at Amir. His hair was wet, and, while he'd pulled his pants on, he'd left his robe off for the walk back to the palace. He had it thrown over one arm now. He'd been too distracted to dress.

*'If you're going to insist on monopolising me, then I shall have to think of a form of payback.'*

*'Oh? What do you have in mind?'*

*She'd straddled him, taking him deep within her, and leaned over him so her dark hair teased his shoulders. 'What if I told you I have no intention of wearing underwear tomorrow, Amir?'*

A smile flicked at his lips as the memory seared his

blood. Desire whipped him. It was practically daylight, and still he found he couldn't wait to see her again.

'Yes, sir. There's been an intelligence report. A band of vigilantes is forming in the foothills.'

Amir heard the words with a heavy heart, the statement jolting him back to the present, regretfully pushing all thoughts of Johara and her promise from his mind. 'Well, that didn't take long.'

'No, sir.' Ahmed's voice was similarly weighted.

'Damn it.' Amir dragged a hand through his hair. 'Give me twenty minutes then meet me in my office. Have Zeb join us,' he said, referring to the head of the security agency.

'Yes, sir.'

'Your hair is like a bird's nest,' Athena chastised with a smile. 'What in the world happened?'

Johara smiled, remembering every detail of the night before. 'I went swimming.' The words emerged before she could catch them. Her eyes met Athena's in the mirror. 'Alone. Last night. I found a stream and it was so hot, and no one was around...'

Athena stared at Johara as though she were losing her mind. 'Your Highness...'

Johara sighed, reaching up and putting a hand on Athena's. 'It's fine. No one saw me.'

She could see the fight being waged inside Athena. Their relationship was strange. While they were friends, it was a friendship that existed in a particular way. Athena would never overstep what she considered to be her place, despite the fact Johara often wished she would.

'What is it, Thena?' She pronounced her friend's name 'Thayna', as she always did when she wanted to set aside their professional roles and be simply two women who'd known each other a long time.

Athena's smile, though, showed the conversation was at an end. 'I was just thinking how to style it. A bun will hide the mess.'

'These are your parents?' She stopped walking, staring at the beautifully executed portrait, her eyes lingering on every detail.

'Yes.' At her side, Amir was very still. 'Painted the year of their marriage.'

'She's beautiful.' And she was. The artist had captured something in his mother's features that made Johara feel a tug to the other woman. She shifted her gaze to Amir's, conscious that servants surrounded them so keeping a discreet distance and a cool look pinned to her face. 'You have her eyes.'

He returned her look but it was futile. It didn't matter how cool either of them attempted to appear, heat sparked from him to her, making her fingertips tingle with an impulse to reach out and touch. She ached to drag her teeth across his collarbone, to flick her tongue in the indentation of his clavicle, to run her fingertips up his sides until he grabbed her and pinned her to the wall...

Her cheeks flushed, and she knew he recognised it because his attention shifted lower in her face and a mocking smile crept over his mouth—mocking himself or her, she didn't know.

She turned away from him, moving a little further down the hallway, her gaze sliding across the next painting—another couple. 'My grandparents,' he supplied. The next had her feet stilling, to study it properly.

'It's you.'

It jolted him—the painting had been done when he was only a small boy. 'How can you tell?'

'Your eyes,' she said seriously. 'And your smile.'

Ahmed had moved closer without either of them realising, and caught her observation, a small frown on his face. 'I beg your pardon, Your Majesty.' He addressed Amir alone.

'What is it?' Amir's impatience was obvious.

'There's an update, on the matter we discussed this morning. Zeb has the information. He's waiting in your office.'

Amir's brow creased in consternation but he nodded, turning back to Johara. 'I have to deal with this.'

Disappointment crested inside her. Perhaps Amir sensed it because he lowered his voice, though Ahmed stood at his elbow. 'I won't be long.'

It was too obvious. Heat sparked in Johara's cheeks. She looked away, nodding with what she hoped appeared disinterest. 'It's no bother, Your Majesty. I have plenty here with which to occupy myself.'

Amir didn't stay a moment longer than necessary. He turned on his heel and stalked down the corridor. Johara watched until he'd turned a corner, before realising that Ahmed was still there, his eyes intent on her face.

She forced a polite smile. 'The artwork here is first class.'

'Yes, madam.'

Frosty. Disapproving. She turned away from him, telling herself she didn't care. She continued to tour the gallery, each painting deserving far more attention than she gave it. She couldn't focus on anything other than Amir.

'My mother used to play the piano,' Amir said quietly. 'She was very good. When I was a child, I would listen to her for hours.'

Johara reached for another grape, grateful that they were—finally—alone. It had taken a heck of a lot of logistics but they'd managed to find a way to give all of their servants the slip, so that they could now sit, just the two of them, in his beautiful private hall that he'd brought her to the first morning she'd arrived. The morning he'd asked if she was pregnant. How much had happened since then!

'Do you play?'

He shook his head. 'No. I think her musicality escaped me.'

'Music can be taught,' she pointed out.

'The techniques can be, but not the passion and the instinct.'

Johara smiled. 'Remind me never to play if you're in attendance.'

'You play piano?'

'Yes.' She reached for another grape, but before she could pluck it from the vine he caught it and held it to her mouth instead, his eyes probing hers as he pushed it between her lips. Passion and desire were like flames, licking at the soles of her feet.

'Strangely, it was one of the things I excelled at.'

'Your dyslexia didn't make it difficult for you to read music?'

'Impossible.' She laughed. 'But I hear something and can play it.'

'I'm impressed.'

'Don't be.'

He lifted another grape to her mouth.

'It's just the way my brain is wired.'

'I want to hear you play.'

She leaned closer, pressing a kiss to the tip of his nose. 'And yet, I just said I won't play for you.'

'And what if I ordered you to?' His voice was mock-demanding.

She laughed. 'You and what army?'

He moved closer, grabbing her wrists, pinning them above her head as he used his body to press her backwards. 'Haven't you heard? I'm King of all I survey.'

'Including me?' she asked, breathless, lying on her back with Amir on top of her, the weight of him so pleasing, so addictive.

'Definitely you.'

'Ah, but I'm not one of your subjects,' she reminded him. 'I'm the enemy.'

He stared at her, his look serious. 'Not my enemy.'

It was strangely uplifting, but she didn't want to analyse the meaning behind his statement, because it would surely lead to disappointment. She kept her voice amused.

'My allegiance has to be earned.'

He smiled lazily, releasing one hand while keeping her wrists pinned easily in the other. He traced a line down her body, over her breasts, finding the peaks of her nipples and circling them before running his hand lower, and lower still, to capture the fabric at the bottom of the long dress she wore.

'I can think of one way to ensure loyalty.'

'Oh?'

'Let me see, first, if you are a lady of honour.'

She laughed. 'A what?'

'If you are true to your word.'

'Oh!' Heat stained her cheeks. She held her breath as his fingers crept up the satiny skin of her inner thigh and found what he was looking for—nakedness. She had gone without underpants for him. And she'd hoped he'd remembered her parting statement, and that the thought had driven him as wild as it had her.

His answer was everything she'd hoped for.

'Well?' she asked huskily.

'Just as promised.' He spoke with reverence. Their eyes met and something shifted inside her heart.

His dark head dipped down, his tongue stirring her to a fever pitch of longing, making her ache for him, reminding her of the maze, of everything they'd shared together since, of everything they were. Pleasure, passion, power; her blood was exploding with needs, her pulse too fast to be contained. She pushed up, needing him, wanting more than he could offer, craving the satisfaction she knew it was within his grasp to give. His mouth moved faster and she shattered, her fingertips driving through his hair, her mouth capable of shaping only two syllables: *Am* and *Ir*. Over and over and over she cried his name, as though it were an invocation that could ward off what they both knew was coming.

But she refused to think of the future, about what would happen in two days' time, when her tour was at an end and the flight took her back over the mountains to Taquul, and the future that was waiting for her.

She couldn't think about that. Not when there was this pleasure to be relished and enjoyed.

He knew they needed to move, to leave this sanctuary. He was Sheikh and, despite the fact he answered to no one, he couldn't simply disappear for hours at a time without arousing suspicion. His absence would be noticed. So too, he imagined, would hers.

But the weight of her head on his chest was so pleasant. Just for a little while longer, he wanted to keep the doors to this room shut, to lie as they were: naked on the scatter pillows, the heady fragrance of trees and flowers and the sound of flowing water creating their own world and atmosphere. It was a *masjid* first and foremost and here he felt that he was worshipping Johara as she deserved to be worshipped.

'Will you come to my room tonight?'

The question surprised him—he hadn't intended to ask it, but he didn't regret it.

'Sure.' Her voice, though, was teasing. 'I'll just let your guards know I'm popping in for a quick roll in your bed. That won't raise any eyebrows whatsoever.'

He laughed, shifting so he could see her face. 'There's a secret way.'

She met his gaze. 'Into your room?'

'Yes.'

'Why?' And then, realisation dawned. 'For exactly this purpose.'

Another laugh. 'Yes.'

'So you…sneak lovers in…regularly?'

He heard her hurt and wondered at his body's response to it. He wanted to draw her into his arms and tell her she had nothing to be jealous of. He'd never been with a woman like her. He doubted he ever would be again.

'No, Johara. Never.'

'Oh. Then why…?'

'Because my room has been the Sheikh's room for many hundreds of years.' He lifted his broad shoulders. 'And whichever palace concubine my predecessors decided to amuse themselves with would arrive via a secret tunnel.'

Her jaw dropped. 'You're not serious.'

Her innocence made it impossible not to smile. 'Perfectly.'

'But…'

'But?'

'Well, it's a security risk, for one,' she huffed.

'It is not a corridor anyone knows about.'

'Want to bet?'

He arched a brow, waiting for her to continue.

'It seems to me like the kind of thing your enemies would pay a lot of money to learn about.'

'The palace is guarded like a fortress.'

'I know that.'

'It's safe.'

'I know that too.' She gnawed on her lower lip, her eyes clouded, but after a moment she sighed, surrendering despite her first response. 'Well? How do I find it?'

# CHAPTER ELEVEN

'THIS PLACE IS…'

She looked around, wishing she didn't find the room so incredibly sumptuous and sensual. 'I mean…'

His smile was sardonic. 'Yes?' But he knew how she felt. Shirtless, wearing only a pair of slim-fitting black trousers, he prowled towards her, capitalising on the overwhelm a space such as this had given her.

The carpets were a deep red in colour, the furnishing a similar colour, velvet, with gold details. There were chairs but in the middle of the space, making it very obvious exactly what the room was to be used for, was the most enormous bed Johara had seen. It could easily accommodate ten people.

Her mouth felt dry as she stepped towards it, studying it with a curiosity she couldn't resist.

'What's that?' She ran her finger over an ornate brass hook that hung in the centre of the bed's head.

'For handcuffs.'

She spun around to face him, oddly guilty. 'Handcuffs?' The question squeaked out of her.

He prowled closer, and the nearer he got, the faster her pulse went. She bit down on her lip as he grabbed her wrists, rubbing his thumb over them. 'Or rope. Or silk. Whatever your preference.'

Her eyes moved back to the bed, as desire ran the length of her spine.

'Does it tempt you?'

She shivered quite openly now, lifting her eyes to his, uncertainty in their depths. Yes, she wanted to say. It tempted her—a lot. But only with him! It was a fantasy she'd never had before—never even thought to have. But with Amir, the idea of being tied up and made love to was, perhaps, the most intoxicating thing she'd ever contemplated.

So she clung to outrage instead, because she was aware of how dangerous her supplication had become, how completely she'd surrendered to Amir and his ways.

'I just can't believe there's a place like this in your palace. A harem!'

His smile showed he knew exactly how she felt, and why she was intent on denying it.

'It hasn't been used since my great-grandfather's reign.'

She looked away, her eyes betraying her and straying to the hook once more, her nipples straining against the silk fabric of her bra.

She was fighting a losing battle.

'So what do you do when you're dating a woman?' she prompted, needing to focus on something other than this overtly sexual room, and the hook that would accommodate handcuffs just perfectly.

He tilted his head, waiting for her to continue. 'Are you asking if I bring women here?' he prompted, gesturing to the bed.

'God, no.' She shook her head urgently, not wanting *that* image in her mind. 'I just meant…do you date, publicly? Can women come to your room?'

'I can do whatever I want,' he said gently. 'I'm Sheikh.' He pressed a finger to her chin, lifting her face to his. 'It is for you that we must be secret about this—and for the sake of the peace treaty.'

She nodded. 'So if I were just some woman you'd met, you'd have me delivered to your room whenever it suited?'

His laugh was little more than a growl. 'You make it sound so archaic. So one-sided. If you were just a woman I'd met,' he corrected, 'I would invite you for dinner. We would share a meal and then I would ask you if you wanted to come to my room. The choice would be—as it is now— yours.'

Her heart turned over in her chest. She had the suspicion she was being combative and she didn't know why. Something was needling her, making her frustrated and wanting to lash out.

'I'm sorry,' she said truthfully, lifting her fingers to his chest and pressing them there. 'I don't know why I'm acting like this. I just didn't expect this room to be so—'

'Confronting?' he suggested. Then, 'Unpalatable.'

She shook her head, not meeting his eyes. 'Palatable,' she corrected, so quietly it was barely a whisper.

In response, he pulled her hard against him, and before she could draw breath he was kissing her as though everything they cared for in this life depended on it. Her body moulded to his like it was designed to fit—two pieces carved from the same marble. She felt his heart racing in time with hers, thudding where hers was frantic, a baritone to her soprano.

Time and space swirled away, concepts far in the distance, as he stooped down and lifted her easily, kissing her as he cradled her against his chest, carrying her through this room and into a corridor that was wide but dimly lit. She felt safe. She felt whole.

She relaxed completely, a beautiful heaviness spreading through her limbs. When they entered his room, she spared it only a cursory glimpse, and took in barely any of the details. It was similar to the suite she'd been provided with, but larger and more elaborate. It was also quite spartan. Where hers was filled with luxurious touches, his had been pared back. The mosaics on the floor were beautiful, but there was no art here. Just white walls, giving the windows all the ability to shine, with their view of the desert. Or, as it was now, of the night sky beyond.

He placed her gently onto the bed then stood, looking at her, his eyes showing a thousand and one things even when he said nothing.

Johara smiled and reached for him—her instincts driving her—and he came, joining her in the bed, sweeping her into his arms once more and kissing her until breathing became an absolute afterthought.

*'You don't have to do this, sir.'*

*'I want to.' Twelve-year-old Amir fixed his parents' servant with a look from the depths of his soul. It was a look of purpose and determination. It was a look that hid the pain tearing him into a thousand little pieces.*

*'I have identified their bodies, for security purposes,' Ahmed reminded Amir softly, putting a hand on Amir's shoulder. His touch was kindly meant; it was then Amir remembered Ahmed had children of his own, not too far apart in age from Amir.*

*'I want to see them.'*

*He spoke with a steely resonance, and it gripped his heart. There was much uncertainty. In the hours since his parents' death, he'd had to grapple with the change in his circumstances, the expectations upon him. He felt deeply but showed nothing. He was a leader. People looked to him.*

*'Amir,' Ahmed sighed. 'No child should have to see this.'*

*He drew himself to his full height. 'I said I want to see them.'*

*It was enough. Even Ahmed wouldn't argue with the Sheikh of Ishkana—for long.*

*'Yes, sir.' He sighed wearily, hesitated a moment then turned. 'This way.'*

*The corridor was dimly lit but muffled noise was everywhere. The palace had woken. The country had woken. News had spread like wildfire.*

*They were dead.*

*At the door to the tomb where their bodies had been brought to lie, Amir allowed himself the briefest moment of hesitation, to steel himself, and then stepped inside.*

*Three people were within. Lifelong servants. People who felt his parents' loss as keenly as he, who grieved with the same strength he did.*

*'Leave me,' he commanded, his eyes falling to his father's face first. He didn't look to see that he'd been obeyed. He knew that he had been. Only Ahmed remained, impervious perhaps to the Sheikh's commands, or perhaps knowing that, despite the appearance of strength, a twelve-year-old boy could not look upon his parents' crumpled bodies and feel nothing.*

*He kneeled beside his father, taking his hand, holding it, pressing his face to it, praying for strength and guidance. He moved to his mother next, and it was the sight of her that made a thick sob roll through his chest.*

*She looked asleep. Beautiful. Peaceful. He put his hands on either side of her face, as though willing her to wake up, but she didn't.*

*It was the worst thing he'd had to do, but seeing his parents like that became the cornerstone of his being.*

*The war had killed them. Taquul had killed them. The Qadirs...*

* * *

He woke with a start, his heart heavy, a strange sense of claustrophobia and grief pressing against him, before realising he wasn't alone.

He pushed the sheets back, staring at Johara in complete confusion. It took him a second to remember who she was, and then it all came flooding back to him—their affair, their intimacy, the way he'd started to think of her and smile at the strangest of times.

What the hell was he doing? His parents' visage was so fresh in his mind, the hatred he'd felt that night—and here he was, with a Qadir...

No. Not a Qadir. Johara.

Her name was like an incantation. It relaxed him, pulling him back to the present, reminding him of everything they'd shared in the past week.

She was a Qadir, but she was so much more than that. When he looked at her, he no longer saw her family, her place in the Taquul royal lineage, her birthright; when he said her name he saw only her, not the uncle for whom she'd been named, the uncle who had orchestrated his parents' murder.

But guilt followed that realisation. He'd promised his parents' dead bodies he would never forget. He'd promised them he would hate the enemy for ever, and here he was, seeking comfort in Johara's arms, craving her in a way he should have been fighting against.

He moved to the windows, the ancient desert a sight that comforted him and anchored him, reminding him who he was. He breathed in its acrid air, letting it permeate his lungs. He was a Haddad. He was of this country, this kingdom, he served the people of Ishkana and nothing would change that.

What he and Johara were doing was... He turned towards

the bed, her sleeping body making him frown. He couldn't describe how he felt about her, and this. He knew only that there was a greater danger here than he'd ever imagined.

A knock sounded at the door—loud and imperative. Amir saw that it disturbed Johara and winced, crossing to the door quickly, grabbing shorts as he went and pulling them on. With one quick look over his shoulder, he pulled it inwards. Ahmed stood there, but he was not alone. Zeb, and several guards, were at his back.

Amir pulled the door shut behind himself, shielding his bed and lover from view before consulting his wristwatch. It was almost four. Only something serious would have brought anyone—particularly this contingent of men—to his room at this hour.

'What is it?'

Ahmed nodded. 'There's been an attack.'

Amir tensed. 'Where?'

'In the *malani* provinces.'

His eyes swept shut. Anger sparked inside him. 'How many?'

'Two confirmed dead so far.'

He swore. 'Insurgents?'

Ahmed looked towards Zeb. 'Taquul insurgents,' he said quietly. 'They set off a bomb outside a nightclub.'

Many times in his life had he been told news such as this. He braced for the inevitable information. 'How bad?'

'It's an emerging situation. The damage is being assessed.'

'Whose bomb?'

'That's not clear,' Zeb murmured. 'It has the markings of a state device, though the timing...'

'Yes.' Unconsciously, he looked over his shoulder. It was impossible to believe anyone in Malik's military would be foolish enough to launch an attack while Johara was deep in Ishkana.

'What scale are we talking?'

Ahmed winced. 'It's bad, sir. A building's collapsed.'

Amir swore.

'I've put the border forces on alert.'

Amir stiffened. It was protocol. Zeb had done the right thing, and yet the familiarity of all this hit him like a stone in the gut. Just like that, he could see the peace evaporating.

'We need more information.'

'Sir?' Ahmed's brows were furrowed.

'Was this the act of a rogue military commander, or the insurgents in the mountain ranges looking to profit from ongoing unease between our people, or a state-sanctioned skirmish in disputed land? We need to understand what the hell happened and why, before we respond.'

'But you will have to respond,' Zeb insisted. 'We don't have all the details yet but this was a vicious peace-time attack. Your people will expect—'

'My people want peace,' Amir said quietly, thinking of the sadness he'd seen in the eyes of the man who'd thrown coffee at Johara. 'Not a knee-jerk retaliation that springs us back into the war.'

Silence met the statement.

'The Princess—' Zeb's expression was uneasy. He looked to Ahmed before continuing. 'She would be a good bargaining chip. To ensure Malik apologises, takes responsibility...'

Amir felt a surge of disgust and then rage. 'Even if he had nothing to do with it?'

'I find it hard to believe an attack of this kind could occur without his involvement.'

'This is what we will discover. But in the meantime Her Highness remains our honoured guest. No one is to speak to her of this, to touch her, to even think of using her in any way. Understood?'

Zeb frowned. 'It is my job to advise you on the best military strategies…'

'Fine. You've advised me.'

'The death toll could be in the hundreds. You must act, sir. I have the eleventh division mobilised. They could retake one of our strongholds in the mountains—'

'No.' He shook his head, then in a tone designed to placate, 'It's too soon.'

'Too soon? The destruction. The inevitable death count—'

'We are no longer at war.'

'What is this if not an act of war?' Zeb pushed with obvious impatience.

Amir fixed him with a stare that was designed to strike fear into the other man. It worked. Contrition overtook his expression. While Amir allowed—and appreciated—a lot of latitude from his advisors, he remained the ultimate power holder.

'We don't have enough information to know yet.'

'But if it was state-sanctioned?'

Amir considered that. He had met with Malik and seen in his eyes the same desire for peace that lived in Amir's heart. They both wanted this, for their people. 'We'll discuss that if we come to it.'

'And you'll respond accordingly?'

Amir compressed his lips, not inclined to answer that without having more of an idea as to the circumstances of the attack.

'The Princess should be held until we know,' Zeb pushed. 'Detain her, show our people that we're not feeding our enemies cake and wine…'

'She is not the enemy,' Amir said cuttingly. 'And I have already told you—no one is to bring her into this.'

'She is in it, though,' Ahmed said gently. 'Her presence alone requires some kind of action.'

Ahmed's words reached inside Amir and shook him, forced him to see clearly the tenuousness of Johara's place here in the kingdom. He had come to know her, beyond the fact she was a Qadir and a princess of Taquul, but why should he expect his people to feel as he did? She could easily become a focus for anger and revenge. His gut rolled with a burst of nausea; his skin felt hot and cold all over.

He turned back to the men. 'I want a meeting in the tactical rooms. Fifteen minutes. Discover what you can in the meantime. I need answers. And I want to speak to Malik Qadir. Arrange that as soon as possible, Zeb.' His eyes met Ahmed's. Something passed between them. Understanding. Agreement. 'Let me be clear here—my goal is to maintain the peace.' He softened his tone. 'For too long we have answered violence with violence; I understand your instincts now are to do the same. But that will only perpetuate what we've always known. The fight for peace will be won with diplomacy, not military force.'

He paused, knowing what he had to do and hating the necessity of it. But for her safety…to prevent anything ever happening to her as had happened to his parents? An image of his mother's face filled his mind, as she'd been the last time he'd seen her, in the tombs beneath the palace. Fear hardened into resolve. Johara would be protected at all costs.

'Johara Qadir will leave the country immediately.' He faced Zeb. 'Her safe passage is the most important job you will have tonight, Zeb. If anything happens to her—'

'I know. It will inevitably renew the war.'

Amir waited until they were gone before pushing the door to his room open. Johara was awake now, looking at him, her eyes huge and hair tousled. He wasn't sure what she'd heard, but it was clear she knew something was amiss.

She stood as he walked towards the bed, her nakedness taking his breath away even then.

'Something's wrong?'

He contemplated not telling her. He contemplated saying nothing, but she deserved to know. Besides, her brother would undoubtedly contact her imminently.

'Yes.'

'What is it?'

He ground his teeth together, moving towards her. 'There was an attack. A Taquul bomb in one of the northern towns.'

Her features showed surprise and then sorrow. 'You said this would happen.'

'Yes, but I had hoped…' He shook his head. He hadn't, really. He'd known that peace was a Sisyphean task, yet still he'd pushed for it, worked towards it, knowing his people deserved at least a chance. He still believed that. For their sake, he had to quell this, ensure it didn't form the beginning of more conflict. But the attitude of his chief military advisor showed what a battle he was waging—even within his own government.

'Was anyone hurt?'

'Yes.'

'Killed?'

'The exact number is unknown but we expect the count to be high.' She dipped her head forward, and he knew she felt as he did—sorrow. Futility. Anger.

'You have to go.'

She nodded, looking around for her clothes. 'Yes. I shouldn't have fallen asleep. What can I do?'

He stared at her, committing everything about her to memory. He could never see her again. These last few days had been something he could never put into words, but it had to end. She wasn't simply a woman with whom he could enjoy a no-strings affair. He wanted her too selfishly. In another day or two, he wouldn't be able to relinquish her. It had to be now. To his people, and his government, she would always be the enemy. He was putting her at risk every minute he kept her here.

'How can I help?'

Her words were some kind of balm. No one had offered him help—and so simply—all his life. But he pushed the offer aside. 'You misunderstand, Johara. You need to leave Ishkana. I have arranged your transport. You are to leave now, in the dead of night, before the country has awoken to this news.'

Her mouth dropped open.

'That's... No.'

Another surprise. People didn't say 'no' to him. 'You misunderstand me again. I'm not asking you to leave.'

Her eyes narrowed. 'You're ordering me?'

He expelled a sigh, moving across the room and pulling out some clothes. He understood her resentment of that— all her life she'd been ordered around and yet she deserved so much better. He didn't want to be just another person who sought to control her. 'I'm telling you what is going to happen. You cannot be here if war breaks out. The risk to you is too great.'

'War won't break out. My brother and you will work together to prevent that from happening.'

'We don't know yet that this bomb wasn't detonated with your brother's permission.'

She gasped. 'You can't seriously think—'

He shook his head. 'No.' He frowned. 'But war with Taquul is familiar.'

'All the more reason for us to challenge that assumption.'

He shook his head with frustration. Why wouldn't she understand? 'There are powerful members of my government already demanding retribution.'

'You can't do that.'

He ground his teeth together. 'I have to do what is best for my country.'

'And that's peace. We both know that.'

'Yes, Johara, but peace may not be possible.'

She shook her head. 'I refuse to believe that. Let me stay here with you, standing by your side showing that we are committed to a peaceful outcome.'

The image she created was vibrant but impossible. Zeb's response had shown him that. *Detain her.* A fierce reaction resonated along his spine. 'Your place is in Taquul with your people.'

Her eyes sparked with anger. 'Can't you see that's what's wrong with all this? *Your* people. *My* people. They're all damned people, living side by side. Isn't this peace about breaking down barriers, Amir? Wasn't that the purpose of my being here?'

His heart had kicked up a notch. He dragged trousers over his boxers without looking away from her. 'This changes things.'

'It doesn't have to.' She moved towards him with urgency. 'You said, from the outset, there would be difficulties. This is one of them. Are you truly intending to fall at the first hurdle?'

'No.' He reached for a shirt. 'But having you here complicates matters. You have to leave.'

'Why? For whom does it complicate anything?'

'You represent something my people have been taught to hate, and also fear.'

'Me?' She dug her fingers into the space between her breasts; his gut twisted at her look of obvious disbelief. 'I'm just one woman, a woman who's here with an open heart and mind, wanting to improve relations. Your people will see that—just don't push me away. Let me stay. Show your citizens that you and I are both invested in the peace process, that we believe it will succeed...'

'And what if Malik and I cannot agree on this? What if war is inevitable? You think my military will not expect me to keep you as a prisoner?'

She gasped. 'You would never do that.'

'No.' He dragged a hand through his hair, frowning. 'Of course I wouldn't, and that's the problem. You compromise me. This, what we've been doing, has made me forget.' He softened his tone, moving closer. 'But I can't forget.' He lifted a hand to her cheek, touching her for what he knew would be the last time. 'We created a perfect void, you and I. A magical space removed from anything and anyone else. But nothing about this works when the world intrudes. The reality of who we are and what our countries require of us is there, banging at the door. Wake up and hear it, Johara. This has to end and you need to leave.'

He felt her shiver, her body trembling against his hand. 'You're wrong.'

He took a step back. 'This was wrong. I thought we could separate what we were doing from the circumstances of who we are, but I never will. We stand on the brink of war once more. Your people. My people. You, and me. You are a Qadir.'

She shook her head, tears filling her eyes, so he felt pain throb low in his gut. He angled his face away for a moment, unable to see her cry.

'Is that all I am to you?'

He closed his heart against her hurt. 'No. But it's the part of you I have to focus on.'

Silence hung between them, heavy and accusatory. He fixed her with a determined gaze.

'I promise that I will protect you with my dying breath but even that isn't enough to guarantee your safety. I have forbidden my military commander from using you as a pawn in this, but I cannot control this to my satisfaction. You are at risk every minute you remain here, Jo.' The diminutive of her name slipped out in his need to convince her.

'I'm not afraid,' she insisted, her eyes showing fierceness.

'You should be.' He blinked and saw his parents' bodies. His blood turned to ice. 'I will not have your death on my conscience.'

'Then let me absolve you of that. I'm choosing to stay— this isn't your responsibility.'

But she would always be his responsibility. It was inevitable. He didn't want the burden of protecting her; he couldn't lose her because of his selfish desire to have her at his side.

Johara brushed a hand through her dark hair, drawing his attention to her face. 'I won't leave; not now. My visit is scheduled to end tomorrow. Let me stay until then, keep to my schedule. Please, Amir. We cannot capitulate to what's likely to be a few rogues. Why can't you see that? It's exactly what they want! Surely this attack was designed in the hope of disturbing the peace—'

He held a hand in the air to silence her, his blood slamming through his body. 'And what better way to disturb the peace than to harm you? You think that even if you stayed I would ever allow you to keep to your schedule? To leave the palace when the mood is like this? No, Johara.' He refused to soften even when faced with her obvious hurt. 'The night we met, I thought you idealistic. But you are also naïve. You have been sheltered, to some extent, from the ravages of this war. You do not understand the lengths men will go to—'

'How dare you?' She glared at him down the length of her nose. 'How dare you speak to me as though I am—' she stopped abruptly, her face filled with torment '—

stupid?' she finished on a sob, pressing her palms to her eyes.

He stood perfectly still, because if he moved, even a little bit, he knew he would crumble altogether. He wanted to cross to her and pull her to him, to wrap his arms around her and hold her tight, to kiss her until this all faded away into nothingness. To tell her that whoever had told her she was stupid because of her dyslexia was mad, because she was the smartest, most courageous person he'd ever known. But he would not weaken. She needed him to be strong; his country needed him to be strong.

Her eyes narrowed, her lower lip trembling, but when she spoke it was in a tone that was pure steel. 'You think you're the only one who's watched his country suffer at the hands of the enemy? I know what we've done to each other! I've lived it, too! That's why we need to stop it. Work together—'

'As your brother and I will do,' he said, determined to turn her away. 'If this was a rogue attack from the mountain people then we will work together to—reason with them and understand them, just as you urged me to understand the man who threw coffee at you. They have played their part in this war and perhaps they have motives we don't comprehend. You've made me see that, Jo. You've changed how I view conflict, people, war. You've changed me.' The admission cost him. It emerged thick and throaty, dark with his emotions.

He paused, bracing himself for what he needed her to know. 'You cannot remain. You are a liability.' He knew he had to be firm, harsh, to get her to see sense. Feeling as though he were dropping off the edge of a cliff, he spun away from her. 'And you're a distraction I don't want, Johara. I need you to go now.'

# CHAPTER TWELVE

'YOU'RE A DISTRACTION *I don't want, Johara. I need you to go now.*'

She stared at his back, his intractable words beating her in the chest. Her eyes swept shut; she struggled to breathe. Hearing these things at any time would have been difficult, but naked in his room, she felt vulnerable and exposed, disbelieving too, as though what he was saying went against everything they'd become.

'The fate of my country hangs in the balance. Of course I can't just run away from that.' She looked around for her clothes, and finally saw them discarded near the foot of the bed. She stalked towards them, scooping them up and pulling her pants on quickly. Her fingers shook, making it difficult to clasp her bra into place. 'And you don't know me at all if you think I'm the kind of person who would quit at the first roadblock.'

'Then do what you must in the bounds of Taquul but you will leave Ishkana, and leave now, before the kingdom awakes to this news.'

'And they'll think I've deserted them! They'll think my opinion of the peace is fragile when it's not! I believe in this peace as much as I believe in this—what you and I share.'

His eyes closed for a moment, as though he was physically rejecting that sentiment. 'They will be far more concerned with whether or not the war is about to break out again.'

'You're making a mistake.' She knew that to be the case. Every cell in her body was screaming at her in violent protest. Leaving was wrong. Not just Ishkana, but Amir. All week she'd braced herself for the necessity of that, and she'd known it would be hard, but, seeing him with the weight of the world on his shoulders, she finally understood what had been happening to them. Ever since that night in the maze.

She lifted a hand to her mouth, smothering a gasp and turning her back on him while she analysed her head, her heart, everything she was feeling.

It was a secret affair, one they'd agreed would have clearcut boundaries, but Johara's heart…it hadn't realised. Not really. She'd fallen in love with him, with all of herself. The desert sky was still an inky black, the stars overhead sparkling, though now it was with a look of mischief. They'd known what they were doing in the maze, contriving for these two people to see one another and give into that cataclysmic desire. Qadirs and Haddads, unbeknownst, hidden, lovers.

At the very edge of the horizon, where sand met sky, whispers of purple were radiating like flames, promising the break of a new day. Soon it would spread, licking upwards, covering the heavens in colour, and then it would begin. How they acted on this day would determine so much.

She spun back to face Amir. His back was still turned. The sight of him like that, closed off to her, sparked a thousand emotions in her gut. Something inside her snapped, but underneath it all was the wonderment of her realisation.

'What if I stayed?' she said quietly, moving towards him, circumnavigating his frame so they were toe to toe, eyes clashing.

'I won't allow it, and nor will your brother.'

Anger exploded in her gut. 'Neither of you can control me,' she said fiercely.

'This isn't about control. It's about your safety.'

'You're saying you can't keep me safe until this is over?' she challenged him, so close she could feel the exhalations as he worked to control his temper.

'I'm saying your safety would become all I could think of,' he contradicted, putting his hands on her shoulders. 'And I need to focus on *this*—the country—with all of my attention. In Taquul, you will be safe.'

'Maybe I don't just want to be safe, trapped in Taquul, dull yet protected,' she responded. 'Maybe I'd rather be at risk here with you, than anywhere else in the world.'

The words were thrown like a gauntlet. They stared at each other, the meaning behind her statement impossible to miss.

She waited, needing him to speak, but he didn't, and so she asked, quietly, her voice just a whisper, 'Do you really want me to leave, Amir?' She pressed her hand to his chest, feeling the thudding of his heart, wondering if it was beating for her.

'I *need* it.'

She shook her head, pain beginning to spread through her. Why couldn't he see what was right in front of him?

'I'm not afraid.' She tilted her chin defiantly. 'You overreacted earlier this week, when the man threw a coffee cup at me, and you're overreacting now. I'm not made of glass.'

'Overreacting? Did you not hear me, Jo? I've just had the chief of my military agency telling me to *detain you*.' A shiver ran down her spine at the ugliness of that—how quickly people could turn! 'If it turns out that this attack had *any degree* of government assistance then those calls will become louder. Here in Ishkana, to almost all of my people, you *are* the enemy.'

Stricken and pale, she trembled. His eyes swept over her, spreading nothing. No warmth. She felt cold to the core of her being.

'You will leave this morning, instead of tomorrow afternoon. Understood?'

'No!' She shook her head in a last-ditch effort to make him see things as she did—or had. She couldn't deny the kernel of fear that was spreading through her. But she had to be brave—more was at stake now. If he knew how she felt and what she wanted, would it make a difference?

'You're the one who doesn't understand. I don't want to leave now. I don't want to leave tomorrow. I want to stay here in Ishkana with you, for the rest of my life, however long that might be. Anything else is unacceptable to me.' She pressed her hands to her hips, adopting a stance that was pure courage and strength when inside she was trembling like a leaf.

His expression was impossible to interpret. Dark eyes met and held hers, and he said nothing for so long that her stance began to weaken, one hand dropping to her side, a feeling of loss spreading through her.

'It's impossible.'

'There would be difficulties,' she corrected. 'But what we have is worth fighting for.'

'If things were different,' he said quietly, his hands lifting to catch her face, cradling her cheeks as he held her so he could see everything that crossed her expression, 'I might want that too.'

It was both the bursting of light and hope within her and the breaking apart of it too. 'Things don't need to be different. I'm here with you now. Does it make any sense for me to be elsewhere?'

His eyes swept shut. 'There's no future for us, *inti qamar*. We've always known that.'

Her heart was in pain. 'Don't you see what I'm trying to tell you?'

He moved a finger to her lips. 'Don't say it.' His Adam's apple jerked as he swallowed. 'Please don't say it. I don't wish to hurt you by not answering with what you would hope to hear in return.' He padded his thumb over her lower lip.

'So then say it,' she whispered. 'I know you feel it.'

'You're wrong.' He shook his head. 'I fought this. I fought you.' He had. When she'd first come to Ishkana he'd tried so hard to stop any of this from happening. 'I should have fought harder.' He stepped back from her, and again she had the sense that he was ending the conversation, making an arbitrary decision that there was no more to say.

It violated everything she felt and wanted. She stamped her foot as he crossed to the door. He was leaving.

'I love you, Amir.' He stopped walking and stood completely still. 'I have fallen so completely in love with you, and not just you—this damned country of yours. I want to stay here with you as your wife, to live my life at your side. Whatever the risks, I want to be here with you.' His back was ramrod straight. 'I love you.'

She felt as though she were paused mid-air, waiting to have a parachute pulled or to drop like a dead weight towards earth. She didn't move. She waited, her lungs burning with the force of breathing, her arms strangely heavy.

'Loving me is—'

She held her breath.

'I don't want your love.'

She flinched.

'I will never return it.' His eyes bore into hers, the seriousness of what he was saying eclipsed by a look that showed her he meant every horrible word he said.

'Then what exactly have we been doing?'

He clamped his lips together, his jaw pressing firm. 'Not falling in love.'

She shook her head; she couldn't believe it. 'I have been.' She swallowed past a wave of bitterness. 'And nothing you say will make me change my mind on that.'

His response was to walk away from her, across the room. At the door, he turned to face her. 'Forget about me, Johara. Go home to Taquul, live your life. Be happy. Please.'

The helicopter lifted from the palace, and he watched it take off into the dawn sky. With one call he could have it summoned back to the palace. A word to a servant and the pilot would respond, bringing the helicopter—and its passenger—back to him. *I want to stay here with you as your wife.*

It was impossible.

If this morning's outbreak of violence had demonstrated anything it was that the people of Taquul and Ishkana would never tolerate anything of the sort. *Detain the Princess.*

If he weren't Sheikh? And she weren't a princess?

No. He wouldn't lose himself in hypotheticals. He was Sheikh Amir Haddad of Ishkana and his allegiance was—and always would be—to his country.

He wouldn't think of her again.

'It makes sense, Jo.'

She sat very still, listening to her brother, her eyes focussed on the spectacular view framed through the windows of this room. Desert sand, the crispest white, spread before them, meeting a sky that was a blisteringly bright blue.

It was just as it had been from the ruins.

So much of Taquul was like Ishkana.

'You must be able to see how right this is. It's what our parents wanted, it's what I want, what he wants. I think deep down it's even what you want.'

'Well,' she couldn't help drawling her response, 'I'm glad you've given what I want *some* thought, seeing as I'd be the one marrying him.'

'You used to like Paris,' Malik said with a shake of his head, coming to sit beside her. The smell of his tea reached her nostrils.

'I still like Paris,' she agreed. 'I consider him a friend. But I don't intend to marry him.'

Malik sighed. 'What's got into you?'

She turned to face him, her eyes clear. 'What do you mean?'

'You've been…different…since you got back from Ishkana.'

Got back. Returned. Came 'home'. All perfectly calm ways to describe the fact she felt as though a rocket had blasted her world into pieces.

'I felt the same way about this before I left. I have never intended to marry Paris. Not really.' She sighed. 'I can see the sense of it. I can tell it's what you want, and yes, I can see why. But I won't marry him.'

'He cares for you.'

*I love you.* He hadn't said anything back. Did that mean he didn't love her? Or that he *couldn't* love her?

It didn't matter. Four weeks had passed. Four weeks. With effort, work and a lot of the reason, sympathy and diplomacy Johara had advocated for, peace was being forged, and it was strengthening with every day that passed. Life was normal again. Except it wasn't. In the middle of her chest there was an enormous black hole. She went through the motions each day, imitating the woman she'd once been. But while her body had returned to Taquul, her heart and soul had remained behind in Ishkana. She doubted the two would ever reunite.

'I can't marry him,' she said, more strenuously.

'Why not?'

Why not? The truth was screaming through her. She stood uneasily, jerkily, moving to the window. The maze was around the corner. If she leaned forward, she'd be able to see just a hint of its verdant walls. She closed her eyes, nausea rising inside her.

'I *am* different.' The words were barely a whisper. She heard the rustle of clothing as her brother came to stand behind her. 'Something happened in Ishkana and it's changed me. I might have been more malleable once. I might even have agreed to this, to please you, and because yes, I can see that it makes a sort of sense. But not now. I can't. Please don't ask me again.'

'What happened, Jo?' There was urgency in his question. 'Did someone hurt you?' She heard the fear beneath the statement. Why couldn't they stop worrying about her? As though she were so fragile, and couldn't look after herself.

'I was treated as an honoured guest,' she assured him. 'No one hurt me.'

And because the words had been pressing down on her like an awful weight for a month now, she said them aloud, needing to speak them to make them real, and to understand them better. 'I fell in love.' She angled her face towards her brother's. 'I fell in love in Ishkana. The idea of marrying Paris—or anyone—makes my blood run cold. Please don't ask it of me.'

'Fell in love?' he repeated, frowning, as though this was an entirely foreign concept. 'With whom?'

Was there any sense in lying? She bit down on her lip, searching for what she should say or do.

But Malik swore, shook his head. 'No. Not him.'

'Yes.' She twisted her fingers at her side, seeing her brother's shock and wishing she hadn't been the instrument of it, and also not caring, because inside she'd grown numb and cold.

'Johara, you cannot be serious.'

She bit down on her lip. 'I love him.'

'This man is—he is—'

'What is he?' she challenged defiantly, anger coursing through her veins. 'The war is over.'

'But the sentiments are not.' He sighed angrily. 'We were at war a long time. You might be ready to forget that but our people won't. There's been too much loss. Too much hurt. It's going to take time and you, a princess of Taquul, cannot simply do as you wish.'

'Of course I can.' She held his gaze levelly, her expression firm. 'I refuse to be bound by a war that has ended, by a war that was started a century ago. I refuse to hate a man I hadn't even met until a few weeks ago. I love him—and you cannot, will not, change my mind or my heart.'

Malik glared at her with a mix of outrage and disbelief. 'I forbid it. I forbid any of this. You will marry Paris and that's the end of it.' He stared at her for several more seconds then turned, stalking towards the door. He slammed it behind him; she didn't so much as flinch.

Amir told himself he wouldn't ask about her. This day wasn't about Johara. It wasn't about him. This was an event marking six months of hard-fought-for peace, a meeting with Malik Qadir, to show the world that the two leaders were intent on progressing matters. It hadn't been smooth sailing, but each little outbreak had been quickly quelled. All-out war had been avoided.

*'Let me stand by your side. Let them see us united.'*

He heard her voice often. Her promises. Her offer. Her desire.

*'I love you.'*

He wouldn't ask about her.

Within minutes, this would be over. A handshake in front of the media, and then they'd slip into their separate cars, go in separate directions, lead separate lives. Because they were Qadir and Haddad and that was what they did.

Malik had her eyes.

Amir felt as though he'd been punched in the gut. But hadn't it been that way since she'd left?

The documents were signed—more trade agreements, a relaxation on sanctions, the beginning of an economic alliance that would strengthen both countries. The business was concluded.

'Leave us.' Amir surveyed the room, encompassing Taquul and Ishkana aides in his directive.

Malik gave a single nod to show his agreement.

There was the scraping of chairs, the sound of feet against tiles, the noise as the door opened to the corridor beyond, and then they were alone; silence fell once more.

'The agreement is in order.' Malik's voice was firm. 'Our people will benefit from this.'

Amir nodded. He wouldn't ask about her.

'And it is timely too,' Malik said, standing, extending his hand to bring the meeting to an end.

If he was going to ask, it would need to be now. *How is she?* The words ran through his head, demanding an answer. He needed to know as he needed to breathe. Nothing more—just *how is she*? Was she happy?

So much of his own happiness depended on that.

'My attention can now be given over to the details of my sister's marriage.' Malik said the words simply, without any hint of malice. He couldn't have known that his statement was an instrument of intense pain to Amir. He kept his face neutral, but his body was tense, like a snake ready to strike.

'Marriage?'

'Yes.' Simple, with a smile. No ulterior motive. 'You met her fiancé, Paris.'

Amir nodded, standing, his chest constricting. 'Yes, of course. When is the wedding to take place?'

'Next week.' He held his hand out for Amir to shake. Amir stared at Malik's hand for several seconds, a frown on his face. He wanted to say so much! He wanted to ask questions, to know everything.

But he didn't have any right to ask.

'Wish…her well from me.'

A week came and went. Amir kept busy. He worked twenty-hour days, involving himself in every single ministerial portfolio. Very little went on that concerned his people of which he was not aware. He reviewed education initiatives, went through medical funding with a fine-tooth comb, oversaw high-level military meetings, and all the while he refused to pay attention to the days that were passing. He wouldn't think about Johara.

He didn't deserve to think of her.

She had offered herself to him—her heart, her love, her service to his country—she had given him everything she had to give and he had told her to go. He'd told her to have a happy life. And that was what she was doing—with Paris.

He couldn't think about what she would have looked like on her wedding day; would she have smiled as she walked down the aisle? Was she nervous? Excited? Was she truly happy?

He couldn't think about what would happen after. Man and wife, the life they'd lead. He couldn't think about her being kissed by another man, touched by him. He couldn't think about any of it.

He'd made his decision, and even as he'd told her to leave he'd known he would regret it. He'd expected this. He owed it to both of them to hold the course.

This was for the best.

'Did they ever tell you how they met?'

Amir frowned, lifting his gaze from the wedding portrait of his parents, a decoration that had sat on his desk for so long he barely looked at it any more, focussing on Ahmed. The older man had been leaving, their meeting concluded. In fact, Amir had thought he had already left.

'No.' Amir shook his head. 'They didn't.'

'I'm not surprised.' Ahmed's smile showed affection, but something else—strain. His eyes swept over Amir.

'I was only twelve when they died. It wasn't something we'd discussed.'

'It was the night your father's engagement was supposed to be announced.'

Amir frowned. 'They hadn't met before?'

'No.' Ahmed moved to the photo, picking it up off the desk and looking at it thoughtfully. 'She was a guest at the party, the cousin of a diplomat. Your father bumped into her—spilled a drink on her skirt, if I remember correctly—and the rest was history.'

'You're saying he was supposed to marry someone else until that night?'

'I'm saying within half an hour of meeting your mother

he insisted the engagement agreement be set aside. They were inseparable.' Ahmed sighed.

Amir held his hand out, and Ahmed put the photo in it. The happiness in his parents' eyes was palpable. Through the veil of time he could feel the joy that had been captured in this moment.

'I know how happy they were,' Amir agreed.

'Yes. They were happy.' Ahmed frowned, sighed heavily once more, so Amir looked towards the older man with a frown, wondering what was on his mind. 'I often think about that. Would they have changed anything if they'd known what would happen?'

Amir stiffened in his seat, replacing the photo on the edge of his desk with care. 'It's impossible to know.'

'No.' Ahmed's smile was wistful. 'It's not. I believe that even if they'd been told on their wedding day what fate awaited them, they would not have shied away from it. Not when it brought you, and the time they had together.'

Amir's chest felt tight.

'I'm sorry, Your Majesty. At my age, the brain tends to become reflective.'

Ahmed moved towards the door. Before he could open it, Amir said, 'My mother paid a high price for that happiness.'

Ahmed frowned. 'I think if she was here she'd say it was worth it.'

Amir often dreamed of his parents. That they were drowning, or on fire, or falling from a cliff, and in every dream he reached for them, his fingertips brushing the cotton of his mother's clothes, or the ends of her hair, grabbing without holding, so close but ultimately ineffectual.

He knew what was at the root of the dreams: a disbelief that he hadn't been able to save them. A desire to go back to that night and do something, anything, that would change the twist of fate that had taken them from him.

His powerlessness had sat about his shoulders for a long time, and he'd never really accepted it.

This dream was different. Johara, in a maze. Not like the maze in Taquul, this had white walls, and as she ran through it the corridors became narrower and narrower, so that he could never reach her. Whenever he got close, she'd slip away again, disappearing no matter how hard he looked.

He woke with a start, his breath rushed, his forehead covered in perspiration.

*She's getting married.*

*'I love you.'*

*'I want to stay here with you.'*

He swore. Anger flooded his body. He ached for her. He felt her everywhere he looked, but she was gone.

He hadn't been able to catch her; he'd failed her.

# CHAPTER THIRTEEN

BEING BACK IN Manhattan was a balm. It was temporary, but it was enough. She stifled a yawn with the back of her hand, glad the evening—the launch of a new therapy space and classroom funded by her charity—had been a success. And for a brief moment, as she'd walked through the room and smiled and spoken to the assembled guests, she'd almost felt like herself again.

Almost.

It was impossible to forget. It was impossible to feel whole when so much of herself was locked away in a space she couldn't access. She'd stopped counting the days since she'd left Ishkana. When it had passed ninety, she'd known: it was too long. He wasn't going to change his mind—he was glad she'd left. He'd forgotten about her. He'd drawn boundaries for their relationship and he was sticking to them with a determination that was innate to him.

Day by day she'd concentrated on Taquul, on taking on a role there, on seeming as though she were fine and focussed on a life that no longer held any appeal for her. She didn't speak about Ishkana or Amir, not even with her brother, and Malik never asked. At least he'd dropped the matter of her marrying Paris—for now. She went through the motions, day in, day out, breathing, eating, sleeping, smiling, when inside she felt as though she were withering and dying.

She used to try not to think of Amir but that was ludicrous—like trying to stop one's heart from beating. It was something she did reflexively so now she didn't even bother to fight it. She accepted that he would always be a part of her, even when he wasn't. She accepted that she would always look for him, think of him, reach for him—and that she'd never again see him or touch him.

Pain was her constant companion, but so what? She could live with it; she would live with it, because even pain was a reminder of him. And in the meantime, she could still make something of her life. She would always know that he was missing, but she refused to be cowed by that. In time, she'd grow strong again.

Perhaps she was already strong? She'd refused Malik's attempts to organise her marriage. She'd come to New York when he'd clearly wished her to stay. She was carving out the best life she could. And one day, she'd be happy again. Never complete, but content.

She had to be. There had been too much loss, grief, sadness and death for her to waste her life. She wouldn't allow herself to indulge in misery.

Her car pulled to a stop outside the prestigious high rise she called home while in the States, her security guard coming to open her door. She ignored the overt presence of guards flanking the door—the apartment was home to many celebrities and powerful politicians; such security measures were normal. Her guards walked her through the lobby. She barely noticed them.

Almost home now, she let the mask slip for a moment, allowing herself to feel her loneliness and solitude without judgement. The elevator doors pinged open and she stepped inside. One of her guards went with her, as was protocol, but before the doors closed another man entered. Unmistakably, he was of a security detail, but not hers.

A second later, the walls seemed to be closing in on her as a second man entered the elevator. Johara couldn't breathe. Her eyes had stars in them. She pressed her back to the wall of the elevator, sure she was seeing things, or that she'd passed out and conjured Amir from the relics of her soul, because he couldn't possibly be right in front of her, inside the elevator, here in Manhattan?

His dark eyes glowed with intent, his face a forbidding mask that made her knees tremble and her stomach tighten. She opened her mouth to ask him something—to ask if it was really him—but she couldn't. No words would form.

'I'd like a meeting with Her Highness.' He addressed his comment to her guard.

Her stomach flipped.

The guard looked to her. She could see his doubts— the peace was new. He didn't want to offend this powerful sheikh, but nor could he consent to this highly improper request.

She had to say something. A thousand questions flooded her. Anger, too. What was he doing here? Why had he come? It had been too long. Too long! Didn't he see how she'd changed? Couldn't he tell that inside, behind the beautiful dress and the make-up and the hair, she was like a cut flower left in the sun too long? She angled her face away from his. In the circumstances, his handsome appearance was an insult. How dared he look so good? So virile? So strong and healthy, as though he hadn't missed a moment's sleep since she left?

'I'm tired,' she said—the words ringing with honesty because they were accurate. She was exhausted.

'Yes.' It was quiet. Sympathetic. He *could* see what she

hid from the rest of the world. He could see inside her heart and recognise its brokenness.

She swallowed, hurting so much more now that he was here. The elevator doors closed but the carriage didn't move. Not until Amir reached across and pressed a button.

'This is important.'

Resistance fired through her. What she'd said to him, the night she'd left, had been important too. He hadn't listened. He'd made up his own mind and nothing she'd said could change it. She'd told him she loved him and he'd turned his back on her as though she meant nothing.

'I'm tired,' she said again, shaking her head. Her guard moved closer, as though to protect her. Amir stiffened and waved away his own guard. Most people wouldn't have noticed, but she was attuned to every movement he made. She saw the tiny shift of his body, the strengthening of every muscle he possessed.

His gaze bore into hers; she knew he registered everything she felt, and she didn't try to hide it. She returned his stare unflinchingly, because she wanted him to feel what he'd done to her. It was petty but necessary.

A muscle jerked in his jaw and a moment later he nodded, a look of acceptance on his features. 'Tomorrow, then.'

Her stomach squeezed. Tomorrow felt like a year away. She'd never sleep if she knew he wanted to speak to her. What could he possibly have to say?

It had been too long.

She bit down on her lip and damn it! Tears filled her eyes. She blinked rapidly, clearing them as best she could.

'We don't have any business together, Your Majesty.' The words were shaky. 'If it's a state concern, there are more appropriate channels—'

'It isn't.'

She had to press her back to the wall, needing its support.

The elevator stopped moving and Amir's guard stepped out, keeping one hand pressed to hold the doors open.

'This is a private matter.' His eyes didn't leave her face. 'This level is my apartment. Here is the key to my room. I'll stay until five p.m. tomorrow. If you find you would like to hear what I have to say, then come to me. Any time, Johara. I will wait.'

She stared at the key as though it were a poisonous snake, her fingertips twitching, her heart aching, her brain hurting.

'It's your decision,' he said quietly, and the gentleness of the promise had her reaching for the key.

She didn't say anything. She didn't promise anything. She couldn't. She felt blindsided, utterly and completely.

He turned and swept out of the elevator, but he was still there, even as the doors closed and it crested one level higher. She could smell him. She could feel him. Just knowing he was in the same building was filling her body with an ancient pounding of a drum, or the rolling in of the sea, waves crashing against her, making her throb with awareness, need, hurt, pain, love, and everything in between.

At three in the morning, she gave up trying to sleep. She pushed out of bed and walked towards the window, staring out at the glistening lights of New York. Even at this hour, the city exuded a vibrancy she'd always found intoxicating. But not now.

She barely saw the lights. All she could think about was Amir. Was he staring out at the same view? Thinking about her? Why was he here?

*This is a private matter.*

What could that mean?

Her heart slammed into her ribs—hard—then she turned

back to the bed, looking at the table beside it. His key sat there, staring right back at her.

Her heart flipped.

What was she doing?

Instead of standing here asking an empty bedroom why he was there and what he wanted, she could go down and demand he tell her. That made more sense.

Before she could second-guess herself, she grabbed her silken robe and wrapped it around herself, cinching it at the waist, then reached for the key. There was no risk of being seen by a nosy guest or paparazzi; she had the whole level of the building.

At his door, she hesitated for the briefest moment. She lifted a hand to knock, then shook her head, pressing the key to the door, pushing it inwards as she heard the buzz.

It was immediately obvious that he wasn't asleep. The lounge area was dimly lit. He sat in an armchair, elbows pressed to his knees, face looking straight ahead. The moment she entered, he stood, his body tense, his expression dark.

He wasn't surprised though. He'd been waiting for her. The realisation made her stomach clench.

'Why are you here?' It was the question she most desperately needed an answer to.

'To see you.'

It was the answer she wanted and yet it wasn't. It gave her so little.

She moved deeper into the apartment, the similarities to hers in its layout disorientating at first.

'Why?'

More was needed. More information. More everything.

'Please, sit down.'

She eyed the armchair warily, shaking her head. She felt better standing.

'Would you like a drink?'

She made a groaning noise of impatience. 'Amir, tell me…'

He nodded. He understood. He crossed to her, but didn't touch her. She could sense the care he took with that, keeping himself far enough away that there was no risk of their fingers brushing by mistake.

'I came to New York because it was the easiest way to see you.'

She frowned.

'Your brother would not send you back to Ishkana.'

She swallowed.

'You invited me?'

'No. But after he lied about your marriage to Paris, I read between the lines. You told him about us.'

Her jaw dropped. 'He what?'

'He told me you were to be married. At first I believed it to be true.'

She shook her head. 'He was wrong to do that. I never agreed. I would never agree.'

'I know.' His tone was gentle, calming. But she didn't feel calm. Frustration slammed through her.

'You told him about us, and he doesn't approve.'

She ground her teeth together. 'Whether he does or doesn't is beside the point. Malik has nothing to do with us.'

He studied her for several long seconds.

'He's your brother,' Amir said quietly.

'Yes. But I'm a big girl and this is my life. I make my own decisions.'

'I wanted to see you,' Malik said quietly. 'But arranging a visit to Taquul and coinciding our schedules proved difficult. Particularly without alerting anyone to the purpose of my visit.'

'Yes, I understand that.' She frowned.

'When I heard you were coming to New York, I followed.'

*I followed.* Such sweet words; she couldn't let them go to her head.

'Why?'

His smile was a ghost on his face. His eyes traced a line from the corner of her eye to the edge of her lips and she felt almost as though he were touching her. She trembled.

'Before you left Ishkana, I should have explained everything better. Only I didn't understand myself then. I couldn't see why I acted as I did. It took losing you, missing you, hearing that you were to marry someone else and knowing myself to be at the lowest ebb of my life only to pass through sheer euphoria at the discovery that you were not married. It took all these things for me to understand myself. I couldn't explain to you that night, because I didn't know.'

She swayed a little, her knees unsteady.

'I didn't ever decide to push you away. I never consciously made that decision, but it's what I've been doing all my life, or since my parents died at least. I have many people that consider me a friend yet I do not rely on anyone. Not because I don't trust them but because I don't trust life.' His smile was hollow. 'I lost my parents and I have been permanently bracing to experience that grief all over again. Until I met you, I shielded myself the only way I knew how—I made sure I never cared about anyone enough to truly feel their absence.'

Her stomach felt as though it had dropped right to the ground outside. Sadness welled up inside her. 'That sounds very lonely.'

'Loneliness is not the worst thing.' He brushed her sympathy aside. 'But you made it impossible to not care. I tried so hard not to love you, and yet you became a part of me.' He stopped talking abruptly, the words surprising both of them. 'Losing you would have been almost the worst thing that could happen to me—feeling that pain again would have been crippling. But so much worse if it were my fault. When you told me you wanted to stay with me, as my wife, I wanted to hold you so close and never let you go—but what if? What if something happened to you, and all because of my selfishness?'

Her heart was splintering apart for him. His fears were so understandable, but all this heartbreak…

'And I'm a Qadir,' she said quietly, trying to hold onto a hint of the bitterness that had been their stock in trade for generations.

He returned her stare unflinchingly. 'You're the woman I love.'

Her breath caught.

'And I am still half terrified that my love will ruin you, but I have realised something very important in the long months since you left the palace.'

She waited, impatient, desperate.

'You were right that night. This should have been your decision. You know what the risks are to our marriage, and you know that it will change many things for you, including, perhaps, your relationship with your brother. But these are your choices to make, not mine. I pushed you away, as I push everyone away, because that seemed better than taking this gamble. Yet it isn't mine to take.'

His voice was deep, gravelled.

'Only let me assure you that if you wish to make your life with me, I will do everything within my power to keep you safe and make you happy.'

She was silent. Dumbfounded.

'I know I hurt you.' Now, finally, he touched her. The lightest brush of his fingertips to hers. 'It was something I swore I wouldn't do yet in trying to protect you that's exactly what happened.'

She tilted her face away, tears stinging her eyes. 'You did hurt me,' she agreed softly. 'You pushed me away at a time when you could have used my support. You made me irrelevant. You're not the first person to do that, but it hurt the worst with you because I expected so much more.'

He groaned. 'I acted on instinct.'

She bit down on her lip, nodding. 'And I went home, and I waited, and I thought of you, and I have missed you every single day and you've been nowhere. It was as though it never happened. And now you're asking me to forget, and feel as I did then?' Her heart was battered and mangled and yet it was also bursting. Her defiant speech felt good to throw at him, but it wasn't really how she felt. She watched her words hit their mark, the pain in his face, the apology she felt in his eyes.

'I came here knowing you might not want what you did then. But still I had to explain. I didn't ask you to leave because I didn't love you. I loved you too much to have you stay. And I love you now, too much to fight you. Just know that you will always be my reason for being, Johara. Whether you're with me or not, everything I do will be for you.'

He lifted her hand to his lips and kissed it lightly, and she tilted her head back to his, facing him. 'I love you.'

He offered the words so simply, and they pushed inside her, shaking her out of the state she was in. This was really happening. He was standing in front of her pouring his heart out and she was holding onto the anger she'd felt. Was she doing exactly the same thing he had? Pushing him away because she was scared of being hurt again?

Maybe love always brought with it a sense of danger—and the gamble made the pay-off so much sweeter.

'So what are you saying?' she asked quietly, surprised her voice sounded so level when her insides were going haywire.

'Is that not obvious?'

She shook her head. 'I think I need you to say it.'

He nodded, his Adam's apple shifting as he swallowed. 'I wish I could go back to that night and change everything I said and did. I wish I had pulled you into my arms, thanked you for what you were offering and walked hand in hand with you to deal with the problems that faced *us*. Not me. *Us*. About *our* countries.' Her lips parted as she drew in a shaky breath.

'But I cannot go back in time, and I cannot change what I did then. So I am promising you my heart, and my future, and everything I can share with you. I am asking you to marry me, if you can find it in your heart to forgive me. I am asking you to be not just my wife, and the mother of my children, but a ruler at my side. You are brilliant and brave and your instincts are incredible. I would be lucky to have you as my wife, and Ishkana would be blessed to have you as its Queen. I'm asking you to look beyond the past to the future that we could have. And in exchange I promise that I will never again fail you. I will never again fail to see your strength and courage, to understand what you are capable of.'

Tears fell unchecked down her cheeks now. He caught one with the pad of his thumb, then another, wiping her face clean.

'Don't cry.' The words were gruff. 'Please.'

She laughed, though, a half-sob, a sign of how broken and fixed she felt all at once.

'Damn it, Amir, I wanted to hate you,' she said, stamping her foot. 'I have missed you so much.'

'I know.' He groaned, pulling her towards him, holding her close to his body. 'That is mutual.'

She listened to his heart and knew that it was beating for her, just as it always had. She stayed there with her head pressed to his chest, listening, believing, adjusting to the reality she was living, to the happiness that was within reach. They both had to be brave, but the alternative was too miserable to contemplate.

She blinked up at him, smiling. 'Let's go home, Amir.'

He made a growling sound of relief, pleasure, delight, and then he swooped his lips down to kiss her. 'Yes, *inti qamar*. Let us go home.'

'You can't be serious.'

Amir couldn't take his eyes off Johara. Through the glass of his bedroom, he watched her sleeping and felt as though nothing and no one could ever hurt him. She was here, in Ishkana, where she belonged. Seven months ago he'd pushed her away, believing the best thing he could do for her was arrange safe passage to Taquul. How wrong he'd been. And how fortunate he was that her heart was so forgiving...

'We flew back a few hours ago.' Behind him, the sun was beginning to break into the sky. 'It's all agreed.'

'You cannot marry her. I forbid it.'

'Your lack of consent will hurt Jo, Malik, but it will do nothing to change our plans.'

Silence met his pronouncement. If the past had taught them anything it was that neither wanted to risk another outbreak of violence. They both knew the cost too well. Malik might be furious, but he would not threaten military action.

'You must have kidnapped her. Taken her against her will.'

Amir straightened at the very suggestion. 'I will never, in my life, do *anything* against your sister's will. She came here because we are in love, Malik, as you are well aware.' The gentle rebuke sat between them. It was the reason, after all, that Malik had lied about an impending marriage to Paris.

'Love,' Malik spat with disbelief. 'She is a princess of Taquul. Her place is here.'

'Her place,' Amir corrected with a smile that came from deep within his heart, 'is wherever she wants it to be.'

Inside, Johara caught the statement through the open door, her eyes blinking open. She listened, her breath in a state of suspension as the man she intended to spend the rest of her life with spoke to—she could only presume—her brother.

'I insist on speaking to her.'

'Yes, of course,' Amir agreed. 'She is still asleep, but I have no doubt she will wish to speak to you about this. The purpose for my call is simple—I wanted to alert you to the state of affairs and to caution you against saying or doing anything to upset her.'

'Is that a threat?'

'A threat? No. It's a promise. If you push her away, you will lose her completely, Malik. She has chosen where she wants to be, and with whom.' He sighed. 'I love your sister. I plan to make her very happy by giving her everything she could ever want—and we both know that is for us to be, if not exactly friends, capable of existing harmoniously.'

Silence met this statement.

'She and I are to marry. She will carry my children, the heirs to Ishkana. They will be your nieces and nephews. Can you think of anyone who will benefit from continued estrangement?'

* * *

Inside the bedroom, Johara smiled, her eyes fluttering closed. She was exactly where she wanted to be and, with all her heart, she knew that the decision she'd made had been the right one. The only one she could ever make. Her heart, the skies, fate and future had guided her here—it was where she was meant to be.

## EPILOGUE

Amir had been wrong. He had believed his people, and the people of Taquul, would revolt at the very idea of a union between himself and Johara. He had braced for that, and prepared Johara for the inevitable splashback.

There had been none.

Nothing but euphoric delight and anticipation. Every detail of their union was discussed at length. He could not turn on the television without catching some talk-show host speculating about which tiara she would wear down the aisle, and whether the jewel for her ring would be of Taquul or Ishkana.

Billboards were pasted across the city with a smiling photo of Johara, welcoming her to Ishkana. Despite the pain his people had felt—or perhaps because of it—they welcomed her, knowing that lasting peace was truly at hand. With this marriage, the war became impossible. Their union bonded the countries in a way no peace treaty alone ever could. They were family now. His children would be a mix of them, and of their countries, and he had every intention of their being raised in the light of both countries and cultures.

Separation was not the way forward. Unity was. Just as Johara had said.

In the end, she wore a tiara that had belonged to her

mother, and a wedding ring that had been his mother's. Her dress was made of spider's silk, lace and beads, and when she walked towards him, he felt as though it were just him and her, and no one else in the world. When she walked towards him, he felt as though he might be about to soar into the heavens.

She smiled at him and he felt a thousand and one things—gladness, love, pleasure, relief, and a small part of him felt sorrow that his parents would never know her. But in a way, their happiness would be a part of this, because through their example he'd finally understood that being fearless was a necessity to love.

A year after their wedding, to the day, they were blessed with the birth of a son. Two years later, twin daughters followed. And for all the years into the future they'd hoped for, peace, happiness and prosperity favoured not only Amir and Johara, but the people of their kingdoms as well.

There was, as it turned out, never a story with less woe than that of Amir and his Jo.

\* \* \* \* \*

# FAST DEAL

**FAYE AVALON**

For Mum, who's always been
partial to a 'naughty' story

# CHAPTER ONE

A COUPLE MORE MINUTES and he'd put a stop to it.

While the woman dancing on one of the low-level tables was nowhere near indecent, the suggestive way she was moving her hips to the music signalled things could be heading that way.

Connor Fitzpatrick sat back in his chair at the rear of the bar, nursing a whisky. His lower back complained, likely due to all the late nights he'd been pulling. He should be making time for the gym rather than running herd on a group of women who, from their laughter, had undoubtedly been upping his bar profits considerably.

While that was always good, it wasn't as if either of his London clubs needed much in the way of a boost. They were going great guns. He looked around the packed club with its soft ambient lighting, deep, black leather sofas and stylish features in chrome and glass. This club had been his first and had quickly gained favour amongst the young and fashionable. That was why he had been well placed to act when providence had smiled on him and dropped the property he'd been patiently waiting to buy—and then destroy—right in his lap.

About bloody time. Now he could get closure, payback, revenge. Whatever the hell anyone chose to call it.

The deal he'd made with Damian McBride had taken some ducking and diving, but Connor had no scruples about putting on the emotional screws. Offering over the market value hadn't hurt, either, which was why Connor was only a signature away from owning the now defunct Cabacal Club, the place that symbolised the lowest point of his life.

He had no idea what he'd do with it. Maybe just gut the place, or let it fall to rack and ruin. He didn't give a fuck.

It was no skin off his balls. And he should know, since they'd already been sliced and bruised enough for one lifetime. For the past five years he'd placed his focus squarely on building his business, taking pleasure in the rapid success his clubs had brought him. Now the acquisition of the property at the heart of his near-downfall would provide the last soothing layer of balm to heal old wounds right over.

He sipped his whisky, letting it drive down the bile of memories as his gaze drifted back to the woman still making full use of the table. While he liked his patrons to enjoy themselves, this one's impromptu dance wasn't exactly the kind he encouraged. No denying she had curves, displayed as they were in tight white jeans and a sleeveless grey top that had a zipper down the front, opened to reveal some tantalising cleavage.

Still moving, the woman pushed her hands underneath her long mane of dark-blonde hair, lifting it away from her neck and letting it cascade back down over her shoulders. The way she shimmied, her body undulating in perfect time to the music, had his already alert cock throbbing against the fly of his suit pants. Shit, this was all he needed. A frigging hard-on courtesy of Ms Footloose up there.

She held her arms out to the side, gyrating in a way that reminded him of a belly dancer he'd once encountered during a pub crawl with his mates. He had very happy memories of that night, especially the one where he'd peeled away all seven layers of flimsy gauze—in private, of course—before he and said belly dancer had fucked the living hell out of each other.

He took a healthy slug of his drink as he continued to watch the current show, imagining sliding down the zipper of her top to reveal breasts perfect for his hands and mouth. Since he could see the faintest outline of nipple, he'd bet she wasn't wearing a bra. He imagined feasting on her breasts, ruthlessly licking her nipples, then slowly stripping her out of those jeans. He wondered what kind of underwear she favoured. Those skimpy, lacy deals, perhaps? Or maybe she wore none at all.

He swallowed, his fingers curling tightly around the glass as his gaze zoomed in on her ass, looking for a distinct panty line. Shit, he had a full-blown throbbing erection now. And if he did then he'd bet nearly every other guy in the place did too.

Since he prided himself on running classy establishments, he knew the time had come to call a halt. With considerable reluctance, and hoping to hell his erection wasn't visible to all and sundry, he tossed back the remainder of his drink, placed the glass on the table and stood. Instantly, one of his security men was at his side.

The man glanced over at the group of women. 'You want me to deal with this, boss?'

Connor shook his head. It didn't matter how many times he told Nigel not to call him 'boss', the man was old school, an ex-copper, and seemed to prefer formalities. 'No.' Connor let out a long exhale. 'I'm heading home anyway, so I'll sort it on my way out. Keep an eye on them, though, and if they attempt a replay or start to get rowdy call them a cab.'

Nigel tapped two fingers to his temple. 'Consider it done.'

Connor walked across to the table, hoping that the raunchy dance hadn't offended his other customers. From his brief glance around the club, most seemed to be taking the unexpected entertainment in a genial manner.

As he neared the table, the woman reached down and took off one shoe. It was one of those lethal, spiky heels that looked as if it should come with a health warning. Not that he didn't enjoy seeing them at the end of a woman's leg—sexy as hell, especially when they wore nothing else.

Encouraged by her friends, the woman started twirling around, wobbling precariously on the one remaining heel. She bent, obviously intent on removing the other shoe, but toppled and stumbled back against him.

As Connor reached out to catch her, something lanced across his neck. He inhaled sharply, his fingers reflexively digging into her waist as she fell to her knees, still holding the recalcitrant shoe.

'Oh, shit. I'm so sorry.'

Caught in the startled green of her eyes, his hands tightened around her waist, holding her steady.

'You're bleeding. I've hurt you,' she said.

He tore his gaze away from hers long enough to turn his head, the spike of her shoe dangerously close to his head. 'It's fine. Just get that thing away from me before you poke my bloody eye out.'

Using his shoulders as leverage, she swivelled around, then sat on the edge of the table and put her shoe back on. All the while she peered at his neck. 'I'm really sorry.'

Connor touched his hand to the spot she was staring at, aware of the slight sting there. He wasn't sure if that sensation was because of the wound itself, or the intensity of her study, but when he drew his fingers away they were streaked with blood.

She reached up. 'You're bleeding on your shirt collar.'

Connor stepped away from where she was about to touch his neck. 'I've bled on worse things. Don't worry about it.'

From the small bag she had strapped across her body, she pulled out a wad of tissue. 'Here, press this hard to the wound. It will staunch the bleeding.'

He found himself doing as she said. It was those hypnotic green eyes. Or more likely the concern in them.

That unsettled him. Pulled up too many memories. He'd rather she poked his eye out with that insane heel than make him remember things he'd sworn to forget.

'Thanks,' Connor said. He turned from her, intending to head to his office at the back of the club, and almost bumped into Nigel.

'Have you got a first-aid kit somewhere?' she demanded of the burly bouncer, before turning back to Connor. 'We should make sure the wound is clean and dress it properly. There's no telling what germs are on the heel of my shoe—you might be infected by something nasty.'

'I'm sure I'll survive.'

'There's a kit in the office,' Nigel said, tilting his head towards the door, and Connor could have sworn the man was battling a grin. 'It'll be fully stocked with everything you need.'

Connor narrowed his eyes, fully intending to remind Nigel of his duty of care towards his employer, especially the part about protecting him from pushy females. 'Great. Then I'll thank you both for your unwarranted concern and be on my way.'

He was almost at his office door, and trying not to think about those eyes, those curves, all that bloody hair, when he felt her behind him.

Still pressing the wad to his neck, he looked over his shoulder and raised his eyebrows. 'I'm a big boy. I can take it from here.'

She shook her head, sending those luxurious locks brushing against her shoulders and—fuck—across her breasts. 'You really should let me have a look. I'm a qualified first-aider.' She glanced towards the door, then back at him. Her eyes went wide. 'Are you the manager, or something?'

'Or something,' he said, acknowledging that her cagey look was likely due to concern that she'd be charged with bodily harm. 'Look, it's okay. No harm done. I'm not about to press charges.'

Still, she hesitated, looking from him to the door and back again before moving right past him and into his office.

Connor closed the door, watching as she took a cursory look around before heading over to the three-tiered filing cabinet in the corner. 'Is this where you keep the first-aid kit?'

Damned if he knew. 'Probably.' He walked over, unlocked the cabinet and, as he knew the first two drawers were jam-packed with business files, slid open the bottom one. His efficient assistant had placed a green box at the back of the drawer, clearly marked with the universal symbol for first-aid supplies.

Before he could reach for it, the woman bent down and grabbed it from the drawer. 'Sit,' she instructed, crossing to the desk and sliding out his black leather chair. 'Let me take a closer look.'

Connor frowned. He should tell her to get the hell out of his office, remind her that he could deal with his own bloody cut, and if he wanted to sit in his damned chair he would—he didn't need a pushy siren giving him instructions. Instead, he found himself walking to the chair and sitting like a well-trained canine. His only excuse was that the sooner he let her do her nursing stint, the sooner she would be gone. At least, that was what he told himself.

She reached out to remove the bloodied wad at the same moment he did. Their fingers brushed, hands touching. Okay, nothing wrong with a little spark of chemistry, a zing of sexual awareness. Some very definite fire in the blood, and below the waist.

The subtle snatch of her breath as they touched, the way her heated gaze held his a moment too long before dropping to his mouth, confirmed she wasn't immune to that zing. One glance at her grey top confirmed his theory. Those nipples he'd imagined licking to peak were already reflecting the very outcome he'd visualised.

Maybe he was being too hasty in his desire to be rid of her. For the past several weeks, he'd been on a rollercoaster, his attention tightly focused on a driving need to buy the Cabacal and lay to rest old ghosts. He couldn't blame his body for starting to retaliate against having its physical needs denied for too long.

From her table-dance earlier, she was definitely a party girl, probably up for some fun, and the way she was sending his hormones on this happy journey signalled she was exactly the kind of woman to break his no-sex streak. Fun-loving, easy-going, obviously in touch with her own sexuality. Add this definite mutual attraction to the mix and it boded well for a little private party of their own.

She tossed the tissue into the waste bin, then she placed her hands on her knees and bent to peer at the wound with an intensity reserved for someone inspecting a new kind of species.

When she reached for the first-aid box she'd placed on the desk, Connor couldn't resist a quick glance down her top.

Nice, he thought, as his extremely interested cock responded with appropriate pleasure. He averted his gaze as she turned back. Instinct had him folding his hands in his lap in a bid to hide the evidence, but he was too late. Her eyes dropped to his hands before she returned her attention to his neck. 'You don't have to hide that,' she teased, dabbing the cut with a cotton ball. 'Was my dance responsible? Or just the fact I'm wearing a low-cut top?'

He liked her directness. Liked that she didn't seem at all interested in playing games, or pretending there wasn't a massive flood of pheromones renting the air between them. Appearances could be deceptive, of course, but it was refreshing to find a woman who seemed straightforward and down-to-earth.

Her directness warranted some of his own. 'It started with the dance, then you bent over the filing cabinet and then you bent over me. What's a man to do?'

She smiled, still dabbing. 'Can't blame you, I suppose. Men are such basic creatures.'

'Come on.' He winced as she touched a sore spot. 'You're not telling me your intention wasn't to get the men out there fired up?'

Not a hint of insult showed on her face, feigned or otherwise, nor in her actions. He liked that too. 'Why should it always be a woman's intention to turn on a man? Can't she simply enjoy moving her body for her own pleasure?'

'Fair enough, but why choose a crowded club to do it?' He waited until she looked at him. 'Or do you always like an audience when you give yourself pleasure?'

Tiny spears of colour bloomed in her cheeks, and she caught her bottom lip between her teeth. He enjoyed watching that spectacular mouth, maybe even more than the fact he'd managed to set her back a step.

His enjoyment was short-lived when she reached out to the box again. 'If you're trying to shock me, you'll have to do much better than that.' She undid the cap of a bottle with blue liquid and poured some onto a fresh cotton ball.

He grinned. 'You didn't actually answer my question.'

With a sexy pout that had his erection throbbing beneath his hands, she held the now doused cotton ball aloft and considered. 'Do I like an audience when I give myself pleasure? Hmm. Well, to be honest I usually do that in private. For my eyes only.'

She jerked down the collar of his open-necked shirt, smiled sweetly at him then stabbed him with the fire of hell. He shot back in his seat and grimaced. 'Whatever kind of bloody healing balm is that?'

All innocence and patience, she continued to administer to his neck, earning from him several more sharp intakes of breath as she worked. 'Men are such babies. And here I was thinking you were a grown man.'

'I'm man enough, sweetheart, with all the parts to prove it.' Suddenly irritated, both by the sting from that bloody liquid and the image of her pleasuring herself without him being there to see it, he reached up and curled his fingers around her wrist. 'I reckon I'm cleaned up well enough by now.'

She glanced down at his hand before bringing her gaze back to his. 'Are you allergic to plasters?'

'No.' Even if he were, he'd suffer through it if it meant getting this torture over with. Not just suffering at the hands of her less than gentle nursing techniques, or the growing temptation of sampling her very appealing attributes. It was also the way it made him wonder when a woman had shown this much concern for his welfare, if ever.

The sting of that liquid had not only cleaned the cut but had shaken him back to reality. Yeah, okay, he wanted her. He *really* wanted her. But the timing sucked. His priority was getting home, grabbing some long overdue sleep, checking final figures and documentation, then preparing himself for the six a.m. conference call with Damian McBride.

Normally, Connor would take his chances. What was one more sleepless night? Especially if he had the opportunity to share a bed with a hot woman. But he couldn't afford to take any chances with tomorrow's meeting. It was too important to him. He'd waited too long. He had every intention of making Damian draw up that contract pronto so they could both sign on the dotted line.

Which meant he had to call a halt to this extremely pleasant interlude and get his ass back home. He sucked in a breath. 'Won't your friends be wondering where you are?'

'They know where I am. They would have seen me come back here with you. If I'm not out in a reasonable amount of time, they'll call the cops.'

He realised he still had hold of her wrist, noticed how his hand fitted easily around the circumference of all that soft flesh. With considerable reluctance, he released her. Shit, but he really wanted to seduce his dancing queen, find out if all that bared skin was as silky as it looked. Let his hands slide easily over those sexy dips and curves as he kissed her full lips and drove them both insane.

'Well, stick the plaster on, and maybe you should go back and join them. I'd just as soon not have the cops banging on my door, if it's all the same to you.'

She laughed, took off the protective wrapping of the plaster then bent down to place it on his neck. He deliberately kept his gaze averted as she moved closer to smooth the plaster down at the edges, but her scent washed over him. Floral and earthy at the same time. Feminine and sultry. He wanted to draw her close, breathe her in.

Luckily, she straightened. 'There. Good as new.'

He was tempted to tease her, ask if she thought he'd be left with a scar. But, as he figured he had enough of those already, he declined. Some things weren't easy to joke about.

Since he didn't intend delving any deeper into that aspect of his past right then, he pushed such thoughts away and kept his focus trained on her.

He made a long, slow perusal of her as she stood there staring at his neck. Her tank top had ridden up, revealing a creamy strip of flesh around her midriff, causing saliva to pool in his mouth. And, maybe it was his imagination but the atmosphere was hot and enticingly tempting.

In the grand scheme of things, who said a man needed eight solid hours sleep anyway? He'd existed on far less than that during his thirty years on the planet and, while tomorrow's stakes had never been this high for him, there wasn't much that could go wrong. The negotiations had been undertaken, the sums agreed.

In which case…

Connor eyed her up and down, making sure she couldn't mistake his intention. No point wasting valuable time with unnecessary rituals and peripherals, like pretending they both weren't interested in each other.

'Since you've taken such good care of me, why don't I buy you a drink?'

'A minute ago, you were trying to get rid of me.'

Yeah. And he would wonder for ever what particular brain malfunction had brought about that insane notion. There was being cautious and there was being a complete dickhead. What man with his head on straight denied himself a quick roll in the hay with a hot and willing woman?

'I was just making sure we were thinking along the same lines.'

'Which are?'

'You. Me. A bottle of whatever is your pleasure.' She bit her bottom lip again and he could see cogs turning, wheels spinning. Determined to get her agreement, he tapped a finger to the plaster and pursed his lips in a pitiful manner. 'You can't surely be considering abandoning me so soon? I might start bleeding again.'

She laughed, a deep rumble of sound that shot fresh heat through his blood and promised extremely good times ahead. He leaned forward and reached out to take her hand, noticing how her fingers stiffened momentarily beneath his before relaxing. Not wanting to push things too hard too fast, he let go of her. 'Why don't you go and tell your friends you won't be needing the cops?'

She raised her eyebrows, amusement evident in her eyes. 'That might be a little premature.' She replaced the lid of the first-aid box. 'But say I agreed to one drink, I've got a feeling you wouldn't be satisfied with that. Am I right?'

He knew instinctively that he needed to change tactics, maybe back off a little. Despite that she seemed to be matching him in the verbal banter stakes, it was hard to deny her tentative manner as she'd asked him what his intentions were. He hoped to hell he wasn't making her uncomfortable.

Not that she'd appreciate any kind of subterfuge either.

Straight-shooter, he reminded himself. She didn't play games. 'Look, let me tell you where I stand. I think we've got this mutual thing going. I'd like to buy you a drink and see where it leads. If it leads us beyond that drink, then I'll be an extremely happy man.'

Her breasts hiked as she sucked in a breath. While he hadn't shocked her, he'd pushed her off-balance. He kind of liked that. There was a certain satisfaction in unbalancing a confident woman. From nowhere came the unsettling thought that right then he was almost as desperate to get her affirmative response as he was that contract from Damian McBride. What the hell was that about? Perhaps he really had been without female company for too long.

She didn't respond but kept eyeing him as if she was trying to figure him out. He chanced an easy smile. When she screwed up that delicious mouth, he held his breath, willing her not to back out now. Not when he had images of her doing incredible things with that mouth.

Slowly, she picked up the box and took it back to the cabinet where she bent and slid it into the lower drawer. His throat went dry at the sight of her perfect ass in those tight-fitting white jeans.

She closed the drawer and stood. Her back went ramrod straight as she looked at the captioned photograph on the top of the filing cabinet. The one taken when he'd received an industry award last year.

He walked over to stand next to her, making sure not to crowd her.

'Look, I think you're a woman who likes to call it straight and, since we both know there's a strong physical thing going on here, why waste time pretending otherwise?'

She continued to look at the photograph, then took another deep breath and turned to look up at him, making his pulse kick like a frigging donkey.

After a brief hesitation, she placed her palm

against his chest, and he swore her guarded eyes
went a darker green. 'I do like straight talking, but
I also like to think around things.'

'Then start thinking.' He winked, smiled. 'Make
it fast.'

Another hesitation, then she laughed. Shit. He really liked that laugh, the way she paused before she
got the joke and then the laugh bubbled from deep
in her throat.

'Trust me, as much as I'm tempted, it's not a good
idea. For a variety of reasons.'

'Name one.'

She blinked, as if she hadn't expected the question. 'Well, we don't know each other. Like you said,
the response is physical.'

What the fuck was wrong with that? 'Physical
responses can be the best ones,' he said with a wag-
gle of his eyebrows. 'Less chance things get complicated.'

She laughed again, her eyes meeting his for long
moments. It made him wonder if she was enjoying
their flirtatious banter as much as he was but was
determined to hold back, to fight against their obvious attraction. 'You may be right about that.' Her
smile was a little wistful as she reached up to tap
the plaster. 'Make sure to keep that on for a while.'

What the hell did that mean? Was she giving him
the old heave-ho? He wasn't prepared to let her walk
away that easily.

Maybe he really had come on too strong. She

said one of the reasons this was a bad idea was because they didn't know each other. Well, that he could remedy.

'So, about that drink.'

She was at the door, her back to him and with her fingers wrapped around the handle. For what seemed like an age during which Connor held his breath, she stood there, no doubt taking her time to deliberate.

Then she turned to look over her shoulder at him. 'I'll meet you at the bar.'

# CHAPTER TWO

LOLA MCBRIDE TUGGED DOWN the edge of her top so that it covered her midriff and perched on a stool at the bar. Her friends were over on the small dance floor, having fun, but Lola needed a few minutes. Away from Connor Fitzpatrick's hormone-inducing presence, she was able to think again, to breathe again.

She still hadn't recovered from seeing that photograph of him on top of the filing cabinet, and the caption declaring Connor Fitzpatrick an entrepreneur to watch. Finding out *he* was the owner of the club and not just the manager had taken the wind right out of her sails. She'd imagined someone older, embittered, hardened, somehow. And while the man she'd just spoken to wasn't one you'd want to mess with—the hint of steel in his grey eyes alluded to that—he'd been kind of playful, flirty and...sexy.

She hadn't factored in the possibility that Connor Fitzpatrick would be insanely gorgeous and that they'd share an intense and instant sexual attraction.

What the devil had she been thinking, flirting with him right back, egging him on?

That was most definitely not part of her plan.

She'd expected to come here, suss out the joint and in the process have a little post-graduation fun with her friends. It never hurt to check things out, nor did it hurt to size up the man who would play a vital part in her achieving her goal.

But meeting him tonight and being attracted to him hadn't remotely figured in her plans. How was it that one glimpse of him had heated her blood and shot lurid little messages to every one of her nerve endings?

Lola tapped her fingers on the bar. Think... She had to think.

Damian would be in Singapore for another couple of weeks, plenty of time for her to get Connor's agreement to her plan before her brother got wind of it. If Damian found out, he would stymie it in the same way he'd stymied all her attempts to get the Cabacal property back. Her brother hadn't even done her the courtesy of looking at her business plan. He had just flat-out told her it wasn't a viable proposition, that the competition was fierce and that it would likely fold sooner rather than later. He'd told her to put her first-class business degree to better use than some airy-fairy notion of running a fitness studio.

The fact Damian had actually used 'airy fairy' in relation to her long-held dream had incensed Lola more than anything—perhaps even more than hav-

ing to fulfil the requirements of her trust fund. She'd
achieved the business degree and post-graduate qual-
ification demanded by her late father, yet she still
wasn't able to run her own show until her twenty-
fifth birthday.

Despite pleading with Damian to hold off putting
the property on the market for six months, until she
would be in a position to buy it for her studio, he'd
gone right ahead and entered into negotiations with
Connor Fitzpatrick.

Connor was owed, Damian had said. It was poetic
justice that the property should be his. Lola knew
that Connor had worked for her late uncle as manager of the Cabacal, and that he had been a victim
of her uncle's treachery as much as her mother had
been. All that aside, she didn't think Connor had as
much right to the property as she did. Built by Lola's
maternal great-grandfather for his beloved wife, the
Cabacal had been handed down the female line of
the family, right until her mother had been cheated
out of it by her only brother, Lola's uncle.

Now Lola had made it her mission to get the property back where it belonged.

While she appreciated the tenacity that Connor
had shown in outbidding two other serious buyers, it
didn't make things easy for her. So, denied using the
front door to achieve her goals, she had no option but
to go around the back. That meant ensuring that, if
Connor bought the property, she could convince him
to sell it to her as soon as she had the money from

her trust fund. She'd need to show him that her need to own the property was greater than his.

It was a long shot, of course, but she could hopefully sweeten the pot with an excellent financial incentive. Whatever it took, she was going to get her late mother's inheritance back, and in doing so would right a cruel wrong, rebalance the books and put the universe back on its axis.

She'd come close to jeopardising her plans by falling into lust with Connor, but how in heaven was a girl supposed to resist those eyes, or the way his dark hair brushed against his very kissable neck? Not to mention the impressive width of his shoulders, or the breadth of a quite spectacular chest.

Tempted to break her non-drinker status, she eyed the cocktail one of the bartenders was currently making and wondered if she should order one.

Despite her spontaneous dance routine—thanks to an equally spontaneous game of truth or dare—she hated the nightclub scene. It was in total contrast to what she loved. Keeping fit, active, healthy. Eating the right foods, nurturing her body, making sure she treated it so that it would serve her well.

During her enforced academic studies she'd moonlighted as a fitness instructor, taking part-time courses in health and wellbeing and massage therapy, eventually qualifying as a yoga instructor.

It had been her mother's dream. Now it was hers.

Deep in thought, Lola sensed a ripple of something around her and became aware of Connor a moment before he slid onto the stool next to hers. Her whole body responded sensually as his scent and his aura washed over her. 'What's your poison?'

As if by magic, a bartender morphed before their very eyes and was waiting expectantly. 'Virgin mojito, please.' When Connor raised his eyebrows, she shrugged. 'I'm not a fan of alcohol.'

As the bartender went off to fill the order for their drinks, Connor swivelled his stool towards her. 'You said there were a variety of reasons this was a bad idea,' he said, leaning his forearm on the bar. 'The first was that we don't know each other. What's the second?'

Distracted by the brush of his thigh against hers as he swivelled towards her, Lola swallowed. She didn't want to feel his muscular strength against her legs, notice the way his shirt collar flirted with his amazing neck or glimpse the light sprinkling of dark hair escaping the V of his opened shirt.

'I don't do one-night stands.'

She blurted it out, as much for her own benefit as his. If she kept that particular mantra at the front of her mind, she might just make it through this conversation without making a grab for that shirt opening and hauling him against her for a blistering kiss.

He raised his eyebrows. 'Sometimes it pays to broaden your horizons.'

Not right then, it didn't, Lola thought with a degree of desperation, trying hard to keep hold of her withering resolve. Thankfully, their drinks arrived, and Lola took a healthy swig of hers. Her body was doing the most incredible things. Her breasts felt so tender they actually tingled, and her nipples were hard buds scraping against the fabric of her top. As for between her legs…well, talk about achy and throbbing.

She glanced to where Connor's fingers leisurely stroked his glass, unable to keep from imagining just what kind of damage those fingers could inflict on her. If just the thought of that could turn her on, what would the reality do?

Okay, men had turned her on before, and a couple had turned into lovers. Neither one of them had made her body feel as if it was being twisted inside out.

'Why don't we backtrack here?' Connor said after taking a swig of his beer. 'What's your name?'

Lola couldn't think of any reason why she couldn't tell him. If by the slimmest possibility Damian had mentioned her to Connor, he would have referred to her as Louise, and not by her nickname.

Even so, she kept a careful watch for any hint of recognition. 'It's Lola.'

He gave a slow nod. 'Sexy. Like you.'

Remembering that she wasn't supposed to know his name, she raised her eyebrows. 'And you?'

'Connor,' he said, and held out his hand. 'Good to meet you, Lola.'

She slipped her hand into his and felt a definite punch of reaction from her breasts to her core.

Still playing along with the pretense that she had

no idea who he was, Lola sipped her drink again. 'So, this is your place? You're the owner?'

'Yeah,' he said matter-of-factly, but there was caution in his eyes. 'Is that a problem?'

Lola shrugged. 'Of course not. You must be quite the entrepreneur, though. The location alone makes this place a prime piece of real estate.'

His expression morphed from caution to amusement. 'What are you? An estate agent?'

With a smile, she shook her head. 'Just been doing some research. I'm planning to start my own business.'

He took another drink of beer. 'What kind of business?'

It was on her lips to tell him, but this question put her on shakier ground. Damian might have let it slip that his sister wanted the Cabacal property with the view to opening a health studio, but she couldn't imagine that was really a possibility, seeing as her brother barely acknowledged her dream. Still, it didn't hurt to be circumspect. She didn't want Connor putting two and two together, at least not until she'd had the chance to figure out his plans.

He leaned forward, obviously sensing her hesitation. 'Come on, it's only fair. Tit for tat. You know I own this place.'

She huffed. 'That didn't take much working out. You might not have *owner* emblazoned on the door of your office, but I would have guessed from the way your security chap sprang to attention when I scratched you, or the way the bartender popped up from nowhere as soon as you appeared, even when I'd already been waiting a full five minutes to be served.'

His eyebrows drew together. 'You'd been waiting that long?'

Realising how that sounded, she waved her hand in dismissal. 'A figure of speech. I was just making a point.'

'Even so…' He turned towards the bartender. 'He'll have to go.'

'No.' Lola reached out and grabbed Connor's wrist. 'He's lovely, and he's rushed off his feet, just like the rest of your bar staff.'

She drew back with a frown when Connor turned towards her with a grin. Releasing her hand from his wrist, she gave him a haughty look. 'Funny.'

He kept his gaze on hers. 'And it was hardly a scratch.'

'What was?'

With a mock-pitiful expression, he stroked his thumb across the plaster on his neck.

Lola laughed. She really liked his quick humour. 'Oh, for pity's sake.'

He leaned forward, serious again. 'Speaking of pity, are you going to put me out of my misery, Lola?'

Her stomach clenched along with her inner thighs. 'Don't do one-nighters, remember?'

'That was when we didn't know each other.'

She willed her hands not to tremble as she reached

for her drink and sipped the soothing liquid. 'You think knowing each other's names takes care of that?'

'We've shared a whole lot more.' He slid his hand across to where she held her glass and lightly stroked his fingers over hers. 'I know you're a qualified first-aider. That you care about my bartender keeping his job. That you're probably the only woman I've ever met who can do an erotic dance on a nightclub table without the aid of alcohol.' His eyes narrowed slightly, the grey darkening as he looked at her. 'And I know that you're sexy as fuck.'

She kept her focus on his hand, that slow, sensual slide of his fingers over hers. Hell, but she really wanted to know how it would feel to have those fingers toying with other parts of her body. Like her nipples, her breasts, her sex...

She drew her hand away from his intoxicating touch. 'None of which qualifies as an in-depth getting-to-know-you session.'

He winked. 'It's a great start.'

This really wasn't a good idea. It could badly affect her plans. What if they had sex and it all went wrong? Even if it didn't, how would he react when he knew who she was and what she wanted? It was already getting messy. If she told him now, he'd feel manipulated. How much worse would it be if they had sex and then she told him?

She knew of his history with her uncle—knew he'd been cleared of the embezzlement charges brought against him five years ago. Even though she had long since severed all ties with that side of the family, no doubt Connor would react unfavourably to her when he learned of the connection. She'd planned to reveal her identity alongside an explanation of what had happened to her mother, hoping that Connor would see some parallel with his own situation and be sympathetic to her plans to get the Cabacal back.

But things had taken an unexpected turn with this insanely inappropriate attraction between them.

She looked down, already regretting that she couldn't let this go any further. 'If things were different, I'd be on the same page as you.'

'I think we're already on the same page...about a lot of things.'

The way he said it put her on alert. Did he already know who she was? Had Damian spoken to him about her, warned him she might try something like this? Since she'd been deliberately cagey about her plans, she couldn't see that was likely.

Her stomach slid uncomfortably as she met his eyes. 'What things?'

He grinned. 'Aside from the extremely pleasant sexual attraction we have going? Looks like we're both actively looking to acquire property.'

This was the perfect place to just blurt everything out and hope that he'd understand. Except something stopped her. If she found out a little more about his reasons for acquiring the property, and what he intended to use it for, she might have a better understanding of how to set about convincing him that her reasons were more justified. Knowledge was power, right?

Watching him closely, she raised her glass to her lips. 'Are you expanding your business?'

His casual shrug was in opposition to the dark flash in his eyes. 'Haven't decided yet.'

'Then why are you acquiring property?'

There was a definite change in his demeanour now. No trace of the easy charm, or the sexy glint in his eye. 'Fate dropped an opportunity in my lap. A property became available that I've wanted for a while.'

'For another nightclub?'

'Like I said, haven't decided.' He twisted his glass, round and round, seemingly mesmerised by the movement…and maybe old, painful memories. Then he gave another casual shrug, as if to toss those old memories aside. 'There's no rush to do anything with it. It's been empty for a few years.'

An optimistic band of hope settled around Lola's heart. If he had no direct plans for the building and would allow it to remain empty for the foreseeable future, then surely it wouldn't be too much of a wrench for him to sell it on to her when the time came?

'We've gone off-course,' he said, his mood changing back to its easy, flirty style. 'Why would I want to talk bricks and mortar when I'm in the company of a beautiful woman?'

'Are you saying that women can't talk bricks and mortar?' she challenged. 'That we can't talk business?'

He held up his hands. 'Nope. Not saying that. Some of the hardest negotiators I've dealt with are women.'

She sensed he meant that and wasn't just tossing her a line. 'I'm pleased to hear it.'

He lowered his hands, grinning. 'All I'm saying is that I'd like to negotiate something else entirely right now.'

She laughed and tucked hair behind her ear. 'You're just too predictable.'

'I can live happily in that knowledge, especially if it gets my hands on you.'

The feeling of wanting his hands on her, of wanting hers on him, was almost overwhelming. She knew that Connor would be a fabulous lover.

No doubt his innate confidence would extend to the sack, making what they shared powerful and explosive. She was drawn to that confidence, to his easy wit, his ability to tease without seeming to belittle.

She chose that moment to glance over Connor's shoulder and caught the crazy butt-wiggles and thumbs-up signs her friends were giving her from across the bar. When she looked back at Connor's ruggedly handsome face, and the dark seduction in his eyes, she felt like doing some butt-wiggling herself. Except she couldn't. He was way out of bounds.

Of her friends, only her flatmate Emily knew her

plans, knew the history behind them. Lola looked over at Emily now, saw the concern in her friend's smile and gave a subtle shake of her head. She looked back at Connor. 'I'll just be a minute.'

As she swivelled on the stool, he leaned forward. 'Don't break my heart and dump me before you've even given me a chance.'

She laughed at his puppy-dog expression and stood. 'I just need to…' She pointed towards the cloakrooms. 'I'll be back. Even if it's only to tell you that we're no longer on the same page.'

He slapped a hand to his chest, and Lola laughed again, heading to the ladies' room as Emily did the same.

Emily didn't waste any time as they walked through the door together. 'I've been talking to Nigel and he told me that's Connor Fitzpatrick. Did you know? Have you told him who you are?'

'Yeah, that's him, and no, I didn't tell him. Couldn't find the words. I did have a hairy moment when I thought he might already know, but since he hasn't told me to piss off I'm pretty certain he doesn't.'

'He didn't look much like he was planning to tell you to piss off.' Emily nudged Lola's elbow. 'More like he was planning to rip your panties off and have you right there on his bar.'

'Bloody hell. Don't put that image in my head. I'm trying to contain myself as it is.'

'If he were anyone else, I'd say go for it. I mean,

hot dude, nightclub owner, single, probably got all his own teeth.' Emily slicked on fresh lip gloss and looked at Lola in the mirror. 'You know I'm worried.'

'There's no need. All I'm doing is trying to buy a property. If my stupid brother wasn't such a prick, he'd let me buy it straight from the estate and then I could go ahead with my plans and have guilt-free sex with Connor Fitzpatrick. It would be a win-win.'

'You know what I think. That you should just walk away from everything and start fresh.' Emily sighed and shrugged. 'But then you wouldn't get the property or the sex.'

'I can't do that, Em. I need the Cabacal back.'

Emily tucked her lip gloss in her bag and turned so that her back was to the counter. 'We never factored in you fancying the guy. This makes it ultra-complicated. You really should just walk away and think of another way to get what you want.'

'I know.' Somewhere between leaving Connor and entering the cloakroom, Lola had grasped just how crazy an idea this was. Not just having sex with Connor but asking him to let her have the property. 'I'm going to head home and rethink all of this. Find another way.'

'Good. Look, the others are going to party for a while longer, by the looks of things, so why don't I come home too and we can hash things out?'

'No. You stay. Enjoy yourself. I'll get a taxi back.'

Lola usually appreciated her friend's input when she was working around a problem. But tonight she wanted some alone time to think of another way to make her plans come to fruition after her interaction with sexy Connor Fitzpatrick. After that, some solitary self-pleasuring while watching late-night-TV porn was on the cards.

Lola checked her watch. 'First thing tomorrow, I'm going to call Damian, put on the emotional screws if I have to. I'm going to make him read my business plan, look at my projections and convince him that I'm deadly serious about doing this. He can't refuse me. I won't let him. If I need to, I'll get lawyers involved, prove that our mother was cheated out of that property. If nothing else, it will delay the sale for a while. Maybe even for six months.'

Lola felt distinctively nauseous at the prospect of going head to head with her stubborn brother again, but her determination didn't waver. It was a hellishly long shot, but Lola was prepared to take it.

She said her goodbyes to Emily and, since she didn't want to see Connor again, headed straight for the exit.

Hopefully, she wouldn't have to wait too long for a taxi. She had new plans to formulate…and a date with a silver bullet vibrator.

# CHAPTER THREE

THE DOORMAN SET ABOUT hailing her a taxi, although at this time of night Lola knew she might have to wait a while. She shivered as the cool air brushed over her bare arms, but the chill did nothing to diminish the heat still burning inside her, and the smoulder of desire for the man with gun-metal-grey eyes and deep, gravelly voice.

Lola shivered again, but this time it had nothing to do with forgetting to collect her jacket before she'd left the club. It had everything to do with her fevered thoughts about one incredibly sexy club owner.

She shot off a quick text to Emily asking her to grab her jacket, and almost dropped her phone when the voice came from behind.

'So, you decided to dump me after all.'

His voice rippled along her spine, setting all her nerve endings alight. She turned, meeting his equally powerful gaze. 'Yeah, well. I decided we'd slipped off the same page after all.'

Bloody hell. How was she supposed to resist him when he moved up this close to her, when she had to look up several inches even while wearing these treacherous heels?

In the relative safety of the ladies' room, with her bestie giving her support, deciding to leave him behind had seemed easier—the right decision. Now, with him here while she gazed into those gorgeous eyes, she was so damn sunk.

'That's a pity,' he said, sliding his hands into his trouser pockets. 'And just when I'd decided to go all out to seduce you with my winning ways.'

Okay, he was teasing her, but she really wished he was being serious. She wanted him to pull out all the stops. Not that he'd have to try too hard. She was already ninety-nine percent seduced, and it was only a pesky one percent that kept her from throwing caution to the wind.

'Can't have that,' she said, trying to bite back a smile. He didn't need any more encouragement. 'I wouldn't want to be responsible for robbing women of one more bad boy trying to make good.'

'It's true, then? Women really do like bad boys?'

'Of course. But then you already know that. Hence the dirty sparkle in your eye.'

He grinned. 'That dirty sparkle is all for you, sweetheart.'

If Lola had thought her blood was burning hot, it damn near raced through her in a fiery inferno now. 'I'm not really one for bad boys.'

'I'd have thought women who dance on tables don't want any other kind.'

With immense effort, Lola turned her attention back to the road, hoping the doorman would succeed in getting a taxi pronto and save her from herself. 'Don't believe all you see. My friends were all feeling punch-drunk at having been released from the shackles of university life, and they reminded me of a promise I made three years ago when I said that as soon as I graduated I'd be so happy that I'd dance on a table. What you saw was a woman letting her hair down after having it pulled up tight for too long.'

Bloody hell. Why had she told him that? What was it about him that made her spill so easily?

He tugged gently on the ends of her hair. 'Looks like it's well and truly down to me.'

'Yeah, well, looks can be deceiving.'

'Not with you. It's one of the reasons I'm attracted. You tell it like it is. No bullshitting.'

Guilt rippled along her spine and her heart gave one solid, culpable thump. 'I can bullshit with the best of them when I need to.'

'Nope. It's not your style, and believe me, I can tell.'

The feeling intensified. 'Maybe you don't know women as well as you think.'

A guarded look came into his eyes, then it was gone as he moved closer. 'I reckon I know you. You're a woman who knows what she wants. And, from experience, I know women who set their mind on something tend to get it.'

Lola was too busy basking in the compliment to concern herself with the damning truth of what he'd said.

She had waited the best part of her life to have someone—anyone—imply that she was strong-willed enough to make her own decisions, to choose what was best for her. She supposed that was what happened when you were raised by a headstrong father and an even more headstrong older brother.

Yet here was Connor, actually giving her the one thing she'd wanted for ever. An acknowledgement that she was not only capable of knowing what she wanted but was resolute enough to carry through with her plans.

It warmed her right through, heightened her confidence and solidified her determination to call Damian tomorrow morning and get him to sell the Cabacal direct to her. If Connor could see how competent and determined she was, surely she could convince Damian. She felt a little bad she'd be going behind Connor's back, but he didn't seem too interested in doing anything specific with the place.

Besides, all was fair in love and property acquisition, right?

There was another bonus, too. By persuading Damian to let her purchase the property, it meant Connor Fitzpatrick wouldn't be an obstacle. Which meant her reasons for keeping him at arm's length were null and void. Was there a reason to deny them both the pleasure of enjoying each other any longer?

Just like that, she felt her earlier resolve not to indulge in a one-night stand crumble. If she was ever going to break that rule, then this was certainly the time to do so. She couldn't imagine a man more likely to give her a good time than Connor.

She eyed him—that glorious neck, the wide, muscular chest and those powerful thighs. She thought of how Connor's thighs had brushed against her knees while they had chatted at the bar, imagined how amazing it would be to feel his legs tangled with hers when they were both naked.

She took a deep breath as a taxi pulled up to the kerb and leaned down to give the driver instructions before turning back to Connor. 'There's a hotel near my place with a pretty decent lounge and excellent bar service. We could share a nightcap.'

The lights from the club entrance caught the glint in his eyes. 'My place has the same. I've also got a great view.'

She returned his smile. 'I'd really love to see it.'

Connor gave the driver fresh instructions then slid into the taxi beside Lola. He was tempted to throw whatever money he had in his wallet at the poor man and order him to put his foot down on the pedal. On arrival, he'd simply haul Lola from the car, toss her over his shoulder and head up to the penthouse.

But something niggled.

What had changed her mind? She'd been happy to dump him, to leave his club without telling him why. She'd even given him a categorical no when he'd propositioned her.

Even as he cursed himself, he knew he wouldn't rest unless he understood the reasons for her change of heart. He was not usually one to look a freaking gift horse in the mouth, but past experience had made him wary. He had to know, had to make sure she wasn't playing him.

He'd been played before, and look how that had ended. At first Caroline had seemed like the perfect woman: beautiful, accomplished, loving, attentive. The daughter of his mentor, the man who had given him his first big opportunity in the world of business. Little had Connor known, when he'd accepted the manager position at their family's flagship casino, that he'd basically set himself up for the ultimate fall. He'd remained blissfully unaware of Caroline's ulterior motives, her desire to manipulate and use him. It wasn't until the police had come calling that Connor had realised he'd been set up, not just by his mentor, but by the woman he'd thought he loved.

Since then he'd been wary of history repeating itself, which was why he rarely got involved with women beyond easy, brief, sex-only deals. So, despite the fact that his body thrummed with the need to get his hands on Lola, he made himself sit back as the cab driver negotiated the busy late-night traffic. 'One question.'

Surprise lit her face. 'Okay.'

'What's with the about turn? No one-night stands, remember?'

Lola hiked up one shoulder. 'Can't a girl change her mind?'

'In my experience, if a woman changes her mind it usually ends up biting the man in the ass.'

She laughed, but there was an edge to it. 'Like I said before, I like to think my way around things. That's what I've been doing, and now what I want has changed.'

He had a feeling they weren't just talking about sex, but since they'd arrived at his place he shelved the conversation for now. From the throbbing in his pants, he had more urgent things with which to concern himself.

This was only a one-nighter, but it didn't mean he wouldn't keep his wits about him.

As soon as the taxi drew to a halt, Connor stepped out and went around to hold the door for Lola. He paid the driver, vaguely registering the man's thanks for the generous tip. He turned to Lola. Although he resisted hauling her over his shoulder, he couldn't stop from reaching for her hand. Her fingers curled tightly around his, and he pulled her to his side. Her generous lips slid into a smile and she looked up at him with eyes filled with temptation.

He managed to pull his gaze from hers long enough to jab the code into the security panel of the foyer door, then he hurried her through the marble-floored entrance hall and towards the bank of lifts.

While they waited, she pulled gently at the edges of his plaster with her free hand. 'That's dried up already. You must heal fast.'

He needed a moment to get his thoughts straight, as he was totally focused on the arrival of the damn lift and getting her up to his place pronto. 'It'll take more than a four-inch heel to put me down.'

She made a low, smoky sound in her throat that did interesting things to his rapidly escalating libido. 'How about six-inch ones?'

The vision of her wearing even higher heels made his abs clench. 'On you? That would not only put me down, it'd knock me clean out.'

'Have you got a shoe fetish?'

'Don't give a rat's ass about shoes, only the legs they accentuate.' Deliberately, he kept his gaze locked on hers. 'Especially yours.'

'A leg man, then.'

Still he kept his eyes on hers. 'Legs, breasts, ass and pretty much everything between. I'm not particular.'

Again, that laugh. He was tempted to ditch waiting for the lift and negotiate the twenty floors up to his apartment on foot.

'I don't believe that for a moment,' she said with a tilt of her head. 'I have a feeling you're very particular.'

He reached out and touched the ends of her hair that were so damned close to her breasts and those hard nipples poking through her top, which he *really* wanted to touch. 'What about you? Chest? Pecs? Butt?'

'My favoured attribute depends on the man.'

He stabbed at the lift button again, his chest tightening with the need to get his hands on her. 'How so?'

'Well, I like some men for their bodies. Others for their intellect. Others still for their ability to make me laugh.'

After a quick mental tot, he grinned. 'Never had any complaints about my body,' he said waggling his eyebrows. 'And, while I can't split the atom, I can hold my own in most conversations. As for making you laugh? I've heard that dirty laugh of yours enough times to know I score high in that regard.'

She gave him another sample of said dirty laugh. 'Okay, three strikes and you're not out.' She eyed him wryly. 'Yet.'

'Is there another set of manly attributes on your list?'

'Can't think of any straight off. Of course, there's sex. The whole "satisfying a woman in bed" thing.'

Connor swallowed. Yeah. He really liked the way she shot straight. 'That would make it four strikes, and still I'm not out.'

She huffed. 'You've got a healthy enough ego, I'll give you that.'

'No point indulging in false modesty. From what I've been told, I seem to have an uncanny ability to make a woman happy between the sheets.'

She took in a breath and let it out on a less than steady sigh. 'Ah, theory. Or maybe just hearsay. Me?

I like evidential proof. I've always been a practical girl.'

He glanced down at her cleavage. Hard not to when her breasts were moving up and down as her breathing rate increased. 'I'll bet.'

His own breathing was unsteady and, had his cock not been restrained by his trousers, it would have joined in the fun. As it was, it pressed painfully against his zipper.

He resisted a muttered expletive as he stabbed the lift button yet again, his legs almost sagging with relief when the doors pinged open.

He took Lola into the small space and, unable to resist any longer, pushed her against the far wall, then placed his hands either side of her head. He brought his mouth a whisper from hers.

'It's time to put theory aside, Lola.' He brushed her lips lightly, making sure to press his hips against hers to let her feel the force of his desire. 'And hearsay.'

'Fine by me.' She wrapped her arms around his waist, moving her hips in a subtle motion and almost making him lose it. 'Like I said, I've always favoured the practical.'

# CHAPTER FOUR

LOLA HAD HEARD the expression that you could reel from someone's kiss, but she'd never given much store to it. Yet as Connor took her mouth she…reeled. Her knees all but buckled and fire zipped in her veins. She wasn't sure if the way her stomach somersaulted was because of the kiss or because the lift had arrived at Connor's floor.

'Hmm. I really like the practical,' she said, disengaging herself from Connor's arms and stepping back from him to get a few moments to steady herself. 'Much better than the theory.'

'Me too,' he said as, taking hold of her hand, he led her from the lift and out into the small hallway. There was only one door that she could see, and they headed towards that.

Connor slid the key card into the slot and let Lola enter first. He was right about the view. Across the wide living space, floor-to-ceiling windows dominated and the lights of central London flickered around them.

'Wow.' She walked across to get a better look.

'This is amazing.' Instinct had her looking across to the east and towards the area that housed the Cabacal property. Discomfort flared that she was kind of deceiving Connor by not coming clean about who she was. He seemed a decent enough guy. But as this was just a one-off deal, and she would likely never see him again, there didn't seem any real harm.

Connor came up behind her and wrapped his arms around her waist so that they both looked out at the view. He hadn't switched on any lights in the apartment, so what there was came from the reflection of the flickering London skyline beyond.

She loved the feel of his arms around her, the scent of him and the sheer animal magnetism that was uniquely his. One hand came up to cup her breast.

'You don't waste any time,' she said in a droll tone as his other hand cupped her other breast. 'I thought you might be the savouring kind.'

'I am,' he said, nuzzling her neck and making her tremble. 'This is me savouring.'

He squeezed her breasts lightly and rocked his erection against the curve of her ass.

'You feel damn good, Lola.'

The husky, muffled tone shot reaction from her breasts to her core. She moved her hips, not wanting him to have all the fun, and her reward was a needy groan. 'You feel damn good too, Connor.'

He kept one hand on her breast and slowly slid the other down to cup her between her legs. Lola moved against him as he gently touched her, encouraging him to increase the pressure. Thankfully, he took the hint.

'I was planning to take this slow,' he said in a low, sexy drawl. 'But the feel of your ass against my hard-on is kind of making that impossible.'

Reaching up and back, Lola locked her hands around the back of his neck, the movement pushing her breasts forward so that the hand cupping her breast squeezed lightly. 'Sometimes slow is overrated.'

He pressed harder against her, encouraging her to open her legs a little.

'I've got you for one whole night, which means we can do fast, slow and everything in between.'

She recalled what he'd said back in the bar about the benefits of broadening horizons, and if she was broadening hers then she was damn well going to enjoy every moment of it. 'We're still talking theory,' she teased. 'You might still be out on that fourth strike.'

He spun her around, stealing her breath. 'Not going to happen,' he warned as he hiked her up into his arms. She squealed, wrapping her legs around his waist and clinging to his shoulders as he took her through to his bedroom located directly off the living space, quickening his pace as he went.

Another huge room, Lola thought as he set her down on the bed. Another room with amazing views from floor-to-ceiling windows. 'Are the walls in every room of your apartment made of glass?'

'Just two,' he said, yanking the edge of her top

from her waistband. 'Are you planning on talking interior design right now?'

Lola laughed. She really did like his dry wit. It was sexy and a big turn-on.

'I'm just making pleasant conversation.'

Slowly, he drew the zipper of her top down, and she raised her arms as he pulled the top over her head. He took a moment to gaze at her bared breasts, then cupped them, his hands moving in drugging circles, thumbs flicking her nipples and hardening them into tighter buds. She arched, loving the way he touched her.

'You like your breasts touched?'

'Uh, huh.' She hadn't given it much thought before, but now her whole attention was focused on Connor's adept thumbs and skilled fingers manipulating her tender flesh.

He leaned forward, guiding her back until she was lying across the bed. He licked one nipple with the lightest touch but it sent shockwaves right through her body. His tongue felt hot, determined, and she hadn't thought she could feel any better about having her nipple licked until he increased the pressure.

Even as Lola closed her eyes, enjoying his attention, he took the bud into his mouth and sucked. She arched again, higher off the bed this time, resisting the urge to just lie back and let him do what he wanted.

But she had some wants of her own, and that meant getting her hands on Connor. As he continued to kiss her breasts, she pulled his shirt from his trousers and tried to shove it off his shoulders. Connor didn't seem in any hurry to get naked, grabbing her wrists and coaxing her arms back over her head.

He knelt, working his knees between her legs and holding her arms steady, then continued the sexy manipulation of her breasts.

Lola wondered if she'd ever been shot to peak quite so fast before, because she could feel the merciless throb between her legs and knew that it would only take one touch and she'd probably explode.

But Connor didn't release her hands. Instead, he curled his fingers more tightly around hers and anchored her to the mattress.

He moved down, kissing her ribcage, the skin across her waist. Bracketing both her wrists with one hand, he used his free hand to reach between them and unhook the clasp of her jeans. He moved her zipper down a mere inch, touching his mouth to the exposed skin. The only sound came from their deepened breathing. His tongue circled her navel, making the muscles between her legs clench hard.

He caught the zipper fastening between his teeth and slowly pulled it all the way down, then used his free hand to push her jeans open.

It was deliciously erotic and Lola moaned low in her throat.

Connor looked up at her, his grey eyes dark and hooded.

With her wrists still bracketed by his hand, Lola

swallowed and gave a half-hearted tug. 'Do I get to yank your kit off any time soon?'

He grinned, that deliciously sexy hike of his mouth doing amazing things to her equilibrium. 'All night, remember? First I'm having you. My way.'

'What does that mean?'

He trailed a finger down the line of the unfastened zipper towards the top edge of her panties just visible beneath her jeans. She shivered.

'It means I'm going to touch you, taste you, do what the hell I like. After that, maybe I'll let you do the same to me.'

Lola liked the sound of that, but she wasn't going to let him think he was calling all the shots. 'Who says you get to go first? Isn't there some leeway for negotiation?'

'We already negotiated.'

'We did? I must have missed that part.'

He kept his gaze on hers and pushed his hand down the opened fastening of her jeans. Lola sucked in her stomach to ease his way lower, wishing she hadn't worn such tight-fitting jeans. As it was, his fingers were barely inside the lacy edge of her panties.

'My place, my rules.'

'So, if I'd invited you to my place, I'd be the one with the negotiating power?'

He hesitated. 'That's how it works.'

'In whose world?'

'Mine.'

He released her hands but she kept them over her

head, wondering what he planned to do next. Her whole body was on fire, trembling, skin shivering and burning all at once. He lifted her hips and pulled the jeans from her legs so slowly that it made her feel exposed in a way she'd never felt before.

Having tossed her jeans away, he hooked his fingers into the sides of her panties. She thought he was going to tug them off too, but instead he leaned down and pressed his mouth to her lace-covered mound.

It was somehow more erotic having him kiss her with this flimsy barrier between them than if he'd just ripped the panties away and kissed her bare. Her whole body trembled as he hooked his hands beneath her knees and raised her legs so he could get more access to the place he wanted. His mouth was hot, his tongue determined as it flirted with the edge of her panties.

Bringing her hands down from above her head, she tried once more to get the shirt from his shoulders, needing to feel his skin beneath her hands and drive her fingers deep into his firm, hot flesh. But he didn't budge, just kept kissing her with a kind of determined focus.

'Connor?'

Her breathy plea echoed around the space, but Connor ignored it. She hiked herself up onto her elbows, her gaze falling to where Connor worked her so expertly. If the man could make her feel like this with her panties still on, what the hell would he be able to do when she was naked?

She didn't have to wait long to find out. Before she could track what he was doing, he tugged at the lace, dragged it down her legs and tossed it away to join her jeans on the floor.

He spread her, holding her open and looking his fill. She shivered as his head descended, and the first touch of his mouth to her raging heat shook her right through to her core.

She flopped back against the mattress in sensual surrender, her fingers curling into the sheet for purchase. It was like being devoured, like being ravaged, tossed in an erotic sea of pure sensation. All she could do was go with it, let the storm take her wherever it might. She closed her eyes, her muscles jerking with each press of Connor's tongue against her slit.

There was no time to prepare herself, no time to brace against the fury of the spasms that rocked her world. It was amazing, incredible, overwhelming, and as she came down she was already mourning the fact that this was temporary, one night only, no strings. No anything.

Lola flung an arm across her forehead, gasping for breath. 'Bloody hell.'

He inched up, bracing himself on his hands to lean over her. 'Yeah.'

'You're good at that.'

'I'm good at a whole lot more.'

'Condom?'

He grinned. 'Not yet. I haven't finished.'

Since she had her legs open with him lying between them, his impressive bulge pushing hard against her heat, she looked up at him from beneath her arm. 'When do I get my turn?'

'I thought you just did.'

'Funny. You won't even let me take your shirt off.'

'Plenty of time for that.'

She tried again to slip it from his shoulders, but he caught her hand. 'I told you I wasn't finished.' He grinned. 'Unless you want to miss out on my special technique.'

Lola gave him a suspicious look. She wanted to challenge him on his bossy attitude, his determination to get his own way. Getting involved with a man who liked to control to the extent Connor did should have sent out all kinds of warning signals, but her body was sending out its own signals right then. Her skin tingled and her muscles clenched in anticipation. She had to admit that she was intrigued and, as this was only a one-night deal and their paths were unlikely to cross again, she wasn't about to get too hung up on his need to call the shots. 'What special technique?'

He grinned, leaned down and kissed her breasts, taking his time to explore each nipple in turn. Then he moved down her body, kissing her lightly at the waist, exploring her abdomen and around her navel before touching light kisses down her thighs to her knees.

Lola moved in sensual pleasure, driving her fingers into his hair until he started to move up her body again and settled beside her. Their gazes met and Lola loved the deep, smoky look he gave her.

His hand moved down her body, his palm cupping her pussy.

Lola swallowed. She wanted to turn her face away from his intense look, but she couldn't seem to. Slowly, he teased her apart with his forefinger, stroking lightly across her wetness. She held her breath, expecting that he would push in deeper but, when he continued that drugging, barely there movement, she had to suck in a deep breath as her lungs squeezed.

He leaned down and brought his mouth to hers, kissing her in a way that mirrored what he was doing between her legs. Lola felt light-headed and realised she was holding her breath again.

He kissed across her mouth, her jaw, down her throat, but still the pressure of his finger remained light.

She arched her hips a little, coaxing him. He kissed her, this time pressing his tongue between her lips and delving into her mouth in a deep and sensuous exploration of her softness.

Lola moaned, moving her hips again. She was going to start bloody complaining if he didn't take the hint and just...

The breath caught in her lungs as he pushed inside her, swapping his forefinger for his middle finger and sliding in deep. As she closed her eyes, he started a slow push-and-release motion that soon had Lola gasping for air.

She heard herself cry out when he arched his finger, applying a gentle pressure against her clit. This time she really did feel the room spin, and she opened her eyes to see him watching her with those hooded eyes.

'You're right,' she managed between breathy gasps. 'That's certainly special.'

'We're not there yet,' he said in a deep and gravelly tone.

Before she could respond, he flicked his wrist, making his finger spin inside her, backward and forward as he varied the penetration, the pressure.

'Oh, my God…' Lola felt as if her whole body was being twisted as he continued to work her, and she wondered if she could take much more of this intense pleasure. She was riding high again, hurling up towards that precipitous edge, to be flung into the stratosphere with nothing to cling to.

She grabbed for his wrist, wanting the connection, wanting something to keep her from spinning into orbit. It was too late. Because she flew, she spun and all she could do was let go.

Slowly she came down, easing out her body like a sensual cat.

Were one-night stands supposed to rock your world? Were they supposed to make you…feel? Because she *did* feel, all kinds of things—warm, sensual, shaky, unsettled. It hadn't escaped her that he'd put her needs first, that he'd focused on her pleasure. It made her want much more than this single encounter.

Which was crazy, stupid, dangerous…

She pulled herself back from the perilous edge. 'Well, I can officially vouch for the specialness of your technique. Happy now?'

He withdrew his hand. 'Shouldn't that be my line?'

'You don't play fair.'

'You got that right.'

He looked serious, making her wonder at his meaning. All indications were that Connor loved to play, loved to tease, but the way he'd said it, the look in his eyes, alerted her to some deep, hidden meaning behind his words.

'I didn't have you down as a point-scorer.'

He trailed his fingers lightly across her abdomen, then shrugged. 'No point-scoring involved, just hot and dirty sex. Isn't that what you want?'

It was exactly what she wanted, and she really couldn't fathom why she had all these feelings spinning around inside her. Maybe that was what happened when you agreed to have sex with someone you didn't know that well. And when that someone turned out to be so very adept at making a woman's body sing. 'Absolutely. Hot and dirty sex. And now maybe it's time to show you one or two of my own special techniques. It's my turn to get what I want. To have my fun with you, right?'

He narrowed his eyes, as if he was trying to work out her meaning, then he turned and lay on his back. 'Go for it, sweetheart. Do your worst.'

# CHAPTER FIVE

CONNOR HAD KNOWN she'd be a fire cracker in bed, that she wouldn't be shy about stating what she wanted, so why did her words put him on full alert? *It's my turn to get what I want. To have my fun with you, right?*

Maybe because he preferred to be the one calling the shots. It was safer that way. But Lola had so easily shifted the dynamic he liked to set up from the start—the one that gave him all the control.

When Lola straddled him, whatever else he'd been about to think flew out of the window.

She stripped away his shirt and undid the button of his fly. He was burning, his body one hot mass of need. Maybe that was what came of being without physical release for too long now.

Connor pushed away the nudge that warned it had less to do with that and more to do with enjoying this particular woman. Lola. Yeah, she was a fire cracker, all right. She'd said she liked to think things around in her mind, work out the pros and cons before making a decision. It seemed when this woman had done the weighing up she went straight for what she wanted.

And, right then, that appeared to be him.

The determination in her eyes set his blood on fire, sending a lightning bolt of raw desire through his system as she yanked down his zipper.

Her hand slid inside his trousers, her fingers playing just above the head of his cock. His abdominal muscles jerked, and a throbbing need to be inside her vied with his decision to let her take her fun. It was only fair. Yet, at the same time, he knew he needed to keep his instincts sharp because something about Lola could make him take his eye off the ball. And that was never going to happen again.

Was he getting to be such a suspicious bastard that he was seeing spooks where none existed? This thing between them was scratching an itch, right? It was just sex. Going nowhere.

*Just sex. Going nowhere.*

That became a mantra as she ran her free hand lightly over his chest, his pecs, across his shoulder, making every single muscle tremble beneath her touch. Light. Smooth. Devastating.

'You have great definition,' she said, making him lose the ability to breathe as her fingers inched closer to the tip of his erection. 'Gym?'

He shook his head, unable to tear his gaze away from the lusty look in her eyes. 'No time.'

She plucked at his nipple while her other hand

played dangerously close to where he wanted it. 'What do you do to keep fit?'

He grinned, although his chest was tight with anticipation of what she would do next. 'Fuck.'

Her hands stilled; her eyes went wide. 'Really? You must do that an awful lot to get this kind of result.'

He was about to defend himself against the subtext that he was some kind of man-whore when she grinned.

'I suppose you think you're quite the comedienne,' he said, waiting with what he considered stoic patience for her to start working his body again. His muscles had no such fortitude, and his cock jerked as his abs clenched.

She kept her gaze on his and, with a very feline smile, placed her palm flat on his chest so she could lean slightly forward, then pushed her other hand down into his boxers and wrapped her fingers around his cock.

Connor swallowed at the feel of her solid grip, marvelling at the strength in her small hand. She rotated her hips and, though her pussy wasn't touching him, his dick reacted as if it were.

He reached out, wrapped his hands around her hips and tried to bring her against him. She shook her head and tutted. 'Not yet. We have all night, remember?'

He narrowed his eyes at the way she batted his words back at him. When she started moving her hand over his erection, slow and easy, he called on some more of that stoic patience.

His breath caught, his chest tightened and he almost shouted his relief when she sat back and tugged at his waistband. 'Let's have these off, shall we?' she said, as she yanked both his trousers and boxers from his hips with surprising strength of purpose.

He raised his hips, already toeing off his shoes, and then sat up to help dispose of his remaining clothes. She straddled him again and placed both palms on his chest before looking down to where his dick stood at attention. 'Impressive,' she said. 'Makes me want to play.'

Before he could get a coherent thought into his frazzled brain, she inched down his body, her breasts jiggling and making him want to take them in his mouth again, to savour all that ripe and silky flesh.

Then he didn't even try for any kind of thought as she bent down, her hands on his thighs, and she licked across his head.

His throat went tight along with his body, and he arched his back, encouraging her to take more of him. She continued the slow slide of her tongue across his tip, her fingers pressing into his thighs as if to anchor him where she wanted him.

Briefly, Connor closed his eyes, his hands tight fists against his sides. She took him a mere inch into her mouth, her tongue wrapping around him, before withdrawing and again giving her attention just to the tip.

He was about to protest…make that plea…when she ran her tongue lightly down the length of him, at the same time sliding her hands higher up his inner thighs until she could cup his sac.

His breath came in desperate gasps now, his ribcage locked as his muscles tightened almost painfully in his chest.

His fisted hands pushed hard against the mattress as she took him fully into her mouth, her soft lips curling around him, the light graze of her teeth a delicious friction as she moved up and down his length. Her hair trailed across his thighs and slid over his lower abdomen as she worked him slowly, then harder.

When his balls grew tight, he reached out for her, sliding his fingers into her hair and raking her scalp, encouraging her to release him. He wasn't going to last, and he didn't want to lose it with her mouth wrapped around him.

While he wasn't a stranger to a woman going down on him, or letting her take things to their natural conclusion, for some reason he didn't want that tonight. It made him feel too raw…

He didn't have time to question that, given he was seconds away from shooting his load. Instead, he sat up and grabbed for her arms, pulling her away from him.

She looked a little surprised, her green eyes wide, her soft lips full and pink from being wrapped around his cock.

'Need to be inside you,' he growled, reversing their positions until she lay on her back. 'Can't wait.'

He closed his eyes as his erection throbbed, trying to get his act together long enough to grab a condom from the bedside drawer. It didn't help that he was lying between her legs, her slick heat against his length and her breasts pressing against his chest.

He opened his eyes and reached out, fumbling for the drawer. Seconds later he had the condom rolled on, and he looked down at her.

A smoky green layer of pure lust filled her eyes as he eased her legs wider, then slid his hands beneath her backside to tilt her hips upward.

He pressed forward and, her eyes still on his, she arched her neck. Her lips parted and, barely inside her, he leaned down and kissed her, pressing his tongue inside her mouth. She gave a low sound in her throat as he released her mouth.

He slid deeper, her warmth and wetness aiding his way, her muscles drawing him in and clamping tight around him. Vaguely, it registered in that moment that he was powerless against the magnetism that seemed to burn between them.

But it was only sex.

To prove that he drove himself to the hilt, stealing the breath from them both, thrusting inside her as his mind switched off and his body took control.

A burning sensation hit the base of his spine, barrelling around to his pelvis, down the length of his cock. He wanted to hold off, make this last, but he was too far gone.

He managed to get a hand between them, pressing a finger to Lola's clit. Her frantic moan ripped away the last of his restraint and sent him over the edge.

He came. Pumping into the condom. Encouraged by Lola's needy rendering of his name and the clenching of her muscles as she gripped him tight.

He looked down at her as they both fought for air. Her face was flushed, her eyes heavy-lidded, and she looked so bloody beautiful it stole what little air he'd managed to grab into his tight lungs.

*What the fuck just happened?*

He moved back from her as if she were possessed by some strange power that could contaminate him. 'Okay?' he asked lamely.

She nodded, looking a little dazed. 'Yes. You?'

'Me?' He sucked in air, willed his breathing to settle and eased further away. 'I'm always okay. I make sure of it.'

Lola battled to regain a little balance. If she was going to break her rule about one-night stands, she couldn't have done it in a more spectacular fashion.

Maybe there was something to be said for casual hook-ups after all, especially if the sex could be as amazing as they'd just shared. She hadn't expected it to be quite so intense, so…breath-taking.

There'd been a connection between them, something she couldn't quite label as anything else, but maybe that was all part of the brief and temporary nature of a one-nighter. It was her first—how would she know?

What she did know was that it had been far more than she'd anticipated, even though she'd anticipated a whole lot of fabulous with Connor.

As he was already heading to the bathroom, Lola stretched, managed a deep breath and would have let it out on a contented sigh if something hadn't niggled.

Connor had seemed to be enjoying her oral skills until he'd unexpectedly called a halt by pushing her away at a vital moment.

Okay, she didn't have a mountain of experience when it came to sex, but she liked it well enough, and thought she could find her way around a man's body.

Emily had once declared that some men didn't like a woman to go all the way when it came to blow jobs because it made them feel vulnerable. Was that what had happened? Had Connor been annoyed that she'd tried to force him to lose control?

Since he was the epitome of strapping, confident male, she couldn't quite make the fit, but he'd certainly yanked her away from him fast enough.

Maybe an ex had hurt him in the past. Had a woman made him feel vulnerable? She thought back to when she'd suggested he might not know women as well as he thought he did. Remembered that guarded look he'd given her, and the cryptic

comment about women who set their mind on something tending to get it.

Maybe that was at the heart of his need to control.
To keep a tight handle on proceedings.

*My place. My rules.*

If Connor was deep into the control thing there
was no way she wanted any more of that. She'd already had a lifetime of it. Men who liked ordering
her around, who pressed their own agendas on her
life, all the time citing that they were acting in her
best interests.

Men like her father and her brother.

Okay, they loved her and wanted the best for her,
but come on… When were they going to step out
of the prehistoric age? Her father had been the kind
who thought it was his absolute right to manage the
lives of his wife and daughter, to provide for them,
protect them. The problem was, his idea of protection and provision had been beyond autocratic. Like
something out of Victorian times. According to him,
he'd known what was best for the women in his life
and that was that. End of story.

Unfortunately, her brother had inherited that same
attitude. Damian had always been a chip off the old
block, but in the three years since her father had
passed away her brother had upped his game and
taken on the mantle of family despot.

Once, although she'd fought against their unreasonable decisions, she'd had little choice but to go
along with them. That was no longer the case. Now

she was running her own show, and there was absolutely no room for more dictators in her life.

So why in heaven's name was she attracted to the same type of man? Why was she already wanting more than one night with Connor? More of that amazing, world-rocking sex?

And why was she ruining an intensely enjoyable evening by over-thinking?

All she needed to know right then was that he made her body hum. He lit her up in all the right places, and several she didn't even know she had. Being with Connor had given her an excellent yardstick by which to measure future sexual experiences.

Connor chose that moment to come back into the bedroom. Lola's mouth went dry as she feasted on his tall, muscular physique, and the easy way he strolled towards the bed with a predatory look made her want to reach out and yank him back pronto.

While she wasn't into control or dominance by men in general, she hadn't realised how much of a turn-on Connor's assertiveness could be. At least where sex was concerned.

'You've got a look in your eye,' he said as he settled on his side next to her. 'Makes me want to do things.'

Lola fluttered her lashes. 'That's why we're here, isn't it?'

He bent his elbow, supporting his head with his hand. 'Want anything? Drink? Something to eat?'

She shimmied against him. 'What I want you can't get from the kitchen.'

He brought his free hand to her stomach, flattening his palm over her navel and making her muscles clench. 'In that case…'

Lola placed her hand over his, determined to enjoy what was left of their hot night and see it as entrée into her new life. From the old to the new. From tyranny to liberation.

Tomorrow, she would go head to head with her brother over the Cabacal, convince him that she meant business. She'd show him how serious she was about her future plans, how determined she was to make a go of it, and she'd get him to change his mind. Whatever it took.

Then this night with Connor would be relegated to the ranks of one naughty, exhilarating, extremely hot encounter with her very own bad boy.

# CHAPTER SIX

'WHY ARE YOU so determined to be difficult?'

Lola had spent the past twenty minutes video-calling her brother and pleading her case but Damian hadn't budged. She'd outlined her business plan, given him detailed figures and targets, walked through the accounts she'd kept for the last year while she'd been teaching yoga part-time—but he hadn't been swayed.

Frustrated beyond measure, Lola had then threatened to instigate proceedings to contest her late uncle's legal ownership of the property, citing how it had essentially been stolen from their mother. Damian had quickly poured cold water on that, reminding her that it had been contested at the time and that, since her mother had been considered of sound mind when she'd signed over the property, it had been deemed a lawful, if not moral, transaction.

Their father had been angry, although not particularly sympathetic. He'd blamed his wife for not having taken proper care of her assets and allowing the property to fall into her brother's hands. He hadn't

been in the least bothered that the property meant
far more to her mother than its financial value. That
she'd intended it to provide a studio for health and
wellbeing, a place where people could escape the
increasing frenzy of city life.

Not only had her mother suffered the heartbreak
of being duped by her only brother, whom she'd
trusted and adored, she'd also lost what was to have
been Lola's inheritance. Witnessing her mother's dis-
tress, Lola had vowed to one day make her mother's
dream come true and open a fitness studio in the
Cabacal property. Sadly, she'd lost her mother soon
after making the vow, but her determination to fulfil her promise had never wavered.

'This property has done nothing but cause problems for this family,' Damian said. 'It caused a huge
rift between us and Uncle Guy's family that I can't
ever see healing, especially now Caroline has been
released and has decided to move to Dubai.'

Lola couldn't find any compassion for her. She'd
never liked her cousin and thought her spoiled and
mean-spirited. Caroline had always protested her
innocence in the embezzlement charges, but Lola
didn't believe that claim for a second, and neither
had the judge who had sentenced her to four years
in prison.

'I don't want the rift healed,' Lola said. 'I'll never
forgive Uncle Guy for what he did to Mum, and I'll
never understand how you could accept the role of
executor of his will.'

'Because there's nobody else,' Damian said, running a hand through his short, dark hair. 'Do you think it's been easy handling his affairs? He's left a mountain of debt, and the only real asset available for me to work with is the Cabacal.'

Lola could see the turmoil in his green eyes, and she knew that for the past six months since their uncle had died, he'd worked hard to negotiate the estate, and if her brother was finding it problematic then it really was complicated. Damian might be controlling and a bloody pain in her backside but he was one of the most astute businessmen she knew.

'Which is why my offer to purchase the property makes sense. You can have my trust fund, which basically makes me a cash buyer. There aren't too many of those around. Any other buyer and you'll have to wait for loans and mortgages to come through before you get an injection of cash.'

'I promised Dad that I'd take care of you,' he said in a tone that indicated he was fast losing his patience. 'That means not letting you waste your trust fund on some venture that'll see you broke before you even blink.'

'How can you say that? Along with my business degrees, I'm a specialist in therapeutic yoga and relaxation techniques. That puts me in a solid position to make my plans work.'

'New health clubs come and go so fast, it's hard to keep track,' he said, his eyes narrowing. 'The demand for gym classes might be high, but there are far too many establishments offering them already.'

Lola wanted to scream. Gym classes. *Gym classes*. Her brother really hadn't been listening to a word she'd said. She wanted so much more for her clients than a good workout. She wanted a place they could unwind from the stresses of life. A soft place to fall when life became overwhelming.

Lola held fast to her own patience. 'When are you back in London?' she asked, undaunted by Damian's persistent refusal to be reasonable. 'Promise me you won't do anything concrete until I can go through all my projections with you face to face. You'll see how thorough they are, and how serious I am about this.'

'Fitzpatrick is offering over the asking price, and the estate needs every penny it can get.'

'It shouldn't even form part of Uncle Guy's estate. It wasn't his to own. You can't feel good about this.'

'What I feel isn't the issue,' Damian said with a sigh, leaning back in that way of his that signalled he was done with the current topic of conversation. 'Mum signed away the property without telling Dad or even seeking legal advice. Nobody does that.'

'And nobody expects their brother, their own flesh and blood, to steal from them either.'

'Look, Louise. The sale of the Cabacal's a done deal. Connor Fitzpatrick wants the property and he's in a position to buy it. I spoke with him crack of dawn this morning and we agreed final details. Apart from his signature on the contract, and the transfer of his funds into the estate, it's in the bag.'

'You spoke to him this morning?'

When had that happened? She and Connor had been active pretty much all through the night and they'd shared breakfast. The only time they'd been apart was when she'd taken a shower.

Her heart took a major dive. Not just because her plans to obtain the Cabacal first-hand were fading into oblivion, but now she'd slept with Connor. If her only option was reverting to Plan A, and getting him to sell to her when she was in a position to buy, she'd have to tell him who she was. Now he'd think she'd used him and would likely tell her to go take a hike, or something much worse!

Her chest tightened as her breath hitched beneath her ribcage. She didn't want him to think her a liar, a manipulator, a cheat, but he would, and that made her feel hollow inside.

She called on her yoga background, reminding herself that the ancient practice taught calmness even in the midst of challenging situations. She took a deep breath and let it out slowly through her mouth as she mentally counted to six.

She couldn't believe that Damian had gone ahead with the sale to Connor, and it hurt so much to think that he wouldn't even consider her plans for the property. But since it was fruitless arguing with Damian any longer, she ended the call.

With a huge sigh of frustration, she sat back and

thought about what Damian had told her about Connor. He'd said Connor was owed the property, and despite feeling she was owed too, this intrigued her. What exactly had gone on between Connor and her uncle that Connor would offer above market value to purchase the Cabacal? Why would he want any reminders of his past there? Why would he want anything more to do with it?

If she'd been falsely accused of embezzlement, she would want to erase the whole sorry episode from her mind.

But then it wasn't really her business. Her business was to work out her next steps.

She sipped her coffee, considering. She could go ahead with her original plan, and ask Connor to sell the Cabacal to her, or she could start looking at other properties.

No. The latter wasn't an option. If she gave up on the Cabacal it would be like letting her mother down.

Her mother had been a gentle soul, less interested in profit and loss than she was in helping people and making them happy. Having her soft heart used against her by a money-grabbing brother, who'd known his sister wouldn't question whether he had anything other than good intentions, had been unconscionable.

Furious, Lola shoved the coffee away. The fight wasn't over yet. There was no way she was backing off. One way or another, she was getting her mother's property back.

Which meant there was only one thing for it.

Plan A was back on the table.

Connor would think she'd had sex with him in an attempt to seduce him into selling to her. He'd never believe she'd slept with him because she wanted to, because she was attracted to him, because she liked him.

She had to make him understand why she needed the Cabacal so much, and convince him that she'd only given in to the attraction between them once she'd believed she could convince Damian to sell her the property outright. The fact her plan had gone belly-up had now left her in a precarious position.

Speaking of precarious positions... Her mind skipped back to last night. The sex had been hot, no arguing with that, but being with Connor had been... fun. Despite the blip when she'd glimpsed that edgy side to him—something locked down, unfathomable, untouchable, controlling—she'd really loved his quick wit, his playful manner. He was exciting, adventurous. He'd made sex fun as well as wickedly erotic.

She hadn't experienced that before.

Her first time had been with a fellow undergrad who had been studying applied mathematics and had done everything, including sex, with precision and measured skill. It hadn't been the most exciting way to lose her virginity, but at least he was thorough.

Her second lover had been a guy she'd met while doing her MBA. He'd been studying for a doctorate and she'd had a feeling he'd enjoyed their conversations more than the sex, although when he had applied himself the sex generally had been satisfactory.

At least, that was what she'd thought until last night.

From now on, considering her plans, she'd have to keep any future interaction with Connor on a hands-off basis.

Regardless of anything else, she had to come clean.

She went into her tiny bedroom and started dressing for her midday yoga class, knowing that afterwards she'd have to contact Connor. She wasn't certain what concerned her the most. Facing his hostility when she told him the truth, or hurting him by doing so.

Whatever it was, she'd just have to deal with it.

Connor left his brother Logan's law office satisfied that the paperwork Damian McBride had emailed over to him was in order. Even though he liked Damian, and knew that the man was not a great fan of his late uncle or his business methods, Connor wasn't taking any chances, which was why he'd asked his brother to take a look at the contract.

While Logan specialised in family law, he'd worked for major players in the world of politics and commerce and for A-list celebs. Connor was satisfied that, if his brother gave the okay, all was solid and above board.

He thought about celebrating his win by heading across London to view his soon-to-be acquisition. He could stand and stare at the place, imagine it being bulldozed. At first Connor had thought about renovating; the place hadn't been empty long enough that it couldn't be rescued. But the thought of tearing it down was just too satisfying to dismiss.

Maybe he'd ask to operate the wrecking ball, take the first swing to demolish concrete and stone. How satisfying would that be? Perhaps, as the first brick crumbled, as the first wall fell, he would gain that elusive sense of liberation from his past. Feel his anger and frustration fade as the building leveled.

He'd rebuild, of course. No sense buying prime real estate in the capital and doing nothing with it. Apartments, perhaps. Something far removed from what it had been five years ago—an outwardly high-end casino which, he'd painfully discovered, had been used for nefarious purposes.

His hands fisted, chest tightening. He wanted that damn place. He wanted every last piece of what it had been and what it represented obliterated from the face of the earth.

Images came unbidden, filling his head with old and painful memories. Caroline standing beside the baccarat table, her green eyes lit with the knowledge that she'd successfully primed him to take the fall for her father's and her duplicity. The realisation that she'd professed to love him only to stab him in the back. The cops arriving to read him his rights...

Deliberately, he uncurled his fingers and took a deep breath. No point looking back. Everything was set to move forward to his satisfaction. Which made today a fucking good day.

He considered walking to the nearest of his clubs. His back was acting up this morning and a walk usually eased it. He could use the time to finalise details of Logan's stag party, make sure everything would be on point for his brother's last shot at freedom. Why the hell he wanted to tie himself down, Connor had no idea. Okay, Connor liked April well enough, and his future sister-in-law seemed like a good person. Most importantly, she made his brother happy.

Logan was a hero in Connor's book. His oldest brother had done everything in his power to keep their family together when their parents had taken off, leaving five children to fend for themselves. That, and the fact that Logan had saved him from the lash of his father's belt too many times to remember.

His brother was the only person Connor trusted.

He hailed a cab, sat back, and closed his eyes. The sun played across his lids, helping his muscles relax. He fought the pull of sleep as the cab trundled through the busy traffic, his drugged thoughts rolling back to the previous night and the reason for his current fatigue.

Lola.

Shit, but that woman was something else. Hot. Adventurous. Inexhaustible.

And fuck was she flexible, he thought with a grin. Bending her body with effortless ease and making him lose his damn mind as she took him to paradise…

Paradise? When had he ever used words like that? It was sex. That was all it was. Good, dirty, passionate, energetic sex.

His cock strained against his zipper and he shifted. He'd known he wouldn't be disappointed. When she'd left that morning, she'd made absolutely no demands to see him again. No hints that, although they'd agreed only to one night, maybe there could be more. No suggestions that they could hook up again some time if they were both at a loose end.

None of that. They'd shared breakfast. She'd kissed him, tossed him a smile and left his apartment. She was a female version of him. For some reason, that pissed him off.

He'd fought against her wanting to direct proceedings, yet he really shouldn't have concerned himself. She'd shown a determination to satisfy them both. The problem he'd had was more to do with her inherent softness, and he was suspicious of that. Who could blame him? He'd promised himself he'd never again be taken in by face value attributes. Yet Lola seemed genuine, which in itself rang warning bells and cautioned him to keep his instincts sharpened.

While she shot from the hip, she had conflicting layers: strength, gentleness, wildness, caution. All part of the fascination that made her so damn sexy, but which confused the hell out of him. Not that he should concern himself with that, either. They'd both understood it was temporary and no-strings sex.

Yeah…so why was he leaning forward and tapping the glass to direct the driver to her place? Except he didn't know exactly where *her place* was, apart from what he'd overheard her tell the driver last night which was basically just the street and general location. What the hell was he going to do? Knock on every door until he found out where she lived?

Part of him warned he was pushing things, crossing a line by trying to track her down. The thing was, he wanted to see her again. *Really* wanted to see her again. Now that he had her in his head, he couldn't resist the opportunity for another meet. He wanted more of those conflicting layers, another chance to get a handle on who she really was.

More fool him.

Fifteen minutes later, the taxi pulled up outside one of several tall terraced houses in a long row of similar residences. Connor paid the fare and got out.

As the taxi sped away, he stood on the pavement and surveyed the nearest building, wishing he'd thought to grab her mobile number so he wouldn't be standing like an idiot on a busy London street in the middle of the goddamn day, wondering what the devil his next step was.

But asking for her number would have suggested he wanted more. Would have given her the impression he was interested in seeing her again.

*Yeah, and standing outside her place isn't doing that at all, is it, Einstein?*

Connor pushed back his jacket and slid his hands into his trouser pockets, looking up at the property like some kind of demented estate agent, hoping it housed Lola's place.

With no real plan, he strolled up the half-dozen stone steps and glanced at the panel by the side of the door. He scanned the list of names but didn't see Lola's.

So, what did he do? Press every bell and ask for her? How the heck would that sound, some stranger pressing bells and requesting a woman in the middle of the day? Not suspicious at all.

Ten minutes later, he was sure that someone had probably already called the police. He'd tried to use his best appeasing tone and had been surprised at the trusting nature of several occupants he'd already tried. Other occupants seemed less unsuspecting.

One woman had demanded his name, his mobile number and the exact nature of his business before telling him to get lost when he'd said he was looking for a woman called Lola.

By the time he hit pay dirt, he was sure that he'd be hauled away in a wailing cop car any moment and would spend the night in the nearest nick. As he pressed what he decided would probably be the last button before he called it quits, memories hit him. A cold cell, echoing walls, drunken shouts of innocence from his neighbours.

He remembered the icy slab he'd slept on, the numerous questions, the looks of suspicion aimed at him from police officers, until Connor had finally caved and asked for his lawyer.

It had seemed like hours before Connor even knew what he'd been charged with—longer still until

Logan had arrived and demanded to know what the hell was going on.

He'd listened with a kind of disembodied disbelief as they'd outlined the charges and had realised he'd been framed, used as a scapegoat.

But that hadn't been the worst of it…

'Hello?'

He jerked back, almost toppling off the top step as the husky, familiar tone slapped him dead centre in his chest.

'Hey, Lola.'

There was a long silence, during which Connor wondered if he'd imagined hearing her voice, but then she spoke. 'Connor? What are you doing here?'

'I was passing. Thought maybe I could buy you lunch.'

Another silence, during which Connor started to question the wisdom of what he was doing. What the hell was happening to him that he found himself this attracted to a woman that he'd act so out of character? Okay, so it wasn't the first time he'd actually pursued a woman he liked, but this?

Was this bordering on stalker-ish?

Maybe his wanting to find out more about her had something to do with those layers. Her intriguing blend of assertiveness, strength, hesitancy, and doubt. It was an explosive mix in a woman, and it fascinated the hell out of him.

'How did you know where I lived?'

He jolted as her question drew him from his reverie. 'Heard you tell the taxi driver last night,' he said, more than a tad embarrassed at the admission.

Yet more silence. 'Give me five minutes.'

Turning, he sat on the stone step, both anticipating seeing her again and wondering what in God's name he was doing. He should have left it. Should have enjoyed their one night of great sex. Moved on.

She arrived faster than he'd anticipated, considering that a woman's five minutes could often stretch to infinity.

The door opened and he stood, turning to face her. She wore a white tee with a red diagonal flash across her breasts that announced *Forever Fit* in script lettering, and a snazzy pair of leggings that looked as if she'd poured herself into them. Her hair, all that glorious hair, was pulled back and up into a kind of messy bun.

She had a battered holdall flung over her shoulders.

Connor raised his eyebrows. While she looked sexy as hell, she was hardly dressed for lunch at Lavini's where he'd planned to take her.

'Sorry, but I can't do lunch,' she said, reading his thoughts. 'I've got a class.'

He should have been relieved. Should have shrugged, said 'Another time,' and walked away, but instead he slipped his hands into his pockets and stayed where he was. 'Quick coffee?'

She glanced at the big white watch on her wrist. 'Yeah, that would work. But mine would need to be decaf.'

'Where's your class?' he asked, taking the holdall from her before heading down the stone steps onto the pavement. 'We'll find a coffee shop nearby.'

She pointed along the road to a building that looked like a community centre. 'Just across the road.'

'Right.' He let her lead the way, wondering what the hell she had in the bag that made it feel like a dead body.

'What kind of class?' he asked as they crossed the busy road.

'Lunch time yoga.' She eyed him, an amused look in her sexy green eyes. 'Want to join us?'

He raised his eyebrows. 'Do I look like I want to join you?'

She eyed his suit, then laughed with that throaty sound that shot straight to his balls. 'Funny, but it's always the people who could use it most that are the most derogatory. Almost like they're scared to actually relax.'

'I relax,' he felt compelled to point out. 'I just prefer not putting myself into complicated positions and cutting off my air supply when I do so.'

She shook her head, the bun on top wobbling precariously. 'Another misconception. Some of the most effective poses are incredibly simple. Yoga teaches controlled breathing and only some of the practices involve holding your breath.'

'If you say so.'

This time she tutted, her expression making him wonder if he'd hit a nerve of some kind. As they'd arrived at the double entrance doors, and Lola was keying in security numbers on the pad beside them, he thought it best not to follow up his insights into the ancient practice.

Several people milled around in the entrance hall, and a couple of them waved to Lola. She went through more double doors and into a small coffee bar. Most of the tables were taken, so she headed to a bench counter that looked out onto a small garden area.

She sat on one of the high stools. 'This okay?'

Connor gladly put the bag down between them, then sat next to her. 'Yeah, great.'

Amused, she looked at him as he settled in. 'You have to go and order at the counter.'

He narrowed his eyes, but couldn't stop the smile. 'What happened to equality?'

'You invited me, remember? That means you go get the coffee. I'll have a small decaf Americano.'

Yeah. He really liked her directness. No side. No games. Maybe that was part of the attraction? What you saw was what you got. And he'd been watching closely.

He turned, almost falling off the stool. She gave a throaty laugh which, combined with the sight of her in all that close-fitting workout gear, went straight to his cock.

He wasn't sure how he was supposed to make it to the counter without disgracing himself but, as everyone seemed happily engaged in their own conversations, he walked off to place their order, hoping to hell nobody checked out the vicinity of his groin.

# CHAPTER SEVEN

OF ANY SCENARIO Lola could have imagined, the very last one was having Connor turn up on her door step.

Her first thought was that he'd discovered who she was, but that didn't seem to be the case.

She had gone over half a dozen potential starts to the conversation she knew they needed to have about the Cabacal, but one look at him standing there looking drop-dead gorgeous in his business suit, his blue shirt opened at the collar, and she'd forgotten every single one.

She turned and watched appreciatively as he ordered their drinks, knowing that the impressive breadth of his shoulders had nothing to do with the impeccable tailoring of his jacket and everything to do with his muscular perfection. She glanced at his neck, wondering if beneath his collar he sported evidence of the fact that she'd taken big, greedy bites of it.

Her gaze slid down to his backside and she swallowed, recalling how firm he had been as she'd clenched her hands over his taut flesh, encouraging him to drive deeper inside her.

She blew out a breath and turned away. God, it was getting hot in here.

Seconds later, he was back. He slid onto the stool, grimacing a little as he settled there. 'What time's your class?'

She checked her watch. 'Forty-five minutes yet. I usually like to get here an hour before, but since I had a busy night, and a late start this morning, I'm a little out of sync.'

He grinned and looked at her as if he was remembering every dirty thing they'd done together. 'You like to warm up before class?'

Even if she did, she wouldn't need it today. Her body was impossibly hot already. 'I like to set up before class starts.'

He raised his eyebrows. 'You're the instructor?'

'Is that so unbelievable?'

He shook his head, his gaze travelling down her body and then back again. 'No, but I thought you'd just finished uni. Which was the reason you were dancing on my table last night.'

'I have just finished uni. Bachelors and then an MBA.'

'Where does yoga come in?'

'I did a part-time teacher training course. Practical and theoretical. It was almost like taking another degree.' She blew out a breath. 'It's a very profound and intricate subject that involves learning about anatomy, physiology and the philosophical side, too. I love it.'

Connor smiled, leaning forward to clasp his hands on the table. 'I can see that from the way your eyes light up.' His gaze held hers with such intensity that Lola felt the punch of it right down in her solar plexus. 'Are you planning to make a business out of it?'

'Uh-huh. I'm going to run my own studio.'

Habit had her bracing herself for what she feared might follow. Would Connor be like her father, like Damian, and try and convince her of the error of her ways?

'Your own studio,' Connor said, smiling at the waitress who brought their coffee. 'What are you planning to offer your clients?'

'Remedial yoga, relaxation therapy, Pilates, and therapeutic massage.'

Connor took a small sip of his coffee, pursing his lips as he nodded. 'What size studio do you have in mind? Are you planning to start off just by yourself, or will you take on other tutors immediately?'

Since there was no hint of censure in his questions, Lola leaned forward. 'I want to offer a variety of courses and therapies right from the start. There are a few well-qualified teachers on the circuit who are interested in taking on more work. But I intend to be really hands-on and not stick myself behind a desk doing admin.'

He nodded again. 'Yeah, I get that. It takes some organisation but it's doable.'

Lola caught her bottom lip between her teeth, her face pleasantly warm from the realisation that Connor seemed genuinely interested. It was so refreshing not to have to defend or explain her choices.

'That's what I'm thinking. I've done really detailed planning, based on my research of health clubs from a variety of UK cities, projected out for the next few years. That should give me a really good head start, and some leeway for changing things up if necessary.'

'That's why you're looking at property? Potential locations for your studio?'

She found it hard to look at him, knowing that now was the perfect time to come clean. To admit her plans for the Cabacal. 'Yes.'

'Found anything suitable yet?'

She raised her head, met his eyes. 'I have. A perfect property. Perfect location.'

'That's great.'

Her stomach gave a ridiculous lurch, leaving nausea in its wake. 'It would be, but there are complications.'

'What kind?'

She kept her eyes on his, trying to find the right words to minimise the damage of her confession. 'Somebody else is interested.'

'Then make sure the agents know that you're even more interested,' Connor said. 'Make them an offer they can't refuse.'

She thought of Damian. How she'd tried to convince him to sell direct to her. 'You make it sound easy.'

'If it's what you really want, go for it. Don't give

up until you've exhausted all possibilities. Until there's nowhere left to go.'

'Is that what you would do?'

A determined look came into his eyes. 'Every time.'

Lola knew they were both talking about the same thing, and again she wondered why he wanted the Cabacal property so badly. If it held bad memories for him, wouldn't he want to walk away, have nothing more to do with it? Or maybe it was more a case of laying old ghosts to rest. In which case, if she remained patient it wasn't unreasonable to think that he'd be willing to sell it to her.

Connor shrugged. 'You just need a plan of action. I'd imagine a woman who studies for a business degree, an MBA, and trains as a yoga teacher at the same time isn't exactly lacking in the smarts department.'

It was a strange and pleasurable sensation that filled her chest, for a moment pushing away the uneasy feeling that had settled there at the thought of coming clean about who she was. She really liked his faith in her abilities, that he considered her smart. It was refreshing to have a man who thought her capable of going for her dreams.

Yet layered beneath the pleasure of that was the nudge of guilt. He'd supported her as she'd laid out her plans to him, encouraged her to go for what she wanted, all the time unaware that those plans and wants were in direct opposition to his own.

On top of that, he'd told her that he liked her direct approach, yet here she was continuing the deceit. Her only defence was that she was really starting to like him, and she didn't want her time with him to come to an abrupt halt when she told him the truth.

He looked at her for several unsettling moments, then flashed a devilish grin. 'So, yoga,' he said, looking at her over the rim of his cup. 'That explains why you're so freaking flexible.'

Lola's body reacted to the sexy implication, an arrow of heat firing through her veins. She clenched her fists in her lap, annoyed that she'd let the perfect opportunity to tell him who she was slip past. She'd chickened out.

Wrong time. Wrong place. A coffee bar in the community centre, a short time before she was supposed to instruct a class in the art of relaxation, was not exactly the best place to confess all.

Admitting her identity to Connor would open a whole can of worms that would need explaining. While she hadn't outright lied to him, Connor wouldn't see it like that. It would be a double whammy for him. Not just because she'd been economical with the truth about who she was and what she wanted, but also because of her family connection to the man who had brought false embezzlement charges against him.

That connection was tenuous, especially considering Lola had distanced herself from that side of the family after what had been done to her mother, and over the years she had cut herself off completely from them with absolutely zero interest in their lives or what happened to them. Still, as Connor rightfully harboured a lot of ill-feeling towards her uncle, she knew her blood relationship would matter a great deal. Some people thought the apple didn't fall far from the tree.

She saw a couple of her students enter the building. 'I have to go,' she said, swigging down the last of her drink. 'People are arriving.'

Should she suggest another coffee meet-up? They needed to talk some more. Talk, not have sex.

Connor reached for her hand. 'I had a great time last night.'

Blood raced through her veins and sexy memories flooded her mind. 'So did I.' She reached down for her bag. 'But it was a one-nighter, remember?'

As disappointing as it was, she couldn't have sex with him again. It was one thing giving in to her hormones when she'd thought she wouldn't see him again but, now that they were essentially in direct conflict over the Cabacal, another hook-up was out of the question.

He squeezed his fingers around hers as she tried to pull away. 'It wasn't good enough to repeat?'

Sneaky bastard. She wanted to say something pithy, something that would wipe that cocky grin off his face. 'I surely don't need to stroke your ego by admitting that it was fantastic, do I?'

'Fantastic is always worth another go-round.'

Her core muscles clenched and she felt the pull in

her blood. 'I'm betting you can't afford the distraction any more than I can.'

'As distractions go, great sex always wins out.'

'Not always.'

'Why don't you let me take you to dinner tonight? Let me prove it.'

Hell, no. She wouldn't survive another evening with Connor and his particular brand of seduction. Dinner could so easily lead to so much more, and before she knew it they'd be in bed again. She was finding it hard enough to resist that smile of his as it was, the one that hiked up one corner of his mouth and made him look rakishly sexy. The gleam in his steely grey eyes that gave off a very definite bad-boy vibe. Not to mention the pure male energy that came off the man and surrounded her, swamped her, made her want to fall into his arms, despite her better intentions.

Absolutely not. No way. End of story.

She had to stay immune to him. She couldn't allow him to spin his magic over her again.

'What do you say, Lola? Want to be distracted again?'

*No. No. No.*

She took a deep breath. 'Okay.'

Lola turned away from the mirror and smoothed down the front of the simple dark-blue shift. She'd chosen the dress for its modest neckline and knee-length skirt, hoping it gave off a specific 'dinner with a friend' vibe.

In the time it took to shower and spritz herself with an innocuous floral body spray, she had to remind herself that having sex with Connor again was most definitely not on the cards. She had to keep him at arm's length—absolutely no flirting.

What she planned to do was use their time together to get to know him better. Find out what made him tick. She might be able to discover more about his reasons for wanting the property so badly, and what plans he had for it. If they were based entirely on drawing a line under his past experiences, to put those old ghosts to rest, then she might have a better chance of getting him to sell it to her.

In the grand scheme of things, since they'd already slept together, keeping the truth from him just a little longer surely didn't matter that much. While she wasn't entirely comfortable doing that, she had to believe that the means justified the ends.

Getting the Cabacal back meant everything to her. It was more than righting a wrong; it was her real link with her past, with her mother.

So many of her childhood memories were tied up in that building. Parties her grandparents threw there, where she and her friends dressed up in pretty dresses and imagined they were film stars.

Being allowed to watch from the little balcony at the back of the club with her mother while famous singers performed for the cream of London society.

Watching her adored grandparents, smiling at each other and so in love as they danced together on the club's crowded dancefloor.

As her throat tightened, she reached out for the fitted denim jacket she kept on a hook by the front door, took a fortifying breath and made her way out. She'd chosen basic black pumps tonight—far more practical, since she didn't possess a car and usually took the tube or walked.

Emily was working a shift, which spared Lola having to explain that she was seeing Connor. She knew her friend still worried about Lola's Plan A, and would have given Lola an earful if she'd known what was going on.

The nearest tube station was around the block from the West End restaurant Connor had chosen, and her chest hitched when she saw him waiting on the pavement by the entrance. The jolt to her system wasn't entirely unexpected. The man certainly made an imposing sight. Well over six feet of nicely honed muscle, confidence oozing from the set of those impressive shoulders and an aura of strength emanating from his masculine frame as he stood surveying his surroundings with his hands in the pockets of his trousers.

As he was looking the other way, Lola stopped and took a moment to compose herself, to remind herself that she had a very definite plan for the evening, and that plan did not involve ending up in bed with him again.

Despite her self-talk, her mouth fairly watered as she watched him, as she took in the sight of all that male energy and leashed power. The muscles between her legs clenched in sympathy with her plight, and heat burned through her veins. It was as if her body already mourned the loss of all that excitement, adventure and erotic pleasure.

She started walking towards him and, as if he'd sensed her, he turned and met her gaze. Her stomach went into freefall.

'Hey.'

He leaned down and kissed her lightly, his scent washing over her and making her insides do crazy, stupid things. Bearing in mind that her intention was to keep things light, she failed miserably as she met his kiss and deepened it a little.

He grinned. 'How was your class?'

'Good. How was your afternoon?'

He nodded. 'Busy. Productive.'

Meaning that he'd been looking over the final contract for the Cabacal property before signing on the dotted line? A sinking feeling played in her stomach.

'Hope you're hungry.'

She was, and not just for food. Oh, hell. Why was she letting her desire for Connor overpower what she had to do?

Focus. She had to keep focused. 'I'm famished. Didn't have time to grab much of anything today.'

'Let's remedy that.'

Their table was on the mezzanine level in a secluded booth that nevertheless gave a bird's eye of the diners on the lower level.

'I've heard about this place,' Lola said. 'I thought they were booked out for months. How did you manage to get a table?' She raised her eyebrows. 'Or maybe you have a standing reservation?'

He smiled at her over his menu. 'Yeah, it's a necessity. Have to make sure I accommodate my revolving door of hot lovers.'

She really liked his ability to make her laugh. 'In which case you must have some recommendations as far as the menu is concerned.'

He kept his gaze on hers for long moments, during which her pulse kicked up. He had the sexiest eyes, all that steely grey that turned to smoke when he was aroused. Like now. 'Depends what menu we're talking about.'

'The one with food on it.' She shook her head, then went back to perusing the offerings. 'You've got a one-track mind.'

'And yours went straight there. Explain that.'

She kept her attention on the menu but lowered her voice. 'We're not having sex again tonight, Connor.'

He likely wouldn't want it anyway if he knew what secrets she harboured.

'In that case, I'd better give the oysters a miss.'

Lola made the mistake of glancing up and smack into the depths of that sexy grin. The man was too delicious to resist. Was there anything quite so irresistible as an intelligent and devastatingly gorgeous male with the hint of bad boy about him?

'I have no idea how anyone can eat them anyway.'

'I should have known,' Connor said with a shake of his head as he placed his menu down. 'You're going to tell me you're a vegetarian.'

'No, I'm not, actually. Not that there's anything wrong with that.'

He pursed his lips, holding up his hands. 'No argument from me.'

'I'm actually pescatarian.'

'Ouch.' He mock-frowned. 'Sounds painful.'

'It means I eat fish.'

'Okay.'

'Nothing with batter around it, though.'

'Whatever you eat, you look good on it.'

She put down her menu. 'Thanks. But still not having sex.'

Connor was laughing as the waiter arrived. Lola ordered the steamed haddock and seasonal vegetables, asking for a plain white sauce. Connor chose steak. Rare.

When they were alone again, he raised his wine glass and nodded to her sparkling water with its slices of lemon and lime. 'You're sure you wouldn't like something other than water. A mocktail, maybe?'

Lola picked up her glass. 'This is fine. I'm not especially fond of the taste of much else, to be honest.'

'Don't drink. Don't eat battered fish. If I didn't know otherwise, I'd think you didn't have any vices.'

Lola tried not to return his grin as he raised his glass to his lips, but there was just something too deliciously naughty about him that made that near impossible.

'Any more news on the property front?' Connor asked. 'About those complications, I mean.'

Lola frowned at the question. 'Not really. It's a bit of a stalemate at the moment.'

'What agents are you using? Maybe I can help.'

Why did he have to say that? Why did he have to be ultra nice and offer his help? It only piled on the feeling of being the biggest cheat. And what did she say to that anyway?

*Actually, Connor. You can help. You can sell me back the property I've been deceiving you about from the get go.*

She had visions of him tossing her over the balcony of the mezzanine, and she wouldn't blame him. She'd endure just about anything if it meant getting the Cabacal back, even Connor's wrath if she had to.

Since her throat was tightening up, she took a sip of the tart water. 'That someone I told you about has beaten me to it. Offered a really competitive price.'

'Do you still want the place?'

She made herself meet his gaze. 'Yes.'

'Then keep at it. Like I said, anything's possible if you want it bad enough.'

'The person buying it really wants it too. In fact, I think he might even have already signed the contract.'

Part of her wondered if he'd say how coincidental

that was because he'd also signed a contract today. But he didn't.

'Call the agent. Find out. You need to know for sure. If the buyer's stalling, you can get in fast with a counter-offer.'

She thought of Damian. Even if Connor hadn't signed yet, even if for some reason things had stalled, her pig-headed brother wouldn't budge. He wouldn't let her counter-offer because he wanted to ensure she didn't get to follow through on her plans, just as her father had tried to thwart her mother's dream.

'City people won't have time for such foolhardy nonsense,' her father had said one night, when Lola had been listening at the top of the stairs as their argument had become more heated. 'They're too busy making sound investments, keeping abreast of financial dealings, to worry about bending and stretching and chanting some mantra after a long day. If they want to let off steam they'll take a run along the Thames, or find the nearest bar that sells a decent malt.'

Her mother's protests had fallen on deaf ears, just as Lola's had with Damian. The two men had been cut from the same cloth.

But Connor hadn't been. He'd been supportive and had even offered to help her.

Before guilt could run its scratchy claws down her spine again, Lola asked, 'Would you ever stall on buying a property you wanted?'

'Can't see the point. You want it, or you don't.'

So the chances were that there wasn't a hold-up with Connor signing the contract. Which meant the transaction had likely already gone through.

She took a steadying breath. 'What if you bought a property then decided it wasn't actually what you wanted? That the reason you'd bought it was no longer valid?'

She watched him closely as he pursed his lips, considering. 'Hard to say what I'd do. Never been in that position before. But as long as it turned a profit, I'd find a way to make it work.'

*As long as it turned a profit.* Surely Connor was driven by more than financial gain in his acquisition of the Cabacal? There had to be more of an emotional reason for him, based on his history with her uncle. It couldn't primarily be because the property would make him money.

'Anyway, where is it?'

Lola had to refocus. 'Where's what?'

'This property you want so badly.'

'It's way across town.' She knew he'd probe and was thankful when the waiter chose that moment to bring their food. It gave her some thinking time. 'But there are a couple of other properties I've seen that show promise.'

Why the hell had she said that? If she let Connor believe that, it would weaken her position when she came to negotiate with him. But right then she had to get his attention away from the real property she wanted. Because she wasn't ready to tell him. While she hated lying to him, she still needed to know more about him and his reasons for wanting the Cabacal.

Should she allude to her own reasons for wanting it? Not directly, of course. She couldn't come right out and say she wanted it yet. But if she could allude to the reasons, demonstrate how important it was to her, he might be more accepting of her behaviour when she eventually told him.

God. She hated the thought of things ending between them. She liked the way he took her seriously, how he encouraged her to go for what she wanted. She really liked his company, liked being with him. He gave her more confidence to go for what she wanted, which was kind of perverse, considering the situation.

'I'd never recommend you compromise,' Connor said, slicing his steak. 'That's an easy out.'

Lola speared a green bean. 'Don't you ever compromise?'

Chewing, he shook his head. Then he swallowed. 'Not if I can help it. Compromised once and it bit me in the ass, big time.'

Did this have something to do with her uncle? Trying for nonchalance, Lola cut into her fish. 'That can't have been good.'

'It wasn't, but it taught me a valuable lesson.'

'Which was?'

'Trust your instincts. Don't get screwed.'

That hit her right in the centre of her chest. Was that what he'd think she was doing? Screwing him?

And not in a good way. What were his instincts tell-ing him right now?

'Those other properties you looked at,' he said, giving no indication anything was currently amiss in the instinct department. 'Have you seen them at night?'

'No.'

'It's a nice evening,' he said. 'Let's take an excur-sion after we've eaten and you can show them to me.'

Her heart jolted at the quick-fire suggestion. 'To-night? In the dark?'

'Yeah. It's worth checking out the areas at night since I assume you'll be offering classes until late?'

'Yes, that's likely to be my busiest period.'

'So you'll get a feel for each place that'll differ greatly from the one you'll get during the day.'

Despite the moment of panic at Connor's sugges-tion to see the properties, it was hard not to enjoy his obvious interest in her plans. The fact he'd ac-tually give them some thought, and wanted to help her with the practicalities was incredibly addictive.

Just like him.

But then he was a businessman. That interest was innate.

'Makes sense,' Lola said, thankful she'd taken the opportunity at least to research other proper-ties as back-up options. She hadn't wanted to imag-ine the worst-case scenario—that she would never get the Cabacal back—but if despite her best efforts her plans for acquiring the property collapsed she had every intention that the health centre would still go ahead.

'Great.' Connor picked up the menu. 'The chocolate torte here is the best you'll ever taste.'

'Then make it two. I never share dessert.'

# CHAPTER EIGHT

THEY DROVE THROUGH the streets of London towards the address Lola had given for the first property.

Parking being what it was in London, they had to leave Connor's convertible and walk a few streets to the first property. It was in a relatively quiet back street, with not particularly good lighting.

'See, this was my point,' Connor said as he slipped his hands in his pockets and looked up at the terraced building with its fairly dilapidated windows and doors. 'You wouldn't want to think about somewhere like this for your studio.'

As Connor looked around, Lola tried to think of relevant points to illustrate why this was a place she'd seriously been considering. 'It's close to a tube station, though. That's an important consideration.'

'Yeah. Really important. But it's too quiet. Not enough footfall. You'd need good security lighting, state-of-the-art security generally. Maybe even someone manning the entrance. That would hike your start-up costs.'

Looking around, Lola agreed. She hadn't factored

in major overhauls to the outside of the properties, aside from general sprucing up, and Connor was right: there were too many dark areas once the surrounding small shops were closed up at the end of the day. Security would have to be a priority if she ever considered this place.

She thought about the Cabacal and its surrounding area. It was in a really busy, well-lit area with trendy bars where people milled about at all hours of the day and night. Security there wouldn't be much of an issue beyond the basic requirements of lighting, good locks and a building alarm. She certainly wouldn't need to hire a night guard.

The next property was an easy fifteen-minute walk. Connor reached for her hand, his fingers tightening around hers, drawing her close. His scent wafted on the evening air, doing delicious things to her insides and making her move even closer to him as they walked. She needed to focus.

'What sort of things would you look for when property hunting?' Lola asked, as casually as she could. 'I suppose it depends on what use you intend, of course, but would you always have an idea of that at the point of purchase?'

She glanced over as he considered her question. With a bit of luck, he'd give something away regarding his plans for the Cabacal, and she'd have more information on which to build her case to convince him to sell to her.

He pursed his lips. 'Can't say I always know, although I'd have a general idea seeing as night clubs are my business.'

'Then any other property you acquire would always become a night club?'

'Not always.'

Before she could probe deeper, they turned a corner and the next property came into view.

Lola tucked away her frustration that she hadn't been able to glean more.

'This has more going for it, location-wise,' Connor said as he perused what was this time a two-storey concrete block, freshly painted and with new windows and doors. 'Although it's not as close to a tube station. Plus, there's noise from that bar across the road, which might cause you some problems if you're trying to create a relaxing atmosphere.' He glanced at his watch. 'It's still relatively early, so things are likely to get livelier, especially at weekends.'

Lola looked towards the bar, her rueful smile indicative of the fact she might never have given that much thought. 'Good point. There's so much to consider.'

Again, she thought of the Cabacal. The trendy bars nearby were unlikely to get especially raucous since they attracted a different crowd, mostly after-work professionals who were stopping by to discuss business with a colleague, or taking the opportunity to enjoy a quick drink before heading home. Close to public transport, relatively quiet, yet busy enough that she wouldn't have to worry about extra security measures. Even if the Cabacal hadn't meant so much to her, she would be hard-pressed to find a property more suited to her plans.

'You've got your priorities straight,' Connor said, cutting into her thoughts. 'Location and access. Once they're in place, you can build on everything else. Where to next?'

As they walked to the final property, Lola had to admit that having Connor's take on the properties was insightful and incredibly useful, and his willingness to help her by giving valuable advice only seemed to increase the gnawing sense of guilt about lying to him.

She had no intention of purchasing any of these properties. She wanted the Cabacal. Yet she couldn't shake off the feeling of connection that was growing with Connor. He seemed genuinely interested in helping her. He was able to make suggestions and give insights, but in no way did he ever undermine her. He never dismissed her ideas out of hand, but somehow managed to make her question them herself to get things clear in her own mind.

She was starting to like him more and more as the evening went on.

The last of the properties was in an even quieter area than the first one. It was smaller than the others, but there was no denying it had a certain charm.

'I thought this one might work because there's

a tube nearby and it has good bus links,' Lola said. 'But I think it's probably too quiet. Too small.'

Connor came to stand beside her after he'd taken a cursory look at the front of the building. 'Yeah, it's quiet, but you could use the back entrance at night. Busier there and plenty of people around. And, while it might be small, there could be the possibility of extending into the next building at some stage.'

'Hmm. And I do want to expand the business in the future.'

Lola studied the building, thinking that at some time down the line this type of building might be an option, but right then there was only one place she wanted.

'Does it give you a good feeling,' Connor asked. 'Those instincts, remember?'

She looked up at him and met his gaze. *He* certainly gave her a good feeling. And all her instincts told her to grab him and kiss the life out of him. He was so incredibly gorgeous, standing there in the muted light of a quiet street, his hair ruffled by the breeze, his dark eyes filled with that sexy gleam. All big and masculine in a tailored jacket that fit him to perfection, his tie rakishly loosened so he could unfasten the top button of his shirt.

Her mouth positively watered just looking at him.

It wasn't just the way he looked, although that had the power to steal her breath clean away. It was much more than that. With every moment she spent with him she felt the attraction grow. He didn't dismiss her dreams but seemed intent on helping her achieve them. He encouraged, supported, offered her his own insights. It was such an alien concept to her, having that encouragement, that support. How could she even try to resist him?

She wanted him. *Really* wanted him.

As if reading her thoughts, he stepped forward. 'You've got a dirty mind.' He grinned and slid his arms around her waist. 'Here I am, trying my hardest to keep my mind on business, and you're looking at me as if you want to do very wicked and erotic things to me.'

His chest grazed her breasts as he pulled her closer and her nipples hardened to tight peaks.

'No harm in looking.' She hesitated for just a second, then slid her arms around his neck. 'I really like you, Connor. Just remember that.'

He grinned. 'Okay.'

Then his mouth took hers in a desperate, heated kiss.

He circled her closer to the building, kissing her mouth, her jaw, her throat, and soon she was a quivering mess of need.

'Why don't we take a closer look at the entrance?' Connor suggested as he placed open-mouthed kisses on her neck.

They moved into the stone-floored entryway and Connor angled her back against the door. She searched around frantically, looking for security cameras. 'This is insane, Connor.'

'Yeah.' He pressed her to the door. 'Let's be in-sane together.'

'I hope we're not being caught on camera,' she managed as his erection prodded her and she opened her legs a little. 'I don't want to be on *Crimewatch*.'

'I already checked,' he said between those heated kisses, his hands moving to clamp around her hips. 'No cameras.'

He levered up her dress, pressing his knee be-tween her legs and coaxing her to widen them even more. 'We can't do this, Connor. Not here. What if someone walks by?'

'We'll wish them a pleasant evening and tell them to sod off.'

He grinned, quick and sexy.

Even as she spun between pure lust and the deca-dence of having sex in a public place, Lola couldn't find it in her to stop Connor from reaching for her panties.

He stepped back so he could shimmy them down her legs, and all the while Lola kept searching around for hidden cameras. She gave a quick laugh as she stepped out of her panties, and Connor shoved them in his trouser pocket.

'Oh, hell. I can't believe I'm doing this.'

Connor grabbed his wallet from his jacket pocket and took out a condom. He unzipped his fly, the rasping sound in the quiet of the London back street doing nothing except to spur him on. He couldn't wait any longer. He needed her now.

When he'd covered himself, he pushed her back deep into the door-well, satisfied that they were as sheltered as possible and offering up a silent plea that they'd not be disturbed. Lola grabbed for his shoulders and raised one leg to wrap it around his waist.

'Thanks be to the yoga gods for a flexible woman.'

Lola laughed and tightened her leg against him as she dug her hands into his shoulders.

'You haven't even scratched the surface of my flexibility.'

He grinned, squeezing her backside as his cock pressed against her heat. When her foot slid down his spine, pressing on that sensitive area of his back, he reached around and positioned her foot to ease the discomfort. Although, when she hiked up her hips and all her wetness curved around his erection, he didn't think he was capable of feeling anything other than his blood rushing through him in a frenzied blast of lust.

'Shit, Lola.'

Her response was to bring her hand down between them and curl her fingers around his cock. She closed her eyes and dropped her head back against the door, her hips curving upward, encouraging him to slide inside her.

He wanted to torment her, make her beg for him to take her. He wasn't sure how he did it, but he managed to string things out, even as his cock throbbed and that lust in his blood gathered strength. Leaning down, he kissed her neck, letting his teeth graze against her delicate throat.

Still her hips bucked and she gave an urgent, 'Connor…'

'What?' His voice sounded low, grazed, as if his throat was raw. 'Tell me what you want.'

'You know,' she complained, her fingers squeezing his thickness, her foot pressing into his back, her hips grinding as she tried to get him inside her. 'I'm not going to spell it out.'

She didn't have to, not when her wet heat was like a siren call to his dick. There was only enough torment he could take, only enough resistance he could manage.

He tapped her hand away, replacing it with his own as he positioned himself and pushed hard, deep and was inside her as she gasped and clung to him.

He pumped hard, each shove pushing her harder against the door, which answered with a shaky, clanging sound that indicated an unsustainable lock.

Each time he shoved into her she caught her breath, the sound travelling to her throat in a needy groan.

'Connor… Oh, God. Connor…'

She held him tight, her muscles gripping his cock, her fingers digging into his shoulders.

He drove into her like a freaking train, but in his defence she was making him bloody crazy with her tight, hot body and those needy gasps and moans.

Each time he pushed deep, the door gave way a bit, and in the small slice of his brain that still functioned with some coherence he had the thought that maybe the door wouldn't hold out much longer against the determined battering they were subjecting it to.

He placed his hands on her hips, squeezing tightly both to go even deeper inside her and to hold her safe in his arms in case the door gave way.

He came hard, over and over, as he felt her answering response.

He dropped his forehead to hers, their gasping breaths echoing around the silent back street.

'Do you think someone heard us?' Lola asked as she caught her bottom lip between her teeth. 'I think I was making a lot of noise.'

'Yeah,' Connor said as he withdrew from her. 'You were sounding off loud enough to wake the dead.'

She slapped at his shoulder. 'You weren't exactly quiet.'

She looked so thoroughly fucked, her hair all mussed, her lips full from his kisses, not to mention her dress up around her waist. He zipped himself, then leaned down and lightly kissed her. 'Let's go back to my place and really put on a show.'

She hesitated for a moment in the process of pulling down her skirt, and he knew those cogs and wheels were turning and trying to come up with an excuse. 'I should get home. I've got some lesson plans to write up and other admin to do.'

He noticed she didn't meet his eyes and wondered if she was thinking the same thing he was thinking. That one-night stands were supposed to last one night, but neither of them seemed able to stick to that. They both wanted more.

He didn't want to dwell on what 'more' was. Didn't want to think around why he couldn't seem to get enough of her.

All he knew was that this was starting to turn into more than sex. He couldn't remember the last time he'd enjoyed being with a woman this much. Lola was easy to be around and maybe that was part of the attraction. She knew what she wanted. She was focused, intelligent, and fun. No side.

He'd enjoyed looking at those properties with her, getting a handle on what she was looking for and what she wanted for her business.

She had plans, dreams, and he sensed an innate determination to achieve those plans and dreams. That energy bounced off her like a living thing. It was addictive.

She was addictive.

Fuck.

Reality check. 'Look, I know this has been pretty intense,' he said as nonchalantly as he could manage while he battled with the idea that he wanted more with Lola than blow-the-doors-off sex. 'But in my experience this kind of chemistry burns out faster when acted upon and not denied.'

She reached into her bag and pulled out a tissue

for him to use to dispose of the condom. After he'd taken care of that with a visit to a refuse bin a few yards away, he came back to find her straightening her clothes.

There was a tightness in his chest and his breathing felt uneven. Unusual for him to feel stress after a great bout of sex, but something about Lola unsettled him. He wondered if it was because she might be about to say no. To walk away.

He wasn't ready for that. He hadn't been lying when he'd suggested letting this thing between them burn out naturally, except he was no longer sure it was that simple. Regardless, the last thing he wanted was to have her stick in his system and not be able to do a thing about it.

His mind flashed back a few years to the moment he'd realised Caroline had been manipulating him. Shit. That had hurt like nothing else. Maybe if he hadn't been so damned obsessed with her, hadn't allowed himself to fall too fast and too hard, he might have seen the signs, might not have gone against his instincts to slow down, take his time getting to know her better. Instead, he'd plunged straight into the deep end of the pool, only to come up gasping for air and finding himself in the role of scapegoat.

He'd been a damned fool, and his only defence was that he hadn't been thinking straight. When a man didn't think straight because of a woman, there was usually hell to pay. He'd learned his lesson, and that lesson included keeping things temporary, light, easy. Fuck a woman and get her out of his system before she had chance to take up residence there.

He knew he needed to do that with Lola, but it wasn't a real problem. This time he was giving the deep end of the pool a wide berth, and there was no chance of falling in. His eyes were open, and he wasn't about to be taken for a fool. Never again.

'How about I help you with that admin work you mentioned?' he said. 'Then you can stay the night and I'll make you breakfast.'

She looked up at him, her direct green gaze indicating she was trying to resist him but failing miserably. He really liked that she wasn't clingy and needy but was instead independent and focused on her own plans. Her determination to make her dreams a reality was refreshing, more so because she didn't seem the type to step on anyone to do it. He should know, since he'd been privy to enough treachery and deceit to last him a lifetime.

'You're a difficult man to say no to, Connor.'

'Then don't say it.' He slid his hands in his pockets. 'Look, this is fun, right? And that's what we both want. No strings, no commitment?'

She nodded.

'It doesn't have to mean anything for either of us beyond good sex. We're not making it into anything else. It won't go on for ever.'

Why did he keep saying this? Was he trying to convince her, or himself?

Caution filled her gaze, only adding to his own

sense of confusion and panic. What the hell was wrong with him? If she said no, he would let her go. No hard feelings. Nothing lost. He'd forget her, and the sex, soon enough. He'd make bloody sure of that.

'You're right,' she said with a nod. 'It doesn't have to mean anything else. It doesn't have to affect anything else. It's just sex, and it certainly won't go on for ever.'

Having her shoot his own words back at him pissed him off, and made him want to press her right back against the door and show her just how long it could go on.

It was bad enough that he wanted another night with Lola, but he feared he was already planning the night after that. And the next. He was at risk of stepping onto dangerous ground. What had happened to quick, easy sex-only arrangements? The kind that ensured he didn't have to look beyond what was on the surface. He didn't have to bother working out a woman's motivations or wonder what the hell she might be plotting or planning. He didn't need to figure out what her end-game was, and how it might bring him to his fucking knees.

Once bitten was more than enough for any man, and he'd vowed that he'd never let himself be vulnerable again. That he'd never totally trust. And, family excepted, he never had.

He stepped away from Lola so fast that he stumbled on the kerb.

He winced as his back muscles protested, and

Lola's hand reached out at the very moment he righted himself.

'Connor. Are you okay?'

He grimaced, his hand shooting to his lower back as pain ripped through him. 'Yeah, fine.'

'You're not fine. I've seen you flinch a few times now. What's wrong with your back?'

'Nothing. Just kicks up from time to time.'

She came around behind him and put her hand on his lower back. 'Where does it hurt?'

She pressed and prodded, making Connor think that if his back hadn't hurt before it certainly would after she'd finished with him.

'Your muscles feel really tight. I can help with that.' She came back in front of him. 'Let's stop by my place on the way to yours and I'll grab a few things.'

Tired of this particular conversation, Connor drew her closer, placing his arms around her. 'The only thing you need to bring is you. I'm planning to keep you naked and very contented for the whole night.'

'And what if your back seizes up?' she asked, cocking her head to the side. 'You're not going to be much use to me then, are you? Think about it. I'll be naked and there'll be nothing you can do about it.'

Connor drew in a breath. 'When you put it like that…'

# CHAPTER NINE

EMILY WAS STILL OUT when Lola rushed up to their flat. She grabbed a few supplies then scribbled a note telling her friend that she wouldn't be home again that night.

Lola knew she needed to put Emily's mind at rest about what was going on. They'd spoken on the phone earlier that day when Lola had admitted that her conversation with Damian hadn't gone well. She knew Emily was worried about her spending time with Connor while this secret lay between them. So was she.

*It doesn't have to mean anything for either of us beyond good sex. We're not making it into anything else.*

Would he feel that way when he knew the truth? Would he shrug off what they'd shared as something that didn't matter? That didn't have to influence a business transaction between them?

She feared he wouldn't be able to do that. Hadn't he also said that he found it hard to trust?

Nausea settled in her stomach at the knowledge that she would be responsible for adding another cruel layer to his trust issues. The very last thing she wanted to do was hurt him and the longer this went on between them without her admitting who she was, the worse it would be for Connor.

And for her. Because she was getting herself in too deep. She was starting to really care about him, and about the consequences for him if she continued this charade. There was also the possibility that the longer she delayed telling him the truth, the more likely he was to refuse selling the Cabacal to her.

Despite everything, she couldn't seem to not want him. Couldn't deny herself the opportunity to spend another night with him.

Soon, everything would change between them, so couldn't she just have this one last time?

She wanted it. So much. And she was going to take it. She slipped a change of underwear in her bag, along with some toiletries from the bathroom, then headed back out to where Connor was waiting for her. She knew that she should have invited him up, but she didn't want him seeing anything that might make him suspicious. It was safer to let him wait in his car. Thankfully, he hadn't pushed.

The fact he had showed no interest in seeing where she lived confirmed that he saw this as a temporary thing between them. That it would burn itself out. There was no need for him to concern himself with the inside of her flat, or anything else in her life that didn't relate to their time between the sheets.

The thought sat heavily in her chest.

Perhaps this was a good thing. If he wasn't invested in anything they shared other than excellent sex, then her eventual revelation wouldn't hit him as hard. She might not add to his trust issues as deeply as she'd feared.

That was a cop-out, but it went some way towards alleviating her guilt. But only some way, because the spectre of her deceit was always lying there just beneath the surface.

Yet she didn't want that spectre to ruin what time she did have with Connor.

On arriving at his apartment, Connor busied himself getting drinks while Lola went into his bedroom and unpacked her bag.

When he came in with their drinks, he stopped dead. 'What's all this?'

She looked to where he stared at the bottles of essential oils she'd unpacked on his side table, the scented candle and oil burner, and the huge towels she'd fetched from the bathroom, one of which she'd placed across the centre of the bed. 'I'm giving you a massage.'

He frowned. 'Why?'

'Because your back muscles need one.'

A pained look passed over his face. 'My back muscles are fine.'

'They will be when I'm finished with them. This is one of the things I'm trained to do, remember? Therapeutic massage.' She bit back a grin. 'Honestly, anyone would think you're about to undergo a form of torture.'

'They'd be right.'

Now she did laugh. 'Get your kit off, lover. Then come and lie face-down on this bed.'

He raised his eyebrows, then took a large swig of his drink before placing their glasses down on the other side of the bed. 'That was going to be my line.'

Lola pouted. 'Poor baby. Would it help if we were both naked? Would that make this whole torturous experience less objectionable to you?'

'Wouldn't hurt.'

They eyed each other across the bed and, saying nothing, Lola reached behind her to pull down the zip of her dress. She slid the material off one shoulder, then the other.

Connor watched transfixed as she let the dress fall to her waist, revealing her bra. He only moved when Lola raised her eyebrows expectantly, and he slowly began unbuttoning his shirt.

It was Lola's turn to be mesmerised. With his heated gaze still fixed on hers, he tugged the unbuttoned shirt from his trousers to reveal the amazing muscled perfection of his chest. Her mouth positively watered as she imagined sliding her oiled hands over all that hard, masculine strength.

He tossed the shirt to the floor, then grinned. 'You next.'

Enjoying the game, she reached around and pulled the zip further down her back so the dress slid over her hips and to the floor. Then it was her turn to wait. But Connor didn't move.

'Haven't you forgotten something?' he asked with an arch of his eyebrow.

She glanced down at herself, then realised what he meant. She looked up, met the wicked gleam in his eyes then unhooked her bra. Only when she tossed it away, revealing her breasts to his hungry gaze, did he unhook his belt and draw it from the waistband of his trousers.

His slow striptease was really turning her on, and she hoped by the time they were both naked that she'd still be coherent enough to administer his massage.

When he was down to his boxers, he stood waiting again. 'Take them off. Make it slow.'

The now-familiar burn in her lower belly intensified, joining the throb of anticipation between her legs. But she couldn't let herself be distracted; she needed to work on Connor's back first. Ease some of that tension she'd felt beneath her hands when she'd checked him out.

Nevertheless, she'd promised him that they could both be naked when she massaged him. So she hooked her fingers into the sides of her panties and slowly lowered them down her legs to the floor, where she stepped out of them.

From across the bed, she heard Connor's breath hitch, saw his nostrils flare and his erection jerk hard against his boxers. He yanked off his boxers, his cock standing proud and ready.

Lola took a moment to enjoy the sight of him,

the exceptional physique and potent appeal, then she nodded. 'On the bed.'

She thought he would protest, say something like *You first*, but he did as she said. She had to wonder if his instant compliance was more to do with the prospect of having his sexual needs satisfied rather than having his non-sexual physical needs fulfilled.

She coaxed him into a prone position, noting how he pillowed his head on his folded arms and then turned so he could watch her. She poured some of the massage carrier oil into the bowl she used for mixing, then added several drops of lavender essential oil and some cooling eucalyptus, before pouring the mixture into an empty glass bottle.

'Smells like crap.'

She glanced down at him as she swirled the contents in the bottle. 'Open your mind to possibilities. This is going to make you feel really good.'

'If your intention is to make me feel good, then I've got a better idea. One that involves you lying beneath me with my cock inside you.'

'You've such a way with words, Connor. Romance just oozes from you, doesn't it?'

He turned his head a little more, a questioning glint in his eyes, making her wish she could take back what she'd said. Because romance didn't come into this thing between them; it was purely physical. It didn't matter that she was starting to want more. That she was enjoying the way he treated her like a woman who knew her own mind, who had good ideas, whose dream he validated and supported. It didn't matter that she enjoyed his quick wit, his attentive manner.

Because he didn't feel the same, and once he knew the truth she might not be able to convince him that what she felt for him wasn't all a lie. So this, right now, was all that mattered. Being with him, attempting to ease his discomfort, enjoying him.

Everything else could wait just a little longer.

She cleared her mind so she could tune in to Connor's needs. She picked up a small hand towel and placed it beside Connor's shoulders, then grabbed the bottle of mixed oils and got onto the bed.

He looked amazing. All that lean and honed muscle across his back, the wide shoulders, carved shoulder blades and well defined arms. She wanted to touch every square inch of him.

'This is more like it,' he said as she straddled him and her wet heat pressed against the crease of his buttocks. 'Your hot little pussy pressed against me is all the massage I need.'

'Try and switch off your thoughts,' Lola instructed, trying not to react to the feel of Connor's toned body against her. 'Soon, you'll be feeling so good that you could go all night.'

He gave a low hum, making her smile.

She rubbed her hands together, warming the oil between her palms before placing them either side of his lower spine.

His muscles tightened a fraction, then released as

she moved her hands in slow, circular movements. 'Put your attention on the area I'm touching and imagine your muscles relaxing.'

'Uh-huh.'

She smiled at his muted response, sliding her hands along his spine in a slow up-and-down then circular motion.

'How's that?' she asked softly when his breathing deepened, slowed.

'Not bad,' he said after a moment. 'You've got magical hands.'

'You're really tense around here.' She worked on the area beneath his waist. 'How did you hurt your back?'

His muscles tightened a fraction. 'Old history.'

'I'd really like to know. It might help me understand just how deep a massage I need to give you.'

It wouldn't necessarily help her to do that, but Lola really wanted to know more about him, and getting him to talk while he was in a relaxed state would likely be the best opportunity she would have for that to happen.

'Got into some scrapes while I was in foster care.'

Lola straightened. She hadn't expected him to say that, but now that he had she was intrigued.

'Father took off when we were kids. Mother left to go find him. The five of us kids were placed in care. Wasn't long before I acted up and they transferred me out, away from my siblings. Maybe I deserved it. I was a cocky little bastard.' He went silent for a moment, then drew in a long breath. 'You stopped stroking. I was enjoying it.'

'Sorry.' She began working his muscles again, taking extra care as myriad feelings vied for attention. Her heart squeezed at the image of a scared little boy acting up because he didn't know what was happening to him, to his family. Not only losing his parents, but being separated from his siblings.

Anger simmered deep inside her at a system that didn't recognise the effect of that kind of trauma on a child. 'You've got four brothers and sisters?'

'Yeah. Logan's the eldest. I'm next. Then there's Aiden and Ty, who are in the forces, and Colleen's the baby. She's at uni.'

She forced herself to keep her strokes light. 'How did you hurt your back?'

He raised his shoulders in a lazy shrug. 'Took a tumble down the stairs, courtesy of a bigger kid's boot.'

Her chest burned. 'Little shit.'

'Him, or me?' His low scoff should have eased the anger inside her, but it didn't.

'What happened after that?'

'Wasn't long before Logan got himself a job. Got us all back together again.'

Lola hadn't met Connor's eldest brother, but already she liked him without reservation.

She couldn't imagine that kind of childhood. Her father and brother were controlling, but she knew they loved her, protected her. And her mother and grandparents had adored her.

After a few moments, Connor stretched a little. 'Have to admit, that feels really good.'

'Tension and stress will tighten your back muscles and cause pain, especially since you have a weakness in that area. You really should take time to learn to relax.'

'Yeah.'

She continued to work on his back, warming and pouring more oil to aid her manipulation of his muscles. She could feel them loosening by degrees, his breathing really deep and his body relaxed.

She thought about what he'd told her, about the circumstances of his injury. Although anger still burned through her, she knew it wouldn't aid her massage ability, so she took some deep, cleansing breaths and willed her hands to relax.

She loved touching him, helping him, and it didn't hurt that she could feast on his spectacular body at the same time.

Unable to resist, she leaned down and pressed a light kiss to his neck, then across his shoulders and down his spine. The fragrance of the oils combined with Connor's own exquisite scent flooded her nostrils. She shifted back a little and kissed each of his ass cheeks. This guy was certainly built.

'Do I get to pour oil over you and kiss your ass next?'

It made her laugh. 'How does your back feel?'

'Good. Why don't we test it out?'

Deeply moved by what he'd told her, she wanted to help him even more. That, and the fact she was enjoying the feel of Connor's hot and pliable flesh beneath her hands. 'There's something else we could try that might help you relax deeper.'

'Now you're talking.'

'You might like this even more. It has dual benefits.'

'I'm all ears,' he said, turning to look at her with slumberous, sexy eyes. 'Well, not all ears. I'm pretty much a whole lot of cock at the moment too.'

To confirm his statement, he turned onto his back.

Lola laughed and shook her head. 'So I see.'

She straddled him again, making sure to keep away from his erection which threatened to press against her heated core. 'Have you heard of Tantric sex?'

'Yeah,' he said, his hands on her hips. 'It's the kinky stuff, right?'

'No. It's really slow sex. It can lead to incredibly powerful orgasms.'

That got his attention. He raised his eyebrows, his hands leaving her hips to cup her breasts, his thumbs stroking slowly across her hardening nipples. 'Tell me more.'

'It's been around for thousands of years. It involves prolonging arousal.'

'Go on. I'm riveted.'

She kept her face impassive because she needed him to understand the real nature and purpose of the practice. 'You have to stick with it, Connor. Have to step out of your comfort zone. You can't change your mind halfway through and go for the whole wham-bam thing instead. It involves a lot of slow, steady touching.'

'I can do slow,' he said, illustrating his point by languidly sliding his hand across her stomach. 'And I can do steady.'

'I'll need to teach you a full yogic breath. Controlling your breathing is a fundamental part of Tantric sex. Now, are we doing this or not?'

He shifted on the bed, as if getting comfortable. 'Go for it.'

'Okay.' Still straddling him, she got comfortable herself, thinking how bizarre it was teaching someone how to breathe deeply while you were both stark-naked and one of you had a massive erection. 'Close your eyes. Concentrate on your exhalation.'

Surprisingly, he picked up the technique really fast, and before long was taking good, deep breaths.

He opened his eyes. 'When do we get to the good stuff?'

'This is the good stuff. It's not just about getting off. Do you know what chakras are?'

He grinned. 'Kinda'

She talked him through each one, pleased that he paid attention, although his hands found her hips again, his fingers possessively digging into her.

Closing her eyes, she deepened her own breathing. When she opened them again it was to find him watching her. 'You're so fucking beautiful.'

It knocked her sideways for a moment. Not just because of what he'd said, but the way he'd said it.

As if he was seeing deep inside her, looking past the superficial to what lay deeper beneath the surface.

It unsettled her, pushed at the guilt that she'd tried to put away for one more night. When he tried to pull her down against him, she batted his hands away. 'You're losing focus.'

He gave a lazy grin. 'I like my focus.'

'I'm going to touch you really slowly,' she said, battling to concentrate. 'You're going to breathe through it, and you're going to concentrate on being in the present. If you feel like you're going to come, pull the energy up from the base of your spine to the top of your head.'

He raised his eyebrows, his grin widening. 'The top of my head?'

'Connor. Are you going to take this seriously?'

He sobered, but she knew it took everything he had. It was his first introduction to esoteric practices and it was natural for people to be circumspect when they didn't know what to expect.

She took in a deep breath, filling her lungs with the fragrant oils and the heady scent of Connor, then placed her hands on his chest and slowly circled her hands over his skin, teasing his nipples.

It didn't take long before he cupped her breasts, brushing his thumbs across her nipples and sending delicious thrills through the entire length of her body. She shifted against him, rubbing her heat against his impressive erection, but making sure to take it really slowly and sensually, reminding herself that this was about the journey, about exploring each other, about making it last.

Soon they were both breathing heavily, with no thought of control, or of stringing things out. Connor curled his fingers deeper into her hips and held her tight as he flipped them both until she was on her back and he was leaning over her.

'Your back...'

'Is feeling great,' he ground out as he slid his hand between her legs. 'Those magic hands of yours.'

He had magic of his own, Lola thought while she still could. In his hands, and just about everywhere else. He pushed his finger in deep, sliding in and out in a slow and drugging rhythm until Lola was trying to delay her own orgasm.

She didn't want this to end. Not just the slow and easy way they were together like this, but her time with Connor. Deep inside her she knew she was on borrowed time, and she couldn't deny the truth of that even as Connor brought her closer and closer to the edge.

Not wanting to let that truth take root, she focused on what she'd told him and slowed down her breathing as her inner muscles began to contract. She pulled the energy from between her legs, imagined drawing it up her spine to the top of her head and found herself gasping for both air and control.

Connor withdrew his hand and reached out for a condom. Vaguely, Lola knew he'd covered himself and she opened her legs as he moved between them.

With his hands braced either side of her shoulders, he looked at her, their gazes connecting and holding, and Lola felt something move through her that was at once powerful, amazing and discomfiting. She sensed that Connor was fighting to keep control. He was trying hard to do what she'd told him and take this really slowly.

'Think I've just about reached the end of my journey,' he said as he nudged her opening. 'So, unless you object, I'm heading straight for my destination.'

Lola wanted to tell him it was okay, that she'd reached the end of her journey too. She was primed to take him inside her, to feel the length of him fill her and take them where they both needed to go.

Journey's end.

Instead, he took it slowly, his gaze locked to hers as he pushed in an inch before he withdrew, then another inch, and again a withdrawal. It was exquisite: the friction, the heat, the sheer girth of him. Each time he pushed forward, she gripped him hard, holding tight as he withdrew and earning a deep groan.

Like her, she knew he hovered at the edge of orgasm and, loving his attempt to keep things slow for as long as possible, she wanted to return the favour.

Reaching between them, she called on her theoretical knowledge of the practice and pressed her fingers beneath his balls. She was rewarded with a sharp, 'Fuck'.

'Sorry…'

He held above her, gritting his teeth, his eyes

squeezed tight for a few moments. Then he opened them and shook his head. 'Don't apologise. That's taken the edge off.'

'Really?' She released her hands and brought them to his shoulders. 'It was supposed to.'

He pushed inside her, a little deeper this time, before withdrawing again. 'Are you close?'

As if he had to ask. Surely her gasps and moans were indicative of her nearness to orgasm? But she nodded. 'Yes.'

Still moving slowly, but making sure he didn't push too deep, he dropped a kiss to her mouth. 'Want me to stop for a while? Slow things down?'

When she shook her head, gripping his shoulders tighter, he brought a hand down to her knee and raised her leg higher. The movement allowed him to push deeper and this time he drove in all the way.

Lola gasped and clung to him. 'Oh, hell. That's…'

The angle at which he penetrated her allowed him to rub against her slick walls and hit the exact spot where she didn't think any amount of Tantric knowledge would stop her from coming. She was powerless. Completely and desperately defenceless against the spasms that flung her over some metaphoric wall where everything was shot with colour, light and pure sensation.

*Nirvana*, she thought as the orgasm went on and on. This had to be the closest to nirvana anyone could get on this earthly plane.

With each shove inside her, Connor grunted, then

he was coming too, and she could feel each frenzied release reverberate inside her.

Their gazes clashed again and held. Their breathing was unsteady, gasping.

Connor blew out a long breath through his mouth, then dropped his forehead to hers. 'That was…some journey.'

Lola managed a smile as she reached up and brushed the back of her fingers along his stubbly jaw, her hands not quite steady. In fact, nothing about her felt steady. Her world had been rocked, shaken. 'Destination was pretty good too.'

His gaze held hers and for an instant she glimpsed something raw and unexpected in his grey depths. Had he been as affected by what they'd just shared as she had been? Had he experienced a tumble into the unknown, a wrench away from the norm? Whatever it was disappeared beneath the flash of his grin. 'How long before we can take the return trip? That squeezing thing you did was pretty neat.'

'I didn't do it right,' Lola said, still trying to make sense of what she'd glimpsed in his eyes. 'You came too soon afterward. Maybe I didn't press hard enough or long enough. Done right, you're supposed to be able to go for hours before climaxing.'

Connor's eyebrows rose. 'Anywhere I can press to stop you from coming so fast?'

'It's not so vital for women. Multiple orgasms, remember?'

'Even so. This Tantric thing has something to recommend it. Maybe I'll make a study of it.'

For some reason, his statement made her feel ridiculously pleased. Probably because he actually seemed serious, although she did wonder if he was just being glib. Whatever, she loved the fact that he hadn't dismissed it as being out there or new age, and seemed willing to keep an open mind.

She wanted to tell him they could do lots more practising, but that spectre of guilt hung between them. After her revelations she doubted there'd be any kind of relationship between them, let alone one that involved experimental sex.

A hollow feeling settled in her stomach, but she wasn't about to let it ruin what had been an amazing experience, so once more she locked it down inside her and refused to dwell on what she couldn't have.

Connor eased away from her and rolled onto his back. He didn't look at her as he asked, 'Have you tried anything like this before?'

'No. Any knowledge is theoretical.' She rolled onto her side and hiked onto her elbow, looking down at him to gauge his reaction. 'Although I have considered learning more about it and maybe adding it to my repertoire. I could give lessons.'

His head whipped around and the look of horror on his face was priceless, until he realised she was ribbing him.

'Give me some time to recover and I'll help you with a lesson plan.'

# CHAPTER TEN

LOLA WOKE IN the early hours with Connor's arm around her shoulder, her head on his chest. She hadn't planned to stay the night again, but that Tantric session seemed to have wiped them both out.

She angled her head to look up at him and saw he was in a deep and seemingly restful sleep. The urge to wake him was strong; she couldn't seem to get enough of being with him. But she left him to it. The quality of sleep after a massage was often the purest form of rest. Not to mention the benefits of a hefty session of good and wholesome sex.

Carefully, Lola got off the bed and, as Connor's shirt was the nearest item of clothing, she shrugged into it, loving how his smell wrapped around her.

She fastened a couple of shirt buttons at her waist, checked the candles and oils had burned right out, then made her way to his kitchen. Interesting. His counters were clear, the whole space pristine-clean. Perhaps not unusual for a man who probably didn't spend much time at home. Despite that he'd taken some time having coffee with her in the middle of

the day, she sensed he was a workaholic, and probably spent more time travelling back and forth between his two clubs than anything else.

Lola found a glass and poured herself water. She
turned and leaned back against the sink, her gaze
landing on the breakfast bar in front of the large
floor-to-ceiling window that looked out over the
capital as it came awake in the soft glow of early
morning.

On the black marble counter lay a scattering of
papers, and on top of the pile was a copy of what
looked like the agent details for the Cabacal property. Lola walked over and picked up the document,
scanning the photos and the descriptions beneath
them. She stroked lovingly across the photographs
of the old Art-Deco-style building, remembering vis-
its with her mother when she was a child. Back then
her grandparents had been alive and the building had
housed a small exclusive cabaret club.

But Lola's mother had always planned that when
it became hers she would turn it into a fitness and
wellbeing studio with the sole intention of helping
people live better, healthier lives. It had caught Lola's
imagination from the start, and she'd listened with
rapt attention as her mother had declared what the
various rooms would be used for: the colours, the
equipment, the classes she'd planned. Lola had been
inspired, and from then on it had become her dream
too. Until her devious uncle had changed everything.

Saddened by old memories, she placed the details

back down, noticing the wad of official-looking documents off to the side.

The contract, Lola thought. For the sale of the property.

She tilted her head, trying to get a good look at the papers without actually touching them, all the while instructing herself to turn around and walk away. Was Connor in the process of reading through the document before he signed it? Wouldn't that be done in a lawyer's office? Why did he have the paperwork at home? Left so haphazardly on the breakfast counter? Was this just a mock-up of the real thing that Damian had sent?

Lola took a breath, then put down the glass. It wouldn't hurt just to take a peek, would it? She wasn't sure why she was torturing herself, but morbid fascination drove her onward. Maybe there was something in the contract, some clause, that could provide her with ammunition to persuade Connor to sell the property to her when she was in a position to buy it. Her fingers crept dangerously close to the bottom edge of the paper, but she pulled them back.

She couldn't do it. It wasn't right. It was intrusive, invasive and downright dishonest.

Connor had been good enough to try and help her with the properties he thought she was interested in. He'd taken her to each one and pointed out pluses and minuses. Okay, they'd punctuated their viewings with some very enjoyable back-street sex, but that wasn't the point.

He'd been interested in helping her. Which meant that she had no business snooping. Besides, she knew what was in the contract, the terms of the agreement. Damian had told her, labouring the point: full and final sale. As if she needed reminding.

It was strange, really. Connor was obviously willing to pay an extremely competitive price for the place, yet he'd admitted to having no real plans for it, and had even considered allowing it to remain empty for the foreseeable future. He hadn't really seemed that interested in it.

What exactly was the pull of the place for him? Why did he feel compelled to own it?

She knew how strong that compulsion could be, and although the property held wonderful memories for her she imagined Connor would rather forget what had happened to him.

As she mused about reasons, her hands found the countertop. Before she could stop herself, she nudged back the edge of the papers and flicked through them. All legal jargon, with the usual sections and clauses. No mention of intended use anywhere that she could see, but that wasn't unusual. If Connor planned another nightclub, it wasn't so far removed from the casino that her uncle had used it for.

Her eyes almost popped out of her head when her gaze fell on the agreed purchase price. How much? It wasn't just over the market value advertised but was more than Lola's trust fund could cover. Her heart took a dive along with her stomach. How was she supposed to persuade Connor to sell to her at a much lower price than he had agreed to pay for it?

Disheartened, Lola let the pages fall back and straightened the contract on the counter. But beneath it was more papers. She didn't even think about not looking now. Surely there was nothing else that could surprise her? Slowly, she drew out the remaining documents.

Pages of blue letterhead held a series of price quotations for construction work. Yes! Now she might get an idea of what Connor planned to do with the place.

The top quote was for some restructuring at the club where she'd first met him, to add a small rear patio area with lighting and outside heating.

The quote underneath made her heart stop.

*To carry out demolition work at premises in south west London currently known as the Cabacal Club.*

Demolition? Was he having it torn down?

Lola stared at the quote, reading every word over and over, as if she might have misread them. As if that word 'demolition' was actually something else. But it wasn't. He was having the property demolished.

She couldn't seem to swallow, couldn't stay the nausea that swam in her stomach. For long moments she just stood there in the quiet of Connor's kitchen, staring at the words which now blurred as her eyes went damp.

She shoved the quotes back beneath the contract

and stepped away from the counter, as if doing so would make what she'd just seen disappear. She sniffed, squeezed her eyes shut as anger coated the nausea.

There was no way she would stand back and let this happen. No way she'd let him destroy that wonderful old building.

She snatched up the property details again, knowing what a travesty it would be to tear down all that old architecture, all that wonderful marble and inlaid panelling. She thought about how her great-grandfather had built the property as a testament to the love he felt for his wife. How it had stood for almost a century, through turmoil and change, only to be obliterated from the face of the earth because Connor wanted some kind of payback.

If he went ahead and tore it down, then her mother's dreams for the property would be gone for ever, because then there was no way Lola could make them happen.

She smoothed her hand over the details again, searching for some way to convince him to change his plans and preserve the old building. If he really didn't want it, then why couldn't he sell it on to her? She had to talk to Connor. Had to tell him about her mother, how she'd been cheated out of the property. Maybe she could make him see that, like him, her mother had been a casualty of her uncle's treachery. That if he allowed her to buy the Cabacal back he'd be helping her put things right.

She heard a sound behind her and turned to see

Connor lazing against the door frame, his eyes languid, like a man just roused from sleep, but with an intensity in his gaze that was hard to miss.

Her first instinct was to lash out at him, demand he tell her what the hell he was thinking, demolishing such a wonderful building, but she couldn't do that. He might, quite rightly, do some lashing out of his own. He still didn't know who she was, or what the building meant to her. And that was down to her own cowardice in not telling him before now.

As it stood, he had every right to do what he wanted with his new purchase. But she wasn't going to give up without a damn good fight.

Connor didn't like how he'd woken from a deep, relaxing sleep and his first thought had been Lola. What they'd shared had been intense and unsettling. Not just the slow sex stuff, but the way she'd gotten him to open up about his past. He rarely talked about that. The last time he'd been persuaded to reveal his past, it had been used against him.

He'd learned long ago that women had their own agendas. They could wheedle every little bit of information from you and then twist it and turn it to accommodate their own desires.

Sounds from the kitchen stopped his thoughts from spiralling downward. He needed a distraction, and that meant getting Lola back to bed for some early-morning activity. He found her deep in thought and poring over some papers. His papers.

The sharp nudge of suspicion squeezed his chest.

What the hell was she doing reading his personal documents?

'Found something interesting?'

Lola started, the papers fluttering to the floor. 'Sorry.'

She picked them up quickly, then stacked them on the counter, her eyes not meeting his. It hiked his suspicion several notches, until he realised that he'd left the property details for the Cabacal in full view, and it was probably perfectly natural she'd take a look, given she was searching for a property of her own.

Was he just being paranoid?

'You should drink some water,' she said, coming across and handing it to him. 'You need to rehydrate after a massage.'

'I know what else I need after a massage.' He took the water, noting how her hands trembled a little. Was she unnerved because he'd startled her? Caught her snooping? He felt that poke of suspicion again, until he reasoned that this was Lola, not Caroline. Lola had always been upfront and had never given him reason not to trust her.

Yeah. He was likely being paranoid.

He placed the glass down and slipped his arms around her.

'My shirt looks good on you.'

'It was the nearest thing I could find.'

Although she laid her hands on his biceps, her manner was reserved, her voice tight. She didn't meet his eyes. He frowned, placing his hand beneath her chin and coaxing her to look at him. 'Everything okay?'

She gave a wan smile. 'Of course. How are you feeling?'

'Good.' Actually, he felt more than good. He felt fucking amazing. Except he knew there was most definitely something wrong with her. Was she still concerned with his wellbeing?

He didn't need that, or want it. He could look after himself.

From nowhere came the memory of concerned eyes looking down at him. That look had warmed all his cold parts until he'd discovered the duplicity, the treachery that could lie beneath feigned concern and the need for a scapegoat. Caroline had been an expert at deceit, making him believe she cared for him when all the time she'd been making plans behind his back to destroy him.

Shit. He needed to get his attention away from the past. Lola had stirred up things with her questions last night, and it was fucking up the good times. Good times he wasn't quite ready to end.

That knowledge was troubling in itself, but at least he had his finger on the pulse. Had his wits about him. He knew what he was doing. And right now that meant coaxing her back to bed, enjoying some early-morning sex. And in doing so he'd put a smile back on both their faces.

He popped open the three buttons at her waist, then slipped the shirt from her shoulders.

'The effects of your magic hands are wearing off a little. I'm thinking you should give me a refresher.'

He tossed the shirt to the floor and, wanting to demonstrate just how good his back felt, he hiked her up into his arms.

She stiffened against him, but her hands landed on his shoulders. 'You should take care for a while. No sudden movements.'

'Told you,' he said as he strode back to the bedroom. 'It's fine.'

'Just take things slowly for a while so you can gauge how it really is.'

'Oh, I can do that.' He deliberately misinterpreted her meaning, turning to the bed and taking his time lowering her down. 'There. Slow.'

Lola sighed as he moved over her, but her demeanour felt stilted. 'You really need to pace yourself. When you're stressed, you don't take the time to think things through. That's when you can end up making snap decisions that are irreversible. It never hurts to consider things from all angles.'

He searched his memory banks for a conversation they'd had which would make sense of what she'd just said, but found nothing. 'No need for concern on that front. I'm a man who considers every single angle.' Wanting to ease whatever was bothering her, he waggled his eyebrows. 'Or hadn't you noticed.'

'Connor, I'm really sorry for snooping, but I couldn't help noticing the property details on your counter.'

'Yeah. I saw you reading them.'

She took a huge breath. 'Are you really thinking of having that building demolished?'

He felt the punch in his solar plexus. He didn't much care about her looking at the property details, but he certainly didn't like the fact she'd gone through his private correspondence. It didn't pay to let anyone think they had more of a part in your life than you were prepared to give them. And Connor wasn't prepared to give an inch. When he gave that inch, the shit tended to hit the fan. 'That's my business.'

'Like I said, I'm truly sorry, but it's such a wonderful building.'

Not for him, it wasn't. The sooner the place was razed to the ground, the sooner he could draw a solid line under the past and start a new chapter.

'It's called progress,' he said, rolling onto his back. He felt irritated, both by her prying and by the fact she'd made him think back too much in the space of a few short hours. He'd felt too comfortable sharing things with her last night, and there was no space for that in their relationship. Their time wasn't meant for conversation, it was meant for hot, dirty sex.

She hiked onto her side and looked down at him. 'Progress doesn't mean destroying what's good about the past.'

'Believe me, there's nothing much good about that.'

'That's surely not true? Even with what you told

me last night, there had to be some good things, some good memories.'

'Yeah.' He thought about the moment Logan had brought his siblings out of foster care so they could live as a family again. It had been the happiest moment of his life. 'Maybe one or two.'

'Have I told you about my mother?'

Dangerous territory, Connor thought. Hadn't he warned himself against this? Against shooting things between them to another level?

'My mother was a yoga instructor,' Lola said before he could distract her. 'At the time she started teaching, the premise was way out there. My father didn't understand. He used to call it hippy nonsense. When he knew I wanted to follow the same path as my mum, he was livid. He insisted I get a business degree, obviously hoping that during my time at university I'd come to my senses.'

Connor frowned. He didn't hold with the idea of a parent manipulating a child and controlling them. Not that his father had been Dad of the Year. His old man hadn't been bothered enough to stay in his kids' lives, let alone try and manipulate them.

'At first, I wanted to tell my father to get stuffed. That I didn't need the carrot of a trust fund to achieve my dreams. But then I realised having a business degree was a wise step to take, considering my plans, and I certainly wouldn't have been able to afford to run my own studio if I didn't have the trust fund. So, like it or not, I was kind of over a barrel.'

Connor thought that she eyed him with the same look that a person watching an angry snake would have. Cautious. Wary. He had a feeling she thought he would judge her for doing her father's bidding. For accepting the trust fund.

'We have to take our breaks where we can,' he said with a shrug. 'No point looking gift horses in the mouth. And we're all products of our childhoods, like it or not. And sometimes not just our child-hoods.'

'What do you mean?'

He gave another shrug, not wanting to indulge in any more revelations about his past, but she looked so unsure, he wrapped his arm around her and coaxed her to lie back. When she settled against him, he drew her close so that her hand settled on his chest.

'My own particular gift horse came at a time when I was trying to prove something,' he said. 'Prove that I was better than my old man. That I could stick to something, make something of myself. Got myself involved in a situation where I should have trusted my instincts and walked away.'

'But you didn't?'

'No. I didn't have a trust fund dangled in front of me, but the carrot was too juicy for me to walk away from. I got the opportunity to work for a man who ran a string of successful casinos throughout Lon-don. He took me under his wing, eventually offered me manager at his flagship club.'

He couldn't be certain, but he thought he felt her

tense a little against him. Then she shifted, relaxed, and he wondered if he'd imagined it.

'For a while things were great, then something happened and everything changed.' Beneath the steady stroke of Lola's fingers, Connor's chest tightened as he thought again of Caroline, of how she'd slowly coerced him to do her bidding and how he'd slowly begun to tie the noose around his own neck.

He took a breath, working to find the words to give Lola the potted version, and avoid having to dig too deep into the nitty-gritty. 'The guy I worked for was involved in some dubious dealings and, when he slipped up, I was right in the firing line.'

'What happened?'

'I was arrested.'

She didn't react, not even a snatched breath of shock, a momentary gasp or incredulous flutter of eyelashes. All she did was keep stroking her fingers soothingly across his chest.

'I was falsely accused of embezzlement,' he found himself confessing. 'Took my eye off the ball and managed to get myself into a shit-load of trouble. My fault. Should have kept my finger on the pulse, trusted those instincts.' He shrugged. 'Still, lesson learned.'

'I can't believe you can say that so calmly,' Lola said as she looked up at him. 'You were arrested for something you didn't do.'

'It was a hard lesson learned. Taught me to rely on my instincts and never doubt them again. I chose to trust someone I shouldn't have trusted, even after I'd started having doubts.'

She quickly looked away, then rested her head against his chest. Maybe it was because she wasn't pushing for more information that he found his tongue loosening even more.

'That property I just bought was the one I used to manage. I poured everything I had into that place and it came to represent what I wanted in life. Success. Personal achievement and satisfaction. Wealth.'

He took a moment to catch his breath as it backed up in his lungs. 'I thought I had a tight handle on everything that went on in that casino, but my arrogance made me myopic. Looking back, I realise I didn't want to acknowledge what my instincts said. I wanted to go on believing everything was legit because, if it wasn't, what did that say about my judgement?' He sighed, as if to help disperse the tension lodged in his chest. 'But I couldn't ignore it forever. The dodgy dealings…the dirty money. Before I could confront the owner, tell him I knew what was happening, the police arrived to arrest me.'

Her fingers stopped gliding over his chest. 'That's terrible.'

He thought again of Caroline. Of what she'd done. He'd fallen in love with her, assuring himself that she felt the same. He'd been bloody besotted with her. That was the only reason he could think of for his temporary insanity. The truth was he'd trusted her. He hadn't for one moment considered she had an ulterior motive. That motive being setting him up as the fall guy when the shit had hit the proverbial fan.

It was only when he'd been arrested that he realised he'd been set up to take the fall.

It was a story as old as freaking time: man trusts a woman too readily and ends up getting his balls sliced.

'How long before the police released you?'

'Pretty fast. Luckily they found evidence to prove I'd been set up. After what happened, I just wanted to see the place gutted, obliterated.'

'I'm so sorry, Connor.'

Lola's heartfelt words and her gentle touch were so comforting that Connor pulled her over him. He wanted to see her face, look into her eyes, have her as close to him as he could get her.

Her softness, her understanding, was like a balm to him. Perhaps a woman like her could make him believe that things could be different. That he could let go of that defensive wall he'd built around himself. Maybe even learn to trust again.

As she straddled him, she placed her hands on his chest and leaned down. 'You really didn't deserve what happened to you.'

She slipped her hands to his shoulders, leaning further down and placing a kiss to his mouth. It was tender, the pressure firm and determined. Connor felt something shift inside him. It had been a long time since he'd felt so raw, so pulled apart. Longer still since he'd allowed himself to remember the finer details of what had happened that night five years ago. He layered the painful memories beneath his desire to draw the line under that part of his life, to take his own brand of revenge on the family who had tried to destroy him by becoming the owner of what was the symbol of his downfall.

Lola's kiss seemed to soften all the rough edges, soothe the turmoil those memories had unleashed. She was making him wonder about a better way, if maybe his desire to stick that final pin in the bubble of bad memories was worth the angst. Would he do better to let it go? Move on?

A thought came to him. Lola had wanted a studio in central London, and the properties she'd shown him were so different from the Cabacal he couldn't imagine it would suit her needs. Yet, what better way to draw that line under his past than see the property used for positive means? A place where people could go to be de-stressed, rejuvenated, invigorated.

It seemed fitting somehow.

He would run it past her. She could always say no.

But right now wasn't the time for that particular discussion. Not when she was kissing along his jaw, down his throat. Tender yet determined kisses that sent blood through his veins in a frenzy that belied the softness of her touch.

He'd think on it some more. Maybe drop a few hints along the way as to whether she'd be interested in using the Cabacal for her studio. He didn't want to make her feel uncomfortable. He should probably first try and discover what level of trust fund they were talking about. Since she was looking at central London for a venue, he couldn't imagine she was sitting on anything other than a substantial sum.

Maybe he'd offer to rent it to her first, then she could take her time deciding if it was going to be the right fit.

He'd give it some more thought. Maybe sound her out first.

Until then…

He placed his hands around her hips, anchoring her as she straddled him. She straightened, all that amazing hair tumbling around her shoulders, brushing against her nipples.

She stroked the back of her hand across his cheek. 'I'm so sorry for what happened to you, Connor.'

'Hey, it's not your fault,' he said as her green eyes went misty. 'We've all got our story to tell.'

'Maybe.'

He hated that she looked so sad, so reflective. Things had gotten far too heavy. His confess-all moment had dampened the mood. This wasn't what either of them had signed up for.

He held tightly to her hips and reversed their positions, making her laugh. 'I'm starting to think you've got a problem with me being on top.'

'I don't have a problem with any position you're in,' he said, leaning down to take one very desirable nipple into his mouth. 'As long as that position involves you being naked.'

He glanced up, expecting to find her expression one of mock censure, but instead she had that pensive expression again.

He tapped his finger to the worried lines between her eyebrows. 'What's with the solemn look?'

'Just thinking.' She took a breath. 'Nothing is ever black and white, is it? You think you've got things sussed, that you really know what you want, and then it all comes crashing down and you end up having to rethink it all out again. Find a new way to achieve your plans.'

'Huh?' Connor wasn't entirely sure what she meant, but then it wasn't exactly his brain that was spinning its gears right then.

She shook her head. 'Ignore me. Just thinking out loud.'

With a smile, she reached for him. 'Why don't we find something to do until the sun really breaks through? Then you can make me breakfast.'

Connor could get on board with that. He breathed a sigh of relief, sensing they'd left the deep and meaningful discussion behind and were now back to the fun stuff. He knew his way around pre-breakfast activities of the between-the-sheets variety, and he could certainly negotiate that far better than the heavy talk that had left Lola looking so downcast.

He moved between her legs, intent on really putting that smile back on her face.

# CHAPTER ELEVEN

LOLA HAD KNOWN most of what Connor had told her, and she'd kind of filled in the blanks herself about what she hadn't known. But having *him* tell her what had happened to him—hearing the anger, the hurt and, yes, the self-loathing in his tone—made it so much worse. Her uncle, a man he'd looked up to, who had basically mentored him, had allowed him to be charged when he was completely innocent.

As the tube she was travelling on entered a tunnel, she looked beyond the window and into the darkness. It kind of suited her mood.

If she'd hated her uncle before because of what he had done to her mother, she hated him even more now because of what he'd done to Connor. She knew it was bad to have feelings like that, and she knew she should try and turn her anger into something more constructive. She remembered that saying about how being angry at someone was like drinking poison and expecting the other person to die.

The problem was, she couldn't help it. Her uncle had been so manipulative and cruel. He'd cheated her mother out of her dreams and he'd almost cheated Connor out of his liberty. He'd made Connor question himself when all Connor had wanted was to do a good job, be a good manager and make some of his dreams come true. She didn't think she could ever forgive her uncle for that.

She'd felt so close to Connor as he'd told her of his past, as he'd opened up to her, yet the guilt was never far away. He still didn't know who she really was or what she wanted. After he'd been so honest about his own past, she'd had the perfect opportunity to come clean, but she couldn't do it. She couldn't hurt him further by admitting that she had also deceived him. Instead she'd wanted to comfort him, hold him, make love to him and provide a salve for his wounds.

Admitting the truth became harder the more time they spent together, yet no matter how bad she felt it didn't seem to stop the wanting.

Somehow her own feelings had grown past the purely physical and had developed into something deeper and more profound. There was so much about him that she respected and admired.

His single-mindedness, for instance. His ability to forge through adversity and come out the other end, determined to make the most of it. He'd had what sounded like a rotten childhood, and then he'd been badly betrayed and falsely accused by someone he'd thought he could trust. Yet he'd refused to be beaten down by his experiences and instead had used them, learned from them and made the most of his opportunities.

Maybe Damian was right. Connor was owed the Cabacal. For him, it was symbolic, and he deserved to have the satisfaction of owning the property that had been instrumental in bringing him down so low.

But that didn't mean she would stop fighting for the property. While she understood what it represented for him, there was no way she was going to stand by and allow him to raze the building to the ground.

'You're a chatty little thing this morning.'

Lola turned to see Emily's raised eyebrows as they travelled towards Clapham where Lola taught three yoga sessions on Mondays, finishing early afternoon. Emily attended the first of Lola's classes and then headed back for her shift at a local coffee shop.

'Sorry.' Lola shook her head. 'Just trying to work things out.'

'Things? As in, certain sexy nightclub owner?'

Lola sighed. 'Him and other stuff.'

Emily had tried to convince Lola that she should walk away from both the Cabacal and Connor. She thought Lola was in too deep and that whatever she did from then on would only cause her hurt and pain. She'd argued that if Lola walked away now she would never have to admit the truth of who she was or reveal her original plans.

For Lola, neither was an option. She couldn't walk

away from the Cabacal and she couldn't walk away from Connor.

What they'd had on that first night was meant to be fun, but somehow it had morphed into far more. At least for her. She'd started to imagine building a relationship with him even before he'd given her glimpses into his past. He didn't share things easily, but he'd shared them with her.

Slowly, she'd been falling for him.

'I'm a bloody idiot,' Lola murmured to herself, but the nudge to her ribs signalled that Emily had heard.

'No, you just fell hard for a hot guy who happened to see you as an intelligent woman capable of achieving her dreams. He's probably the first man in your life who's actually supported you rather than thrown obstacles in your way.'

The concern in Emily's eyes made Lola feel worse. She hadn't betrayed Connor's confidence by telling Emily what had happened to him, or his reasons for wanting the property. That really *was* his business. But she had told her friend that she was really starting to like him.

'I should have come clean to Connor right from the start. Maybe he would have understood.'

'And maybe he wouldn't.'

'True,' Lola said, her heart weighing heavily beneath the enormity of what she knew had to be done. 'But I have to tell him the truth.'

He deserved that. If afterward he didn't trust her enough to continue to be with her, or if she lost the

Cabacal in the process, he still deserved to know everything.

Her heart clawed at her throat, stealing her breath. There was no other way.

She had to tell Connor.

All her classes were full that day, but it didn't keep her from thinking about her impending confession and its potential consequences.

She intended to talk to Connor as soon as her work day was over. There was absolutely no point in delaying any longer.

Connor was a reasonable man, wasn't he? Surely he'd allow her to explain what she'd done and why she'd done it? He knew what it was like to be exploited, used. Surely he would see that her mother had been treated the same way, and how important it was for Lola to make things right.

She'd make him see, make him understand, and she wouldn't stop until she did.

It was hard to imagine not seeing him again, not having him in her life. But the possibility sat like a heavy brick on her chest, making her stomach feel hollow.

Without him, there would be a big yearning gap now. Because she'd let him sneak right under her skin and straight into her heart.

While she packed up her things after her class, her phone buzzed. Since they'd exchanged numbers before she'd left his place earlier, she wasn't entirely surprised that it was Connor.

'Finished for the day?' Her heart leapt at the sound of his deep voice, its rich tone edged with velvet. 'If you don't have any plans, maybe we could meet up. There's something I'd like to show you.'

She couldn't be distracted by the fact he wanted to see her, or that he'd remembered her classes ended early on a Monday. She had to keep focused. 'Connor. I need to talk to you.'

'Then why don't you grab a taxi and come on over?'

Before she could ask where he was, he rattled off an address which made her heart stop.

He was at the Cabacal.

Mixed feelings vied for attention: the pleasure of seeing the property again…the pleasure of seeing Connor again…but taking priority was the fact she'd be revealing her identity to him in the very place they both wanted. The place that stood between them.

If he didn't plan to demolish the building before, he certainly would after she'd told him she'd been lying to him.

Lola spent the taxi journey mentally rehearsing how to start the conversation she'd been dreading, her nerves escalating with each moment that passed. To make matters worse, what should have taken fifteen minutes took more than double that thanks to emergency road works. Unable to sit still any longer, Lola paid the driver, gathered her bags and walked the remaining half-mile to the property.

It was a good area, bordering the River Thames,

and, while busy, it was not so heavily populated with visitors as the rest of the city.

The weather was fine, so the sun sparkled on the surface of the water, reminding Lola of the times when she and her mother had come to visit and had chosen to sit on the stone steps leading down to the water's edge, where they'd talk about anything and everything.

It wasn't just memories of her mother that constricted her heart as she sat and looked out over the river now. It was the possibility she might lose Connor. What if she couldn't convince him that she had never meant to hurt him by keeping her identity a secret? What if he saw her silence as a sharp betrayal and was determined not to forgive her?

Her vision began to blur but since tears wouldn't solve anything, she inhaled deeply, gave herself a metaphorical dusting down then stood. She'd come here for a reason. She had to get on with it.

A short walk brought the Cabacal into view. She'd seen the outside several times while it had been unoccupied, but even neglect couldn't diminish the sheer beauty of the exterior. Like a sponge, Lola soaked up the architectural details. Art Deco in style, with a flat roof covering its geometrical shape, angular corners and large curved windows. Testament to an elegant time now long since past.

She wondered how the interior chrome, decorative glass motifs and beautiful limestone floor would look. Probably dulled and sullied—five years of neglect would do that—but likely still as stunning beneath the surface. It bordered on criminal, allowing a beautiful place like the Cabacal to rot this way.

It was even more criminal to have it demolished, although she intended to fight that possibility with everything she had. There had to be a way to make Connor change his mind.

'Hey.'

Lola swung round, dropping her yoga bag in the process, and her gaze met Connor's. Dressed in a sharp business suit, he stood at the side entrance of the property, smiling.

He strolled towards her, his sexy grin warming the icy little pockets of discomfort that had settled inside her. 'You look good,' he said, sliding his hands around her waist and pulling her close up against him. 'Smell good, too.'

How was it that he could set all her nerve endings alight just by breathing? How could he make every thought and worry disappear so that all she could think about was being in his arms?

He leaned down and took her mouth in a deep, passionate kiss, his hold on her tightening as the kiss went on. She tried to resist, tried to break away from him, but his pull on her was just too great. So she sank into the kiss and just let herself be with him while the inevitable confession nudged at her conscience.

When his hold on her eased a fraction, he looked down at her and smiled. 'How was your day?'

Her hands lay heavily on his shoulders, as if the weight of what she held inside her fused at that point. She hoped those broad shoulders would withstand the battering they would receive so that they could both find a way through the resultant storm.

'I really need to talk to you.'

'Same here.' His sexy wink turned her already feeble legs to mush. 'Want to see inside?' He picked up her yoga bag and grabbed her hand.

Thanks to her mental rehearsal in the taxi, she thought she'd had her moves all planned out, but he'd stripped all that away. 'Inside?'

'Yeah, as in through the front door. Then I get to kiss you the way I really want to kiss you, out of the glare of prying eyes.' He brought her closer again, his smile fading as he looked at her. She felt the punch of his intense gaze right down to her toes. 'I've really missed you.'

His hoarse tone had an awkward edge, as if he'd summoned the words and their meaning from a deep, dark cellar which he hadn't opened in a very long time.

Why was it so difficult for him to say them? Had he said them once before, and they'd been thrown back in his face? Perhaps by an ex who had hurt him and caused him pain?

But he'd said them to her, and they had the power to close up her throat, to bring tears to her eyes and to make her heart ache for something she hadn't even known she wanted.

But she did know what she wanted. She wanted him. More than anything else.

He brought his hands down to link with hers. 'Come on. I'll show you around.'

'Connor…' She tightened her fingers around his and pulled him back as he started to move. She couldn't go inside without having told him. It would only be delaying the inevitable. But then this might be the last chance she'd have of visiting the Cabacal, the last time she'd get to walk through the wonderful old place and relive precious memories.

It was too compelling to resist. So she loosened her hold on him and nodded. He took a bunch of keys from his pocket, selected two and used them to open the locks on the double doors.

He stood back and Lola stepped into the vestibule.

A gazillion memories tumbled over themselves as she took in the pink marble inlays and chrome fittings. She had a vision of her grandfather escorting her inside when she'd had lunch there as a special treat for her tenth birthday. She'd worn a pretty blue and cream floral dress, the detail of which was as vivid right now as it had been on that day.

As memories swamped her, she pushed them away. Because it was too much. She already felt raw and emotional, especially as Connor stood beside her and said nothing. She had the crazy notion that he knew—that he realised the place had a special meaning for her. But that was impossible. She hadn't had the guts to tell him yet.

His phone buzzed, breaking through her frenzied thoughts and the eerie silence of the empty space. She turned to see him checking the display. 'I need to take this,' he said. 'Look around. I'll be right back.'

As Connor went outside, Lola stepped through into the main hall. She froze. While the vestibule and entrance were unchanged from what she remembered when her grandmother had been alive, the main hall provided evidence of what her uncle and his greedy hands had done. Most of the stunning architectural features remained intact, thank God, but there was no trace of the beautiful, elegant interior her grandmother had created. In its place were the garish and showy remnants of the casino.

Taking a breath, she wandered further into the space. Since she'd never seen the appeal of gambling, Lola didn't know to what use the dusty, discarded tables had once been put. Poker? Black jack? The only game she recognised was roulette, with its distinctive wheel still in evidence.

At the far end of the main hall was a bar, its rich mahogany surface covered in layers of dust and grime, its shelves now empty, having once held glasses and alcoholic beverages showcased by the old etched mirrors running along the length of the back bar.

As she walked towards it, she glanced up to the mezzanine and spotted some old slot machines juxtaposed with a smaller bar which, she imagined with some cynicism, had allowed punters to refill their drinks with as little disturbance as possible to their game-playing.

Her footsteps echoed on the dusty limestone floor as she wandered past the bar and towards the wall that had once held clear windows looking out over the river. That would have been the first change she'd have made, Lola thought somewhat innocuously. Reinstating those wonderful views.

She turned back to look around the hall. It would have been an amazing space in which to run her studio. The main hall could easily have been partitioned into smaller units without losing the sense of light, of space. On fine days she could've thrown the windows open, maybe even had a deck built on the grassy ledge outside for outdoor classes when the weather allowed.

She wandered into one of the annexes off to the side, imagining it as a cloakroom with lockers for her clients. Then into another room that would have been perfect for storing class equipment.

Before long she would have removed all traces of the travesty her uncle had made of the space, but in the absence of being able to do that she was damn sure she was going to make certain that Connor didn't get to obliterate the property completely. She couldn't bear to think of all its lovely architectural features lying in a pit of rubble on the beautiful limestone floor.

She heard Connor, his voice getting louder as he neared the door to the main hall. 'Okay, I'll wait for you,' he said to the caller. 'It'll save me a trip to your office.'

Steeling herself for the conversation to come, Lola came back into the main hall as Connor tucked his phone back in his pocket.

'What do you think?' he asked, coming to stand beside her. 'It's a big space, but it'd be easy enough to have it made into smaller areas. The two pillars at the sides aren't load bearing, so they could be removed easily enough, which means that the smaller annexes could be knocked together.'

Lola found it hard to concentrate on the rest of what Connor said. She was too busy trying to make sense of what she'd already heard. Why on earth was he waxing lyrical about the potential of the place?

Her heart stuttered. 'You're not going to have it knocked down?'

His eyebrows rose. 'Well, no. Not if you think it would work for you.'

She swallowed, her throat so tight it was hard to breathe. 'Work for me?'

Had she slipped into some alternative reality? A parallel universe? What the hell was he talking about? She didn't even want to consider what she *thought* he was talking about.

'Like I said, those pillars aren't a problem, and if you want the hall sectioned off some good stud walling would be an easy enough fix.' With his hands in his pockets, he strolled around the room. 'How many people are you planning to have in each class?'

Lola's heart was flipping about like a mad thing, but she couldn't take his words at face value. She searched his face but there didn't seem to be any artifice in his expression or demeanour. No suspicion in his eyes telling her he'd found out who she really was and was messing with her. Connor didn't play those sorts of cruel games. If he'd known who she was, she would have seen it in his eyes, would already be facing his wrath.

'Ten students per class is the norm,' Lola said, her throat like sandpaper. 'Twelve, tops.'

Connor nodded thoughtfully. 'This space could easily accommodate those numbers.'

As she still wasn't entirely sure what was going on, whether or not he had some sort of agenda, Lola kept her gaze steady on his. 'I don't understand.'

He shrugged. 'I've got a property, you need one. None of the others you showed me seemed suitable. This one does. I'm willing to rent it out to you until such time as I'm ready to sell it and you're happy it'll work for you. Unless you already know it won't work.'

Lola bit her bottom lip. Everything she'd planned for had fallen into her lap. Just like that. So how come, instead of celebrating her luck, she had a hollow feeling settling in the pit of her stomach? He was willing to do this for her when she hadn't even had the decency to tell him who she was, and that this very scenario was the outcome she'd been planning all along.

'It would work perfectly,' she said as guilt clawed its ugly way around her heart.

She couldn't let this continue, couldn't let him make this huge gesture until she had come clean. He would no doubt retract his offer. And she wouldn't blame him.

Yet she had to make this right.

'Connor. I can't tell you how much I appreciate what you're offering me. But we really need to talk.'

'Hold that thought,' he said, already moving towards the entrance door as his mobile buzzed. 'I just need to take care of some business. Hand over some papers. If it's the cost of renovation that's worrying you, we can work that out.'

It was only delaying the inevitable, yet Lola was glad of the breathing space. The chance to formulate her words in a way that would cause Connor the least damage, the least hurt. She was about to throw his generosity back in his face, and she hated what that might do to him. He'd already been manipulated and betrayed by her uncle, and the fallout had taken him years to work through. How would she feel when she not only opened up all those old wounds, but inflicted even more new ones?

She wrapped her arms around herself, as if to stop her insides from spilling out. It felt as if she'd been flayed right through to the core of who she was because she couldn't bear the thought of hurting Connor this deeply.

She heard him speaking with someone outside, a

vague shiver of recognition trembling down her already icy spine.

The door swung open and Connor walked through, closely flanked by Damian.

As Lola met her brother's angry gaze, she knew any chance she had of making Connor understand had just disintegrated like dust on the limestone floor.

# CHAPTER TWELVE

ANY FOOL WOULD have noticed the tension that snapped between Damian and Lola. Just as any fool would have noticed the colour leeching from her beautiful face.

Connor looked between them, his eyes narrowing. 'What the hell's going on?'

Damian kept his attention on Lola. 'That's what I'd like to know. Maybe you'd like to explain, Louise.'

*Louise?*

'What are you doing here, Damian?'

The man raised his eyebrows, showcasing the confusion in his eyes. 'The real question is, what are *you* doing here?'

'Somebody better start explaining,' Connor said, his chest squeezed so tight that his ribs started to ache. 'And soon.' They obviously had some kind of history, and clearly not good. Were they once lovers? That possibility made him want to pound his aching chest in a direct display of male possession so that Damian knew with absolute certainty that Lola was his now.

Lola seemed to have turned even paler. 'This is none of your business, Damian. You should leave.'

A hint of perception replaced confusion in Damian's now narrowed eyes. 'Have you gone behind my back? After everything I said?'

Gone behind his back doing what? What the fuck was going on?

'You didn't give me any choice.' On the surface, Lola sounded firm, but Connor heard the hitch in her voice. 'This wasn't what I wanted. It certainly wasn't what I planned.'

Damian turned to Connor. 'Have you agreed to anything?'

'About what?'

Damian took a deep inhalation. 'My sister can be very persuasive.'

His *sister*?

Connor looked between them again, his gaze settling on Lola even as his head buzzed. Lola was Damian McBride's sister? What the fuck?

Why hadn't she told him? She must have known he was doing business with Damian over the Cabacal, which meant…

Shit. It meant she'd been lying to him.

His head pounded and the straitjacket that was now around his ribcage tightened further. He needed to think. To work this out, make sense of it.

'Lola?'

Strands of hair fell free of the messy bun as she shook her head. Her eyes were over-bright, shining with the truth of what his fevered brain was slowly, painfully, figuring out. She'd lied to him. All the time they'd been together, she'd had her own agenda. And he'd slowly been falling for her, allowing the wall around his heart to crumble brick by brick, allowing himself to contemplate the possibility that he might be able to open himself up enough to trust a woman again.

Fucking idiot.

'Connor. I need to explain everything to you.'

He thought he'd known pain before. As a child abandoned by his parents, as a budding entrepreneur betrayed by the man he'd considered his trusted mentor, as a lover cruelly manipulated by the woman he'd thought himself in love with. All those things had cut him like a thousand blades, but nothing…not one of those things…had ripped him apart like the pain of knowing that Lola had willingly, blatantly deceived him.

His blood was a torrent of rage as it swept through his veins. 'Damn right you need to explain. Start with why you lied to me. Right from the start. You fucking lied to me.'

Her throat contracted, her eyes deep pools of agonised green, but no way would he let his guard down. For all he knew, it was another act. Another attempt to manipulate him, draw him in, make him soften. Right now, he wanted answers. He wanted the truth.

'I always intended to tell you who I am, but first I

wanted to get to know you, to understand your reasons for wanting the Cabacal.'

Damian stepped forward. 'I told you Connor was owed. That should have been good enough. Why didn't you let it go?'

Lola turned to her brother, the paleness of her complexion highlighted by the spears of heat that flashed across her cheekbones and echoed in her eyes. 'You wouldn't even listen to me. Wouldn't even give me the chance to buy this place back. It belongs to our family, to me. You should have given me the option.'

Connor didn't want to know the ins and outs of who she thought was the legal owner. All he cared about was getting answers. From Lola.

'What were you hoping to gain from your lies?' he demanded, ignoring the way she flinched.

'At first I hoped to get you to agree to sell it on to me when my trust fund becomes available in six months' time.'

She threw a look at Damian, who had paced over towards the window, before bringing her gaze back to Connor's. Connor's mind was still trying to process everything. He was battling the sense of betrayal. The lies. The deception.

The need for answers to so many questions.

'That first night, at my club, you knew who I was?'

'Yes.' Her voice sounded thready, as if she couldn't quite catch her breath.

'And what? You thought you'd get me nice and

mellow? Is that what the dance was for? Work me up, then present me with the dotted line on which to sign?'

His gut burned. He couldn't believe he'd been so gullible. Couldn't believe he'd been so easily duped again. Hadn't he been careful? Hadn't he shut himself off enough not to let a woman close again? History, it seemed, really did repeat itself.

'No. I didn't even know you were in the club when I did that dance. It was a bet, remember? It wasn't until after I'd stabbed you with my heel and saw the award photo in your office that I knew who you were.'

Damian had now moved across to the entrance door, obviously sensing there was more going on than a property war.

A red haze misted across Connor's vision, his anger renewing with each confirmation of Lola's continued subterfuge. 'Wait,' he called, striding across the space to snatch up the papers Damian had left on the old bar before continuing towards the door. 'You'll want these.'

Connor was more determined than ever to own the Cabacal. Damian was right. He was fucking owed. The place had been at the heart of not just one, but two of the most destructive and deceit-filled periods of his life.

'You're sure?' Damian glanced at his sister, then back at Connor.

'Never more so. I want immediate completion on this. No delays.'

Damian nodded, then with a concerned look at his sister took the documents and walked out of the door.

Connor shook his head, hoping to shake some clarity into the chaotic mess that was his thoughts. 'Shit, I virtually played into your hands. Offering to rent you the place. Bet you were close to congratulating yourself on pulling that one off.'

'That's not true at all. Before Damian arrived I was planning to tell you the truth. I never meant to keep it from you this long. I swear I'm being honest.'

His laugh was as hollow as his stomach. 'I don't remember you being too worried about telling the truth that first night at the club when you went all out with the seduction routine. How can I be sure that wiggling your butt at me and shoving your breasts in my face wasn't all part of the act?'

'I told you. When I did that dance, I didn't know who you were. And if we're talking seduction, from what I remember you pressed pretty hard.'

Connor narrowed his eyes. 'And from what *I* remember, you refused me. Then you changed your mind.'

'I was attracted to you but, considering what I planned, there was no way I was going to sleep with you. Then I decided that if I could make Damian change his mind and sell direct to me, there was no reason not to act on the attraction. It wasn't until the next morning, after we'd slept together, that I realised you had both already agreed on a deal and that you were on the verge of signing, or even that you'd already signed. That's when I knew that I had to keep you at arm's length, that I couldn't sleep with you again. Not when I had to go back to my original plan and try and persuade you to sell the property to me.'

With each word, her voice grew stronger. She didn't falter, didn't hesitate. Connor wanted to believe what she was telling him, but he couldn't quite make that leap.

'Yet we ended up having sex again anyway, and I don't remember having to push too hard. What? Did you think it would give you the edge? Sex and business? Quite an explosive combination if you could make it work.'

'I didn't plan it, it just happened. You were pretty hard to say no to. And I certainly didn't intend having sex to give me any kind of edge. I was attracted to you, and I really enjoyed spending time with you. There was no way I ever intended for you to get hurt.'

Connor shoved his hands in his pockets and curled his fingers into his palms. 'Do you know what the really crazy part of all this is? I'd convinced myself that you were a straight-shooter, that you didn't do pretence. I'd been made a fool of before by a woman who I thought was different. Now I realise it must run in the family, that easy slide into deception, the ability to work on a man until he doesn't know which fucking way is up.'

She had the grace to look perplexed. 'I'm not sure I know what you mean.'

'Is that right? You expect me to believe you didn't know about my history with your cousin?'

Her brow furrowed. He wanted to believe she really didn't understand. Once, he might have done. But now he knew differently, and he wasn't buying the act.

'Maybe you swapped stories, is that it? How do I know that she didn't even give you pointers? Tell you my weak spots.'

'Connor, I really—'

'She'd damn well know them better than anybody. Caroline prided herself on reading people.'

The look of shock that passed over her face, that set her back a step, was worthy of an award-winning actress. 'Caroline?' Her hand went to her throat, her face turning pale again. 'What's she got to do with anything?'

Connor knew he shouldn't fall for it, but there was a stupid part of him that wanted to give her the benefit of the doubt. 'She played me,' he said. 'Primed me good and hard, so that when she was ready I walked straight into the trap.'

Her eyes flicked sideways, back and forth, and Connor knew those cogs and wheels were turning. He hated that he knew that about her, detested that he'd allowed her to get under his skin so far that he knew her ways, her expressions, her mannerisms.

Her hand stayed at her throat, her fingers sliding across her collar bone. 'Are you saying it was Caroline who set you up? Who got you arrested? I thought it was my uncle.'

'They came as a pair. She was cunning, manipulative, but it was Daddy who pulled the strings. She was his willing little puppet.'

She looked him square in the eye and, although he fought it, his gut twisted. 'You were lovers?'

Connor kept his face passive. 'Yes.'

She took in a breath, then bit down on her lower lip. 'I always assumed it was my uncle who was responsible for implicating you. I didn't for a moment consider Caroline had a part in it.'

'They carted her off to jail soon after my release, for God's sake. You didn't think she might have had a role in incriminating me?'

'I wasn't in touch with that side of my family, so I didn't know all the details.'

She shook her head, sending more strands loose to float around her face. He had to curl his fingers into his palms to stop from reaching out and brushing them away. Stop himself wanting to tilt up her chin, look into her troubled eyes and tell her everything was going to be okay. Because it wasn't going to be okay. It never could be. Not for them.

Her gaze settled at his throat. 'I'm so sorry, Connor. You must really hate my family. You must really hate me.'

Damn it, but he wanted to. He wanted to tell her to get the hell out of his life. He didn't need reminding that he'd allowed himself to be taken in by yet another scheming woman intent on using him to further her own desires.

Yet she seemed surprised by the knowledge her cousin had been complicit in his downfall. Genuinely concerned about what had happened to him.

Shit. It was making his head explode.

'Let's just put it this way,' he said, deciding he was done with it all. 'It doesn't make a difference to me that you weren't in touch with that side of your family, and I don't give a damn that you say you didn't mean to deceive me, manipulate me. The fact is, you didn't have the guts to come clean and tell me who you were and what you wanted.

'How do you know I might not have been sympathetic? That I might not actually have agreed to what you wanted, had you given me the courtesy of being honest? As it stands, I want nothing left standing of this damn building and nothing more to do with your family, or with you.'

Lola felt the punch of Connor's words deep in her solar plexus. Her insides were being scraped by some kind of vicious knife that wouldn't let up. She couldn't defend herself against his diatribe, because every word he said was right. Except in her heart she hadn't meant to manipulate him. She might have deceived him, but she'd never imagined that it would open so many old wounds for him.

She couldn't believe it was her cousin who had betrayed him so badly. Not that Lola didn't deem Caroline capable of such treachery, but she hadn't even considered the possibility that Connor had been attracted to someone like her mean-spirited cousin.

Lola wondered if she would have been able to keep from confronting Caroline and telling her just how evil she was if Caroline had been easily accessible, and not off hiding overseas after her release from prison.

Although right then Lola had more urgent and important things that she had to try and salvage. The most vital of which was trying to make Connor understand that she had never meant to upset him so badly.

Oh, he was angry, and rightfully so. He had every reason to be. But beneath that anger she knew she had wounded him. He hid it well, but the bleakness in his stormy grey eyes was evident to her. It cut her to the very depths of her being.

'I'm sorry for what I did, Connor. When we met I was really attracted to you and I never for a moment meant to lead you on. I certainly never wanted to cause so much hurt. All I intended was to persuade you to sell the property to me. I didn't realise what it represented to you. I can understand why you want it demolished, but please will you at least take some time to consider if that's really the best thing to do?'

Lola took a breath, trying to find the right words of appeal. She didn't want to fight for the Cabacal so soon after he'd told her about Caroline and how badly her cousin had treated him, but she couldn't afford to remain quiet. She at least had to try to save the property that had meant so much to her mother.

'My uncle cheated my mother out of this property,' she said quickly, unsure how long Connor would let her speak before he marched her out of the building. He was at least going to know what had prompted her to act in the way she had. 'My great-grandfather built it and it's been passed down through the women of the family. My mother planned to run it as a health studio until she was tricked out of her inheritance. I wanted to get it back. Make her dream come true. I know it doesn't change anything, but I just wanted you to know how important it is to me and why I did what I did. You don't owe me a thing, Connor, but please don't destroy this wonderful place without really taking some time to consider.'

When he didn't respond, Lola knew that, while he'd listened to her, he hadn't really taken what she'd said to heart. Maybe she'd hurt him too badly to expect any kind of compassion.

She sucked in a thready breath. 'I don't want you to hate me.'

He raised his eyebrows, piercing her with a look. 'We don't always get what we want.'

His words were like a physical blow aimed straight at her heart, smashing it to pieces. Her blood flowed like ice in her veins; her legs were hollow.

She closed her eyes against the torrent of hurt, before opening them to look straight into Connor's merciless gaze. 'Is there any way I can make this right?'

He shrugged. 'No. I was lied to once by your family. Cheated, deceived, fucking sliced in two. Thankfully, this time I found out before any real harm was done.'

His eyes bored into hers, the steel in their grey depths cold and unforgiving. It broke the final fragile shards of her heart.

In that moment, she knew she had lost him. That there was no making it right, no coming back from the dark place she feared she'd driven him to.

Lola turned and gathered up her bags, then suffered the cold, hard look in his eyes as he glared down at her. 'I really am so very sorry, Connor. Please believe that.'

His nostrils flared as he drew in a breath. 'Bye, Lola.'

She hurried across the space, barely seeing anything as her eyes blurred dangerously. She didn't give much thought to the fact this was the last time she would be inside the Cabacal building, the last time she would get to glance around it as she left it for ever.

All she cared about, all she thought about, was that she had ruined every chance she might have had with Connor. She had destroyed whatever they might have built together.

Just as she knew he would now destroy the Cabacal. She'd seen it in his eyes, heard it in the words he'd spoken.

And she couldn't find it in her shattered heart to blame him.

# CHAPTER THIRTEEN

THE VERY LAST THING Lola wanted to do was have lunch with Damian. Her brother had called numerous times since that day at the Cabacal, but she'd refused to answer or return his calls. She felt a little bad about it, but she'd needed time to herself. She'd needed the break. Time to lick her wounds. Three weeks since her confrontation with Connor, and they were still as raw. Still as painful.

It was impossible to count how many times she'd gone over everything in her head, driving herself insane with thoughts of 'what if she'd done this?', 'what if she'd told him that?'. But it always came down to one thing.

She'd screwed up.

How was it possible to miss someone so much? How could the pain of losing them hurt quite so deeply? She couldn't pinpoint the exact moment that she'd fallen for him. Couldn't isolate the precise instant that she'd slipped from liking him to falling so deeply in love. Because she did love him. With every ounce of her being.

What they'd shared wasn't supposed to be meaningful. Yet it had so quickly morphed into the most extraordinary relationship of her life. And she'd thrown it all away because she hadn't had the courage to tell him the truth.

Now here she was, with her heart broken, and there wasn't a bloody thing she could do about it.

Ruthlessly, she pushed thoughts of Connor aside as she rode the lift to Damian's office. She'd spent far too many hours pining and crying and missing Connor. What good would it do to continue down that route? He didn't want her. He hadn't contacted her.

It was over. She had to move on.

Somehow. Some way.

Yet she knew her brother would want to know the ins and outs of her relationship with Connor, and she braced herself for the barrage of questions no doubt coming her way. Not that she needed to explain anything to him. It was her business. He had no right delving into her personal life any more than she had his. She'd make sure he respected that.

What she did intend to tell him was that she had found a suitable property for her studio. After a second viewing yesterday, she was putting in an offer. He had to realise that she wasn't seeking his permission, but that she was forging ahead with her plans, in her own way, on her own terms.

Oh, she understood that Damian cared for her, that he wanted to look out for her, but there were limits. She'd half-expected to find him waiting outside the Cabacal three weeks ago, ready to confront her, but there had been no sign of him. He'd called that same evening, though, and had found Emily in fierce guardian mode, telling Damian to sod off and mind his own business.

Lola could only imagine her big brother seething through the phone. Damian and Emily had never hit it off, and Lola suspected that her friend had taken great delight in giving the *arrogant and entitled dickhead*—her words—a piece of her mind.

She exited the lift and headed through the classy reception of her brother's investment company and towards his office. Having been waved straight through by his EA, she found Damian looking out of the window, his back to the door as he spoke on the phone.

He turned, finished the call, then came around to draw Lola into his arms. His brotherly embrace threatened to undo her resolve to move on with her life and her breath hitched dangerously. He held on for several moments, then drew back and placed his hands on her shoulders. 'Are you okay?'

As her throat had tightened from the unexpected warmth and support in his gesture and tone, all she could do was nod.

'I thought we could have lunch here,' he said, glancing to the meeting table laid out with coffee and sandwiches. 'There's something I need to talk to you about.'

'That's fine. There's something I need to talk to

you about too.' Lola took the property details from her bag before walking over to place them on the table. She thought it best to tell him her plans before she let him say whatever was on his mind. That way he'd know her mind was made up. 'Do you mind if I go first?'

'Louise.' Damian placed his hand over hers. 'I understand you're still pissed at me, and maybe I can't altogether blame you for that.'

'None of it matters now. I'm just interested in moving on. Which is why I'm putting in an offer for this property.' She nodded towards the details. 'I've spoken with the bank and they're prepared to advance me the deposit in lieu of my trust fund being released.'

She considered moving her hand out from under his but didn't. He was her brother and, despite everything that had happened, she needed him. She loved him.

'You still believe that I was being vindictive by not letting you have the Cabacal.'

'I know you were acting on Dad's wishes, although I suspect you agreed with his reasoning. You don't think I have the intellect to make my own business choices.'

'That's not true.' He looked at her for a long moment, then nodded to the nearest chair. When she sat, he settled beside her and reached for the jug to pour them both coffee. 'Do you know the real reason

Dad insisted on a business degree before you could access your trust fund?'

'Yes. Because he thought I was incompetent, in the same way he thought Mum was. He knew that, like her, I wanted to set up a health studio at the Cabacal, but he didn't think I was capable of making it work. He thought I'd be tossing away my inheritance.'

Damian sipped his coffee then looked down thoughtfully into the dark liquid before he met Lola's gaze again. 'I've learned the hard way that you've got a hell of a backbone, Louise.'

She was so busy basking in the startling compliment that she almost missed his next words.

'Dad never wanted you to know, but I think you deserve the truth.'

'What truth?' Her insides flipped uncomfortably, probably because Damian's expression signalled it wouldn't be to her liking.

'The Cabacal wasn't the only part of her inheritance our mother lost.'

Lola frowned, her breath shuddering. 'I thought it was the whole part. The property.'

'Our grandmother left her very financially secure, but Mother always had a guilt complex about that. She became involved in charity work, sat on committees, was actively involved in fundraising events. Unfortunately, her need to help people wasn't matched by a good head for business. She was easy prey, a target for manipulation by some unscrupulous types. She gave every penny of that inheritance away, and probably would have done the same with the Cabacal, except she'd earmarked that for her studio. It was symbolic for her.'

He took a breath, his face turning ashen. 'By the time father found out and stepped in to try and salvage the situation it was too late. All she had left was the Cabacal.'

Lola wrapped her hands around her cup, needing something to clasp as she tried to make sense of what her brother said. She hadn't known anything about her mother's extra inheritance—had never heard mention of it.

'Dad felt that if mother had invested her wealth wisely and made better business decisions she could have helped even more people, but she just acted rashly and without much thought. Then when she lost the Cabacal—'

'She didn't lose the Cabacal, she was cheated out of it.'

'Dad didn't see it like that, at least not totally. He saw it as yet another instance when mother didn't keep tighter control of her assets. She trusted too easily.'

'Nobody expects their own brother to steal from them.'

'Uncle Guy wasn't exactly trustworthy at the best of times. How many dubious dealings was he involved in? How many start-ups did he have that didn't get off the ground? His own parents didn't trust him to run their affairs, yet our mother decided that he was working in her best interests?'

'We all know how manipulative he could be.'

'Exactly. So you can't blame Dad for becoming paranoid about protecting you. He wanted to ensure you had a good financial grounding so that you'd make sound business decisions. That's why he set up the condition that you get the degree before you get your trust fund.'

Lola frowned. 'Did he make the same conditions for you? Did getting your trust fund require that you meet certain stipulations?'

'Yes. But I had to prove myself in business. Reach certain targets.'

That stopped her in her tracks. 'Really?'

She had always suspected that she'd been singled out, but if it was true that Damian had had to jump through similar hoops then it changed things.

Or did it?

'Then you should have been more understanding of my position. Even after I'd got my degree, proved myself capable, you refused to listen to my business proposal. You should never have withheld the acquisition of the Cabacal from me. You should have talked to me, discussed it as I asked. You wouldn't look at my projections, my ideas, my financial data. You completely dismissed me.'

'I know, and I'm sorry for it. My only defence is that I was still trying to protect you. That property had already caused so much heartache for our family, I didn't want it back in our lives. I didn't want you hurt any more.'

Damian scraped his hand through his hair, then pushed his coffee away. 'I need something stronger.'

He walked to the small bar in the corner and held up the whiskey decanter.

Lola shook her head. 'I don't drink. You'd know that about me if you took the time to find out instead of thinking you have to save me from myself all the time.'

Damian returned to his chair, whiskey tumbler in hand. 'Fair comment.' He sipped his drink. 'I've been wrong to dismiss your plans out of hand, and from what I hear you've got it all down pat. The figures, projections, anticipated profit and loss for the first five-year trading period. Not to mention ideas for promotional activities to set your studio apart from others offering similar things.'

Surprised, Lola raised her eyebrows. 'Where did you hear that from?'

Damian frowned. 'Your friend the ball-breaker, for one. She gave me an earful when I called and asked her to give you the message about lunch today. Told me that if I took my head out of my backside long enough I might learn something. Then, as if I hadn't been reprimanded enough, I got an earful from Connor.'

Lola shot forward as her heart jumped into her throat. 'Connor?'

Damian took another sip and nodded. 'Met him

at the official handover of the keys. Apparently, he's refurbishing the place after all, turning it into another nightclub. I happened to say that it was a good move.' He paused, watching her. 'He asked about you. I told him you weren't taking my calls. That you were still pissed at me.'

Lola's brain had latched onto the fact he'd asked about her, and her insides were currently doing a crazy, hopeful dance.

'He said he couldn't blame you,' Damian went on, unaware that his sister was having difficulty breathing. 'That the least I could have done was listen to your proposal, seriously consider your plans for your business instead of dismissing them like they didn't matter. He said you had a good head on your shoulders, that you thought things out, knew your own mind. According to him your plans to open a studio are sound. He finished by saying I didn't know jack shit about you.'

Lola's hand went to her throat, which was currently threatening to seize up. 'He said all that?'

Damian shrugged. 'Maybe he was right. Somehow it slipped my notice that you're all grown up now. A formidable woman who knows what she wants and goes all out to get it.' He smiled, looking vulnerable, something she'd never associated with her strong, opinionated brother. 'I'd really like to get to know that woman.'

She felt a loosening around her heart and smiled back. 'I'd like that too.'

Damian was half out of his chair before she could finish the sentence and they came together in a hug.

'Forgive me?' Damian asked when they drew back.

'Of course. You're my big brother. I know you're looking out for me and I appreciate it. Just do it a little less often, maybe? And hear me out?'

'Agreed. But maybe I can stick my nose into your business just one more time before I leave the dark side?'

Lola raised her eyebrows, expecting that he'd have something to say about her putting in an offer on the property she'd seen. 'Go on.'

'Hopefully you now understand where Dad was coming from when he placed the stipulation on your trust fund, and now that I've explained my actions you've forgiven me. Don't you think that maybe Connor would understand your reasons if you explained them to him?'

She toyed with the cup. 'I tried. But I've really hurt him. I never meant to, but I have.'

She hated what she'd done. If she'd felt manipulated by her father and brother, how much worse did Connor feel? He'd been manipulated, lied to, betrayed. Twice, she thought as her heart twisted. By her cousin and by her. Did she really think that a few words of apology would make it right?

'What happened to my formidable sister? The one who knows what she wants and goes all out to get it? Are you telling me that sticking to your guns despite everything, and fighting for your own studio, means more to you than making things right with Connor?'

Her head shot back. 'No.'

Connor meant everything to her. Certainly more than any studio. More than anything she had ever wanted, and would likely ever want. Which made him worth fighting for. With everything she had. Whatever it took.

Before she could second-guess herself, she stood, leaned down to peck Damian on the cheek and grabbed her bag as she headed for the door. 'Sorry, can't stay for lunch.'

At the door she stopped and looked back. 'As older brothers go, you're okay.'

She bolted from his office, her breath tight. Had Connor really said those things to Damian about her? That had to mean he would be willing to listen, didn't it? That he'd be open to letting her explain how she felt.

Her brother was right. She had fought for her dream of owning her own studio. But that didn't come close to how much she wanted Connor. Not having him in her life was like a huge slice down the middle of every dream she'd ever had and she wanted nothing more than to stick those parts back together, with Connor at the very centre.

She had to make him see that. Had to make him understand that she'd never intended to hurt him, deceive him. He needed to realise that he could trust her. That she cared only for him.

During the tube journey she planned what she would say, dismissing each and every attempt at an explanation almost as soon as she'd considered it.

She visited both his clubs, but he wasn't at either of them. She struck pay dirt when she bumped into the security man who had been there the night she'd first met Connor. He told her that his boss was busy sussing out his new club premises over on the South Bank and wasn't expected back until that night.

With her heart in her mouth, she hailed a cab and headed straight for the Cabacal.

Connor walked through the property with his foreman. Renovations had started and by rights he should have been pleased with progress so far. News of his plans for his latest club had already garnered interest, and his investors were happy that he was sitting on a potential gold mine.

Yeah, he should be on Cloud Fucking Nine, but the truth was he found it hard to give a damn. Maybe his plans for the place were foolish, but they seemed right somehow. Fitting.

And maybe he was a stupid prick who needed a reality check.

He walked across the newly renovated limestone floor and tried to focus on what he was creating here. He'd always been lucky that he could visualise how something would turn out, and various consultants had agreed that his vision for the place was spot on.

So why the fuck was he thinking of Lola again?

Slowly, his anger towards her had dissolved, and in its place was this damned melancholy.

In retrospect, it might have been better to renovate this building along the lines of his other two clubs, but the idea had entered his head and stuck there. Then he'd mentioned it to Logan and to a handful of other people whose opinions he valued. Spurred by their enthusiasm, he'd rolled with the idea and now there was no going back.

Maybe he'd been naive thinking that he could keep Lola from his thoughts. Every time he stepped foot in the place all he could do was remember how she'd looked wandering around the space, probably imagining how it would feel to run her studio there, in the place that had been in her family for generations and which held her mother's cherished vision. Her expression had turned wistful as she'd run her hands over the soon-to-be-refurbished pillars with their pink marbled inlays.

It had been her dream to run the studio in this building and there was a part of him, way down deep beneath the anger and the hurt, that suffered a sting of remorse that he had been instrumental in denying her that dream.

As for his own dream? He didn't rightly know what that was.

To expand his empire? Open more clubs? Go international?

Maybe.

He looked out through the windows towards the river knowing that, while those things might once have comprised his dream, lately his vision had morphed into something else.

Something far more valuable and precious.

Because somewhere in all this jumbled mess, despite the deceit and the lies, his dream had become… *her*.

Shit. He was a fucking moron. Acting like a love-sick fool.

*Love-sick?*

That hit him with the force of a truck and he came to an abrupt halt. He pulled his wayward thoughts together, or tried to.

*Love-sick?*

It was just a word. One he'd plucked out of thin air. A word with which his treacherous heart thought to torture him. Taunt him. Make him suffer.

Which was fair enough. A man who had allowed himself to trust again, despite his experiences, his promises not to get involved, deserved nothing less. He'd let Lola sneak under his defences. He'd let her take up residence in his head, in his heart, and now here he was. Raw. Disheartened. Dispirited.

Bloody *love-sick*!

Fuck that.

He gave himself a mental shake. All this maudlin introspection was doing nothing for his mood, and today of all days he needed to keep from sliding further into his self-imposed pit of gloom. Tonight was

Logan's stag party, and his brother deserved better than Connor's dark attitude.

His foreman chose that moment to bring Connor the latest sketch for the renovation of the glass panels beside the rear exit doors, the ones that would reinstate the views of the River Thames beyond. The man was an artisan, and Connor felt lucky to have him at the helm of the refurbishment. Determined to focus on his newest acquisition, he gave his full attention to the sketch pad and his foreman's animated explanations.

Until the door to the building swung open...

# CHAPTER FOURTEEN

EVERY SINGLE THOUGHT in his head disappeared when his gaze fell on Lola, and then a barrage of emotions shot through him, each one urging him to go to her, kiss the very life from her, tell her that they could work things out.

Except they couldn't. He knew that. He'd lain awake too many nights these past few weeks, considering things from all angles, but every avenue brought him back to just one.

She'd conned him. Thought to trick him. There was no way back from that.

He met her gaze, noticing the slightly bruised look beneath her eyes. Had she been having trouble sleeping, like him? A well of concern hit him out of the blue and made him want to gather her up and make all her problems go away. Not that he should care. He *didn't* care. All she was to him now was a part of his past that, while painful, had thankfully been brief.

She raised her chin as she walked towards him: upright, resolute, full of confidence. Only those tell-tale shadows hinted at a different story. His peripheral vision shimmered to a blurry haze, his full attention riveted on her and the way she pulled so many conflicting emotions from deep inside him.

With Caroline, there'd been only one emotion. Anger.

With Lola? Damn it, there were too many to count.

She stopped in front of him, her gaze yet to leave his. Terrified he might disgrace himself and pull her into his arms, he slid his fisted hands into his pockets.

'Shall I come back later, boss?'

Vaguely aware of his foreman's presence, Connor nodded, although he couldn't seem to tear his eyes from Lola. 'That'd be great, Sid. Thanks.'

His blood began a slow and steady burn. She was so close that her citrus and floral scent wrapped around him, layering over the smell of newly plastered walls and freshly cut wood.

She took a breath and looked off to the side, past the half-dozen builders working in different areas, until her attention landed on the beginnings of a curved raised floor in the corner. 'I heard you were renovating after all. It's starting to look amazing.' A noise from the opposite side of the room garnered her attention. 'You're having the two smaller rooms incorporated into the main space? It'll look great.'

There was no disapproval in her tone, no sadness evident in her expression. Instead, she looked animated, almost enthusiastic. He wasn't about to let his guard down. 'If you're here for one last try to get me to sell to you, then I'll tell you straight off. You're wasting your time. Because I'm not selling this place to you, or to anyone else.'

Connor wasn't entirely sure how he managed to get all that out, seeing as his damn chest was squeezed so tight. His voice sounded firm, gruff. But inside he was in bloody turmoil.

'That's not why I'm here. In fact, I'm putting in an offer on a place I've found close to where I live.'

'Good for you.'

He wanted to pull her into his arms. He wanted to draw her close, lose himself in her, but he kept his distance.

She looked straight at him, her eyes clear and earnest. 'How's your back?'

His jaw tightened as he clenched his teeth. Her question wasn't welcome, nor was the concern in her stunning eyes. He didn't need a reminder of how amazing his back had felt that night when she'd massaged away the tension in his muscles. When they'd shared parts of themselves, and he'd wondered if things could be different and if he could learn to open up to someone again.

'It's fine.'

Another noise came from the side, followed by heavy banging. 'Can we go somewhere quieter?' she asked, hiking the strap of her bag higher onto her shoulder. 'There are things I'd like to say to you.'

He looked around, barely resisting the urge to

wrap his fingers around her arm as he nodded towards the open terraced doors that led onto the embankment.

A measly slice of sunlight crept through the heavy clouds, only to disappear again as Connor closed the doors behind them. It was quieter out here, although the steady undertone of noise as people went about their business in the capital was a constant hum in the background.

Lola turned to face him. 'I'm going to get straight to the point. I came here for one reason, and I hope you'll listen to what I need to say.'

She spoke with her trademark directness, that openness he'd admired from the start, but which lately he'd tried to convince himself had all been an act.

'I want to apologise again,' she said, her fingers curling more tightly around the strap of her bag. 'What I did was deceitful. All I can say is I was blinded by my own aspirations, my need to right a wrong. I was tunnel-visioned, and because of that I didn't acknowledge that more than one person had been wronged, or that I was hurting the people I really cared about.'

His heart took a ridiculous leap until he told himself she was referring to her brother. That was who she cared about hurting, not him. Damn it. Hadn't he learned anything from all this? Did he still want to hear her say that she cared about *him*?

Shit. He really was his own worst enemy.

'I should have come clean to you right from the start. Just blurted out who I was and, if you'd still been prepared to listen, ask if you'd be willing to consider my proposition. Instead of doing any of that, I just kept on withholding the truth from you.'

She took a breath. 'God. I'm babbling. I've been thinking about what to say to you for ages, working it all out so I'd have the best chance of making you understand that I mean every word. But when I walked in and saw you everything went full out of my head and I'm just—'

'I'd take a breath if I were you. Preferably a full yoga one.'

She stared at him, her breath hitching, then gave a wan smile. 'Have you been practising that?'

'No.' He wasn't entirely sure why he was torturing himself this way, making reference to that night again. Remembering their closeness, her gentleness, as she'd tended to him. What he should be doing was blocking everything they'd shared out of his mind.

'That's a pity.' She raised her chin again, looking him square in the eye. 'I had every opportunity to tell you who I was and you deserved to know.'

She put her weight on one foot, then the other. 'I spoke with my brother today. He told me things about my mother that I didn't know, things that he and my father had kept from me. It hurt me. Not what he told me, but that they'd never considered I had a right to know.'

She swallowed. 'I told you that the Cabacal was

my mother's inheritance. Mum knew my father wasn't interested in her plans to run a fitness studio so she went to her brother, my uncle, for advice. He told her she'd need loans to get the business up and running and said she'd need to use the Cabacal as collateral. She didn't know he was the one loaning her the money, and when she defaulted he took the property. It seemed he'd planned it all along.'

Connor hung tight to her every word, surprising himself with the raptness of his attention. He didn't want to see the parallels between his own situation and Lola's mother's, but it was hard to deny.

Trusting someone and having them deceive you was the hardest blow.

Yet as he looked at Lola he knew that she'd never meant to deceive him. She'd been trying to find a way to honour her mother, to right an injustice. She'd never deliberately set out to hurt him.

Fuck. He wasn't sure which way was up right then.

He knew what it was to be consumed with a need for revenge, that unshakeable drive for retribution. It drove everything—a man's thoughts, words, actions. He'd always felt it was a righteous desire. But now he wondered if that was true.

On the surface, he and Lola weren't that different in their need to pursue what could be considered a noble quest. The righting of a wrong. A balancing of the books. The difference between them was that, unlike his, Lola's attempt to balance the scales wasn't driven by revenge. It was driven by love. For her mother.

'Anyway,' Lola said as he remained silent. 'I just wanted to tell you the reasons behind my actions in the hope that you can begin to understand and maybe in time come to forgive me.'

His continued silence wasn't helping Lola's nerves. It felt good, telling him everything, and she knew she'd done the right thing, especially since his fierce expression had slowly softened. She'd hoped he would at least begin to understand why she'd done what she had, but now she had her doubts. She couldn't begin to gauge his thoughts.

She searched for more to say that might help but her mind came up blank. Then he turned and walked to the railing that separated the embankment from the edge of the river.

He leaned his forearms on the railing. 'Right from the first moment, you've had me turned upside down and inside out. That was the whole problem. I thought I had a handle on women...thought I could read them, see through any pretence.'

He stared across the river, his eyes bleak and his jaw tight. Lola wanted to step up to him and rub at the tension she suspected had moved into his shoulders, slide her hands down his back and, despite his earlier assurances, ease any pain he might have there.

But she knew he wouldn't welcome it, and any pain he felt was likely less to do with physical discomfort and more to do with having his perception of himself and his ability to read people destroyed. By her.

Mirroring him, she leaned on the railing beside him. 'I'm as sorry about that as I am about everything else,' she said, looking down at her clasped hands.

'Don't beat yourself up about that. I'm not blameless in all of this. When I first saw you, my only intention was to get you into bed. I didn't much care about anything else. Not exactly honourable, was it?'

'You'd had a really bad experience.' She could only imagine the way her cousin had used him, leaving him doubting himself and his ability to make sound judgements. 'It's natural that you'd be circumspect after what my family put you through.'

'No excuse.' He turned to look at her. 'If you hadn't got under my skin, I'd have dumped you as soon as I'd got what I wanted from you. I was using you to get what I wanted, so in some ways that makes us similar.'

'You got under my skin too.' Lola took a chance. 'I really wanted you that night. I still do.'

His gaze travelled over her face and butterflies took flight in her stomach. 'You said you're putting in an offer on a suitable place for your studio?'

The question killed off all those butterflies and replaced them with a big, fat hole of disappointment. She'd told him she still wanted him and he'd changed the subject.

'Yes. It's a good location. Plenty of space for what I need.'

Silence stretched until he sucked in a breath. 'I'm having this place restored, and as much as possible, I'm planning to keep the original features.'

'Yes. I can see that.' Her stomach fluttered, and she wanted to fling her arms around him as emotion filled her chest, but his insouciant expression put paid to any such notion. 'That's really wonderful. It should be restored. Thank you.'

As happy as she felt about that, she would much rather he'd told her he'd forgiven her. All her pleasure at knowing her precious Cabacal would be saved disappeared beneath a knot of despondency.

'You don't want to know what plans I have for it?' he asked.

No. She didn't. Because she really didn't care. Not anymore. Whatever he used it for it would now always be a painful reminder of exactly what she'd lost. And that was far more precious than bricks and mortar.

She kept her fingers wrapped around the railing, but she turned to him. 'My myopic need to get this property back has caused me more misery than I ever imagined. By the time I came to my senses, it was too late, and I'd lost something far more important to me. So, whether you decide to demolish it, refurbish it or float it out along the river, I really don't care.'

He pursed his lips, but there was a glimmer that softened the steel in his grey eyes. 'And here I was thinking that I'd maybe invite you to the opening.' He shrugged. 'But if you don't care...'

'Don't be flip, Connor. You'll insult us both.'

He pushed away from the railing. 'I did some checking,' he said as he looked up at the property. 'In your grandmother's time, this was a cabaret club. Quite the place to be seen, apparently. Unique, quirky and booked up months in advance.'

'I remember it really well,' Lola said, her heart a little lighter as she remembered all the times she'd visited the club as a child. How she'd loved exploring all its nooks and crannies, imagining she was one of the glamorous singers up on the stage...

'That raised curve in the corner,' she said, her eyebrows drawing together. 'Is that going to be the new stage?'

He nodded, looking down at her. 'Your brother gave me some old photographs and we're working to restore the interior as close to the original as we can get it.'

Lola's breath caught as the full weight of what he was doing took hold. 'Why are you doing that? Won't it be a reminder for you? I thought you wanted nothing more to do with my family.'

He stepped closer and touched the ends of her fingers with his, making her heart do a strange stuttering thing. 'You don't count your uncle or your cousin as family, and that's good enough for me. What's in the past should stay there.'

She closed her eyes, hardly daring to believe what

he was saying. When she opened them, she saw a warmth in his expression that she'd never expected to see again.

'Connor?'

'What do you say we put everything that's happened behind us and move forward?'

'Move forward? You mean with the renovations?'

He tightened his grip on her hands. 'No, I don't mean the fucking renovations. I mean you and me. Us.'

The heat that radiated through her chest, around her heart, made her breathless, light-headed. 'Us?'

'Yeah.' His throat contracted as he swallowed. 'I'm sorry for not letting you explain. For lumping you in the same league as your cousin. You wanted to right a wrong, and you did it out of love.'

'I never meant to hurt you,' she said, her voice hitching on the last word. 'I would never do that, Connor. Can you forgive me?'

'If you can forgive me.'

When he let go of her hands and slid his arms around her waist, she all but fell against him. She breathed him in, melting into the muscular heat of his chest.

He kissed the top of her head. 'We're a couple of bloody fools, one way and another. We should rectify that.'

'Absolutely.' She held tight, her arms around him, her ear pressed to his chest so she could disappear into the beat of his heart. The words she wanted to say bubbled up from deep inside her, and since she'd already risked too much by withholding the truth from him, she looked up at him and took another chance. 'I love you, Connor.'

His eyes went stormy, but he didn't hesitate. 'I love you too.'

As Lola wallowed in the moment, Connor lowered his head and touched his mouth to hers. The kiss was light, but it sent a fiery need racing through her body, turning incendiary when Connor pulled her closer and turned the kiss from light to passionate and then bordering on indecent.

They only pulled apart when they heard cheering, and turned to see Connor's renovation team on the other side of the windows grinning and applauding.

Connor laughed but didn't let her go. 'Only fitting we should give them a good show, seeing that this place is soon going to be famous for entertainment again.'

'We obviously didn't do a good enough job, since they're already getting back to work.'

'Only because they know I'll dock their pay.'

Lola laughed, but Connor turned serious. 'We're not so far along that I can't change my plans.'

'Why would you do that?'

'If you still want this as a studio, I can—'

Lola touched her finger to his lips. 'That's not what I want. I've got plans of my own now, and I'm excited about them. Besides, my mother would love what you're doing here. She'd see it as a tribute to my grandmother.'

He nodded and drew her in for another heated kiss.

'You know when you asked me how my back was doing?'

She frowned, suspicious. Maybe because of his wicked, sexy grin. 'Yes.'

'Well, come to think of it, I am suffering a few twinges here and there.'

'Really? Maybe I should help you with that. I've got some new massage oils that might be exactly what you need.'

He waggled his eyebrows. 'It's not the oils I need.'

She laughed and leaned into him, looking up into his sinful gaze. 'Then tell me what you need and I'll make sure to have whatever it is permanently on tap. Just for you.'

He grinned. 'Yeah? Then maybe you could throw in some more of that Tantric stuff. I wouldn't complain, neither would my grateful cock.'

'I'll bet. Want to come back to my place? Emily is away for a couple of days.'

'Sounds perfect.' He winced. 'Shit. It's Logan's stag night.'

Lola stroked the back of her fingers down his cheek. 'Come by after. It'll give me time to prepare.'

The glint in his eyes sent little arrows of anticipation straight to her core. 'For what?'

'Let's just say it involves a special relaxation technique I was reading about. You'll probably be in need of that after an evening of strippers and booze.'

He shook his head, his mouth turning up in a hard-done-by grin. 'Strict instructions from Logan. No strippers.'

'Then maybe I'll make up for that and put on a special show for you later. Wouldn't want you missing out.'

'No chance of that.' He dropped his forehead against hers. 'You're everything I need, Lola.'

'And you're everything I need, Connor.'

In the shadow of the building that had threatened to pull them apart, Connor drew her in for another scorching kiss.

Eventually he drew away with that devilish grin on his face. 'So, tell me more about this special technique…'

# EPILOGUE

'WILL YOU PLEASE put that away? You must know it all by heart now.' Lola laughed as she tried to take the small wad of notes from Connor as they waited by the entrance of the reception hall where his brother Logan stood with April, his new bride, greeting their guests.

'I can't remember a bloody word,' Connor said, opening up the notes for his best man's speech again. 'It was bad enough checking my pocket all the time just to make sure the ring was still there, now I've got this fresh hell to negotiate.'

'Just stop,' Lola said, trying not to laugh again as she fixed his tie for the umpteenth time that day. 'You'll be fine.' She looked up into his smoky eyes. 'Do your yoga breathing.'

He gave her a speculative look. At least she'd got his attention off his nerves.

For the last couple of weeks, they'd spent every possible moment together and it had been the happiest time of her life. She loved him so much.

'Not sure I should do that,' Connor said with a

wicked grin. 'Not if I don't want to disgrace myself in front of all these people.'

She finished straightening his tie, then tapped his arm in admonishment. 'It's not supposed to always lead to sex, Connor.' Although, every time she'd instructed him through a relaxing breath-control technique, it almost always had. 'It's supposed to help you calm down.'

He leaned down and kissed her, not concerned at all about the people milling around. When she pulled back, he grinned, but he kept his arms around her. 'That's all the calming down I need.'

'Good. I've never known you this nervous. It's just a speech. I'm sure you've given a few of those in your time.'

Connor kept his gaze on hers, his expression turning serious. 'It's not the speech that's got me all wound up.'

Lola raised her eyebrows. 'What else? Is everything okay?'

He swallowed. 'Yeah. Everything's great. Perfect. Maybe if it wasn't, I wouldn't be this nervous.' He tightened his hold on her. 'I've been looking on this speech as a kind of practice run. For when I'm in Logan's shoes.'

Lola's heart tripped. 'In his shoes?'

'Yeah.' He gave a quick smile. 'How about it, Lola?'

Lola just stared at him, trying to work out if he meant what she thought he meant, or if her crazy, loved-up heart was playing tricks on her. 'How about what?'

'You've got the smarts,' he said, frowning. 'Work it out.'

Oh, hell, she was actually going to cry. She placed her hand at her throat, hoping to stay the waterworks. 'Okay.'

'"Okay" as in *yes*?'

'Uh-huh.' It seemed she had completely lost the power of speech.

He grinned. 'I was thinking we could use the Cabacal for the reception. A private event right before opening night.'

Lola bit her lip, nodding her agreement. She could barely see Connor clearly now.

'I love you, Lola,' he said, pulling her so close against him that he cut off what little air she could get in her lungs. 'So fucking much.'

Looking into his eyes, she felt joy spread through her. Maybe it wasn't the most romantic of marriage proposals, but she'd take it. Just as she'd take everything the future held for them. As long as she had Connor, she had all the romance she would ever need.

And one of these days, maybe she'd teach him to take a full yoga breath that didn't end up with them lying naked between the sheets.

Or maybe not, she thought as she fell joyfully into his kiss.

* * * * *

# PENNILESS AND SECRETLY PREGNANT

**JENNIE LUCAS**

To Pete – Then, Now and Always

# CHAPTER ONE

HE COULDN'T AVOID it any longer. He had to tell her the truth.

From the bed, Leonidas Niarxos looked out the window. Across the river, on the other side of the bridge, Manhattan skyscrapers twinkled in the violet and pink sunrise.

Taking a deep breath, he looked down at the woman sleeping in his arms. For the last four weeks, he'd enjoyed the most exhilarating affair of his life. After years of brief, meaningless relationships with women who had hearts as cold as his own, Daisy Cassidy had been like a fire. Warming him. *Burning him.*

For weeks now—from their very first, accidental, surprising night—he'd been promising himself he would end their affair. He would tell her who he really was.

But he'd put it off, always wanting one more day. Even now, after a night of lovemaking, Leonidas wanted her. As he looked at her, feeling her soft naked body pressed so trustingly against his, his willpower weakened. Perhaps he could put off his confession one more day. Until tomorrow.

No, he thought furiously. No!

He had to end this. Daisy was falling in love with him. He'd seen it in her lovely face, in her heartbreakingly luminous green eyes. She believed Leonidas to be Leo Gianakos, a decent, kindhearted man. Perfect, she called him. She thought he was a store clerk without a penny to his name.

Lies, all lies.

Maybe if he took her to his house in Manhattan first, it might soften the blow, he argued with himself. Maybe

Daisy would be more likely to forgive him in his fifty-million-dollar mansion, while he offered her a life filled with luxury and glamour…

Forget it. Did he really believe that either love or money would make Daisy forgive what he'd done? After he revealed his real name, the only emotions she'd ever feel for him again would be horror and hate.

It had all been stolen time.

She sighed in his arms. Looking down, he saw her dark eyelashes flutter in the gray dawn.

He had to tell her. Now. Get it over with. For her sake. For his own.

"Daisy," he said quietly. "Are you awake?"

Stretching her limbs out luxuriously between the soft cotton sheets, Daisy blinked dreamily in the pale light of dawn. Her naked body was filled with the sweet ache of another night of lovemaking. She felt delicious. She felt cherished. She felt like she was in love.

Was she also in trouble?

Her eyes flew open. *You don't* know *anything's wrong*, she told herself fiercely. *It might be nothing. It* has *to be nothing.*

But her ridiculous fear had already ruined their date last night, when Leo had gone to tremendous expense to take her to a way too fancy French restaurant in Williamsburg. She'd been miserable—not just afraid of using the wrong fork, not just uncomfortable in the formal setting, but haunted by a new, awful suspicion.

*Could she be pregnant?*

"Daisy?" Leo's voice was a husky growl, his powerful body exuding heat and strength as he wrapped one muscular arm around her in the large bed.

"Good morning." Pushing away her fears, she smiled up at his darkly handsome face, silhouetted by the rising dawn.

He hesitated. "How did you sleep?"

Daisy gave him a shyly wicked grin. *"Sleep?"*

Leo gave her an answering grin, and his gaze fell slowly to her lips, her throat, her breasts barely covered by the sheet clinging to her nipples. Over the sheet, his hand brushed her belly, and she wondered again if she could be pregnant. No. She couldn't be. They'd used protection, even that first wild night four weeks ago, when he'd taken her virginity.

But as he softly stroked her body, her breasts felt strangely tender, swollen, beneath his sensual hands...

A sigh rose from the back of his throat as Leo reluctantly pulled away. "Daisy, we need to talk."

Never a phrase anyone wanted to hear. She swallowed. Did her body feel different to him? Had he already guessed her fear? "Talk about what?"

"There's something I need to tell you," he said in a low voice. "Something you're not going to like."

His grim black eyes met hers, over his cruel, sensual mouth and hard jaw, dark with five o'clock shadow.

An awful new fear exploded in the back of her mind.

How much did she really know about him?

After a hellish year, Leo Gianakos had wandered into her life last month like a miracle, like a dream, all dark eyes, tanned skin, sharp cheekbones and a million-dollar smile. From the moment Daisy had first looked at his breathtaking masculine beauty, at his powerful shoulders in that perfectly tailored suit, she'd known he was a thousand miles out of her league.

Yet somehow, they'd ended up in bed. Since that magical day, they'd spent nearly every night together, whenever she wasn't at work.

But it was strange to realize how little she actually knew about him. She didn't know where he worked, or where he lived. He'd always evaded personal questions.

There were all kinds of good reasons why, she'd told herself. Perhaps Leo shared a tiny rat-infested studio with three roommates and was self-conscious about it. After all, not everyone had a wealthy artist friend, as Daisy did, who'd asked them to house-sit. If not for Franck's generosity, Daisy would undoubtedly be sharing a studio with three people, too.

She hadn't pushed Leo for details about his life. They were happy; that was enough.

Now, for the first time, a horrible idea occurred to her. Could there be some other, more sinister reason why he hadn't told her where he worked, or invited her to his apartment? What if—could he possibly be—

"Are you married?" she blurted out, her heart in her throat.

Leo blinked, then gave a low laugh. "Married? If I were married, could I be here in bed with you?"

"Well, are you?" she said stubbornly.

He snorted, his black eyes glinting. "No. I am not married. And for the record, I don't ever intend to be. Ever." His voice dropped to a husky whisper. "That's not the problem."

Daisy stared at him. She was relieved he wasn't married, but…

Leo didn't want to get married? Ever?

She took a deep breath. "I just know so little about you," she said in a small voice. "I don't know where you work, or where you live. I've never met your family or friends."

Pulling away from her, Leo pushed off the sheets and abruptly stood up from the bed. She enjoyed the vision of his powerful naked body in the rosy morning light. She drank in the image of his muscular backside, the strong muscles of his back.

Without looking at her, he reached down to the floor, and started putting on his clothes. Finally, as he pulled on his shirt, he turned back to face her. She was distracted by the brief vision of his muscular chest, laced with dark hair, before he buttoned up the shirt. He looked down at her. "Do you really want to see where I live? Does it matter so much?"

"Of course it matters!" Sitting up in bed, holding the sheet over her breasts with one hand, she motioned around the spacious bedroom with its view of the Manhattan skyline. "Do you think I'd be living in a place like this if my dad's oldest friend hadn't taken pity on me? So please don't feel self-conscious, whatever your apartment is like. Or your job. Whatever it is, I will always think you're perfect!"

Leo stopped buttoning up his shirt. Dropping his hands to his sides, he stared at her across the bedroom, silhouetted by the view of the East River and Manhattan beyond.

She realized he was going to break up with her. She could see it in his grim expression, in the tightness of his sensual lips.

She'd always known this day would come. Leo was ten years older, sexy, tall, broad shouldered and darkly handsome. Daisy had never quite understood what he'd seen in her in the first place. She was so…ordinary. How could a badly dressed, not very interesting waitress from Brooklyn possibly keep the attention of a man like Leo Gianakos?

And if she was pregnant…

No. She couldn't be. *Couldn't.*

Leo took a deep breath. "Would you like to come to my house? Right now? And then…we can talk."

His voice was so strained, it took several seconds for Daisy to realize he was inviting her to his apartment, not breaking up with her.

"Sure." She realized she was smiling.

*No, quick, don't let him see; he can't know I'm falling in love with him.*

It had been only a month. Even Daisy, with her total lack of romantic experience, knew it was too soon to confess her feelings. Turning her face away, she rose from the bed. "I'll go take a shower…"

She felt Leo's gaze follow her as she walked naked across the luxurious bedroom. Entering the lavish en suite bathroom, she tossed him back a single glance.

Before she'd even had time to turn on the water in the enormous walk-in shower, Leo had caught up with her, already rapidly pulling off his clothes. He kissed her passionately as she pulled away from him with a light laugh, drawing him into the hot, steamy water. They washed each other, and he stroked every inch of her. She leaned back her head as he washed her long brown hair. After she'd rinsed, she straightened, and saw the dark heat of his gaze.

Pushing her against the hot, wet tiled wall, he kissed her, and she nearly gasped as her sensitive, swollen nipples brushed against his muscular chest, laced with rough dark hair. She felt the hardness of him pushing against her soft belly, and yearned. Finally, he wrenched away from her with a rueful growl. "No condom," he sighed.

As he turned off the water, and gently toweled her off with the thick cotton towels, in the back of her mind Daisy wondered nervously if it was already too late for that, if she could be pregnant in spite of their precautions.

Taking her hand in his own, he pulled her back to the bed and made love to her, gently, tenderly, after a night during which they'd already made love twice. She told herself it was their lovemaking which caused her breasts to feel so heavy, her nipples so sensitive that she gasped as he suckled her. That had to be the reason. There could be lots of reasons why her cycle, normally so predictable, was two weeks late… She couldn't be pregnant. *Couldn't.*

She pushed the thought away as Leo lightly kissed her cheeks, her forehead. Smoothing back her unruly brown hair, he cupped her jawline with his powerful hands, and lowered his lips to hers. His kiss was hot and sweet against her lips, so, so sweet, and she was lost in the breathless grip of desire. As he pushed inside her, she cried out with pleasure, soaring to new heights before he, too, exploded.

Afterward, Leo held her tight against his powerful body, the white cotton sheets twisted at their feet. Blinking fast, Daisy stared out the window toward the unforgiving Manhattan skyline, and heard the grim echo of his words.

*I am not married. And for the record, I don't ever intend to be. Ever.*

His hands tightened around her. "I don't want to lose you," he said in a low voice.

"Lose me?" She peeked at him in bed. "Why would you?"

He gave a low laugh. It had no humor in it. "Let's go to my house. And talk."

"Talk about what?"

"About…me." His serious expression as he got dressed sent panic through her. Nervously, she pulled on clothes in turn, a clean T-shirt and jeans.

"I'm not scheduled to work today. Are you?"

"I can be late," he said flatly.

"Don't clerks need to be at the store when it opens at ten?" When he didn't respond, she tried again. "You won't be fired if you're late?"

"Fired?" Leo sounded grimly amused. "No." He gave her a smile that didn't meet his eyes. "Shall we go?"

As they left the apartment, he held the door open for her, as usual. He was always gallant that way, making her feel cherished and cared for.

When she was younger, and even now that she was twenty-four, boys her age always seemed to want quick, meaningless hookups, without bothering with old-fashioned niceties like opening doors, bringing flowers, giving compliments or even showing up on time. No wonder Daisy had been a virgin when she met Leo. Ten years older, powerful, and handsome like a Greek god, no wonder she'd fallen into bed with him the first night!

Now, as they left the co-op building, going out into the fresh October morning, Daisy glanced at him out of the corner of her eye. She should have been thrilled he was taking her to his apartment. Instead, she had a weird sense of foreboding. What did Leo want to talk about? And which of her own secrets might tumble from her mouth—her love for him, her possible pregnancy or even the fact that she was the daughter of a convicted felon?

As they walked, sunshine sparkled across the East River with the enormous bridge and Manhattan skyline beyond. She started to head for the nearest subway entrance, two blocks away, when he stopped her.

"Let's take a car."

He seemed strangely tense. Smiling, she shook her head. "You can't seriously want to get a rideshare, after all the expense of that fancy dinner last night. The subway is fine. You don't need to bankrupt yourself trying to impress me." She couldn't help thinking how much she loved him for trying. "You're already perfect."

"I didn't mean a rideshare."

She heard a noise behind him. Frowning, she tilted her head. "Did you hear that?"

"Hear what?"

She looked around. "Sounds like a baby crying."

"I'm sure there are children everywhere here. Its mother will take care of it."

A baby was an *it*? Daisy's forehead furrowed. Then she heard the soft cry again. Weak. More like a whine, or a snuffle. She turned toward the alley behind the gleaming waterfront co-op.

"Where are you going?" he asked.

"I just need to make sure…"

"Daisy, it's not your problem—"

But she was already hurrying toward the alley, following the sound. There had been a newspaper story just the month before about a baby abandoned in an alley in New Jersey. Thankfully that child had been found safely, but Daisy couldn't get the story out of her mind. If she didn't investigate this, and something bad happened...

She followed the sound down the alley and was only vaguely aware of Leo behind her. She saw a burlap bag resting on the top of a dumpster. The sound seemed to come from that. It was wiggling. She heard a weak whine. Then a whimper.

"Daisy, don't," Leo said sharply behind her. "You don't know what it is."

But she was already reaching for the bag. It weighed almost nothing. Setting the burlap bag gently on the asphalt, she undid the tie and opened it.

It was a tiny puppy, a fuzzy golden-colored mutt, maybe two months old, wiggling and crying. She stroked it tenderly. "It's a dog!" Sudden rage filled Daisy. "Who would leave a puppy in a dumpster?"

"People can be monsters," Leo said flatly. She looked back at him, bemused. Then the puppy whined, weakly licking her hand, taking all her attention.

"She seems all right," Daisy said anxiously, petting the animal. "But I'd better take her to the vet to make sure." She looked up at Leo. "Do you want to come?"

He looked grim. "To the vet? No."

"I'm so sorry. Could we maybe get together later? You could show me your apartment tonight?"

"Tonight?" His jaw set. "I'm having a party."

She brightened. "How fun! I'd love to meet your friends."

"Fine," he said shortly. "I'll send a car to pick you up at seven."

"I told you, a car's not necessary—"

"Wear a cocktail dress," he cut her off.

"All right." Daisy tried to remember if she even owned a cocktail dress. Carrying the puppy carefully in her arms, she reached up on her tiptoes and kissed Leo's scratchy cheek. "Thanks for understanding. I'll see you at your party."

"Daisy—"

"What?"

She waited, but he didn't continue. He finally said in a strangled voice, "See you tonight."

And he turned away. She watched him stride down the street, his hands pushed in his pockets. Why was he acting so weird? Was he really so embarrassed of where he lived? Embarrassed of his friends?

She looked down at the puppy in her arms, who whined weakly. Turning on her heel, she hurried down the street, going to the veterinary office owned by one of her father's old friends.

"Dr. Lopez, please," she panted, "it's an emergency..."

The kindly veterinarian took one look at the tiny animal in Daisy's arms and waved her inside his office. After an exam, she was relieved to hear the mixed breed puppy was slightly dehydrated, but otherwise fine.

"Someone must have just wanted to get rid of her. She must have been dumped sometime during the night," Dr. Lopez said. "It's lucky the weather isn't colder, or else..."

Daisy shivered. It was heartbreaking to think that while she'd been snuggled warm in bed in Leo's arms, some awful person had been dumping an innocent puppy in the alley, leaving her to die in a burlap bag.

*People can be monsters.* Leo was right. All Daisy had to do was remember those awful lawyers who'd vindictively harassed her innocent father into prison on those trumped-up forgery charges. Her tenderhearted, artistic-minded father had collapsed in prison, surrounded by strangers. He'd had a stroke and died—

"What are you going to name her?" the vet asked, mercifully pulling her from her thoughts. Daisy blinked.

"Me?"

"Sure, she's your dog now, isn't she?"

Daisy looked down at the puppy on the examining table. She couldn't possibly own a pet. She didn't even rent her own apartment. Franck Bain was due to return from Europe soon, and she'd need to find a new place to live. With her meager income, it was unlikely she'd be able to afford an apartment that allowed a pet. Just thinking of the cost in dog food alone—

No. Daisy couldn't keep her.

But someone had left this puppy to starve. A sweet floppy mutt who just needed a loving home. Could Daisy really abandon her?

Uncertainly, she reached out and softly stroked the dog's head. The animal's big dark eyes looked up at her, and she licked Daisy's hand with a tiny rough tongue.

No. She couldn't.

"You're right. I'm keeping her." She pushed away the worry of expensive vet bills and dog food. "I'll think about a name."

Dr. Lopez tried to wave off her offer of payment, but she insisted on paying. She couldn't live off the charity of her father's friends forever. It was bad enough she'd lived in Franck's apartment for so long, even if he insisted *she* was the one doing him a favor by house-sitting.

She wondered if the gray-haired artist would still think so, after he discovered she'd brought a puppy home.

Leaving the vet's, she went to the nearest bodega and bought puppy food and other pet supplies. Passing another aisle in the store, she hesitated, then furtively added a pregnancy test into her basket, too. Just so she could prove her fears were ridiculous.

After Daisy got the puppy back home and fed, she

stroked her fur. "How could anyone have thrown you away?" she whispered. "You're perfect." Finally, gathering her courage, she left the tiny dog to drowse on the fluffy rug in front of the gas fire and went into the elegant modern bathroom to take the pregnancy test. *Just get it over with*, she told herself. Once she took the test, she would be able to relax.

Instead, she found out to her shock her fears were right. *She was pregnant.*

Pregnant by a man she loved, though she barely knew him.

Pregnant by a man who would never marry her.

Daisy didn't have any money. She didn't have a permanent home. She didn't have a family. Soon, she'd be raising both a puppy and a baby, utterly alone.

She couldn't do it alone. She *couldn't*.

Could she?

She had to tell Leo at the party tonight. The idea terrified her. What would he do when he found out she was pregnant? What would he say? Fear gripped Daisy as she looked at herself in the bathroom mirror.

What had she done by following her heart?

Leonidas Niarxos was in a foul mood as he arrived at his skyscraper in Midtown Manhattan, the headquarters of his international luxury conglomerate, Liontari Inc.

"Good morning, Mr. Niarxos."

"Good morning, sir."

Various employees greeted him as he stalked through the enormous lobby. Then they took one look at his wrathful face and promptly fled. Even his longtime chauffeur, Jenkins, who'd picked him up in Brooklyn—around the corner from Daisy's building, so she wouldn't see the incriminating Rolls-Royce—had known better than to speak as he'd driven his boss back across the Manhattan Bridge.

Leonidas was simmering, brooking for a fight. But he had only himself to blame.

He hadn't been able to tell Daisy his real name.

She'd looked at him with her mesmerizing green eyes, her sensual body barely covered by a sheet, and she'd hinted that seeing where Leonidas lived might make a difference—might give them a future.

At least, that was what he'd wanted to hear. So he'd given in to the temptation to postpone his confession. He'd convinced himself that pleading his case in the private luxury of his mansion, later, after he'd made love to her one last time, might lead to a different outcome.

Now he was paying for that choice. Leonidas Niarxos, billionaire playboy CEO, had just been upstaged by a dog. And he would be forced to confess his true identity in the middle of a political fundraiser, surrounded by the ruthless, powerful people he called friends. Besides, did he honestly think, no matter where or when he told Daisy the truth, she'd ever forgive what he'd done?

Standing alone in his private elevator, Leonidas gritted his teeth, and pushed the button for the top floor.

Daisy was different from any woman he'd ever met. She loved everyone and hid nothing. Her emotions shone on her face, on her body. Joy and tenderness. Desire and need. Her warmth and goodness, her kindness and innocent sensuality, had made him feel alive as he'd never felt before. She'd even been a virgin when he'd first made love to her. How was it possible?

Leonidas never should have sought her out a month ago. But then, he'd never imagined they would fall into an affair. Especially since he'd sent her father to prison.

A year ago, Leonidas had heard a small-time Brooklyn art dealer had somehow procured *Love with Birds*, the Picasso he'd desperately sought for two decades. His lawyer, Edgar Ross, had arranged for Leonidas to see it in his office.

But he'd known at first sight it was fake. He'd felt heartsick at yet another wild-goose chase, trying to recover the shattered loss of his childhood. He'd told his lawyer to press charges, then used his influence with the New York prosecutor to punish the hapless art dealer to the fullest extent of the law.

He'd found out later that the Brooklyn art dealer had been selling minor forgeries for years. His mistake had been trying to move up to the big leagues with a Picasso—and trying to sell it to Leonidas Niarxos.

The old man's trial had become a New York sensation. Leonidas never attended the trial, but everyone had known he was behind it.

It was only later that Leonidas had regrets, especially after his lawyer had told him about the man's daughter, who'd loyally sat behind her elderly father in court, day after day, with huge eyes. He'd seen the daughter's stricken face in a poignant drawing of the courtroom, as she'd tearfully thrown her arms around her father when the verdict had come down and he'd been sentenced to six years. She'd clearly believed in Patrick Cassidy's innocence to the end.

A few months ago, on hearing the man had died suddenly in prison, Leonidas hadn't been able to shake a strange, restless guilt. As angry as he'd been at the man's deceit, even *he* didn't think death was the correct punishment for the crime of art forgery.

So last month, Leonidas had gone to the Brooklyn diner where Daisy Cassidy worked as a waitress, to confirm for himself the girl was all right, and anonymously leave her a ten-thousand-dollar tip.

Instead, as the pretty young brunette had served him coffee, eggs and bacon, they got to talking about art and movies and literature, and he was amazed at how fascinating she was, how funny, warm and kind. And so damn beautiful. Leonidas had lingered, finally asking her if she wanted to meet after her shift ended.

He'd lied to her.

No. He hadn't lied, not exactly. The name he'd given her was a nickname his nanny had given him in childhood, Leo, along with his patronymic, Gianakos.

*Leo*, Daisy called him, her voice so musical and light, and hearing that name on her sweet lips, he always felt like a different person. A better man.

No woman had ever affected him like this before. Why now? Why her?

He'd never intended to seduce her. But Daisy's warmth and innocent sensuality had been like fire to someone frozen in ice. For the first time in his life, Leonidas had been powerless to resist his desire.

But after tonight, when he told her the truth at his cocktail party—hell, from the moment she saw his *house*, when she obviously believed he lived in some grim studio apartment—he'd have no choice but to do without her.

Just thinking about it, Leonidas barely restrained himself all afternoon from biting the heads off his vice presidents and other employees when they dared ask him a question. But there was no point in blaming anyone else. It was his own fault.

Sitting in his private office, with its floor-to-ceiling windows with all of Manhattan at his feet, Leonidas gazed sightlessly over the city.

Was there any chance he could keep her?

Daisy Cassidy was in love with him. He'd seen her love in her beautiful face, shining in those pale green eyes, though she'd made some hopeless attempts to hide it. And she believed him to be some salesclerk in a Manhattan boutique. She loved him. Not for his billions. Not for his power. For himself.

If she could love some poverty-stricken salesclerk, couldn't she love Leonidas, too, flaws and all?

Maybe if he revealed why he'd been so angry about the Picasso, and the horrible secret of his childhood…

He shuddered. No. He could never tell anyone that. Or about his true parentage.

So how else could he convince her to stay?

Leonidas barely paid attention to a long, contentious board meeting, or the presentations of his brand presidents, discussing sales trends in luxury watches and jewelry in Asia and champagne and spirits in North America. Instead, he kept fantasizing about how, instead of losing Daisy with his confession tonight, he could manage to win her.

She would arrive at his cocktail party, he thought, and hopefully be dazzled by his famous guests, along with his fifty-million-dollar mansion. He would wait for just the right moment, then pull her away privately and explain. There would be awkwardness when she realized he'd been the one who'd arranged for his lawyer to press charges against her father. But Leonidas would make her understand. He'd seduce her with his words. With his touch. And with the lifestyle he could offer.

Daisy was living in the borrowed apartment of some middle-aged artist, an old friend of her father's. But if she came to live with Leonidas, as the cosseted girlfriend of a billionaire, she'd never have to worry about money again. He'd give her a life of luxury. She could quit her job at the diner and spend her days shopping or taking her friends to lunch, and her nights being worshipped by Leonidas in bed. They could travel around the world together, to London and Paris, Sydney, Rio and Tokyo, to his beach house in the Maldives, his ski chalet in Switzerland. He'd take her dancing, to parties, to the art shows and clubs and polo matches attended by the international jet set. He would shower her with gifts, expensive baubles beyond her imagination.

Surely all that could be enough to make her forgive and forget his part in her father's imprisonment? Surely such a life would be worth a little bit of constructive amnesia about her father? Who had been guilty, anyway!

Daisy had to forgive him, he thought suddenly. Why wouldn't she? Whatever Leonidas desired, he always possessed. Daisy Cassidy would be no different. He would pull out all the stops to win her. And though he'd never offer love or marriage, he knew he could make her happy. He'd treat her like the precious treasure she was, filling her days with joy, and her nights with fire.

Leonidas had never failed to seduce any woman he wanted. Tonight would be no different. He would make her forgive him. And forget her foolish loyalty to her dead father.

Tonight, Leonidas thought with determination, a sensual smile curving his lips. He would convince her tonight.

# CHAPTER TWO

DAISY LOOKED UP at the five-story brownstone mansion with big eyes. There had to be some mistake.

"You're sure?" she asked the driver, bewildered.

The uniformed chauffeur hid a smile, dipping his head as he held open the passenger door. "Yes, miss."

Nervously, Daisy got out of the Rolls-Royce. She'd been astonished when the limo had picked her up in Brooklyn. Her neighborhood was prosperous, filled with a mix of artists and intellectuals, plumbers and stockbrokers. But a Rolls-Royce with a uniformed driver had made people stare. She'd been dismayed. The fancy French restaurant had been bad enough. How much had Leo spent renting this limo out? He shouldn't spend money he didn't have, just to impress her! She already thought he was perfect!

Although it was true she didn't know everything about him…

Standing on the sidewalk, she looked back up at the five-story mansion. This tree-lined lane in the West Village of Manhattan was filled with elegant houses only billionaires could afford. She craned her head doubtfully. "Is there a basement apartment?"

The chauffeur motioned toward the front steps. "The main entrance, miss. I believe the party has already started."

There was indeed a stream of limousines and town cars letting people out at the curb. An elderly couple went by Daisy, the wife in an elegant silk coat and matching dress, the husband in a suit.

She looked down at her own cocktail dress, which she'd borrowed from a friend. It was green satin, a little too tight and *way* too low in the bosom. Her cheap high heels, which she'd worn only once on a humiliating gallery night where she hadn't sold a single painting, squeezed her feet painfully.

She glanced behind her, longing to flee. But the driver had already gotten back into the Rolls-Royce and was driving away, to be immediately replaced by arriving vehicles, Italian and German sports cars attended by three valets waiting at the curb.

Daisy glanced toward the subway entrance at the far end of the lane, which ended in a busier street. She could make a run for it. Her puppy, who still didn't have a name, had been left in the care of the same friend, Estie, who'd been her pal in art school. Daisy could still go back home, cuddle the dog and eat popcorn and watch movies.

Except she couldn't. With a deep breath, she faced the brownstone mansion. She had to talk to Leo and tell him she was pregnant. Because she needed answers to her questions.

Would he help her raise the baby?

Would he marry her?

*Could he love her?*

Or would she face her future all on her own?

Swallowing hard, Daisy followed the elderly couple up the steps to the open door, where they were welcomed by a butler. As he looked over Daisy's ill-fitting cocktail dress and cheap shoes, the butler's eyebrows rose. "Your name, miss?"

"Daisy Cassidy." She held her breath, half expecting that, whatever the chauffeur had said, she'd been dropped at the wrong house and would be tossed out immediately.

Instead, the butler gave her a warm smile.

"We've been expecting you, Miss Cassidy. Welcome. Mrs. Berry," he glanced at a plump, white-haired woman nearby, "will take you inside."

"I'm Mr. Niarxos's housekeeper, Miss Cassidy," the older woman said kindly. "Will you please come this way?"

Bewildered, wondering who Mr. Niarxos was—perhaps the butler?—Daisy followed the housekeeper through a lavish foyer. She gawked at the brief vision of a gold-painted ceiling above a crystal chandelier, high overhead, and a wide stone staircase that seemed straight out of *Downton Abbey*. They followed a steady crowd of glamorous guests through tall double doors into a ballroom.

Daisy's jaw dropped. A ballroom! In a house?

The ballroom was big enough to fit three hundred people, with a ceiling thirty feet high. The walls were gilded, and mirrors reflected the light of chandeliers that would have suited Versailles. Waiters wearing black tie walked through holding silver trays with champagne flutes on them. On the small stage, musicians played classical music.

Daisy felt like she'd just fallen through the floor to Wonderland. And there, across the ballroom—

Was that Leo in a tuxedo? Talking to the most famous movie star in the world?

"I'll tell him you're here, Miss Cassidy," Mrs. Berry said. "In the meantime, may I get you a drink?"

"What?" It took her a minute to understand the question. Yes. A stiff drink was an excellent idea. Then she remembered she was pregnant. "Uh…no. Thank you."

"Please wait here, Miss Cassidy." The white-haired woman departed with a respectful bow.

Across the crowds, she watched the housekeeper speak quietly to Leo on the other side of the ballroom. He turned, dark and powerful and devastatingly handsome. His eyes met Daisy's, and she felt a flash of fire.

Nervously, Daisy turned away to stare at a painting on the wall. It was a very nice framed print, a Jackson Pollock she didn't immediately recognize. Then her lips parted as she realized it probably wasn't a print. She was looking at a real Jackson Pollock. Just hanging in someone's home.

Although this didn't feel like a home. It felt like a royal palace. The castle of the king of New York...

"Daisy." Leo's voice was husky and low behind her. "I'm glad you came."

She whirled around. He was so close. Her knees trembled as her limbs went weak. "The puppy is fine," she blurted out. "If you were worried."

"Oh. Good." His expression didn't change. He towered over her, powerful and broad shouldered, the focus of all the glamorous guests sipping cocktails in the ballroom. And no wonder. Daisy's gaze traced unwillingly from his hard jawline, now smoothly shaved, to the sharp cheekbones and his cruel, sensual mouth. How could she tell him she'd fallen in love with him? How could she tell him she was pregnant?

"Thank you for inviting me." She bit her lip, looking around at the glittering ballroom. "Whose house is this really?"

His black eyes burned through her. "It's mine."

She laughed. Then saw he was serious. "But how can it be?" she stammered. Her forehead furrowed. "Are you a member of the staff here?"

"No. I work for Liontari."

"Is that a store?"

"It's a company. We own luxury brands around the world."

"Oh." She felt relieved. So he *did* work for a shop. "Your employer owns this mansion? They're the ones throwing the party?"

"I told you, Daisy. The house is mine."

"But how?" Did being a salesclerk pay better than she could possibly imagine? Was he the best salesman in the world?

Leo looked down at her, then sighed.

"I never told you my full name," he said slowly. "Leonidas Gianakos… Niarxos."

He stared down at her, waiting. A faint warning bell rang at the back of her head. She couldn't quite remember where she'd heard it before. From the butler at the front door? Or before that? She repeated, "Niarxos?"

"Yes." And still he waited, watching her. As if he expected some reaction.

"Oh." Feeling awkward, she said, "So who is this fundraiser for?"

Looking relieved, he named a politician she'd vaguely heard of. She looked around the gilded ballroom. This party was very fancy, that was for sure. She saw people she recognized. Actors. Entrepreneurs. And even—she sucked in her breath. A world-famous artist, which impressed her most of all.

What was Daisy even doing here, with all these chic, glamorous people, people she should properly only read about in magazines or social media, or see on the big screen?

"How—" she began, then her throat dried up.

Across the ballroom, she saw someone else she recognized. Someone she'd glared at every day for a month. Someone she'd never, ever forget. A gray-haired villain in a suit.

Edgar Ross.

The lawyer who'd called the police on her father. The last time she'd seen him, he'd been sitting behind the prosecutor in the courtroom. A ruthless lawyer who worked for an even more ruthless boss, some foreign-born billionaire.

"Daisy?" Leo looked down at her, his handsome face concerned. "What is it?"

"It's… It's… What is he—"

At that moment, Edgar Ross himself came over to them,

with a pretty middle-aged blonde on his arm. "Good evening, Mr. Niarxos."

Daisy's lips parted as Leo greeted the man with a warm handshake. "Good evening." He gave the blonde a polite peck on the cheek. "Mrs. Ross."

"It's a great party. Thanks for inviting us." Edgar Ross smiled vaguely at Daisy, as if he were trying to place her.

She stared back coldly, shaking with the effort it took not to slap him, wishing she'd taken a glass of champagne after all, so she could throw it in his face. Including the glass.

"Admiring your most recent acquisition?" Ross asked Leo. For a moment, Daisy thought he meant *her*. Then she realized he was referring to the painting on the wall.

He shrugged. "It's an investment."

"Of course," Ross said, smiling. "It will just have to hold you, until we can find that Picasso, eh?"

*The Picasso.*

It all clicked horrifyingly into place. Daisy suddenly couldn't breathe.

Edgar Ross.

The Picasso.

The wealthy billionaire reported to be behind it all. The Greek billionaire.

*Leonidas Niarxos.*

In the background, the orchestra continued to play, and throughout the ballroom, people continued to talk and laugh. As if the world hadn't just collapsed.

Daisy slowly turned with wide, stricken eyes.

"Leo," she choked out, feeling like she was about to faint. Feeling like she was about to die.

He looked down at her, then his expression changed. "No," he said in a low voice. "Daisy, wait."

But she was already backing away. Her knees were shaking. The high heel of her shoe twisted, and she barely caught herself from falling.

No. The truth was she hadn't caught herself. She'd fallen in love with Leo, her first and only lover. He'd taken her virginity. He was the father of her unborn baby.

But Leo didn't exist.

He was actually *Leonidas Niarxos*. Edgar Ross's boss. The Greek billionaire behind everything. The real reason the prosecutor and the judge had thrown the book at her father, penalizing him to the fullest extent of the law, when he should have just been fined in civil court—or better yet, found innocent. But no. With his money and power, Leonidas Niarxos had been determined to get his pound of flesh. The spoiled billionaire, who already owned million-dollar paintings and palaces, hadn't gotten the toy he wanted, so he'd destroyed her father's life.

A year ago, when her father had been convicted of forgery, Daisy had been heartbroken, because she'd known he was innocent. Her father was a good man. The best. He never would have broken the law. She'd been shocked and sickened that somehow, in a miscarriage of justice, he'd still been found guilty. Then, six months ago, Patrick had died of a stroke, alone and scared, in a prison surrounded by strangers.

Daisy had vowed that if she ever had the chance, she would take her revenge. She, who'd never wanted to hurt anyone, who always tried to see the best in everyone, wanted *vengeance*.

But she'd naively given Leo everything. Her smiles. Her kisses. Her body. Her love. She was even carrying his baby, deep inside her.

Daisy stared up at Leo's heartbreakingly handsome face. The face she'd loved. So much.

No. He wasn't Leo. She could never think of him as Leo again.

He was Leonidas Niarxos. The man who'd killed her father.

"Oh, my God." Edgar Ross stared at Daisy, his eyes wide. "You're Cassidy's daughter. I didn't recognize you in that dress. What are you doing here?"

Yes, what? The ballroom, with its gilded glitter, started to swim in front of her eyes.

Daisy's breaths came in short wheezing gasps, constricted as her chest was by the too-tight cocktail dress. With every breath, her breasts pushed higher against the low neckline. She felt like she was going to pass out.

She had to get out of there.

But as she turned away, Leonidas grabbed her wrist.

"No!" she yelled, and wrenched her arm away. Everyone turned to stare at them in shock, and the music stopped.

For a moment, he just looked down at her, his handsome face hard. He didn't try to touch her again.

"We need to talk," he said through gritted teeth.

"What could you possibly have to say to me?" she choked out, hatred rising through her, filling every inch of her hollow heart. She gave a low, brittle laugh. "Did you enjoy your little joke? Seducing me? Laughing at me?"

"Daisy…"

"You took *everything*!" Her voice was a rasp. She felt used. And so fragile that a single breeze might scatter her to the wind. "How could you have lied to me? Pretending to love me—"

"I didn't lie—"

"You lied," she said flatly.

"I never claimed to love you."

His dark eyes glittered as they stared at each other.

All around them, the glamorous people were frankly staring, tilting their heads slightly to hear. As if Daisy hadn't been humiliated enough last year by the New York press gleefully calling her beloved, innocent father names like *con artist* and *fraud*, and even worse, calling him too stupid to properly commit a crime.

But she was the one who was stupid. All along, she'd known Leo was hiding things from her. She'd ignored her fears and convinced herself he was perfect. She'd trusted her heart.

Her stupid, stupid heart.

Her shoulders sagged, and her eyes stung. She blinked fast, wiping her eyes savagely.

"Daisy." Leonidas's voice was a low growl. "Just give me a moment. Alone. Let me explain."

She was trembling, her teeth chattering almost loud enough to hear. There was nothing he could possibly say that would take away her sense of betrayal. She should slap his face and leave, and never look him in the face again.

*But their baby.*

Her joints hurt with heartbreak, pain rushing through her veins, pounding a toxic rhythm. Her heart shut down, and she went numb. Whatever he'd done, he was still her baby's father. She had to tell him.

"I'll give you one minute," she choked out.

Leonidas gestured toward the ballroom's double doors. She followed him out of the glittering, glamorous ballroom, away from the curious crowd, into the deserted foyer of the New York mansion. Wordlessly, she followed him up the wide stone staircase, to the dark quiet of the hallway upstairs.

She felt like a ghost of the girl she'd been. As they climbed the staircase, she glanced up at his dark shadow, and felt sick inside.

Discovering she was pregnant earlier that day, she'd felt so alone, so scared. Her first thought had been that she couldn't raise a child without him. But now, Daisy suddenly realized there was something even more terrifying than raising a baby alone.

Doing it with your worst enemy.

* * *

As Leonidas led Daisy past the security guards in the foyer, up the wide stone staircase of his New York mansion, his heart was beating oddly fast.

He glanced back at her.

Daisy looked so beautiful in the emerald green cocktail dress, with high heels showing off her slender legs. Her long honey-brown hair brushed against her shoulders, over the spaghetti straps, past the low-cut neckline which revealed full breasts, plumped up by the tight satin. Against his will, his eyes lingered there. Had her breasts always been so big? Just watching the sensuous way she moved her hand along the stone bannister, he imagined being the one she touched, and he stirred in spite of himself.

But her eyes were downcast, her dark lashes trembling angrily against her pale cheeks.

Leonidas wondered what she was thinking. It was strange. He'd never cared before about what his lovers might be thinking. And with Daisy, he'd always been able to read her feelings on her face.

Until now.

She glanced up at him, her lovely face carefully blank. She looked back down as they climbed the sweeping staircase.

This was not how Leonidas had hoped this evening would go.

Thinking about it at the office, he'd pictured Daisy being dazzled by his mansion, by the glitter and prestige of his guests, by his wealth and power. He'd convinced himself that she would be in a receptive frame of mind to learn the truth. That Daisy would be shocked, dismayed, even, to learn his identity, but she would swiftly forgive him. Because he was so obviously right.

Daisy loved her father. But she had to see that Patrick Cassidy had been a criminal, protecting his accomplice to the end, refusing to say who'd painted the fake Picasso. What else could Leonidas have done but have his lawyer press charges? Should he have paid millions for a painting he knew was fake, or allowed someone else to potentially be defrauded? He'd done the right thing.

Obviously Daisy didn't see it that way. He had to help her see it from his perspective. Setting his jaw, he led her down the dark, empty upstairs hallway and pushed open the second door, switching on the bedroom light.

She stopped in the doorway, glaring at him.

He felt irritated at her accusatory gaze. Did she really think he'd brought her into his bedroom to seduce her? That he intended to simply toss her on the bed and cover her with kisses until the past was forgiven and forgotten?

If only!

Leonidas forced himself to take a deep breath. He kept his voice calm and reassuring, just the way Daisy had spoken when she'd held that abandoned puppy in the alley.

"I'm just bringing you in here to talk," he said soothingly. "Where no one else can hear us."

She flashed him another glance he couldn't read, but came into the bedroom. He closed the door softly behind her.

His bedroom was Spartan, starkly decorated with a king-sized bed, walk-in closet and a lot of open space. Through a large window, he could see the orange and red leaves of the trees on the quiet lane outside, darkening in the twilight.

Standing near the closed door, Daisy wrapped her arms around herself as if for protection, and said in a low voice, "Did you know who I was? The day we met?"

He could not lie to her. "Yes."

She lifted pale green eyes, swimming with tears. "Why did you seduce me? For a laugh? For revenge?"

"No, Daisy, no—" He tried to move toward her, wanting to take her in his arms, to offer comfort. But she moved violently back before he could touch her. He froze, dropping his hands. "I saw a drawing of the trial, when your father's verdict was read. It made me feel sorry for you."

The emotion in her face changed to anger. "*Sorry* for me?"

That hadn't come out right. "I heard your father died in prison, and I came looking for you because…because I wanted to make sure you were all right. And perhaps give you some money."

"Money?" Her expression hardened. "Do you really think that could compensate me for my father's death? Some… some *payoff*?"

"That was never my intention, it—" Leonidas cut himself off, gritting his teeth. He forced his voice to remain calm. "You never deserved to suffer. *You* were innocent."

"So was my father!"

Against his best intentions, his own anger rose. "You cannot be so blind as to think that your father was innocent. Of course he wasn't. He tried to sell a forgery."

"Then he foolishly trusted the wrong person. Someone must have tricked him and convinced him the painting was real. He never would have tried to sell it otherwise! He was a good man! Perfect!"

"Are you kidding? Your father was selling forgeries for years."

"No one else ever accused him—"

"Because either they were too embarrassed, or they didn't realize the paintings were fakes. Your father knew he wasn't selling a real Picasso."

"How would he know that? No one has seen the painting for decades. How did that lawyer lackey of yours even know it wasn't real?"

Leonidas had a flash of memory from twenty years before. His misery as a boy at his parents' strange neglect and hatred. The shock of his mother's final abandonment.

His heartbroken fury, as a boy of fourteen. He could still feel the cold steel in his hand. The canvas ripping beneath his blade in the violent joy of destruction, of finally giving in to his rage—

Looking away, Leonidas said tightly, "I was the one who knew it was a fake. From the moment I saw it in Ross's office."

"You." Daisy glared at him in the cold silence of his bedroom, across the enormous bed, which he'd so recently dreamed of sharing with her. "Why couldn't you just let it go? What's one Picasso to you, more or less?"

Leonidas's shoulders tightened. He didn't want to think about what it meant to him. Or why he'd been looking for it so desperately for two decades.

"So I should have just let your father get away with his deceit?" he said coldly. "Allowed him to continue passing off fake paintings?"

"My father was innocent!" Her expression was fierce. "He looked into my eyes and *swore* it!"

"Because he couldn't bear for you to know the truth. He loved you too much."

Anguish shone in her beautiful face. Then her expression crumpled.

"And I loved him," she said brokenly. She wiped her eyes. "But you're wrong. He never would have lied to me. He had no reason—"

"You would have forgiven him?"

"Yes."

"Because you loved him." Leonidas took a deep breath and looked into her eyes. "So forgive me," he whispered.

She sucked in her breath. "What?"

"You're in love with me, Daisy. We both know that."

Her lush pink lips parted. She seemed to tremble. "What…how—"

"I've seen it on your face. Heard it in your voice. You're

in love—." He took a step toward her, but she put her hand up, warding him off.

"I loved a man who doesn't exist." She looked up, her green eyes glittering. "Not you. I could never love you."

Her words stabbed him like a physical attack. He heard echoes of his mother's harsh voice, long ago.

*Stop bothering me. I'm sick of your whimpering. Leave me alone.*

Leonidas had spent three decades distancing himself from that five-year-old boy, becoming rich and powerful and strong, to make sure he'd never feel like that again. And now this.

Senseless, overwhelming rage filled him.

"You could never love a man like me?" He lifted his chin. "But you're full of love for a liar like your father?"

"Don't you call him that. *You're* the liar! Don't you dare even *speak* of him—"

"He was a criminal, Daisy. And you're a fool," he said harshly.

"You're right. I am." Her lovely face was pale, her clenched hands shaking at her sides. "But you're a monster. You took everything. My father. My home. My self-respect. My virginity..."

"Your father made his own bed." He looked down at her coldly. "So did you."

Her lips parted in a gasp.

"I never took anything that wasn't willingly—*enthusiastically*—given to me," he continued ruthlessly.

"I hate myself for ever letting you touch me," she whispered. Her tearful eyes lifted to his. "I wish I could hurt you like you've hurt me."

Leonidas barked a humorless laugh. "You can't."

New rage filled her beautiful face. "Why? Because you think I'm so powerless? So meaningless?"

"No." He wasn't being rude. If Daisy knew about the

pain of his childhood, he suspected it would satisfy even her current vengeful mood.

But she couldn't know. Leonidas intended to keep those memories buried until the day he died, buried deep in the graveyard that existed beneath his ribs, in place of a heart.

"I hate you," she choked out. "You don't deserve—"

"What?" he said, when she didn't finish. "What don't I deserve?"

She turned her head away. "You don't deserve another moment of my time."

Her voice was low and certain, and it filled him with despair. How had he ever thought he could win her?

Leonidas saw now that he'd never make her see his side. She hated him, just as he'd always known she would, the moment she learned his name.

It was over.

"If you think I'm such a monster," he said hoarsely, "what are you still doing here? Why don't you go?"

She stared at him, her arms wrapped around her belly. For a moment, she seemed frozen in indecision. Then—

"You're right," she said finally. She crossed the bedroom and opened the door. He briefly smelled her perfume, the scent of sunshine and roses. As she passed him, he could almost feel the warmth from her skin, from her curves barely contained beneath the tight green dress. "I never should have come up here." She gave him one last look. "As far as I'm concerned, the man I loved is dead."

Daisy walked out of his bedroom without another glance, disappearing into the shadows of the hall. And she left Leonidas, alone in his mansion, feeling like a monster, surrounded by rich and powerful friends, in a world that was even more dark and bleak than it had been before he'd met her.

# CHAPTER THREE

*Five months later*

IT WAS EARLY MARCH, but in New York, there was no whisper of warmth, not yet. It was gray and cold, and the sidewalks were edged with dirty snow from a storm a few days before. Even the trees had not yet started to bud. The weather still felt miserably like winter.

But for Daisy, spring had already begun.

She took a deep breath, hugging herself as she stepped out of the obstetrician's office. At six months' pregnant, her belly had grown so big she was barely able to zip up her long black puffy coat. She'd had to get new clothes from thrift shops and friends with discarded maternity outfits; aside from her swelling belly, she'd put on a good amount of pregnancy weight.

After a six-hour morning shift at the diner, Daisy had already been exhausted before she'd skipped lunch to go straight to a doctor's appointment. But the medical office had been running late, and she'd sat in the waiting room for an hour. Now, as she finally left, her stomach was growling, and she thought with pity of her dog at home, waiting for her meal, too.

She quickened her step, her breath a white cloud in cold air that was threatening rain. She couldn't stop smiling.

Her checkup had gone perfectly. Her baby was doing well, her pregnancy was on track, and after the morning sickness misery of her first trimester, and the uncertainty of her second, now she was in her final trimester. She finally felt like she knew what she was doing. She felt...*hope*.

It was funny, she thought, as she hurried down the crowded Brooklyn sidewalk, vibrant with colorful shops. Her past was filled with tragedy that she once would have thought she could not survive: her mother's illness and death when Daisy was seven, her own failure at becoming an artist, her father's accusation and trial followed by his sudden death, falling in love with Leo and accidentally getting pregnant then finding out he was actually Leonidas Niarxos.

She had decided to raise her baby alone, rather than with a man who didn't deserve to be her child's father, but it was strange now to remember how, five months ago, she'd been so sure she wasn't strong or brave enough to do it alone. But the fight with Leonidas at his cocktail party had made it clear she had no other choice.

And she'd made it through. She was stronger and wiser. She'd never again be so stupidly innocent, giving her heart to someone she barely knew. She'd never be that young again.

Becoming an adult—a *mother*—meant making responsible choices. She'd given up childish dreams of romance, and someday becoming an artist. Her baby was all that mattered. Daisy put a hand on her belly over her black puffy coat. She'd found out a few months earlier she was having a little girl.

Daisy's friends in Brooklyn had rallied around her. Claudia Vogler, her boss at the diner, had given her extra hours so Daisy could save money. She'd forgiven all of Daisy's missed shifts due to morning sickness, and, when Daisy started having trouble being on her feet all day, Claudia had even created a new job for her—to sit by the cash register at the diner and ring out customers. Since most customers just paid their server directly with a credit card, Daisy mostly just greeted them as they came, and said goodbye as they left.

And she was still living in Franck's apartment, rent free. The middle-aged artist had returned to New York a week after her breakup with Leonidas. He'd been shocked, walking into his apartment, expensive suitcase in hand, to discover a puppy living in his home, which was full of easily breakable sculptures and expensive modern art on the walls.

She'd named her puppy Sunny, to remind herself, even in the depths of her worry, to focus on the brightness all around her. But Sunny was an excitable puppy, and she'd already managed to pee on his rug and chew Franck's slippers.

"I'm so sorry," Daisy had choked out, confessing her puppy's sins. She'd half expected him to throw both her and the dog out.

But to her surprise, Franck had been kind. He'd allowed her to keep the dog and told her she could stay at his apartment as long as she liked, since he was leaving anyway, to snowbird at his house in Los Angeles. That had been in October.

She'd fallen to her lowest point in early January, shivering in the depths of a gray winter despair, she'd felt scared and alone.

Franck, returning to New York on a two-day business trip, had discovered Daisy sitting on the fireside rug, crying into Sunny's fur. When she'd looked up, the gray-haired man had seemed like a surrogate for the father she missed so much, and she'd tearfully told him about her unexpected pregnancy, and that the baby's father was no longer in the picture.

He'd been shocked. After vaguely comforting her, he'd left for his studio. He'd returned late, sleeping in his bedroom down the hall.

Then, the next morning at the breakfast table, right before his return flight to Los Angeles, Franck had abruptly offered to marry her.

Overwhelmed, Daisy had stammered, "You're so kind, Franck, but… I have no intention of marrying anyone."

It was true. In addition to the fact that he was so much older, and had obviously asked her out of pity, Daisy had no desire to marry anyone. Getting her heart broken once was enough for a lifetime.

Franck had seemed strangely disappointed at her refusal. "You're in shock. You'll change your mind," he'd said. And no amount of protesting on her part had made him think differently. "But whether you marry me or not, you're welcome to stay here," he'd added softly, looking down at her. "Stay as long as you want. Stay forever."

It had all been a little awkward. She'd been relieved when he'd left for Los Angeles.

But hearing Franck describe how lovely and warm it was in California had given her an idea. She'd had a sudden memory of her father, two years before.

Daisy had been crying after her first gallery show, heartbroken over her failure to sell a single painting, when her father had said, "We could start over. Move to Santa Barbara, where I was born. It's a beautiful place, warm and bright. We could buy a little cottage by the sea, with a garden full of flowers."

"Leave New York?" Wiping her eyes in surprise, Daisy had looked at him. "What about your gallery, Dad?"

"Maybe I'd like a change, too. Just one more deal to close, and then…we'll see."

Shortly after that, Patrick had been arrested, and there had been no more talk of fresh starts.

But the memory suddenly haunted Daisy. Pregnant and alone, she found herself yearning for her parents' love more than ever. For comfort, for sunshine and warmth, for flowers and the sea.

Her mother had once been a nurse, before she'd gotten sick. Daisy liked helping people, and she knew her income as a waitress would not be enough to support a child, at least not in Brooklyn. She needed grown-up things, like financial security and insurance benefits. Why not?

Holding her breath, Daisy had applied to a small nursing school in Santa Barbara.

Miraculously, she'd been accepted, and with a scholarship, too. She would start school in the fall, when her baby was three months old.

Soon after, her morning sickness had disappeared. She'd managed to save some money, and she had a plan for her future.

But now, Franck was due to return to New York next week for good. Daisy couldn't imagine sharing his apartment with him. She needed to move out.

Where else could she live? None of her friends had extra space, and she couldn't afford to rent her own apartment, not when she was saving every penny for baby expenses and moving expenses. It was a problem.

If she'd had enough money, she would have left for California immediately. In New York City, she was scared of accidentally running into Leonidas. If he ever learned she was pregnant, he might try to take custody of their baby. She was desperate to be free of him. Desperate for a clean break.

But she had a job here, friends here, and—as uncomfortable as it might make her—at least at Franck's, she had a roof over her head. She just had to hold on until summer. Her baby was due in early June. By the end of August, she'd have money to get a deposit on a new apartment, and the two of them could start a new life in California.

Until then, she just had to cross her fingers and pray Leonidas wouldn't come looking for her.

*He won't. It will all work out*, Daisy told herself, as she had so many times over the last few months. *I'll be fine.*

The difference was, she'd finally started to believe it.

In the distance, dark clouds were threatening rain, and she could see her breath in the cold air. Quickening her pace, Daisy started humming softly as she hurried home. She'd heard that a baby, even in the womb, could hear her mother's voice, so she'd started talking and singing to her at all hours. As she sang aloud, some tourists looked at her with alarm. Daisy giggled. Just another crazy New Yorker, walking down the street and singing to herself!

Reaching her co-op building, she greeted the doorman with a smile. "Hey, Walter."

"Good afternoon, Miss Cassidy. How's that baby?" he asked sweetly, as he always did.

"Wonderful," she replied, and took the elevator to the top floor.

As she came through the door, her dog, Sunny, still a puppy at heart in spite of having grown so big, bounded up with a happy bark, tail waving her body frantically. She acted as if Daisy had been gone for months, rather than hours. With a laugh, Daisy petted her lavishly, then went to the kitchen to put food in her dog dish.

She didn't bother to take off her coat. She knew how this would go. As expected, Sunny gulped down her food, then immediately leaped back to the door with a happy bark. Daisy sighed a little to herself. Sunny did love her walks. Even when it was cold and threatening rain.

Grabbing the leash, Daisy attached it to the dog's collar and left the apartment.

Once outside, she took a deep breath of the cold, damp air. It was late afternoon as she took the dog for their usual walk along the river path. By the time they returned forty minutes later, the drizzle was threatening to deepen into rain, and the sun was falling in the west, streaking the fiery sky red and orange, silhouetting the sharp Manhattan skyline across the East River. As busy as she'd been, she'd forgotten to eat that day, and she was starving. Seeing her co-op building ahead, Daisy hurried her pace, fantasizing about what she'd have for dinner.

Then she saw the black Rolls-Royce parked in front of the building. A chill went down her spine as a towering, dark-haired figure got out of the limo.

She stopped cold, causing a surprised yelp from Sunny. She wanted to turn and run—a ridiculous idea, when she knew Leonidas Niarxos could easily run her down, with his powerful body and long legs.

Their eyes met, and he came forward grimly.

She couldn't move, staring at his darkly powerful form, with the backdrop view of the majestic bridge and red sunset.

Please, she thought as he approached. Let her black puffy coat be enough to hide her pregnancy. Please, please.

But her hope was crushed with his very first words.

"So it's true?" Leonidas's voice was dangerously low, his black eyes gleaming like white-hot coal in the twilight. He looked down at her belly, bulging out beneath the long black puffy coat. "You're pregnant?"

Instinctively, she wrapped her hands over her baby bump. How had he heard? She trembled all over. "What are you doing here?"

"Are you, Daisy?"

She could hardly deny it. "Yes."

His burning gaze met hers. "Is the baby mine?"

She swallowed hard, wanting more than anything to lie.

But she couldn't. Even though Leonidas had lied to her about his identity, and lied about Daisy's father, she couldn't fall to his level. She couldn't lie to his face. Not even for her child.

What kind of mother would she be, if she practiced the same deceit as Leonidas Niarxos? She felt somehow, even in the womb, that her baby was listening. And she had to prove herself worthy. She, at least, was a good person. *Unlike him*.

"Am I the father, Daisy?" he pressed.

Stiffening, Daisy lifted her chin defiantly. "Only biologically."

*"Only?"* Leonidas's eyes went wide, then narrowed. Setting his jaw, he walked slowly around her, as if searching for weaknesses. He ignored her dog, who traitorously wagged her tail at him. "Why didn't you tell me?"

"Why would I?"

"Because it's the decent thing to do?"

She glared at him. "You don't deserve to be her father."

Leonidas stopped, as if he'd been punched in the gut. Then he said evenly, "You are legally entitled to child support."

She tossed her head. "I don't want it."

"You'd really let your pride override the best interests of the child?"

"Pride!" she breathed. "Is that what you think?"

"What else could it be? You want to hurt me. You don't care that it also injures our baby in the process."

It was strange, Daisy thought, that even after all this time, he could still find new ways to hurt her.

It didn't help that Leonidas was even more devastatingly handsome than she remembered, standing in the twilight dressed in black from head to toe, in his dark suit covered by a long dark coat. His clothing was sleek, but his black hair was rumpled, and his sharp jawline was edged with five o'clock shadow. Everything about him seemed dark in this moment.

"This isn't about you," she ground out. "It's about her. She doesn't need a father like you—a liar with no soul!"

For a moment, they glared at each other as they stood on the empty pathway along the East River, with the brilliant backdrop of Manhattan's skyline against the red sunset. Her harsh words hung between them like toxic mist.

"You only hate me because I told the truth about your father." His voice was low. "But I am not the one you should hate. I never lied to you."

"How can you say that?" She was outraged. "From the day we met, when you told me your name—"

"I didn't tell you my full name. But that was only because I liked talking to you and didn't want it to end." His deep voice was quiet. "I never lied. I never tried to sell a forgery. I am not the criminal."

She caught her breath, and for a moment she felt dizzy, wondering if he could be telling the truth. Could her father have been guilty? Had he known the Picasso was a forgery when he'd tried to sell it?

*I didn't do it, baby. I swear it on my life. On my love for you.*

Daisy remembered the tremble in her father's voice, the emotion gleaming in his eyes the night of his arrest. All throughout his trial and subsequent imprisonment, he'd maintained his innocence, saying he'd been duped just like his wealthy customers. But he'd refused to say who had duped him.

Who was she going to believe—the perfect father who'd raised her and loved her, caring for her as a single parent after her mother died, or the selfish billionaire who'd had him dragged into court, who'd taken Daisy's virginity and left her pregnant and alone?

"Don't you dare call my father a criminal!"

"He was convicted. He went to prison."

"Where he died—thanks to you!" Her voice was a rasp.

"You ruined his life out of spite, over a painting that meant nothing—"

"That painting means more than—"

"You ruined my life on a selfish whim." Daisy's voice rose. "Why would I want you near my baby, so you could wreck her life as well? Just go away, and leave us alone!"

Leonidas stared at her in shock. He'd never imagined that he'd become a father. And he'd never imagined that his baby's mother could hate him so much.

The soft drizzle had turned to sleet, falling from the darkening sky. Nearby, he could almost hear the rush of the East River, the muffled roar of traffic from the looming bridge.

*Just go away, and leave us alone.*

He heard the echo of his mother's voice when he was five years old.

*Stop bothering me. I'm sick of your whimpering. Leave me alone.*

Since their breakup last October, through a gray fall and grayer winter, Leonidas had tried to keep thoughts of Daisy at bay. Yes, she was beautiful. But so what? The world was full of beautiful women. Yes, she was clever. Diabolically so, since she'd lured him so easily into wanting her, into believing she was different from the rest. Into believing her love could somehow save his soul and make him a better man.

Ridiculous. It humiliated him to remember. He'd acted like a fool, believing their connection had been based on anything more than sexual desire.

He couldn't let down his guard. He couldn't let himself depend on anyone's love.

Daisy Cassidy had been the most exhilarating lover he'd ever had, but she was also the most dangerous. He'd needed to get her out of his life. Out from beneath his skin.

So the day after their argument, he'd left New York, vowing to forget her. And he had.

By day.

But night was a different matter. His body could not forget. Against his will, all these months later, he still dreamed of her, erotic dreams of a sensual virgin, luring him inexorably to his destruction. In the dream, he gave her everything—not just his body, not just his fortune, he gave her his heart. Then she always took it in her grasp and crushed it to dripping blood and burned ash.

Two days before, he'd woken after one particularly agonizing dream at his luxury apartment on the Boulevard Saint-Germain in Paris, gasping and filled with despair.

Ever since their affair had ended, his days had been gray. He barely cared about the billion-dollar conglomerate which had once been his passion. Even his formerly docile board was starting to whisper that perhaps he should step down as CEO.

Leonidas could hardly blame them. He'd lost his appetite for business. He'd lost his edge. The truth was, he just didn't give a damn anymore. How long would he be tormented by these dreams of her—dreams that could never again be real?

Then he'd suddenly gotten angry.

He realized he hadn't visited his company's headquarters back in New York once since that disastrous cocktail party. Daisy had driven him out of the city. He'd left his ex-girlfriend in victorious possession of the entire continent. But even on the other side of the world, she destroyed his peace.

*No longer.*

Grimly, he'd called his chief of security at the New York office. "Find out about Daisy Cassidy. I want to know what she's doing."

Then he'd called his pilot to arrange the flight back to New York. He was done running from her. He'd done nothing wrong. *Nothing.* Maybe, once he was back amid the hum and energy of his company's headquarters, he'd regain some of his old passion for the luxury business.

But he didn't relish the thought of Daisy ambushing him at some Manhattan event, or seeing her on another man's arm. He hoped his chief of security would tell him she'd moved to Miami—or better yet, Siberia. Either way, Leonidas wanted to be prepared.

But he'd had no defense against what his security chief had told him.

Daisy Cassidy was six months pregnant, according to her friends. And refusing to say who the father might be.

But Leonidas knew. Daisy had been a virgin their first night, and she'd been faithful for the month of their affair— he had no doubt of that.

The baby had to be his.

Leonidas had felt restless, jittery, on the flight back to New York yesterday, wondering if she'd already known she was pregnant the night she'd walked out on him. Back at his West Village mansion, he'd collapsed, and slept like the dead. But at least he hadn't been tormented by dreams.

Waking up late, he'd gone to the office, but had lasted only two hours before he'd called his driver to take him across the river. He'd waited outside the Brooklyn co-op where Daisy lived, tension building inside him as he tried to decide whether to go inside. Once he confirmed her pregnancy, there would be no going back.

Then he saw her, walking her dog on the street.

Leonidas hadn't been able to tear his eyes away. Daisy was more beautiful than ever, her green eyes shining, her face radiant, and her body lush with pregnancy. She'd gained some weight, and her fuller curves suited her, making her even more impossibly desirable.

Why hadn't she told him she was pregnant? Did she really hate him so much that she wouldn't even accept his financial support for their child? It seemed incredibly reckless and wrong. She could have been pampered in her pregnancy. Instead, by all accounts she was still working on her feet as a waitress, and living in another man's apartment. The same apartment where she and Leonidas had conceived this child. No wonder he felt so off-kilter and dizzy.

Then she'd said it.

*Just go away, and leave us alone.*

Leonidas stared at her, still shocked that the tenderhearted girl who'd once claimed to love him could say anything so cruel. His whole body felt tight, his heart rate increasing as his hands clenched at his sides.

His voice was hoarse as he said, "You really believe I'm such a monster that you need to hide your pregnancy from me? You won't even let me support my own child?"

Daisy's expression filled with shadow in the twilight, as if even she realized she'd gone too far.

"We don't need you," she said finally, and turning, she hurried away, almost running with her dog following behind, disappearing into the apartment building.

*You little monster.* His mother's enraged voice, when he was fourteen. *I wish you'd never been born!*

For a moment, the image of the bleak bridge and water swam before Leonidas's eyes, malevolent and dark against the red twilight. His heart hammered in his throat, his body tense.

Those had been his mother's final words, the last time Leonidas saw her. He'd been fourteen, and had just come from the funeral of the man he'd always believed was his father, when his mother had told him the truth, and that she never intended to see Leonidas again. Heartsick, he'd hacked into her precious masterpiece with a pair of scissors. Ripping the broken Picasso from his hands, his mother had left him with those final words.

She'd died in the Turkish earthquake a week later, and

the Picasso had disappeared. That day, Leonidas had lost his only blood relative in the world.

Until now.

Leonidas looked up at the co-op building, with its big windows overlooking the river. His eyes narrowed dangerously.

Daisy had kept her pregnancy a secret, because she didn't want him to be a father to their baby.

*Why would I want you near my baby, so you could wreck her life as well?*

*Her* life. Leonidas suddenly realized the import of Daisy's words. They were having a baby girl.

And whether Daisy liked it or not, Leonidas was going to be a father. He would soon have a daughter who'd need him to protect and provide for her. This baby was his family.

His only family.

Gripping his hands at his sides, Leonidas went toward the building. He gave a sharp shake of his head to his driver, waiting with the Rolls-Royce at the curb, and went forward alone into the apartment building. He opened the door, going into the contemporary glass-and-steel lobby, with modern, sparse furniture. He headed straight for the elevator, until he found his way blocked.

"Can I help you, sir?" the doorman demanded.

"Daisy Cassidy," he barked in reply. "I know the apartment number."

"You must wait," the man replied. Going to the reception desk, the man picked up his phone. "Your name, sir?"

"Leonidas Niarxos."

The doorman spoke quietly into the phone, then looked up. "I'm sorry, Miss Cassidy says she has nothing to say to you. She asks you to leave the building immediately."

A curse went through his mind. "Tell her she can talk to me now or talk to an army of lawyers in an hour."

The doorman raised his eyebrows, then again spoke quietly. With a sigh, he hung up the phone. "She says to go up, Mr. Niarxos."

"Yes," he bit out. He stalked to the elevator, feeling the doorman's silently accusing eyes on his back. But Leonidas didn't give a damn. His fury sustained him as he pushed the elevator button for the fifth floor.

He straightened, his jaw tight. He was no longer a helpless five-year-old. No longer a heartsick fourteen-year-old. He was a man now. A man with power and wealth. A man who could take what he wanted.

And he wasn't going to let Daisy steal his child away.

The elevator gave a cheerful ding as the door slid open. He grimly stalked down the hall to apartment 502. Lifting his hand, he gave a single hard knock.

The door opened, and he saw Daisy's furious, tear-stained face.

In spite of everything, his heart twisted at the sight. Her pale green eyes, fringed with thick black lashes, were luminous against her skin, with a few adorable freckles scattered across her nose. Her lips were pink and full, as she chewed on her lower lip, as if trying to bite back angry words.

Her body, in the fullness of pregnancy, was lush and feminine. She'd taken off her long puffy coat, and was dressed simply, in a long-sleeved white shirt over black leggings. But she was somehow even more alluring to him than the night of the cocktail party, when she'd been wearing that low-cut green dress, with her breasts overflowing. He'd thought the dress was simply tight, but now he realized her breasts had already been swollen by pregnancy. Pregnant. With his baby.

A baby she was trying to keep from Leonidas, who was here and ready to take responsibility. Who wanted to be a father!

Interesting. He blinked. He hadn't realized it until now.

He'd always thought he had no interest in fatherhood, no interest in settling down. What did he know about being a good parent?

But now he wanted it more than anything.

Daisy tossed her head with an angry, shuddering breath. "How dare you threaten me with lawyers?"

"How dare you try to steal my child?" he retorted, pushing into the apartment without touching her.

It was the first time he'd been back here since their days as lovers. The apartment looked just as he remembered, modern and new, with a gas fireplace and an extraordinary view of the bridge and Manhattan skyline. The only new changes were a slapdash Van Gogh pastiche now hanging in the foyer, and the large dog bed sitting near the fire, where a long-limbed, floppy yellow dog drowsed.

Leonidas took a deep breath, dizzy with the memory of how happy he'd been here, in those stolen hours when he'd been simply Leo, nothing more. This was enemy territory—Daisy's home—but it somehow still felt warm. Far more than his own multimillion-dollar homes around the world.

He felt suddenly insecure.

"You said this is Franck Bain's apartment," he said slowly.

"So?"

"Why has he let you stay so long? Are you lovers?"

Closing the door behind him, Daisy said coldly, "It's none of your business, but no. He was my father's friend, and he is trying to help me. That's all."

"Why would I believe that?"

"Why would you even care?" She looked at him challengingly. "I'm sure you've had lovers by the score since you tossed me out of your house."

But he hadn't. He hadn't had sex in five months—not since their last time together. But that was the last thing

Leonidas wanted to admit to Daisy. He lifted his chin. "I did not toss you out."

"You asked me what I was still doing at your house. And told me to go!"

"Funny, I mostly remember you insulting me, calling me a liar and saying how badly you wished you could hurt me." He gave a low, bitter laugh. "I guess you figured out a way, didn't you? By not telling me you were pregnant."

The two of them stared at each other in the fading red light, an electric current of hatred sizzling the air between them.

They were so close, he thought. Their bodies could touch with the slightest movement. His gaze fell unwillingly to her lips.

He saw a shiver pass over Daisy.

"You're a bastard," she whispered.

Those were truer words than she knew. He took a deep breath, struggling to hold back his insecurity, his pain. He met her gaze evenly.

"You didn't always think so." His gaze moved toward the hallway, toward the dark shadow of her bedroom door. "When we spent hours in bed. You wanted me then. Just as I wanted you."

Her lips parted. Then she swallowed, stepping back.

"You're charming when you want to be." Her jaw hardened. "But beneath your good looks, your money, your charm—you're nothing."

*You little monster. I wish you'd never been born!*

In spite of his best efforts, emotion flooded through him—emotion he'd spent his whole adult life trying to outrun and prove wrong, by the company he'd built, by his massively increasing fortune, by the beautiful women he'd bedded, by his worldwide acclaim.

But Leonidas suddenly realized he would never escape it. Even with all of his fame and fortune, he was still the same worthless, unwanted boy, without a real family or home. Without a father, with a mother who despised him— raised by the twin demons of shame and grief.

He said tightly, "How you feel about me, or I feel about you, is irrelevant now. What matters is taking care of our baby."

Daisy looked at him incredulously. "I know that. Don't you think I know that? Why else do you think I tried to hide my pregnancy?"

"Don't you think our daughter needs a father?"

"Not a father like you!"

Blood rushed through his ears. With her every accusation, the stunned rage he'd felt on the river pathway built higher, making it harder to stay calm. But he managed to say evenly, "You accuse me of being a monster. All I'm trying to do is take responsibility for my child."

"How?" she cried. "By threatening me with lawyers?"

"I never actually meant—" He ground his teeth. "You were refusing to even talk to me."

"For good reason!"

"Daisy," he said quietly, "What are you so afraid of?"

She stared at him for a long moment, then looked away. He waited out her silence, until she finally said in a small voice, "I'm scared you'll try and take her from me. I saw what your money and lawyers did in court, with my father. I'm scared you'll turn them against me and try to take her— not because you love her. Out of spite. Because you can."

She really did think the worst of him. Leonidas exhaled. "I would never try to take any baby away from a loving parent. Never."

Daisy slowly looked at him, and he saw a terrible hope rising in her green eyes. "You wouldn't?"

"No. But I'm her parent, too. Whether you like it or not, we're both responsible. I never imagined I'd ever become a father, but now that she exists, I can't let her go. She's my only family in the world, do you know that?"

Silently, Daisy shook her head.

"I can't abandon her," he said. "Or risk having her wonder about me, wonder why I didn't love her enough to be there for her every day, to help raise her, to love her. To truly be her father."

Looking down at the hardwood floor, she said in a small voice, "So what can we do?"

Yes—what? How could Leonidas make sure he was part of his child's life forever, without lawyers, without threats? Without always fearing that Daisy might at any moment choose to disappear, or marry another man—a man who might always secretly despise his stepdaughter for not being his own?

His lips suddenly parted.

A simple idea. Insane. Easy. With one stroke, everything could be secure. Everything could be his.

It was an idea so crazy, he'd never imagined he would consider it. But as soon as he thought of it, the vibrating tension left his body. Leonidas suddenly felt calmer than he'd felt in days—in months.

He gave her a small smile. "Our baby needs a father. She needs a name. And I intend to give her mine." He met her gaze. "And you, as well."

She stared at him, her lovely face horrified. "What are you saying?"

"The answer is simple, Daisy." He tilted his head, looking down at her. "You're going to marry me."

# CHAPTER FOUR

MARRY LEONIDAS NIARXOS?

Standing in the deepening shadows of the apartment, Daisy stared at Leonidas, her mouth open.

"Are you crazy?" she exploded. "I'm not going to marry you!"

His darkly handsome face grew cold. "We both created this child. We should both raise her." His black eyes narrowed. "I never want her to question who she is. Or feel anything less than cherished by both her parents."

"As if you could ever love anyone!" She still felt sick remembering how he'd once said, *I never claimed to love you.*

"You're right. I'm not sure I know how to love anyone." As she gaped at his honesty, Leonidas shook his head. "But I know I can protect and provide. It is my job as a man. Not just for her. Also for you."

"Why?" she whispered.

Leonidas looked down at her.

"Because I can," he said simply. He took a deep breath. "I might not have the ability to love you, Daisy. But I can take care of you. Just as I can take care of our daughter. If you'll let me."

Daisy swallowed hard.

"But, marriage…" she whispered. "How could we promise each other forever, without love?"

"Love is not necessary between us—or even desirable. Romantic love can be destructive."

Destructive? Daisy looked at his clenched jaw, the tightness around his eyes. Had someone broken Leonidas's heart? She fought the impulse to reach out to him, to ask questions, to offer comfort. Sympathy was the last thing she wanted to feel right now.

"What about marrying someone you despise?" she pointed out. "That seems pretty destructive."

"Do you really hate me so much, Daisy? Just because I was afraid to tell you my last name when we met? Just because, when a man tried to sell me a forgery, I pressed charges? For that, you're determined to hate me for the rest of your life? No matter what that does to our child?"

She bit her lip. When he put it like that…

Her heart was pounding. She thought of how she'd felt last October, when she'd loved him, and he'd broken her heart. It would kill her if that ever happened again. "I can't love you again."

"Good." Leonidas looked down at her in the falling light. "I'm not asking you to. But give me a chance to win back your trust."

Her heart lifted to her throat. Trust?

It was a cruel reminder of how she'd once trusted Leo, blindly believing him to be perfect. How could she ever trust him again?

Daisy looked down at her short waterproof boots. "I don't know if I can."

"Why won't you try?" His face was in shadow. He tilted his head. "Are you in love with someone else? The artist who owns this apartment, Franck Bain?"

"I told you, he's a friend, nothing more!" Daisy kept Franck's marriage proposal to herself. No point in giving Leonidas ammunition. She shook her head fiercely. "I don't want to love anyone. Not anymore. I've given up on that fairy tale since—"

Her voice cut off, but it was too late.

Leonidas drew closer. The light from the hallway caressed the hard edges of his face. "Since you loved me?"

A shiver went through Daisy. Against her will, her gaze fell to his cruel, sensual lips. She still couldn't forget the memory of his kiss, his mouth so hot against her skin, making her whole body come alive.

No, she told herself angrily. No! She'd allowed her body to override her brain once before. And look what had happened!

But she still felt Leonidas's every movement. His every breath. Even though he didn't touch her, she could still feel him, blood and bone.

He looked down at her. "You don't need to worry, then," he said softly. "Because we agree. Neither of us is seeking love. Because romantic love is destructive."

She agreed with him, didn't she? So why did her heart twist a little as she said, "Yes, I guess you're right." She took a deep breath. "That doesn't mean I can just forgive or forget what you did."

"You loved your father."

"Yes."

"He meant everything to you."

"Yes!"

Leonidas looked at her. "Don't you think our daughter deserves the chance to have a father, too?"

She caught her breath.

Was she being selfish? Putting her own anger ahead of their baby's best interests—not just financially, but emotionally?

"How can I know you'll be a good father to our daughter?" she said in a small voice.

"I swear it to you. On my honor."

"Your *honor*," she said bitterly. Her hands went protectively over her baby bump, over her cotton shirt.

He gently put his larger hand over hers.

"Yes. My honor. Which means a great deal to me." He looked her straight in the eye. "I have no family, Daisy. No siblings or cousins. Both my parents are dead. I never intended to marry or have a child of my own. But now… This baby is all I have. All I care about is her happiness. I will do anything to protect her."

Daisy heard the words for the vow they were. Her heart lifted to her throat. He truly wanted to be a good father. She heard it in his voice. He cared about this child in a way she'd never expected.

Her heart suddenly ached. How she wished she could believe him! How lovely it would be to actually have a partner in her pregnancy, someone else looking out for her, rather than having to figure out everything herself!

But could she live with a man who'd done what Leonidas had done? Even if she never loved him—could she live with him? Accept him as her co-parent—trust him as a friend?

His hand tightened over hers. "There could be other benefits to our marriage, Daisy," he said huskily. "More than just being partners. Living together, we could have other…pleasures."

He was talking about sharing a bed. Images of their lovemaking flashed through her, and she felt a bead of sweat between her breasts.

"If you think I'm falling into bed with you, you're crazy," she said desperately. She stepped back, pulling away from his touch. Just to make sure she didn't do something she'd regret, like reach for his strong, powerful body, pull it against her own, and lift her lips to his…

She couldn't. She mustn't!

"I can't forget how it felt to make love to you," he said in a low voice. "I still dream about it. Do you?"

"No," she lied.

His dark eyes glinted. His lips curved wickedly as he

came forward, and without warning, he swept her up into his powerful arms.

"Shall I remind you what it was like?" he said softly, his gaze hot against her trembling lips.

For a moment, standing in this apartment where they'd made love so many times, in so many locations—on that sofa, against that wall—all she wanted was to kiss him, to feel his hands against her naked skin. It terrified her, how easily he made her body yearn to surrender!

But if she did, how long would it take before she gave him everything?

Trembling, she wrenched away. "No."

He looked at her, and she thought she saw a flash of vulnerability in his dark eyes. Then his handsome face hardened. "I'm not going away, Daisy. I'm not going to abandon her."

"I know." She prayed he didn't realize how close she was to spinning out of control. She needed to get him out of here, out of this apartment with all its painfully joyful memories. "I'm tired. Can we talk tomorrow?"

"No," he said, unyielding. "This needs to be settled."

Sunny rose from her dog bed to sniff curiously at Leonidas. The dog looked up at him with hopeful eyes, clearly waiting to be petted. He briefly scratched her ears. As he straightened, the dog licked his hand.

*Traitor.* Daisy glared at her pet. Just when she most wanted her canine protector to growl and bark, another female fell helplessly at the Greek tycoon's feet!

Leonidas stood before her, illuminated by the bright Manhattan skyline and the starry night, and a lump rose in her throat. Did he know how memories of their love affair haunted her?

If it had been Leo wanting to kiss her, she would have already fallen into his arms. If it had been Leo proposing, she would have married him in an instant.

But it wasn't. Instead, it was a handsome stranger, a coldhearted billionaire, the man who'd put her father in jail.

"I can see you're tired," Leonidas said gently, looking at her slumped shoulders and the way her hands cradled her belly. "Are you hungry? Perhaps I could take you to dinner?"

He sounded hesitant, as if he were expecting her to refuse. But after her early morning shift at the diner, followed by her checkup at the obstetrician's office and then walking her energetic dog, Daisy *was* tired and hungry.

"Another fancy restaurant?" she said.

"Whatever kind of restaurant you want. Homey. Casual." Leonidas smiled down at Sunny, who was by now licking his hand and flirtatiously holding up her paw. He added, "You can even bring your dog." He straightened, giving her a slow-rising, sensual smile. "What do you say?"

It was really not fair to use her dog against her. Or that smile, which burned right through her. Daisy hated how her body reacted to Leonidas's smile, causing electricity to course through her veins. She was no better than her pet, she thought in disgust.

But she *was* hungry. And more than anything, she wanted to get Leonidas out of this apartment, with all its sensual memories, before she did something she'd regret.

"Fine," she bit out. "Dinner. Just dinner, mind. Someplace homey and casual. Where dogs are allowed."

Leonidas's smile became a grin. "I know just the place."

Leonidas looked at Daisy, sitting next to him in the back seat of the Rolls-Royce. Daisy's floppy yellow dog was in her lap, sticking her head excitedly out the window. The animal's tongue lolled out of her mouth as they crossed over the East River, into Manhattan.

Sadly, the pet's mistress didn't seem nearly so pleased.

Daisy's lovely face was troubled as she stared fiercely out the window.

But it was enough. He'd convinced Daisy to come to dinner. He'd given quiet instructions to his chauffeur, Jenkins, and sent a text to his assistant. Everything was set.

Now he had Daisy, he never intended to let her go.

It was strange. Leonidas had never imagined wanting to get married, and certainly never imagined becoming a father. But now he was determined to do both and do them well. In spite of—or even perhaps because of—his own awful childhood.

For his whole life, he'd been driven to prove himself. His first memories involved desperately trying to please the man he thought was his father, who called him stupid and useless. Leonidas had tried to do better, to make his penmanship, his English conjugations, his skill with an épée all perfect. But no matter his efforts, Giannis had bullied him and sneered at him, while his mother ignored him completely—unless they were in company. Appearances were all that mattered, and as violently as his parents fought each other, they were united in wanting others to believe they had the perfect marriage, the perfect son, the perfect family.

But the truth was far from perfect. His parents had seemed to hate each other—but not as much as they hated Leonidas. From the age of five, when he'd first noticed that other children were hugged and loved and praised by their parents, Leonidas had known something was horribly wrong with him. There had to be, or why would his own parents despise him, no matter how hard he tried?

He'd never managed to impress them. When he was fourteen, they'd died, leaving him with no one but distant trustees, and boarding school in America.

At twenty-one, fresh out of Princeton, he'd seized the reins of Giannis's failing leather goods business, near bankruptcy after seven years of being run into the ground by trustees. He decided he didn't need a family. He didn't need love. Success would be the thing to prove his worth to the world.

And he'd done what no one expected of an heir: he'd rebuilt the company from the ground up. He'd renamed it Liontari, and over the next fifteen years, he'd made it a global empire through will and work and luck. He'd fought his way through business acquisitions, hostile takeovers, and created, through blood and sweat, the worldwide conglomerate now headquartered in New York.

But none of those battles, none of those hard-won multi-million-dollar deals, had ever made him feel as triumphant as Daisy agreeing to dinner tonight.

This was personal.

Leonidas had never been promiscuous with love affairs, having only a few short-term relationships each year, but the women in his life had often accused him of being cold, even soulless. "You have no feelings at all!" was an accusation that had been hurled at him more than once.

And it was probably true. He tended to intellectualize everything. He didn't *feel* things like everyone else seemed to. Even when he beat down business rivals, he didn't glory in the triumph. Losing a lover made him shrug, not weep.

But he told himself he was lucky. Without feelings, he could be rational, rather than pursuing emotional wild goose chases as others did. The only emotion he really knew was anger, and he kept even that in check when he could.

Except when he'd been Leo.

It was strange, looking back. For the month he'd been Daisy's lover, it had been exhilarating to let down his guard and not have to live up to the world's expectations of Leonidas Niarxos, billionaire playboy. In Daisy's eyes, he'd been an ordinary man, a nobody, really—but somehow she'd still thought him worthy.

And he'd loved it. He'd been free to be truly himself, instead of always being primed for battle, ready to attack or defend. He'd been able to show his silly side, like the time they'd nearly died laughing together while digging through vintage vinyl albums at a Brooklyn record shop, teasing each other about whose taste in music was worse. Or the time they'd brought weird flavors of ice cream home from an artisanal shop, and they'd ended up smearing each other with all the different flavors—chocolate cinnamon, whiskey banana and even one oddly tart sugar dill... He shivered, remembering how it had tasted to suckle that exotic flavor off Daisy's bare, taut nipple.

In the back of his mind, Leonidas had always known it could not last.

*But this would.*

He would marry Daisy. They'd raise their child together. Their daughter would have a different childhood than Leonidas had had. She would always feel wanted. Cherished. Encouraged. Whether she was making mud pies or learning calculus or kicking soccer balls, whether she was succeeding or failing, she would always know that her father adored her.

But marriage was the key to that stability. Otherwise, what would stop Daisy from someday becoming another man's wife? Leonidas wanted to be a full-time father, not a part-time one. He wanted a stable home, and for their daughter to always know exactly who her family was. And if Daisy married someone else, how could he guarantee that any other man could care for Leonidas's child as she needed—as she deserved?

He had to be there for his child. And Daisy.

He had to convince her that he was right.

But how?

Leonidas looked at Daisy, sitting next to him in the spacious back seat of the limo. Convincing her to join him for dinner was a good start. But as they crossed into Manhattan, she still stared fiercely out the window, stroking her dog as if it were an emotional support animal. Her lower lip wobbled, as if she were fighting back tears.

The smile slid away from Leonidas's face. A marriage where the husband and wife fought in white-knuckled warfare, or secretly despised each other in a cold war, was the last thing he wanted. He'd seen that in his own parents, though they'd supposedly once been passionately in love.

He wanted a partnership with Daisy. A friendship. That was the best way to create a home for a child. At least so he'd heard.

Leonidas took a deep breath. He had to woo Daisy. Win her. Convince her he was worthy of her trust and esteem, if not her love. Just as he'd done with Liontari—he had to take their bankrupt, desolate relationship, and make it the envy of the world.

But how?

As the Rolls-Royce crossed into the shadowy canyons between Manhattan's illuminated skyscrapers, the moonlight was pale above them. The limo finally pulled up in front of his five-story mansion in the West Village. Daisy looked up through her car window.

"You call that homey?" she said in a low voice.

He shrugged. "It's home. And very dog friendly."

"Since when?"

"Since now." Getting out of the car, Leonidas shook his head at his driver, and opened her door himself.

But as Daisy got out of the back seat, she wouldn't meet Leonidas's eyes, or take his offered hand. Cuddling her dog against her chest, she looked up at Leonidas's hundred-year-old brownstone, her lovely face anxious.

"I'm not sure this is a good idea."

"It's just dinner. A totally casual, very homey, dog-friendly dinner."

Her expression was dubious, but she got out of the car. Daisy and her dog followed him slowly up the steps to the door, where he punched in the code. They went into the foyer, beneath crystal chandeliers high overhead.

"Where's the butler?" she asked, the corners of her lips curving up slightly as he helped her take off her long black coat.

"He quit a few months ago."

"Quit?"

"I've been living in Paris. He went in search of less boring employment." He shrugged. "I still have Mrs. Berry and a few other staffers, but they've all gone home for the night."

Daisy drew back, her face troubled in the shadowy foyer. "So we're alone?"

He took off his coat, adding it to the nearby closet beside hers. "Is that a problem?"

Her gaze slid away. "Of course not. I'm not scared of you."

"Good. You're safe with me, Daisy. Don't you realize that? Don't you realize I would die to protect you—you and the baby?"

Her eyes met his. "You would?"

"I told you. Our baby is my only family. That means you're under my protection as well. I will always protect and provide for you. On my honor." Remembering how little she'd thought of his honor, he added quietly, "On my life."

As their eyes locked, the air between them electrified. Her gaze fell to his lips. His hand tightened on her shoulder as he moved closer—

The doorbell rang behind them, jarring him. Then he smiled. "That must be dinner."

She looked surprised. "You ordered takeout?"

"My housekeeper's gone home. How else could I serve

dinner? I swore to protect you, not poison you with burned meals."

The edges of her mouth lifted. "True."

For a moment, they smiled at each other, and he knew she was remembering the single disastrous night he'd tried to cook for her in the Brooklyn apartment. Somehow he'd turned boiled spaghetti noodles and canned marinara sauce into a full-scale culinary disaster that had required a fire extinguisher.

Then her smile fell, and he knew that she was thinking of everything that had happened since.

That was a battle he could not win. So he turned to answer the door. Speaking quietly to the delivery person, he took the bags, then turned to face Daisy. "Shall we?"

She looked at the bags. "What is it?"

"Chinese." He hesitated. "I know it used to be your favorite, but if you'd rather have something else..."

"Kung pao chicken?" she interrupted.

"Of course."

"It's exactly what I want." She looked almost dismayed about it.

Leonidas led her through the large, spacious house to a back hallway which led to an enormous kitchen, her dog's nails clicking against the marble floor as she followed behind. On the other side of the kitchen was a small, cozy breakfast room with wide windows and French doors overlooking a private courtyard.

Outside, in the moonlight, a few snowflakes were falling. As Leonidas put the bags of Chinese takeout on the breakfast table, Daisy looked out at the courtyard in surprise. "You have your own yard? In the middle of Manhattan?"

Leonidas shrugged. "It's why I bought this house. I always want fresh air and space."

Daisy's forehead furrowed. "*You* like fresh air?"

He barked a laugh. "Is that so shocking?"

"I just picture you only in boardrooms, or society ball-rooms, or the back seat of a Rolls-Royce or…"

"Let me guess," he responded, amused. "Sitting in the basement of a bank, counting my piles of gold like Scrooge McDuck?"

Her green eyes widened at mention of the old cartoon character. "How do you know who that is?" she said accusingly. "Do you have a child?"

She really did believe the worst of him. His smile faded. "No, but I was one."

"In Greece?"

"I was sent to an American boarding school at nine."

Daisy blinked, her face horrified. "Your parents sent you away? At *nine*?"

"They did me a favor. Believe me." Turning away, he went back to the big gleaming kitchen and grabbed two plates and two bowls, china edged with twenty-four-carat gold. He placed the plates on the table, and the bowls on the marble floor.

Taking three bottles of water from the small refrigerator beneath the side table, he poured water into one of the bowls. Her dog came forward eagerly.

"Are you crazy?" Daisy looked incredulously at her dog lapping water from the gold-edged china bowl. "Don't you have any cheap dishes?"

"No. Sorry."

"We're going to need some, before—" She cut herself off.

"Before our baby needs a plate?" Tilting his head, he looked down at her. "I'm looking forward to it," he said softly. "All of it. I'd like this house to be your home, Daisy. Yours and the baby's. Make it your own. Whatever you want, your slightest desire, it will be yours."

She looked at him with wide stricken eyes, then changed

the subject, turning away to stare at a painting on the opposite wall. "You like modern art."

"Yes," he said cautiously.

"Do you own any of Franck's?"

Leonidas snorted. "He's overrated. I don't know anyone who owns his paintings."

"Well, lots of people must buy them, because he's very successful. He travels first class around the world." She tilted her head. "Everyone loves him."

"Everyone including you?" he said unwillingly.

Daisy looked at him in surprise. "Are you jealous?"

"Maybe."

"You were never jealous before."

He shrugged. "That was before."

"Before?"

"Before you stopped looking at me like you used to." He did miss it, the way Daisy used to look at him. As if he were the whole world to her, Christmas and her birthday all at once. It was a shock to realize that. He'd thought he didn't care if Daisy loved him. In fact, after what he'd seen his parents go through, he'd convinced himself that romantic love was a liability.

*But he missed having her love him.*

"That was a long time ago," Daisy mumbled, her cheeks red. She reached over to scratch Sunny's ears. "Before I found out the man I loved was just a dream."

Leonidas looked down, realizing that his hands were trembling. "We can find a new dream together."

"A new dream?"

"A partnership. Family. Respect."

"Maybe." Daisy tried to smile. "I don't know. But I've lost dreams before. Did I ever tell you how thoroughly I failed when I tried to become an artist?"

"No."

"I didn't sell a single painting. Not even a pity sale." Her cheeks colored. "I don't expect you to understand what it feels like. I'm sure you've never failed at anything."

"You feel empty. Helpless. Like there's nothing you can do, and nothing will ever change for you."

She looked at him in surprise. He gave her a small, tight smile, then started unpacking the takeout cartons from the bags. "I asked my housekeeper to get organic dog food. It's in the kitchen." He quirked a dark eyebrow. "Unless Sunny would prefer kung pao chicken, too?"

"You're hilarious." But Daisy's expression softened as she looked at him. "Sunny already ate. She's fine for now."

"As you wish." As he pulled out carton after carton from the bags, she looked incredulous.

"Will there be a crowd joining us?"

"I wasn't sure if you might be having pregnancy cravings, so I got a little of everything. As well as double of the kung pao." Leonidas handed her a plate, which she swiftly filled with food. He gave her a napkin and chopsticks from the bag, and a bottle of water. He made himself a plate, then sat beside her at the table.

But the truth was, he didn't care about food. He was more interested in watching her.

As they ate, they spoke of inconsequential things, about anything and everything but the obvious. He was mesmerized, watching her eat everything on her plate, then go back for more.

Everything about Daisy drew him—not just her body, her pregnancy-swollen breasts, or the curve of her belly. Everything. The way she drew the chopsticks back slowly from her lips. The flutter of her dark lashes against her cheeks. The graceful swoop of her neck before it disappeared beneath the white cotton collar of her shirt. Her thick brown hair falling in waves over her shoulders. Even her voice, as she teased him about the fundraiser he'd held last year, because his favored politician had lost.

He looked at her. "Will you stay with me?" he asked quietly. "At least until the baby is born?"

Her seafoam green eyes pulled him into the waves, like a siren luring him to drown.

"It's not that simple," she said.

"I know. For you, it is not. But it is for me." Folding his hands, he leaned forward. "Give me the chance to earn your trust. And show you that I can be the partner you need. That our baby needs."

Her cheeks burned red beneath his gaze. He felt out of his element. He knew he should probably play it cool. Act cold. Manipulate, seize control.

But for the first time in his adult life, he could not. Not now. Not with her.

All he could do was ask.

Daisy looked away. "I'm planning to move to California in September. For nursing school."

"Why? You don't need to work." The thought of her moving three thousand miles away chilled him. "I will always support you."

"What if you change your mind?" She snorted. "Do you expect me to just give myself up to your hands?"

An erotic image went through him of his hands stroking her naked body. He took a deep breath. "At least stay with me until September. Let me take care of you while you're pregnant. Give me a chance to bond with our daughter after she's born. Then you can see how you feel."

She bit her lip. "Stay here through the summer?"

He could feel her weakening. "As long as you like. Either way, you and the baby will never worry about money again."

"I'm not asking you to support me, Leonidas."

"You're the mother of my child. I will always provide for you. It's my job as a man." Looking down at her, he said quietly, "You would not try to deny me that."

She chewed her lip uncertainly, then sighed. "I guess I could stay until September. If you're sure you really want me here that long?"

"I'm sure," he said automatically.

"Three months living with a pregnant woman? A whole summer with a crying baby? That won't cramp your style?"

"It's what I want."

"Well." She gave a reluctant smile. "I've imposed on Franck's charity long enough. I might as well impose on you for a while."

"It's no imposition. I want to marry you."

She looked away. Her cheeks burned as she mumbled, "So does he."

Leonidas gaped. "What!"

Daisy rolled her eyes. "It was a pity proposal. He felt sorry for me."

Leonidas doubted pity had anything to do with it. "Did he try to kiss you?"

She looked shocked. "*Kiss* me? Of course not—Franck is old enough to be my father!" But Leonidas saw sudden uneasiness in her eyes, and he wondered exactly what Franck Bain had said to her. He made a mental note to keep the middle-aged artist on his radar.

He was furious that another man had made a move on her. How dared he? She was carrying Leonidas's baby!

But could he blame Bain for wanting her? Any man would want Daisy. It made Leonidas all the more determined to marry her, and claim her as his own.

She tilted her head, looking up at him through dark lashes. "At least you have good reason to want me here. You love our baby." She paused. "I never expected that."

Relief flooded through him. "So you'll stay?"

"With one condition." She lifted her chin. "You have to promise, when I want to leave, you'll let me go."

He saw there was no arguing with her on this point. He

hesitated. Once Daisy was here, living in his house, he believed he'd soon convince her they should marry. They both loved their baby. That was a good enough reason.

He hoped.

"If you'll promise," he said slowly, "you'll never try to keep me from my daughter. Or hide her from me, even if you leave New York."

Biting her lip, she gave a single nod.

Leonidas held out his hand. "Then I agree."

"Me too." Daisy shook his hand. He felt the slow burn of her palm against his, before she quickly drew it away.

"What changed your mind?" he asked quietly.

She looked up at him. "I loved my dad. That was what convinced me. Because you're right. How could I deny our daughter the same chance for a father?"

The father that Daisy had lost, because of him. Leonidas felt a lump in his throat. The ghost of Patrick Cassidy would always be between them. How would they ever get past it?

He said in a low voice, "Will you stay tonight?"

"Yes. So will Sunny. Where I go, my dog goes."

"She's very welcome. Like I said. We're dog friendly." Looking at the dog lazing nearby, he added, "Besides, I think she likes me."

"I noticed," she said wryly. She yawned. "Though I didn't pack any clothes."

"I can send someone back—"

"Wake up one of your employees to send them to Brooklyn and back? I'm not that evil. I'll just sleep naked."

Leonidas broke out in a hot sweat, remembering her bare body against his, the soft sweetness of her skin as she moved against him. He wondered what it would feel like to touch her now, what she looked like naked, so heavily pregnant with his child…

No! He forced the image from his mind. He couldn't seduce her. Not yet. She was still skittish, looking for an excuse to flee. He couldn't give her one. He had to take his time. He had to win her trust.

"Fine. We can pick up your things tomorrow," he said, breathing deeply.

"There's not much to collect." She gave a brief smile. "You don't have to help me. I can just take the subway over."

"Leave you to struggle with suitcases and boxes on the subway? Forget it. I'm helping you."

"Fine," she sighed. She yawned again. "I think I need to go to bed."

He tried not to think about her in bed. "Sure."

"I just need to let Sunny out first." She rose to her feet, opening the door for her dog, who quickly bounded out into the courtyard.

As she stood in the doorway, Leonidas couldn't stop his gaze from lingering over her belly and full, swollen breasts, imagining them beneath her white shirt and black leggings. Turning back, she caught his gaze. He blushed like a guilty teenager.

Clearing his throat, he gathered up the take-out bags and trash, leaving the plates in one of the kitchen sinks. A moment later, after Sunny returned from outside, Leonidas said in a low voice, "I'll show you to your room."

He led her through the kitchen, the dog following them down the hall and up the sweeping staircase to the second floor.

As they passed, Daisy glanced nervously at his master bedroom, where they'd had their blowout fight last autumn. But he didn't pause. He led her to the best guest room.

Reaching inside, he turned on the light, revealing a beautiful suite, elegantly decorated in cream and light pink. "There's an en suite bathroom. All stocked with toothbrushes and toiletries and anything else you might require."

"Do you often have guests?" she asked, smiling awkwardly as her dog went ahead to sniff, scouting out the bedroom.

"You're the first," he said honestly. "Mrs. Berry always seemed to think someone might come to visit. Even though I told her I have no family."

*"Had,"* Daisy said. "Now you do."

His heart twisted strangely. "Right. Good night."

"Thank you," she said softly.

He turned back to face her, standing at the door. "Thanks for staying."

She licked her lips nervously. "Leonidas, you know that… even if someday I agree to marry you, far in the future…and I'm not saying I will…but…"

"But?"

"You know I'll never be yours again. Not like I was."

Never? Leonidas could still remember how she'd felt in his arms. Soft. Sensual. Making love to her had been like fire. And now she was pregnant with his child. Her body was even more lush, with a rounded belly beneath full breasts. He wanted to see her. To feel her. He was hard just thinking about it.

Reaching out, Leonidas cupped her cheek. Her skin felt warm and soft, so soft. "I will do everything I can to win you back," he said softly. "In every way. And soon…"

For a moment, he was lost in the maelstrom of her velvety black pupils. His gaze fell to her full pink lips. He forgot his earlier vow not to seduce her in his thundering need to kiss her, and claim what was his, after months of agonizing desire.

Slowly, he lowered his head—

Daisy jerked back violently. "No." Her eyes were luminous with sudden tears. "No!"

And she slammed the bedroom door in his face.

# CHAPTER FIVE

LEONIDAS DID NOT sleep well.

He tossed and turned, picturing the woman he wanted sleeping in the next room down the hall. So close, and yet she might as well have been a million miles away.

Finally, he saw the early gray light of dawn through the window. Rising wearily from bed in his boxers, he stretched his tired, aching body, as the cool air of the room invigorated his muscles, from his shoulders to his chest and thighs. Going to the window, he pushed open heavy white curtains. Below, he saw the quiet West Village street was covered with a dusting of white. Snow had fallen during the night.

Leonidas's hand tightened on the white curtains. He was furious with himself. Why had he tried to kiss her? How had he ever thought that would be a good idea, in their relationship's current fragile state?

He hadn't been thinking. At all. That was the problem.

He'd let his desire for Daisy override everything else. The stakes were so high. He had to make her feel comfortable here, so she would remain. So they could become friends. Partners. *Married.* For their baby's sake.

Instead, he could still hear the echo of her door, slamming in his face.

How could he have been so stupid? Frustration pounded through him.

Pulling on exercise shorts and a T-shirt from his walk-in closet, Leonidas dug out his running shoes. He peeked down the darkened hallway and saw Daisy's door was closed. He didn't even hear her dog. He wondered how she'd slept.

After going downstairs, Leonidas went out into the gray dawn and went on a five-mile run to clear his head. With most of the city still asleep, he relished the quiet, the only sound his shoes crunching in the thin layer of snow.

Daisy had such a warm heart. He'd seen it in her devotion to her father, to her friends—and their devotion to her. Her kindness. Her loyalty.

He had to win her trust. Prove to her he could deserve it. Even if that meant he had to wait a long time to make love to her.

Even if that meant he had to wait forever.

He could do it. He was strong enough to fight his own desire. He *could*.

Returning home with a clear head and a determined will, he ran upstairs, taking the steps two at a time. He paused when he saw Daisy's door open. But her bedroom was empty. Had she already gone downstairs? Could she have left? Fled the city in the night—

No. He took a steadying breath. She'd promised she'd never try to keep his child from him. And he believed in her word.

But still. He wanted to find her. Going to his en suite bathroom, he quickly showered and dressed in a sleek black suit with a gray button-up shirt. The Liontari corporate office had recently loosened up the dress code, allowing men to skip ties and suits, though of course, the creatives and designers of the specific luxury clothing brands played by their own rules.

But Leonidas had his own strict rule, to always represent the best his company had to offer. And so, he always wore the same cut of suit from his favorite men's brand, Xerxes, altered to fit his unusually broad shoulders, biceps and thighs. He checked the clock. He always had breakfast around seven; he was expected at work in an hour. The thought gave him little pleasure.

Going downstairs, he couldn't find either Daisy or Sunny. Phyllis Berry, his longtime housekeeper, was cooking eggs and sizzling bacon in the kitchen, as she always was this time of the morning.

"Good morning, sir."

"Good morning, Mrs. Berry." Sitting at the breakfast table as usual, he hesitated. "I don't suppose you've seen—"

"Miss Cassidy?" The petite white-haired woman beamed at him as she dished up a plate. "Yes. And all I can say is— finally!"

"Finally?"

"Finally, you're settling down. Such a nice girl, too. And pregnant! You wasted no time!" With a chuckle, she brought the plate of bacon and eggs, along with a cup of black coffee, and put them down on the table in front of him with a wistful sigh. "I can hardly wait to have a baby about the place. The pitter-patter of little feet. And a dog! I must admit I'm surprised. But better late than never, Mr. Niarxos. After all these years, you finally took my advice!"

Raising his eyebrows, Leonidas sipped hot coffee, while he was pretending to skim the business news. "You met Daisy?"

"Yes, about a half hour ago, when she left to walk her dog. Such a lovely girl." Mrs. Berry sighed, then gave him a severe look before she turned away. "Why you still haven't asked her to marry you is something I don't understand. Young people today..."

Leonidas's lips curved upward. *Young person?* He was thirty-five. But then, Mrs. Berry, who'd worked for Leonidas for many years, regarded her employer with a proprietary eye. She seemed to regard him as the grandson she'd never had, and never hesitated to tell him the error of his ways.

He heard the slam of the front door, the dog's nails clacking against the marble floor, and the soft murmur of Daisy's voice, greeting some unseen member of his house staff down the hall. Trust Daisy to already have made friends.

Her dog, no longer a puppy in size but clearly very much in temperament, bounded into the kitchen first, her tongue lolling, her big paws tracking ice and snow from her walk. Mrs. Berry took one look and blanched. She moved at supersonic speed, picking the animal up off the floor. But her wrinkled face was indulgent as she looked down at the dog.

"Let's get you into the mudroom," she said affectionately. "And after we clean your paws, we'll get you properly fed." The dog gave her a slobbery kiss. Mrs. Berry smiled at Daisy, who'd followed her pet into the kitchen. "If that's all right with you, Miss Cassidy."

"Of course. Oh, dear. I'm so sorry!" Daisy glanced with dismay at the tracks her dog had made on the previously spotless floor. "I'm afraid it's a great deal of trouble—"

"No trouble at all," Mrs. Berry said, with a purposeful glance at Leonidas. The crafty old lady was leaving them alone. He wondered irritably if she expected, as soon as she left the room, for him to immediately go down on one knee in front of Daisy and pull a diamond ring out of his pocket? He would have done so gladly, if it would have done any good!

"Good morning, Leonidas." Daisy's voice was shy. She was, of course, wearing the same clothes from yesterday, her long black coat unzipped over her belly. "I saw you come back from my window. Were you running?"

"It helps me relax."

"Does it?" She snorted. "You should walk my dog sometime, then. She'd probably love running with you. She has more energy than I do these days, always tugging at the leash!"

He furrowed his brow. "Is walking her a problem? I could get one of my staff to handle the chore…"

"Chore?" She looked at him incredulously. "It's not a chore. She's my dog. I like walking her. I just thought *she* might like running with *you*."

"Oh." He cleared his throat. "Sure. I could take her running with me." He pictured Daisy walking around the streets of New York in the darkness of early morning, and suddenly didn't like it. "Or I could come walking with you, if you want. Either way."

She blinked. "Really? That wouldn't be too much of a…a chore for you?"

"Not at all. I like her." Leonidas looked up from the table. "And I like you."

She bit her lip. He saw dark circles under her eyes. Apparently she hadn't slept very well either.

"Sit down." Rising to his feet, he pulled out a chair at the table. "Can I get you some breakfast? Are you hungry?"

She shook her head. A smile played about her full pink lips. "Mrs. Berry already made me eat some toast and fruit before she'd let me take the dog out."

Score one for Mrs. Berry. "Good." He paused awkwardly, still standing across from her. "How are you feeling?"

Her lovely face looked unhappy. Her hands clasped together as she blurted out, "I think we've made a big mistake."

Danger clanged through him. "A mistake?"

She tucked a loose tendril of brown hair behind her ear. She said softly, "I don't think I can stay here."

Leonidas stared at her in consternation. Then he understood.

"Because I almost kissed you last night," he guessed grimly. She nodded, not meeting his eyes.

He had to soothe her—make her feel safe. He took a deep breath. Going against all his instincts, he didn't move. Instead, he said gently, "You have no reason to be afraid of me."

"I'm not afraid of you. I'm afraid of—"

She cut off her words.

"Afraid of what?"

Her pale green eyes lifted to his, and he knew, no matter how Daisy tried to pretend otherwise, that she felt the same electricity. Every time her gaze fell to his lips. Every time their eyes met, and she nervously looked away. Every time he touched her and felt her tremble.

She was afraid of herself. Of her own desire. Afraid, if she gave in, that she would be lost forever.

And she was poised to flee. If he didn't reassure her, he'd scare her straight back into Franck Bain's apartment—if not his arms.

Taking a deep breath, he said, "What if I promise I won't try to kiss you?"

Silence crackled as they faced each other in the breakfast nook. Outside in the courtyard, there was a soft thump as snow fell from the branches onto the white-covered earth.

"Would you really make that promise?" she said finally.

"Yes. I'll never try to kiss you, Daisy. Not unless you want me to."

"On your honor?"

He tried to comfort himself with the fact that at least she now believed he *had* honor. "Yes."

Daisy bit her lip, then said slowly, "All right. If I have your word, then…then I'll stay."

He exhaled. "Good." He tried not to think about how hard it would be not to kiss her. How hard it was not to kiss her even now.

He took a deep breath. "I need to go to work today."

"Work?"

"I'm CEO and principal shareholder of Liontari."

"That's a store?"

"An international consortium of brands. You've probably heard of them. Vertigris, for instance."

"What's that?"

"Champagne."

"No. But I don't really drink…"

He was surprised. Vertigris was as globally famous as Cristal or Dom Perignon. "Ridenbaugh Watches? Helios Diamonds? Cialov Handbags?"

Looking bemused, Daisy shook her head.

And all of Leonidas's plans to go into the office flew out the window. He set his jaw. "Okay. I'm taking you out."

"Out?"

"We'll collect your clothes from Bain's apartment, as I promised. Then I'm taking you to a few shops." When she frowned, still looking bewildered, he added, "We can buy a few things."

"What kind of things?"

"For your pregnancy. For the baby."

"You don't need to buy me stuff."

"Think of it as you helping *me*," he said lightly. "Market research. You're a totally virgin consumer. I'd like your take on my brands."

Her cheeks colored at the word *virgin*. "I don't see how my opinion would be useful to you."

"It would be. But more than that, I'd really like you to understand what I do." He gave her a brief smile. "Isn't that what you were asking me? To understand my world?"

"That was before…"

"There was so much I never was able to show you before. We spent our whole time together in Brooklyn." He paused. "Let me show you Manhattan."

Her light green gaze looked troubled, then she bit her lip. "I'm not sure I can leave Sunny alone here…"

"Mrs. Berry can watch her. She's good with dogs." At least, she'd seemed good with Sunny just now. He'd never really thought about it. He'd certainly never lived with a dog before. His parents had despised the idea of pets. "She's very trustworthy." That at least was true.

He could see Daisy weighing that, and wondered if she was setting such a high bar for who was allowed to watch her dog, would any potential babysitter for their daughter need two PhDs and a letter of reference from the Dalai Lama?

"I suppose," she said finally. "As long as we're not gone for too long."

Reaching out, he took her left hand in his own, running his thumb over her bare ring finger. "We could go to Helios," he said casually. "Look at engagement rings."

He felt her shiver and saw the flash of vulnerability in her eyes. Then she pulled her hand away.

"No," she said firmly. "No rings."

Couldn't blame a man for trying. "There must be something you need, you or the baby."

She tilted her head, then sighed, resting her hand on her swelling belly peeking out from the open black puffy coat. "I suppose it would be nice to get a new coat," she admitted. "This morning, I suddenly couldn't zip it up anymore."

As she rubbed her belly, he saw a flash of cleavage at the neckline of her white button-down shirt, and he wondered what touching those breasts would feel like. A very dangerous thing to wonder. He couldn't think about seducing her. Because he was the kind of man that if he let himself think about something, he would soon take action to achieve it.

"But you don't need to pay for it," she said quickly. Inwardly, he sighed. He'd never had so much trouble convincing a woman to let him buy her things. "While we're at Franck's," she continued, "I need to pick up my waitress uniform. I have a shift tomorrow."

Leonidas frowned. "You're not thinking of going back to work at the diner?"

"Of course." Daisy frowned. "Do you really think I'd just quit my job? And leave my boss in the lurch?"

"Why would you—" Gritting his teeth, he said, "You don't have to be a waitress anymore. Ever. I will take care of you!"

She put her hand on her hip. "Are you telling me not to work?"

Raising his eyebrow, he countered, "Are you telling *me* it's comfortable to stand on your feet all day, when you're this pregnant?"

Daisy's expression became uncertain, and her hand fell to her side. "I'll think about it," she said finally. "On the drive to Brooklyn." She paused. "Actually, could we...um... take the subway or something?"

"You don't like the Rolls-Royce?"

She rolled her eyes. "It's a *limo*. With a uniformed driver."

"So?"

"Well, the whole thing's a little bit much, isn't it?"

As much as he wanted to please her, Leonidas wasn't quite ready for the subway. They compromised by having his driver, Jenkins—wearing street clothes, not his uniform—take them in Leonidas's Range Rover.

When the two of them arrived at the Brooklyn co-op overlooking the river, the building's doorman greeted Daisy with a warm smile, then glared at Leonidas.

"You all right, Miss Cassidy?" the man asked her.

She gave him a sweet smile. "Yes. Thank you, Walter." She glanced at Leonidas, clearly enjoying his discomfiture.

"Thank you, Walter," he echoed. The man scowled back. Obviously their last meeting, when Leonidas had threatened Daisy with lawyers, had been neither forgiven nor forgotten.

But Leonidas was even more discomfited, ten minutes later, when, upstairs in Bain's apartment, Daisy announced she was entirely packed.

"That's it?" Leonidas looked with dismay at her two suitcases and a large cardboard box full of books and a single canvas painting. "That is everything you own?"

Daisy shrugged. "I sold most of our family's belongings last year, to pay for my father's legal defense." She hesitated as she said quietly, "The rest was sold to pay for the funeral."

Her eyes met his, and his cheeks burned. Though she didn't say more, he imagined her silently blaming him. When would she realize it wasn't his fault? Not his fault that her father had decided to sell forgeries and needed a lawyer. Not his fault that Patrick Cassidy had died of a stroke in prison!

But arguing wouldn't help anything. Choking back a sharp retort, he tried to imagine her feelings.

He took a deep breath.

"I'm sorry," he said slowly. "That must have been very hard."

Looking down, she whispered, "It was."

Leonidas glanced at the painted canvas resting in the cardboard box. It was a messy swirl of colors and shapes that seemed to have no unifying theme.

Following his glance, Daisy winced. "I know it's not very good."

Reaching down to the cardboard box, he picked up the painting. "I wouldn't say that..."

"Stop. I know it's terrible. I did it my final semester of art school. All I wanted was for it to be spectacular, amazing, so I kept redoing it, asking advice and redoing it based on everyone's advice. I wanted it to be as good as the masters."

"Maybe that's the problem. It looks like a mash-up of

every well-known contemporary artist. What about your own voice? What were you trying to say?"

"I don't know," she said in a low voice. "I don't think I have a voice."

"That's not true," he said softly, looking at her bowed head. He thought of her years of love and loyalty. "I think you do."

Looking up, she gave an awkward laugh. "It's okay. Really. I tried to be an artist and failed. I never sold a single painting, no matter how hard I tried. So I threw them all away, except this one. I keep thinking," she said wistfully, brushing that canvas with her fingertips, "maybe someday, I'll figure it out. Maybe someday, I'll be brave enough to try again." She gave him a small smile. "Stupid, huh?"

Before he could answer, their driver knocked on the door. He'd come upstairs to help carry the suitcases. Leonidas lifted the big cardboard box in his arms. But he noticed Daisy continued to grip the painting in her hands. She carefully tucked it on top of everything else, so it wouldn't get crushed in the back of the Range Rover.

"Do you mind if we stop at the diner before we go back?" she said into the silence. He turned to her.

"Sure."

Her lovely face looked a little sad. "I think I need to talk to my boss."

They arrived at the cheerful, crowded diner, with its big windows overlooking vintage booths with Naugahyde seats. Jenkins pulled the SUV into the loading zone directly in front of the diner.

"Do you want me to come with you?" Leonidas asked.

"No," Daisy said.

Leonidas watched as she disappeared into the busy, bright diner. He thought of the morning they'd first met. She'd taken one look at his expensive designer suit and laughed. "Nice suit. Headed to court? Unpaid parking tickets?" With a warm smile, she'd held up her coffee pot. "You poor guy. Coffee's on me."

They'd ended up spending the rest of the day together. If it had been one of his typical dates, he would have taken Daisy to the most exclusive restaurant in Manhattan, then perhaps out dancing at a club, then a nightcap at his mansion. But he'd known it couldn't be a date, not when he couldn't even tell her his real name.

So they'd simply spent the afternoon walking around her neighborhood in Brooklyn, visiting quirky little shops she liked, walking down the street lined with red brick buildings, ending with the view of the East River, and the massive bridge sticking out against the sky. Daisy greeted people by name on the street, warmly, and their eyes always lit up when they saw her.

It had been a wild ride, one that would put the roller coasters at Coney Island to shame. She'd made him come alive in a way he'd never imagined. Joy and color and light had burst into his life that day, from the moment he'd met her in this diner. It had been like a vibrant summer after a long, frozen winter.

But it could never be like that again. He would never be Leo again. Daisy would never look at him with love in her eyes again.

No. They would be partners. He wouldn't, couldn't, ask for more. Not when he had nothing more to give in return.

Waiting in the back seat of the Range Rover, he tried to distract himself with his phone. He had ten million messages from board members and designers and marketing heads, all of them anxious about various things; he found it difficult to care. He was relieved when he finally heard the SUV's door open.

"Everything all right?" he asked.

"I quit." Daisy gave a wistful smile. "Claudia—that's my boss—said she didn't need me to give notice. Turns out my job sitting at the cash register was not actually that useful, but she couldn't fire a pregnant single mother." She paused. "But now that I've got a billionaire baby daddy…"

Leonidas smiled. "You told her about me?"

She paused, then looked away. "Not everything."

Silence fell as his driver took them out of Brooklyn, crossing back over the bridge into Manhattan.

Leonidas watched her, feeling strangely sad. He fought to push the emotion away. Work, he thought. Work could save them.

"So you haven't heard of Vertigris or Helios," he said finally. "What about Bandia?"

Still looking out the window, Daisy shook her head.

"It's a small luxury brand that does only maternity clothing and baby clothing. We could go there to look for your coat."

"Okay." Her voice was flat.

"Or Astrara. Have you heard of that?"

Daisy finally looked at him, her face annoyed. "Of course I've heard of Astrara. I don't live under a rock."

Finally, she'd actually heard of one of his brands. He was slightly mollified. He maybe should have started with Astrara, as famous as Gucci or Chanel. "Which do you prefer to visit first? Bandia? Astrara? One of the others?"

"Does it matter?"

"Of course it matters," he said. He waited.

Daisy sat back against the seat. "Bandia," she sighed. "It sounds like it has the most reasonable prices."

Leonidas was careful not to disabuse her of that notion as they arrived at the grand Fifth Avenue boutique. After pulling in front, the driver turned off the engine. Tourists passing on the sidewalk gawked at them.

"Even in Manhattan," she grumbled. "Everyone stares at you."

Hiding a smile, Leonidas turned to help Daisy out. "They're looking at you."

Biting her lip, she took his hand, but to his disappointment, dropped it as soon as she was out of the SUV. As they walked into the boutique, Bandia's shop assistants audibly gasped.

"Mr. Niarxos!"

"You honor us!"

"Sir! We are so happy to…"

He cut them off with a gesture toward Daisy: "This is my—" *future wife…baby mama…lover…* "—dear friend, Miss Cassidy. She needs a new wardrobe. I trust you can help her find things to her taste."

"Wardrobe!" Daisy gasped. She immediately corrected, "I just need a coat."

The assistants turned huge, worshipful eyes to Daisy. "Welcome to Bandia!"

"Miss Cassidy, may I get you some sparkling water? Fruit?"

"This way, if you please, to the private dressing suite, madam."

*Perfect*, Leonidas thought in approval. Just as he'd expected. He'd send the CEO of Bandia a note and let her know he approved of staff training levels.

"Madam, what type of clothes do you prefer?" The store's manager hurried to pay her obeisance as well. "Our newest releases for the fall line? Or perhaps the latest for resort?"

Daisy stared at them like a deer in headlights. "I just… need a coat," she croaked.

"Bring everything and anything in her size," Leonidas answered. "So she can decide."

They were both led to the VIP dressing suite, which had its own private lounge, where Leonidas could sit on a white leather sofa and drink champagne, as salesgirls brought rack after rack of expensive, gorgeous clothing for Daisy to try on in the adjacent changing room behind a thick white velvet curtain.

"I don't need all these clothes," she grumbled to Leonidas. "Why should I try them on, when I don't need them?"

"Market research?"

"Fine," she sighed.

Reluctantly, she tried on outfit after expensive outfit. Each time she stepped in front of the mirrors in the lounge, the salesgirls joyfully exclaimed over her.

"You look good in everything!"

"Beautiful!" another sighed.

"I hope when I'm pregnant someday I'll look half as good as you!"

It was true, Leonidas thought. Daisy looked good in everything. As she stood in front of the mirrors in an elegant maternity pantsuit, he marveled at her chic beauty.

"Do you like it?" he called.

Glancing back at him, she shrugged. "It's all right."

"Just all right?"

"It's not very… comfortable."

He frowned. That wasn't something he ever worried about. *"Comfortable?"*

"I prefer my T-shirts and stretch pants," she said cheerfully.

"Keep looking."

Rolling her eyes a little, Daisy continued to try on clothes for the next hour, as Leonidas sat on the leather sofa, sipping complimentary Vertigris champagne—one of Liontari's other brands, from a two-hundred-year-old vineyard in France. His company was nothing if not vertically integrated.

Every time she stepped out of the changing room, to stand in front of the large mirrors in the lounge, Leonidas asked hopefully, "Do you like it?"

Always, the shrug. "It's fine."

"Fine?" A thousand-dollar maternity tunic was fine?

"Not as good as my usual T-shirts. Which, by the way, you can buy three for ten dollars." She tilted her head. "Is this the kind of market research you were looking for?"

Leonidas felt disgruntled. He'd hoped to impress her. Obviously it wasn't working. The only thing that had made Daisy's eyes sparkle was when the salesgirls brought over baby outfits that matched the postpartum clothes, cooing, "This will be perfect after your little one is born!"

Then Daisy looked at the price tag. "Three hundred dollars? For a baby dress that will be covered in spit-up, and probably only worn twice before she outgrows it?" She'd shaken her head. "And it's kind of scratchy. I want my baby to be comfortable and cozy, too!" Then Daisy looked around with a frown. "Don't you have any winter coats?"

The salesgirls looked at each other sheepishly. "I'm sorry, Miss Cassidy," one said. "It's March. We cleared out all the winter clothes for our new spring line."

"It's still snowing, and you're selling bikinis," Daisy said, her voice full of good-humored regret.

"There might be a few coats on the sales rack," one salesgirl said hesitantly.

Daisy seemed overjoyed when one puffy white coat fit her—if anything, it was a little too big. "And it's cozy, too!" Then she saw the price, and her smile disappeared. "Too much!"

"It's fifty percent off," Leonidas pointed out irritably.

"Still too much," Daisy said, but she continued hugging the coat around her tightly, as if she never wanted to take it off.

"We'll take it," he told the sales staff.

"I can't possibly let you pay—"

"You won't let me buy a cheap coat, from my own company? To warm the mother of my child? Are you really so unkind?"

Daisy hugged the coat around her, then said in a small voice, "All right, I guess. Thank you." She looked at Leonidas. "Are you ready to go?"

Finally. He'd convinced her to let him buy *something*. But he'd wanted to buy her so much more. "Not quite." He looked at the salesgirls. "She needs a ball gown."

As the staff left the lounge to gather the dresses, Daisy looked at him incredulously. "A ball gown? You can't be serious."

"I'm taking you to a party on Saturday."

She groaned. "A party?"

"It's for charity." He quirked an eyebrow. "A fundraiser for homeless children. Don't you want to come and make sure they get a healthy chunk of my ill-gotten fortune?"

"Fine," she sighed. A moment later, when the salesgirls rolled a large rack of maternity ball gowns into the lounge, she grabbed the closest one, which was a deep scarlet red. She went back into the private changing room to try it on.

Leonidas waited to see it, practically holding his breath.

But when Daisy pushed back the curtain a few moments later, she was dressed in her white shirt and black leggings. "I'm done."

"But the gown?"

"The gown is fine."

She wasn't going to let him see it, he realized. Disappointed, he said hastily, "You must need new lingerie for—"

Daisy snorted. "I'm *not* trying that on in front of you. Are you ready to go?"

"Aren't there any other things you want to try on? Anything at all?"

"Nope." She turned with a smile to the salesgirls, hugging them. "Thank you so much for your help, Davina, Laquelle, Mary. And Posey—good luck on law school!"

Trust Daisy to make friends, instead of picking out designer outfits. As they left Bandia, going outside to where the SUV waited, Leonidas helped Daisy—now wearing her new white coat—into the back seat, as Jenkins tucked the carefully wrapped red ball gown into the trunk.

Daisy's pink lips lifted mischievously. "I'm sorry I didn't love all the clothes."

"It's fine." But he felt irritated. If not Bandia, surely one of his other luxury brands would make her appreciate his multibillion-dollar global conglomerate! He turned to Jenkins. "Take us to Astrara."

But even the dazzling delights of the famous three-story boutique, as enormous as a luxury department store, seemed to leave her cold. Daisy made friends with the salesgirls, and marveled at the cost of the clothes, which she proclaimed were also "weird looking" and "scratchy."

After that, he took Daisy to a luxury beauty and skincare boutique, which seemed to bore her. "I like the stuff from the drugstore," she informed him.

Finally, in desperation, he took them to a famous perfumery on Fifth Avenue, Loyavault.

As she walked through the aisles of luxury perfume, she seemed dazzled by the lovely colors and bright boxes and lush scents. She bent her head to smell one perfume in a pink bottle, and her green eyes lit up with a bright smile.

"Wow," she whispered.

Leonidas felt the same, just looking at her.

He took the bottle from her hand. "Floral, roses and white jasmine, with an earthy note of amber." They stood close, so close, almost touching. "I'll have them wrap it up for you."

She bit her lip. "I shouldn't."

"I missed your birthday," he said quietly. "Won't you let me get you a present?"

She exhaled, then slowly nodded.

"But after this, we're done shopping."

Giving in to the inevitable, he sighed.

Daisy wasn't impressed by luxury. Or his company. Or him. It hurt his pride, a little. In each store, Daisy had been treated as if she were the queen of England, visiting from Buckingham Palace. Each time, she blushed with confusion, but was soon chatting with the staff on a first-name basis. And before long, the employees seemed to forget the powerful Liontari CEO was even there.

The salesgirls treasured Daisy for herself. He wasn't the only one to see Daisy's bright warmth. She shone like a star.

What a corporate wife she would make!

"Shall we go for lunch?" he asked as they left Loyavault. Outside, the March sun had come out, and the air was blue and bright, as the spring snow started to melt like it had never existed. She looked at him with a skeptical eye.

"Let me guess. Some elegant Midtown restaurant, French and fancy?"

He hastily rethought his restaurant choice.

"There's a place just a block away. It's French, but not fancy. Strictly speaking, it's not precisely French, but Breton. Crepes."

"You mean like pancakes? Yum."

Thus encouraged, he said, "Shall we walk? Or ride?"

"Walk."

They strolled the long city block to the small hole-in-the-wall establishment, tucked into a side street, where it had existed for fifty years. He led her into the wood-paneled restaurant, rustic as a Breton farmhouse, with a crackling wood-burning fire.

Unlike the more elegant restaurants, no one knew Leonidas here. He'd been here only once before, when he'd visited the city on a weekend from Princeton. They had to wait for a table.

But Daisy didn't seem to mind. She took his arm as

they waited together in the tight reception space, and all of Leonidas's ideas of trying to bribe someone for an earlier table flew out the window.

Soon, a wizened host with a white beard led them to a tiny table for two near the fire. He didn't give them menus.

"You want the full?" the elderly man asked in an accented, raspy voice.

Leonidas and Daisy looked at each other.

"Yes?" he said.

"Sure?" she said.

"Cider," the man demanded.

"Just water," Leonidas replied. "Thank you."

After the waiter departed, he looked at Daisy across the table. "You don't really seem to like luxury. Fancy restaurants, fancy cars, fancy clothes."

She suddenly looked guilty. "I'm sorry. I don't mean to be rude…"

"You're never rude," he said. "I'm just curious why?"

"More market research?"

"If you like."

She sighed. "It all just seems so expensive. So…*unnecessary*."

"Unnecessary?" He felt a little stung. "Would you call *art* necessary?"

Daisy looked at him with startled eyes. "Of course it's necessary! It's an expression of the soul. The exploration and explanation of what makes us human."

"The same could be said of clothing. Or makeup or perfume. Or food."

She started to argue, then paused, stroking her chin.

"You're right," she admitted.

Leonidas felt a surge of triumph way out of proportion for such a small victory.

"Here," the white-bearded man said abruptly, shoving plates at them with savory buckwheat galettes, filled with the traditional ham, cheese and a whole cooked egg in the middle.

"Thank you." Daisy's eyes were huge. Then she took a bite. The sound of her soft moan of pleasure shook Leonidas. "It's—so—good," she breathed, and holding her fork like a weapon, she gobbled down the large crepe faster than he'd ever seen anyone eat before. He looked at her, and could think of nothing else but wanting to hear her make that sound again.

"Would you like another?"

"Another?" She licked her lips, and he had to grip the table.

"Save room for—dessert—" He managed to croak out. If only the dessert could be in his bedroom, with her naked, like that time with the ice cream. That would be the perfect end to their meal. Or anytime. Forever—

"Are you going to eat that?" Daisy said, looking longingly at his untouched crepe.

He pushed it toward her. "Please take it."

"Thank you," she almost sang, as if he'd just done something worthy of the Nobel Prize. And she ate that one, too, in rapid time.

Leonidas couldn't tear his eyes away as she lifted the fork to her mouth, before sliding it out again. As she leaned forward, her collar gaped, and he saw the push of her soft breasts against the hard wood of the table—

With a gulp, he looked away. A moment later, the plates were cleared.

"Ready for dessert?" the elderly man barked.

"Yes, please," she said, smiling back at him warmly. "I've never tasted anything so delicious in my life."

The old man frowned, and then his wrinkled eyes suddenly beamed at her. "You have good sense, madame."

Another conquest fell at Daisy's feet. But then, who could resist her?

Not Leonidas.

But he was, stupidly, the only man on earth who'd given his word of honor never to kiss her.

How strange it was, he thought. To want a woman like this, but not be able to touch her, not be able to seduce her. He thought he might literally die if he never possessed her again.

He would win her, he told himself fiercely. He would. And not just for one night, but forever.

"This is so good," Daisy moaned softly over the sweet crepe, drizzled with butter and sugar. Automatically pushing his own dessert crepe toward her, he tried to distract himself from his unbearable desire.

"I'm sorry you didn't care much for the shopping today."

"I liked the *people*... They were very nice."

"Some other day I'll show you more of Liontari's brands. I want you to appreciate my company. It will all belong to our child one day."

Daisy's eyes almost popped out of her head. She actually put down her fork. "Our daughter will inherit your company?"

Hadn't she realized that? Incredible. With any other woman, he thought, his business empire would have been the first thing on her mind. "Of course. It will all be hers."

Her forehead furrowed. "But what if...she doesn't want it?"

Now Leonidas was the one to be shocked. "Not want Liontari? Why would she not want it?"

Daisy took another bite, slowly pulling her fork out of her mouth, leaving a bit of sugar on her lower lip. He was distracted, until she said thoughtfully, "Not every child wants to follow in the footsteps of her parents' professions."

He looked up, annoyed. "It's not just a *profession*. It's a multibillion-dollar conglomerate, with the biggest luxury brands in the world—" He steadied himself, took a deep breath. Daisy couldn't have meant her words as an insult. "Don't worry." He made his voice jovial, reassuring. "I will teach her everything she needs to know. When it's her time to lead, she'll have the board members eating out of the palm of her hand."

"Yes. Maybe. If she wants."

*"If she wants?"* Leonidas repeated incredulously. "Why would anyone not want an empire?" Especially one he'd created out of his own sweat, blood and bone!

Daisy shrugged. "She might find running a corporation boring. Maybe she'll want to be… I don't know…an accountant. An actress. A firefighter!"

He was offering everything he had, everything he'd spent his life pursuing—everything that proved to the world, proved to himself, that his parents had been wrong, and Leonidas Niarxos had value, had a right to be alive.

But Daisy, who had such warmth and concern for strangers, didn't think his empire was worth anything? He thought their daughter might not want it?

He stared at her. "Are you serious?"

"I just want her to find her true passion. Like you found yours."

"My passion?"

"Isn't it obvious?" She gave him a cheeky smile. "Business is your passion."

Her smile did crazy things to his insides. "Business is my passion?"

"The way you've done it—yes. What else would you call it? There's no guidebook for creating a world empire. No business degree could tell a person how to do it."

"What's your passion, then?" he countered.

Her face fell, and she looked down at her plate. "Art, I guess. Even though I'm not very good at it."

She looked sad. He thought again about how she'd treasured that old painting.

Leonidas wanted to reassure her, but he didn't know how. At work, his leadership style was based on giving criticism, not reassurance.

As they left the restaurant, he thought about her words. *Business is your passion.* If that were true, why was it that for the last six months, he'd just been going through the motions at Liontari? He hardly cared about it at all anymore. He had yet to drag himself into the New York office, and the last few months in Paris, he'd barely bothered to criticize his employees.

As they walked out to where their driver waited with the Range Rover, Daisy suddenly nestled against him, wrapping her arm around his.

"Thank you," she whispered, and he felt her lips brush against the flesh of his ear. "For the crepes. The coat. The perfume." Pulling back, she looked at him, her eyes sparkling in the spring sun. "Thank you for a wonderful day."

He looked down at her, his heart pounding at the intimacy of her simple touch.

And suddenly, Leonidas couldn't imagine any passion, any longing, any desire greater than the one he had for her.

# CHAPTER SIX

DAISY STARED AT herself in the mirror of her pretty cream-and-pink guest suite in Leonidas's New York mansion.

A stranger looked back at her, a glamorous woman in a red gown straight out of *Pretty Woman*. The dress caressed her baby bump, showcasing her full breasts, with a slit up the side of the skirt that showed off her legs. Long honey-brown hair hung thickly over her bare shoulders. Her eyelashes were darkened with mascara, her lips as red as the dress, all bought from the drugstore a few months ago. But she was wearing the scent Leonidas had bought her on their shopping excursion three days earlier. Even the shoes on her feet were new. That morning, just as she'd realized she could not possibly wear her scuffed-up black pumps with this dress, new shoes had mysteriously appeared at her door—strappy sandals covered with crystals in her exact size.

"Who are you?" Daisy said to the woman in the mirror. Her voice echoed against the bedroom's high ceilings and white bed.

From the dog bed by the elegant fireplace, Sunny lifted her head in confusion. With a sigh, Daisy said to her, "It's all right, Sunny. I'm all right."

But was she?

She glanced back at her cell phone sitting on the vanity table, feeling dizzy. She didn't just look different now. She *was* different.

When she'd come out of the shower an hour before,

she'd anxiously checked her online bank account to see if her most recent payment, a deposit for nursing school, had cleared yet. Once that money disappeared from her account, she expected to have very little left, so she was nervous about checks bouncing if she'd forgotten anything.

But looking at her bank account, she'd lost her breath. She'd closed her eyes and counted to five. Then she'd looked at her account again.

Her bank account had the scant hundreds she'd expected—*plus an extra million dollars*.

Leonidas had just made her a rich woman.

Why? How could he? She'd never asked for his money! Daisy shivered in the red dress. But she knew it wasn't for her, not exactly. It was to protect their baby, so she'd never worry or be afraid.

*I will always provide for you. It's my job as a man. You would not try to deny me that.*

Especially since she'd denied him other things. Like kisses. When, her first night here, he'd almost kissed her outside her bedroom door, she'd been far too tempted. It had scared her. She'd known, if she ever let him kiss her, that she would surrender everything.

And her life had already become unrecognizable enough. She looked at herself in the ball gown. Could she really keep his money—even for her baby?

It was true she'd already quit her job. When she'd gone to the diner, her boss had been all too happy for Daisy to leave her job, no advance notice required.

"We don't actually need an employee sitting at the register," Claudia had confided. "But I knew it hurt your feet to wait tables, and I couldn't fire you." She'd glanced at the Range Rover through the window. "But look at you now! It's a fairy tale! You said this Greek billionaire even wants to marry you?"

Daisy had winced. "I haven't agreed."

"Are you crazy?" Claudia gazed reverently at the handsome dark-haired tycoon, typing on his phone in the back seat. Then she frowned. "Have you told Franck?"

"I don't know why Franck would care." Daisy had smiled weakly. "I'm sure he'll just be glad to get me out of his apartment,"

"You know he's in love with you."

Daisy rolled her eyes. "He was my father's best friend. He's not in love with me."

Claudia lifted an eyebrow. "Isn't he?"

She'd thought of his strange awkwardness when the middle-aged artist had proposed to her. *Stay as long as you want. Stay forever.*

And now, as Daisy looked in the mirror at the glamorous stranger in the red dress and red lipstick, she felt guilty that she hadn't told Franck she'd moved out and was now living with her baby's father. She didn't look forward to confessing Leonidas's name. Daisy hadn't even shared *that* with Claudia. Her bohemian friends had been her father's friends, too; they hated billionaires in general, but Leonidas Niarxos in particular, after he'd put her father in prison.

They would be horrified if they found out Daisy was having his baby. And if she ever became Leonidas's wife...

She took a deep breath. She didn't want to imagine it. Bad enough that tonight she'd be facing all of Leonidas's friends at a charity ball. They'd probably feel the same scorn for Daisy. They'd ask themselves what on earth the billionaire playboy saw in her. They'd think Leonidas was slumming with a waitress. Worse. Sleeping with the daughter of the convicted felon he'd put in prison.

Swallowing hard, Daisy looked at herself one last time in the mirror. Steadying herself on her high-heeled sandals, she lifted her chin, straightened her spine, and went downstairs.

Leonidas stood waiting at the bottom of the wide stone

staircase. Her heart twisted when she saw him, darkly powerful and wide shouldered in a sleek black tuxedo. Their eyes locked.

"You look beautiful," he said in a low voice as she reached the bottom of the stairs. He visibly swallowed. "And *that dress*."

She gave him a shy smile. "You like it?"

Leaning forward, he whispered huskily, "You make me want to stay home tonight."

She shivered as he touched her, wrapping her faux fur stole around her bare shoulders. Taking his arm, she went out with him into the cold spring night, where Jenkins waited with the Rolls-Royce at the curb.

"Sorry," Leonidas said with a grin. "For tonight, a limo is required."

When they arrived at a grand hotel in Midtown Manhattan, Daisy was alarmed to see a red carpet set up at the entrance, where paparazzi waited, snapping pictures of the arriving glitterati. She turned accusingly on Leonidas. "You didn't say the charity ball was this big of a deal!"

"Didn't I?" His cruel, sensual lips curved upward. "Well. It's all for homeless kids."

Daisy looked with dismay at all the wealthy people walking the red carpet with photographers snapping. "I'll stick out like a sore thumb!"

"Yes." Leonidas looked at her in the back of limo, his black eyes gleaming as his gaze lingered on her red lips and red dress. "You're the most beautiful of them all."

As their driver opened the door, Leonidas stepped out, then reached back to her. "Shall we?"

Nervously, she took his hand. As they walked the red carpet, she clung to his muscled arm, trying to focus just on him, ignoring the shouts and pictures flashing.

"Leonidas Niarxos—is that your girlfriend?"

"Is she pregnant with your baby?"

He didn't answer, just kept looking down at Daisy with a soothing smile. For a moment she relaxed, lost in his dark eyes. Then she heard one of the paparazzi gasp.

"Oh, my God! That's the Cassidy kid! The daughter of the art forger who tried to swindle him!"

At that, there was a rush of questions. She quickened her step and didn't take a full breath until they were safely inside the hotel ballroom.

"How—how did they know who I was?" she choked out.

"They were bound to figure it out." Leonidas's dark eyes looked down at her calmly. "It's better this way."

"How can you say that?"

"There was always going to be some kind of scandal about us. Better for it to happen now, rather than later, after our daughter is born." He put his hand gently on her belly. "That way, it will only affect us. Not her."

It was the first time Leonidas had touched her belly. Even over the red fabric, she felt his gentle, powerful touch, felt his strength and how he wanted to protect them both.

It was strangely erotic.

"Are you ready?" he asked.

Holding her breath, she nodded. His dark eyes crinkled as he took her hand and led her through the double doors.

The hotel's grand ballroom was enormous, far larger than the one in his house, which now seemed quite modest by comparison. A full orchestra played big band hits from the nineteen forties as beautiful women in ball gowns danced with handsome men in tuxedos. On the edges of the dance floor, large round tables filled the space, each with an elaborate arrangement of white and red roses. Crystal chandeliers sparkled overhead.

Leonidas took two flutes of sparkling water from a waiter's silver tray. He handed her one of them, then nodded toward the far wall, his dark eyes gleaming. "Over there are the items that will be up for bidding in the auction to-night. Would you like to go see them?"

"Sure." Anything to give her something to do. To make her feel less out of place. People were staring at her, and she had no idea whether that was because her dress looked strange, or because they'd heard she was the art forger's daughter, or just because she wasn't beautiful enough to be on Leonidas's arm. She knew she wasn't, fancy ball gown or no. He was a handsome Greek billionaire. Who was she?

An ex-waitress. The daughter of a felon. A failed artist. Pregnant and unwed.

Nervously sipping the sparkling water, Daisy followed Leonidas to the long table lining the far wall of the hotel ballroom. Walking past all the items put forward in the upcoming charity auction, she stared at them each incredulously.

There was a guitar that had apparently once belonged to Johnny Cash. A signed first edition of a James Bond novel. Two-carat vintage diamond earrings. A small sculpture by a famous artist. And if the items weren't enough to whet the appetite, there were experiences offered on small illustrated posters: a week at someone's fully staffed vacation house in the Maldives. An invitation to attend Park City Film Festival screenings as the guest of a well-known actor. A dinner prepared at your home, for you and twelve of your best friends by a world-famous chef, who would fly in from his three-Michelin-star Copenhagen restaurant expressly for the occasion.

Walking past all the items, each more insane and over-the-top than the last, Daisy shook her head. Rich people really did live a life she could not imagine.

But on the other hand, it was all for charity, and if it really helped homeless kids…

She nearly bumped into Leonidas, who'd stopped at the end of the final table, in front of the very last item.

"Hey." She frowned up at him. "You nearly made me spill my—"

He glanced significantly toward that last item, his dark eyebrows raised. She followed his glance.

Then her hand clutched her drink. She felt like she was going to faint.

"That's—that's my—"

"Yes," he said. "It's your painting."

It was. Her final project from art school, in all its pathetic mess. Sitting next to all those amazing items that rich people might actually want.

Daisy looked around wildly. The noise and music and colors of the ballroom seemed to spin around her. She felt like she was in one of those awful dreams where you were in the hallway of your school and everyone was standing around you, laughing and pointing, and you suddenly realized you'd forgotten your homework—and your clothes.

She looked up at Leonidas with stricken eyes. "What have you *done*?"

He looked back at her. "Given you another chance."

"A chance at what!" she gasped. "Humiliation and pain?"

"A chance to believe in your dream," he said quietly. "I believe in you."

Shaking, Daisy wiped her eyes. She wanted to grab the painting and run, before any of these glamorous people could sneer at it.

But too late. She stiffened as two well-dressed guests came up behind them.

"What is this?" said the woman, who was very thin and draped in diamonds. "It's not signed."

Her escort peered doubtfully at the painting's description. "It says here that the artist wishes to be anonymous."

"How very strange." The woman turned to call to another friend, "Nan. Come tell me if you can guess who this artist is."

Daisy's cheeks felt like they were on fire, and her heart was beating fast, as if she'd just run two miles without stopping. Leonidas took her arm, and gently led her away from the auction table.

"It's to earn money for the charity. For the kids."

"It won't earn anything. No one will bid on it," she whispered. Why did he want to hurt her like this? She knew Leonidas didn't love her. But did he outright hate her? What other reason could he have to humiliate her, in front of all his ritzy friends?

She felt like she'd been ambushed, just when she'd started to trust him. Leonidas believed in her? How could he, when she didn't believe in herself?

Later, after they sat down at their table for an elegant dinner of salmon in sauce, roasted fingerling potatoes and fresh spring vegetables, Daisy could hardly eat. She barely said a word to the guests sitting around them, in spite of their obvious curiosity about her. She let Leonidas speak for them. Yes, she was his date. Her name was Daisy. They were good friends. He was proud to say they were expecting a child together in June.

And all the while, Daisy was wondering how he could have done this to her.

During the days she'd stayed at his house, he'd gone out of his way to be kind to her. Leonidas Niarxos, the supposedly ruthless tycoon, had spent almost no time at work, other than the day he'd taken her shopping at Liontari's luxury boutiques. Instead, he'd kept her company doing the activities she enjoyed, like walking the dog, watching movies on TV and playing board games. Leonidas had listened patiently for hours as she'd read aloud from her pregnancy book, especially the section titled "How To Be an Expectant Father." She'd started to think he cared. She'd started to think he actually…liked her.

So why was he trying to hurt her like this?

"Cheer up," Leonidas whispered, as dinner ended and they rose to go out on the dance floor. "The auction will be fun."

"Easy for you to say." Daisy tried not to feel anything as he pulled her into his arms. He was so powerful, so impossibly desirable in his sleek tuxedo. As he swayed her to the music, an old romantic ballad from the forties, he was the most handsome man in the world. Damn him.

He smiled down at her, his dark eyes twinkling. "Everything will be fine. I promise."

"Yes, it will," she retorted. "Because I'm leaving before the auction starts."

His smile dropped. "No. Please stay." Licking his lips, he added, "For the kids."

*"For the kids,"* she grumbled. But it was strange. He didn't *seem* like a man bent on her destruction. Was it possible Leonidas wasn't actively trying to wreck her, but honestly believed someone might bid for her awful painting—against all those other amazing auction items?

If he did, he was deluding himself. Just like Daisy had, for years. In spite of getting mediocre marks in art school, she'd always hoped that somehow she might succeed and make a living from art, as her father had. That she'd find her voice, as Leonidas once said.

But she never had. Instead, she'd spent years suffering that terrible hope, getting gallery shows in Brooklyn, Queens and Staten Island through her father's connections, only to sell nothing. Friends *had* offered to come to the shows and buy her paintings, but of course Daisy couldn't allow that. Her friends didn't have money to waste, and anyway, she would have been glad to paint them something for free.

But none of her friends had asked for a free painting. Which could mean only one thing: even her friends didn't like her art, not really.

Even Daisy herself wasn't sure about it. But she'd still tried to force herself to be upbeat, desperately trying to promote her art to bored strangers.

A year of that. Of awful hope, and finally crushing despair. There had been only one good thing to come from her father's trial—a horrible silver lining that she'd never admitted, even to herself. He had needed her, and that had given her an excuse to surrender the horror of her dream.

But now, Daisy was being forced to relive it all. She would never forgive Leonidas for this.

*"Are—you—ready?"* The auctioneer chanted from the stage. There was an excited hubbub from guests at the cleared tables. Women in ball gowns and men in tuxedos sat on the edge of their seats, ready to bid vast fortunes for amusements and whims. *For the kids*, Daisy repeated to herself.

Leonidas put his arm around her. "Try to enjoy this," he whispered. Daisy stared at the oversize arrangement of white and red roses on the table and tried to breathe. Soon this would all be over.

"Let's get started," the auctioneer boomed into the microphone. "For our first item…"

Everything sold quickly—the guitar, the autographed book, the week in the Maldives. The audience was full of smiles and glee, happily getting into bidding wars with their friends, as if they were bidding with counterfeit money, and no amount was too high.

And finally…

"For our last item, we have an unsigned painting, by Anonymous. Do I have a bid?" Even the auctioneer sounded doubtful. "Uh, let's start the bidding at…two hundred dollars."

It was the lowest starting bid of the night, by far. And Daisy knew that no one would even want to give that much. She braced herself for a long, awkward silence, after which

Leonidas would be forced to make a pity bid, to try to save face. He would see he had no reason to believe in her. Even *he* would be forced to admit that Daisy was a talentless hack. She was near tears.

"Two hundred dollars," someone called from the back.

Who was it? Daisy blinked, craning her neck.

"Three hundred," called a woman from a nearby table. She was a stranger. Daisy didn't know anyone here, except Leonidas.

"Five hundred," someone else said.

"A thousand," cried an elderly man from the front.

The bidding accelerated, became hotly contested— even more than the guitar once owned by Johnny Cash. Daisy sat in shock as the number climbed.

Five thousand. *Ten.* Twenty. Fifty thousand. *A hundred thousand dollars.*

Daisy was hyperventilating. Through it all, Leonidas kept silent.

Until…

"One million dollars." His deep, booming voice spoke from beside her. Sucking in her breath, she looked up at him. He smiled back, his dark eyes warm.

"Sold! To the gentleman at table thirteen!"

As people at their table clustered around him, shaking his hand and congratulating him on the winning bid, Daisy trembled with emotion. She couldn't believe what had just happened.

*I believe in you.*

But it hadn't just been Leonidas who'd bid for her painting. He hadn't said a word, not until the end. Other people had bid for it. A bunch of strangers who had no idea Daisy was the artist. She hadn't had to beg them to buy it. They'd all just wanted it.

Was it possible she'd been wrong, and she did have some talent after all…?

Leonidas turned away from his friends. He looked down at her, his dark gaze glittering. "They'll deliver the painting later. Do you want to leave?"

Wordlessly, Daisy nodded.

Outside, the Manhattan street was dark and quiet, except for the patter of cold rain. As they hurried toward the limo waiting in a side lane near the hotel, the rain felt like ice against her skin. Leaning over her, Leonidas tried to protect Daisy from the weather with his arms, with only a small amount of success. They were both laughing as they slid damply into the back seat of the Rolls-Royce.

"Take us home," Leonidas told Jenkins, who nodded and turned the wheel.

"Home," Daisy echoed, and in that moment, the brownstone mansion almost did feel like home. For a moment, they smiled at each other.

Then the air between them electrified.

She abruptly turned away, toward the window, where the lights of the city reflected in the puddles of rain. She felt Leonidas's gaze on her, but she couldn't look at him. Emotions were pounding through her like waves.

Once they arrived at his mansion, she followed him up the steps to the entrance. He punched in the security code, and they entered, to find it dark and quiet.

"Everyone must have gone to bed." He gave a low laugh. "Even your dog must be asleep, since she's not rushing to greet us." He flicked on the foyer's light, causing the crystal chandelier to illuminate in a thousand fires overhead, reflecting on the stately stone staircase behind them.

Taking her fur stole, Leonidas hung it in the closet. He looked down at Daisy, who was still silent. His handsome face became troubled.

"Daisy, did I do wrong?" He set his jaw. "If I did, I'm sorry. I thought if—"

"You believed in me, when I didn't believe in myself," she whispered.

His dark eyes met hers. "Of course I believe," he said simply. "I always have. From that first day at the diner, I saw you were more than beautiful. You're the best and kindest woman I've ever met—"

Reaching up, Daisy put her hands on his broad shoulders, feeling the fabric of his tuxedo jacket, damp with rain. And lifting her lips to his, she kissed him passionately.

A moment before, entering the house, Leonidas had looked at Daisy's lovely, distant face as she'd stood half in shadow. For the first time, he'd questioned whether he'd done the right thing, offering her painting at the charity fundraiser without her knowledge or permission.

But the idea of Daisy giving up her dreams was unbearable to Leonidas. Whether her painting was actually worth a million dollars, or a hundred, he didn't care. He was accustomed to his own despair, but a world where a warm, loving woman like Daisy had no hope was a world he did not want to live in.

So he'd taken the painting from the guest room, and offered it to the charity's auction committee. He'd known if the painting was the last item up for auction, that at least a few people in the audience, after imbibing champagne all night, would assume the painting was an unknown masterpiece, and that others, seeing the bidding war heat up, would not want to be left out, and would swiftly follow suit.

Leonidas would never forget the look on Daisy's beautiful face when her student painting had sold for a million dollars. Not until the day he died.

As they'd left the grand hotel, he'd gloried in the successful outcome of his plan. But she'd been silent all the way home, refusing to meet his eyes. He'd started to have doubts. Perhaps he should have asked her permission. Perhaps—

And so he'd turned to her, as they stood alone at the base of the stone staircase. But even as he'd tried to ask, he'd been unable to look away from her.

Daisy was more beautiful than any art ever created.

Her long brown hair fell over her bare shoulders. Her full breasts thrust up against the low sweetheart neckline of her red column dress, the fabric falling gently over the swell of her pregnant belly. Her dark lashes fluttered against her cheek as her teeth worried against her lower lip, so plump and red.

In the shadows of the foyer, the sparkling light refracted in the hundred-year-old crystal chandelier, gleaming against her lips, her cheekbones, her luminous eyes.

*And then she'd kissed him.*

As her soft lips touched his, he felt a shock of electricity that coursed down his body, from his hair to his fingertips to his toes. His muscles went rigid. He burned, then melted.

He'd been forcing himself to abide by his promise not to touch her. But every day, every hour, he'd felt the agony of that. All he'd wanted to do was kiss her, seduce her, possess her.

But now she was kissing *him*.

With a rush, he cupped his hands along her jawline, moving back to tangle in her hair, drawing her close. He kissed her hungrily, twining his tongue with hers. He felt out of control, as if his hunger might devour them both. He wrenched away, looking down at her. His heart was pounding.

"Come to bed with me," he whispered, running his hand down her throat, along the bare edge of her collarbone. He felt her tremble. Lowering his head, he softly kissed her throat, running his hand through her hair. "Come to bed…"

Her green eyes were reckless and wild. Wordlessly, she nodded. But as he took her hand to lead her to the stairs, she swayed and seemed to stagger, as if her knees had gone weak.

With one swoop, Leonidas lifted her up into his arms. She weighed nothing at all, he thought in wonder. As he carried her up the carved stone staircase, he looked down at her, marveling that she had such power over him.

She'd bewitched him, utterly and completely. As he carried her up the stairs, all the darkness of his world receded. When he looked into her eyes, his heart felt warm and alive, instead of frozen in ice. Beneath the soft glow of her eyes, he could almost believe he wasn't the monster his parents had believed him to be. Maybe he was someone worthy. Someone good.

Leonidas carried her down the hall, into his shadowy bedroom, lit by dappled lights from the window. Outside, the city had fallen into deepening night. Across the street, he could see the illuminated tips of skyscrapers peeking over the rooftops, and beyond that, the twinkling stars, cold and distant.

He lowered her reverently to the king-sized bed. Her honey-brown hair swirled like a cirrus cloud across the pillows. She looked up at him with heavy-lidded eyes, and he caught his breath.

Leonidas dropped his tuxedo jacket and tie to the floor. Kicking off his shoes, he fell next to her on the bed. He slowly removed each of her high-heeled sandals, first one, then the other. Leaning forward, he cupped her face and kissed her tenderly. Her lips parted as he felt her sigh, and it took every ounce of his willpower to hold himself back, when all he wanted to do was possess her. *Now.*

But he held himself back. She was pregnant with his baby. He would not overwhelm her. He would be gentle. He'd take his time. Lure her. *Seduce her.*

And make her his own—forever.

Reaching out, he gently cupped her cheek. His hand stroked whisper soft down her neck, to her bare shoulder.

With an intake of breath, she met his gaze. Her eyes were full of tears as she tried to smile.

"Leo," she whispered.

His heart lifted to his throat.

*Leo.* She'd called him Leo. The name she'd used long ago, before she knew his true identity, back when she'd loved him...

Leonidas shuddered with emotion. Wrapping his arms around her, he pulled her tight. As he kissed her, memories from last fall, when he'd known such joy in her arms, filled him body and soul. The night he'd first kissed her in Brooklyn, the night he'd taken her virginity, all the nights after.

But this kiss was even better.

Because now, Daisy knew who he was. She'd kissed him first. She knew the worst of him, but still wanted him.

Except she *didn't* know the worst. He sucked in his breath. And she must never know...

No. He must not think of it. Not now. Not ever.

He deepened the kiss, until it became rough, almost savage in his need to obliterate all else. Daisy's embrace was passionate and pure, like the woman herself. Being in her arms was the only thing that made him forget...

All thought, all reason, fled his mind as her lips seared his. Part of him almost expected she'd stop him, pull back, tell him she was too good for him—and how could he deny the truth of that?

But she did not pull away. Instead, her lips strained against his, matching his fire. The whole world seemed to whirl around him as he held her, facing each other on the bed. He kissed slowly down her throat.

"Sweet," he groaned against her skin. "So sweet."

Her hands reached for the buttons of his white shirt. When they wouldn't easily open, she reached beneath the fabric in her impatience, and stroked his bare chest. Sitting up, he ripped the shirt off his body, causing the final buttons to scatter noisily across the marble floor, along with his platinum cufflinks.

Turning back to her, he unzipped the back of her red gown and gently pulled it down her body, revealing her white strapless bra, barely containing her overflowing breasts, and then her full, pregnant belly, her white lace panties clinging to her hips.

He tossed the ball gown to the floor. He almost could not bear to look at her, she was so beautiful, looking up at him in the tiny white lingerie that revealed her explosive curves, her brown hair glossy and coiled over the pillows, her green eyes dark with desire.

"Kiss me," she whispered.

A low groan escaped him, and he obeyed. He turned her to face him, kissing her for moments, or maybe for hours. Time seemed to stretch and compress as he was lost in her embrace. He kissed down her throat to the edge of the white satin bra. Reaching around her back, he loosened the clasp, and the fabric fell away. He looked at her breasts, so deliciously full, and holding his breath, he reached out to cup them with his hands.

Her lips parted and her eyes closed, her expression lost in pleasure. He stroked her full nipples, causing them to pebble beneath his touch. Lowering his head, he pulled one into his mouth, swirling it with his tongue, suckling her.

Her hands gripped the white duvet, as if she felt herself flying into the sky. He tenderly kissed around the curve of her full, pregnant belly. Moving back up, he kissed her lips long and lingeringly, before he finally drew back.

Cupping her cheek, he looked down at her with sudden

urgency in the darkness of the bedroom, with the twinkling lights of Manhattan slanted across the marble floor like trails of diamonds.

"Marry me," he whispered. "Marry me, Daisy."

# CHAPTER SEVEN

MARRY HIM?

Daisy's eyes flew open. She was naked, melting beneath his touch. She wanted him; oh, how she wanted him.

But marry him?

"I…" She shivered as Leonidas slowly stroked his warm hand down her cheek to her throat and the crevice between her breasts. Every part of her ached for his touch. Not just her body. Her heart.

Looking at him in the shadowy bedroom, she'd suddenly seen the man she'd loved last fall. Leo. Her Leo. Her lover, with whom she'd spent so many days laughing, talking, kissing in the sunlight, holding hands beneath the autumn leaves. He hadn't taken her virginity. She'd given it to him. Her Leo.

But could she surrender everything? Could she ever forgive herself if she did? What kind of woman would she be?

"I can't marry you," she whispered.

"You know me." His hands stroked softly down her body. Closing his eyes, he rested his head in the valley between her breasts. Surprised, she looked down and placed her hands gently against his dark hair. "I want to be with you. Always."

That couldn't be tears in his eyes. No, impossible. Leonidas Niarxos was ruthless. He had no heart. He himself had said so.

And yet, somehow Leonidas had become her Leo again. His eyes were like pools of darkness glittering with stars, as deep and unfathomable as the night. His body was Leo's. His tanned, muscular chest was powerful, his skin like satin over steel. Daisy's fingers wonderingly stroked his rough dark hair, his small, hard nipples, then down over the flat muscles of his belly.

Leo, but not Leo. Not exactly. She knew too much now. *Leo* had been her equal. This man was more powerful than Daisy in every possible way. He was a famous, self-made billionaire who'd crushed the world beneath his Italian leather shoe, building a global fortune. He was the most eligible playboy in the world, handsome and rich, the man every woman wanted.

And yet—

And yet, in this moment, she saw a strange vulnerability in his black eyes. He watched her as if he expected, at any moment, she might break the spell, and break his heart.

It was an illusion, she told herself.

But as he lowered his mouth passionately to hers, she was lost in his embrace as he wrapped his powerful arms around her. His lips plundered hers, his tongue teasing and tempting. His hands stroked down her body, cupping her full breasts, moving down her full belly to the curve of her hip.

Then his kiss gentled. He held her against his muscular chest as if she were a precious treasure. His hand cupped her cheek tenderly.

"Marry me," he whispered. "And I'll hold nothing back. I will give you everything."

Everything? What did he mean? "You already gave me too much. That money in my bank account—"

"I'm not talking about money."

Then what? Her heart lifted to her throat. He couldn't mean—he might be able to truly love her?

Lowering his head, he kissed her. His sensual finger-tips caressed her bare skin, from her shoulder, to the sensitive crook of her neck. He softly stroked the tender flesh of her earlobe, his fingers tangling in her long hair, as need sizzled through her.

He cupped her breast, rubbing his thumb against her nipple. Leaning forward, he drew her tight, aching nipple into the wet heat of his mouth. She gasped as she felt the hot swirl of his tongue suckling her, the roughness of his chin against her skin.

Pushing her legs apart, he knelt between her thighs on the bed. His broad-shouldered body was silhouetted by the city's dappled light outside. His black eyes gleamed as he slowly pulled her white lace panties down from her hips, like a whisper over her thighs, past her knees and calves, tossing them to the floor.

Shivering with desire, she closed her eyes, her head straining back against the pillows. He spread her thighs wide with his powerful hands, moving his head between her legs. He paused, and she felt the heat of his breath against her skin.

Then, finally, he lowered his head to taste her. His hot, sensual tongue swirled against her, lightly, delicately, then lapping with more force, pushing inside her as she gasped with pleasure. The delicious tension coiled inside her, building higher and higher, until, suddenly, she cried out with joy, rocked by ecstasy.

She was still gasping beneath waves of pleasure when he lifted himself up, holding himself over her belly with his powerful arms. Positioning himself between her legs, he pushed inside her with one deep thrust.

A hoarse groan escaped him as filled her, stretching her to the hilt. For a split second, it was too much.

Then, as he held himself still, allowing her body to adjust, incredibly, new pleasure began to build inside her. He thrust inside her again, slowly. But the muscles of his arms seemed to bulge and shake, and a bead of sweat formed on his forehead, from the effort of holding himself back.

Suddenly, he pulled back. Falling onto the bed beside her, he gently rolled her on top of him.

"Take me," he said huskily, his dark eyes like fire. "I'm yours, if you want me."

If she wanted him?

She wanted him—yes. But he'd never asked her to take control before. Feeling uncertain, she hesitated, her body suspended over his. He was so huge. Then, slowly, she positioned herself, lowering her body, pulling him inside her, inch by delicious inch. The pleasure was almost too much to bear.

Then she looked down at his face.

His expression was worshipful, almost holy, as if he held his breath, as if he were barely holding on to the shreds of self-control. Her confidence grew.

Slowly, she began to ride him. As she picked up rhythm, he gasped aloud, a single choked groan. He suddenly gripped her thighs with his large hands.

"Daisy—slow down—I can't—I can't—"

But she was merciless, driving forward. Pulling him inside her deeply, she increased her speed, going faster and faster. Her full breasts swayed as she rocked back and forward, sliding hot and wet against him, until, gripping her fingernails into his shoulders, she hit another sharp peak, even higher and more devastating than the one before, and she screamed.

He exploded, pouring himself into her with a guttural roar.

She collapsed forward against him, sweaty and spent. He cradled her gently into his arms, kissing her temple.

"Daisy—*agape mou*—"

It had been his old nickname for her, and at that, her heart finally could take no more.

How could she have ever thought she couldn't love him again? How could she have imagined she could ever protect her heart?

Daisy's eyes flew open in the darkness.

She was in love with him. She always had been, even in the depths of her hatred and hurt. She'd never stopped loving him.

Turning to face him on the bed, she looked at his handsome face beneath a beam of silvery moonlight pouring like rain through the window. She whispered, "Yes."

Leonidas grew very still. "Yes?"

Tears filled her eyes, tears Daisy didn't understand. Were they tears of grief—or joy?

Twining her fingers in his dark hair, she tried to believe it was joy.

"I'll marry you, Leo," she said.

They were wed four days later.

The ceremony was small and quiet, held in the ballroom of Leonidas's house—"Your house now," he'd told her with a shy smile. A home wedding was perfect. The last thing Daisy wanted was more attention.

After all the pictures paparazzi took of them together at the charity ball, the story that Leonidas Niarxos had impregnated the daughter of the man he'd put into prison had exploded across New York media. For a few days, photographers stalked their quiet West Village lane. Daisy felt almost like a prisoner, afraid to go outside.

Even after they'd decided to have the wedding ceremony at home, Daisy had nervously wondered how her friends would be able to get through the media barricades.

Then a miracle happened.

The day before their wedding, a scandal broke about a movie star having a secret family in New York, a longtime mistress and two children, while he also had a famous actress wife and four children at his mansion in Beverly Hills. The national scandal trumped a local one, and all the paparazzi and news crews and social media promoters left Leonidas and Daisy's street to stalk the movie star and his two beleaguered wives instead.

Daisy spent her last day before the ceremony finalizing the details with the wedding planner, who'd been provided by Liontari's PR department, and then going to a lawyer's office to sign a prenuptial agreement which, in her opinion, was far too generous. "I'm not looking to get more money," she'd protested to her fiancé. "You've already given me a million dollars."

"That money means nothing to me. I always want you and the baby to feel safe," Leonidas said.

"But the prenuptial agreement would give me millions more. It just doesn't seem fair."

"To who?"

"To you."

Smiling, he'd taken her in his arms. "I'm fine with it. Because I never intend for us to get divorced." Lowering his head to hers, he'd whispered, "You've made me so happy, Daisy..."

They spent the last night before their wedding in bed. Daisy never wanted him to let her go.

And now he never would.

On the morning of their wedding, as she got ready, Daisy was overjoyed to see the spring sun shining warmly, with almost no paparazzi left on the street to bother them.

She invited only about twenty friends to the ceremony. She'd been too cowardly to call Franck in California and tell him she was getting married. She'd decided to tell him after the honeymoon. She told herself she didn't want to have to refuse him, if he offered to walk her down the aisle in lieu of her father. No one could replace her father.

Daisy already felt disloyal enough, marrying the man who'd killed him.

No, she told herself. Leonidas didn't kill my father. He just accused him of forgery.

If only she could believe her father really had been guilty. Because if her father had knowingly tried to sell a forged painting, how could she blame Leonidas for refusing to be swindled?

But her father had sworn he was innocent. How could Daisy doubt his word, now that he was dead? Even now, she felt guilty, wondering if her father was spinning in his grave at her disloyalty.

She would walk down the aisle alone.

Coming down the stairs, Daisy paused in the quiet foyer before entering the ballroom. Giving a nervous smile to the hulking guards who stood by the mansion's front door, providing security for the event, she clutched her bouquet of lilies against her simple white silk shift dress. A diamond tiara glittered in her upswept hair, along with the huge diamond on her finger.

Everything for today's ceremony, including Leonidas's tuxedo, had been carefully chosen from Liontari's various luxury brands, ready to be pictured, packaged and posted by the official wedding photographer onto social media accounts, and released to newspapers around the world.

"You can't buy this kind of press," the PR woman had said, smacking her lips.

Daisy might have preferred something a little less fancy. But Leonidas had already given her so much. He'd barely gone to work all week. When he'd asked her if she minded if their wedding promoted Liontari brands, she'd wanted to help. She'd had only one prerequisite.

"As long as the dress is comfortable," she'd said. And it was, the white silk loose and light against her skin.

With a deep breath, Daisy opened the ballroom doors.

The bridal march played, and all the guests turned to look at her. As she came down the makeshift aisle between the chairs, her knees shook. She wished she'd taken Mrs. Berry's idea and let Sunny walk her down the aisle. But the dog was still so young, not fully trained, and liable to rush off and chase or sniff. She glanced at the dog, sitting in the front row, tucked carefully at the housekeeper's feet. Daisy gave a nervous smile, and the dog panted back happily, seeming to smile.

The emotions of the other guests were more complicated.

On one side of the aisle she saw her own friends, artists and artisans, in wacky, colorful clothes. On the other side sat Wall Street tycoons, Park Avenue socialites and international jet-setters in sleek couture.

The only thing which both sides seemed to agree on was that Daisy was a greedy sellout, a gold digger cashing in, marrying the man who'd killed her father.

She stopped to catch her breath. No. She was just imagining that. No one would think that. She forced herself forward.

But as Daisy walked past the bewildered eyes of her friends, and the envious, suspicious faces of the glitterati, she felt very alone.

Then her eyes met Leonidas's, where he stood beside the judge at the end of the aisle. And she remembered all the joys of the last week. The sensuality. The laughter. The trust. They were going to be a family.

Gripping her bouquet, she came forward. The judge took a deep breath.

"My friends," the man intoned, "we are gathered here today…"

There was a hubbub at the door. Someone was hoarsely yelling, trying to push in. Daisy whirled to look.

A gray-haired man was trying to push into the ballroom, struggling against the two beefy security guards.

*Franck Bain.*

Daisy's lips parted. Why was he here? How had he found out?

"You can't marry him!" the middle-aged artist cried, his shrill voice echoing across the ballroom. "Don't do it, Daisy! I can take care of you!"

Leonidas made a gesture to two other guards hovering nearby, and they quickly moved to assist. The four security guards grabbed the thin man, who was struggling and panting for breath.

"Don't marry him!" Franck gasped. "He's a liar who killed your father—an innocent man!"

As he was forcibly pulled from the ballroom, the double doors closed with a bang.

A very uncomfortable silence fell.

"Shall I continue?" the judge said.

The guests looked at each other, then at the bridal couple. The PR team, who were filming the event live for Liontari's social media feeds, seemed beside themselves with delight at the unscripted drama.

Daisy's heart thundered in her chest. She wanted to fling away her bouquet, to make a run for it—run from all the judgment and guilt, her own most of all.

But her gaze fell on her engagement ring, sparkling on her hand, resting on her pregnant belly. Run away? That would truly be the act of a coward. No matter how much anyone criticized her for it, she'd already made her decision. She was bound to Leonidas, not just by their child, but by her word, freely given four days before.

*I'll marry you, Leo.*

Daisy met Leonidas's burning gaze, and she tried to smile. She nodded at the judge, who swiftly resumed the ceremony.

Ten minutes later, they were signing the marriage certificate. And just like that, they were wed.

Leonidas kissed her as the judge pronounced them husband and wife, but his kiss was oddly polite and formal. As they accepted the congratulations of their guests, Daisy's friends also seemed uncomfortable, their eyes sliding away awkwardly even as they pretended to smile.

At the wedding reception, held on the other side of the elegant ballroom, the very best champagne and liquor was served, all from Liontari's brands. The PR crew gleefully filmed all the glamorous, exotic guests, the wealthy and the beautiful and brightly bohemian, laughing and dancing and eating lobster, pretending to have the time of their lives.

But underneath it, Daisy felt hollow.

*Don't marry him. He's a liar who killed your father—an innocent man.*

The reception seemed to last forever. Leonidas was strangely distant, even though he was right beside her, and after hours of forced smiling, Daisy's face ached. Finally, the last guest drank the last flute of champagne, left the last gift, and departed. Even Mrs. Berry left, with Sunny in tow, leaving only the bridal couple and the PR team in the ballroom.

"You can go," Leonidas told them. The PR woman looked back brightly.

"I was thinking, Mr. Niarxos, we could come on your honeymoon, if you like, and get shots of you two kissing and frolicking on the beach—"

Beach? What beach? Daisy frowned. They hadn't planned a honeymoon. Did the woman imagine them at Coney Island or the Jersey shore? Only if "frolicking" meant shivering to death in the cool March weather!

"That kind of access would be invaluable," the PR woman chirped. "It would almost certainly go viral—"

"No," Leonidas said firmly. "No more filming."

Daisy went almost weak with gratitude as the PR team departed, leaving them alone at last.

Leonidas turned to Daisy.

"Mrs. Niarxos," he said quietly.

She swallowed. Her heart pounded as her husband pulled her closer. She felt his warmth and strength. She felt so right in her husband's arms. This marriage was right. It had to be right.

He lifted a dark eyebrow. "Did you know Bain was going to come here?"

She shook her head a little shamefacedly. "I'm sorry." She bit her lip, her cheeks hot. "I don't know how he found out about the wedding. I didn't tell him—"

"It's all right. I don't blame the man for wanting you."

"You—you don't?"

"Any man would," Leonidas whispered. Lowering his head, he kissed her tenderly. Then he pulled back with a smile. "Our plane is waiting."

"Plane?"

Leonidas took a deep breath. "I told you, if you agreed to marry me, I would hold nothing back. I'm a man of my word."

*Marry me. And I'll hold nothing back. I will give you everything.* When he'd said the words to her, she'd hoped he meant his heart. "So that means a honeymoon?"

He mumbled something. Frowning, she peered up at him.

"What?"

He lifted his head. "I'm taking you to Greece. To the island where I was born." He gave her a crooked smile. "Mrs. Berry has already packed your suitcase."

"What about Sunny?"

Leonidas smiled. "Mrs. Berry has promised to give her the same love she gives her own Yorkies at home."

It was strange not to have Sunny with her, as they left ten minutes later for an overnight flight. After all the drama of the last few days leading up to their wedding, once they were settled on the private jet, Daisy felt her exhaustion. She promptly fell asleep in her husband's arms and did not wake again until an hour before they landed on the small Greek island in the Aegean.

As they came down the steps from their private jet to the tarmac, Daisy looked around, blinking in the bright Greek sun. A burst of heat hit her skin.

It was already summer on this island. She was glad she'd taken a shower on the plane and dressed for the weather, in a white sundress and sandals. Her hair was freshly brushed and long, flowing over her bare shoulders. Even Leonidas was dressed casually—at least, casually for him—in a white shirt with the sleeves rolled up, top buttons undone, over black trousers.

To her surprise, no driver came to the small airport to collect them; instead, a vintage convertible was parked near their hangar, left by one of his staff members.

"Get in," Leonidas said with a lazy smile, as he tossed their suitcases in the back. He drove them away from the tiny airport, along the cliffside road.

Daisy's hair flew in the warm breeze of the convertible, as she looked around a seaside Greek village. She'd never seen anything so lovely as the picturesque white buildings, many covered with pink flowers and blue rooftops, with the turquoise sea and white sand beach beneath the cliffs.

Turning off the slender road, Leonidas pulled up to a gate and typed in a code. The gate swung open, and he drove through.

Daisy gasped when she saw a lavish white villa, spread out across the edge of the beach, overlooking the sea.

"This was your childhood home?" she breathed, turning to him. "You were the luckiest kid alive."

His eyes seemed guarded as he gave a tight smile. "It is very beautiful. Yes."

Parking in the separate ten-car garage, which was almost empty of cars, he turned off the engine. After taking their luggage from the trunk, he led Daisy inside the villa.

They were greeted by a tiny white-haired woman who exclaimed over Leonidas in Greek and cried and hugged him. After a few moments of this, he turned to Daisy.

"This is Maria, my old nanny. She's housekeeper here now."

"Hello," Daisy said warmly, holding out her hand. Maria looked confused, looking from Daisy's face to her belly. Then Leonidas spoke a few words in Greek that made the white-haired woman gasp. Ignoring Daisy's outstretched hand, the housekeeper hugged her, speaking rapidly in the same language.

"She's thrilled to meet my wife. She says it's about time I was wed," he said, smiling.

"Maria helped raise you?"

His expression sobered. "I don't know how I would have survived without her."

"Your parents weren't around?"

"That's one way to put it." He turned to Maria and said something in Greek.

The white-haired woman nodded, then called out, bringing two men into the room. They spoke to Leo and then took their suitcases down the hall.

Leonidas turned to Daisy. "You must be hungry."

"Well—yes," she admitted, rubbing her belly. "Always, these days." She bit her lip. "And I didn't eat much at the reception last night…"

"We can have lunch on the terrace. The best part of the house."

He led her through the spacious villa, which was elegant and well maintained, but oddly old-fashioned, almost desolate, like a museum. She asked, "How long has it been since you've visited?"

He glanced around the music room, with its high ceilings

and grand piano, its wide windows and French doors overlooking the sea. He scratched his head. "A few years. Five?"

"You haven't been home for *five years*?"

"I was born here. I never said it was home." He looked away. "I don't have many good memories of the place. I was away at school from when I was nine, remember. I've hardly come back since my parents died."

She knew he was an orphan. "I'm so sorry...how old were you?"

"Fourteen." His voice was flat. No wonder. It was heartbreaking to lose your parents. Daisy knew all about it.

Her voice was gentle as she said, "Why did you choose this place for our honeymoon?"

"Because..." He took a deep breath. "Because it was time. Besides." He gave a smile that didn't meet his eyes. "Doesn't every bride dream of a honeymoon on a Greek island?"

"It's more than I ever dreamed of." She nestled her hand in his. "I'm sorry about your parents. My own mom died when I was just seven. Cancer. And then my..."

She stopped herself, but too late. Their eyes locked. Would the memory of her father always stand between them?

He pulled his hand away. "This way."

Leonidas led her outside through the French doors. Daisy stopped, gasping at the beauty.

The wide terrace clung to the edge of the bright blue sea, with a white balustrade hovering between sea and sky. On the walls of the villa behind them, bougainvillea climbed, gloriously pink, between the white and blue.

"It's beautiful," she whispered, choking up. "I never imagined anything could be so beautiful."

"I can," Leonidas said huskily, looking down at her. He roughly pulled her into his arms.

As he kissed her, Daisy felt the sun on her bare shoulders, the warm wind blowing against her dress and hair, and she breathed in the sweet scent of flowers and the salt of the sea. She felt her husband's strength and power and heat. He wanted her. He adored her.

Could he ever love her?

He'd told her once that he couldn't. But then, hadn't Daisy said the same after learning his true identity—telling him she could never, ever love him again?

And she'd been wrong. Because in this moment, as Leonidas held her passionately in this paradise, she felt her love for him more strongly than ever.

A voice chirped words in Greek behind them, and they both fell guiltily apart. Maria, the housekeeper, was smiling, holding a lunch tray. With an answering smile, Leonidas went to take the tray from her.

"We'll have lunch at the table," he murmured to Daisy.

The two of them spent a pleasurable hour, eating fish and Greek salad and freshly baked flatbreads, along with briny olives and cheeses. It was all so impossibly delicious that when Daisy finally could eat no more, she leaned back in her chair, looking out at the sea, feeling impossibly happy.

She looked at her husband. As he gazed out at the blue water, his darkly handsome face looked relaxed. Younger. He seemed...different.

"Do you have any drawing paper?" Daisy asked suddenly. He turned to her with a laugh.

"Why?"

"I want to draw you."

"Right now?"

"Yes, now."

He went inside the villa, and a moment later, came back with a small pad of paper and a regular pencil. "It's the best I could find. It's not exactly an art studio in there."

"It's perfect," she said absentmindedly, taking it in hand.

She looked at him as he sat back at the small table on the terrace. "Don't move."

He shifted uneasily. "Why are you drawing me?"

How could she explain this strange glow of happiness, this need to understand, to hold on to the moment—and to him? "Because…just because."

With a sigh, he nodded, and sat back at the table. As Daisy drew, she focused completely on line and shadow and light and form. Silence fell. He sat very still, lost in his own thoughts. As Leonidas stared at the villa, his relaxed expression became wooden, even haunted. To draw him back out, she prodded gently, "So you grew up here?"

"Yes." If anything, he looked more closed off. She tried again.

"You must have at least a few good memories of this place."

"I have good memories of Maria. And the hours I spent on this terrace. As a boy, I used to look out at the water and dream about jumping in the sea and swimming far, far away. Not stopping until I reached North America." The light slowly came back into his eyes. "The village is nice. The food. The people. I was free to walk around the island, to disappear for hours."

"Hours?" She lifted her eyebrows, even as she focused on the page. "Your parents didn't worry?"

"They were happy I was gone."

Moving the pencil across the white page, Daisy gave a snort. "I'm sure that's not true…" Finishing the sketch, she held it up to him with quiet pride. "Here."

Reaching out, Leonidas looked at the drawing. Daisy smiled. It was the best thing she'd done in ages, she thought. Maybe ever. He looked younger in the drawing, happy.

He touched the page gently, then whispered, "That's how you see me?"

"Yes." She'd drawn him the way she saw him. With her heart.

Silence fell, a silence so long that it became heavy, like a dark cloud covering the sun. Then Leo roughly pushed the drawing back to her.

"You've got me all wrong," he said in a low voice. "It's time you knew." He lifted his black eyes. "Who I really am."

# CHAPTER EIGHT

THIS WAS A MISTAKE. A huge mistake.

Behind him, Leonidas could hear the roar of the sea—or maybe it was his heart. He looked at Daisy, sitting across from him at the table.

His wife's eyes were big and green, fringed with dark lashes, and her full pink lips were parted. Her honey-brown hair fell in waves against her bare shoulders, over the thin straps of her white sundress. Behind her the magnificent white villa reached up into the blue sky, with brilliant pink flowers and green leaves along the white wall.

For the last few days, he'd tried to convince himself he was going to tell her everything, as he'd promised. She was his wife now. She was having his baby. If he couldn't finally let down his guard with her, then who?

Then he remembered how he'd felt when that gray-haired artist—Franck Bain—had burst in on their wedding and tried to take Daisy from him.

*Don't marry him. He's a liar who killed your father—an innocent man.*

If the security guards hadn't rushed the man out, Leonidas might have throttled Bain himself. Since the wedding yesterday, the man had been politely warned to leave New York. *Politely* might be an exaggeration. But he had left for Los Angeles and with any luck, they'd never see him again.

But Bain had been right about one thing. Leonidas was a liar. Not about Daisy's father, who hadn't been innocent in the forgery scheme.

But about himself.

For Leonidas's whole life, he'd lied about who he was.

He was tired of pretending. He wanted one person on earth to know him, really know him. And who could be more trustworthy than Daisy?

He wanted to tell his wife the truth. But the idea was terrifying. Even as he'd held his new bride, snuggled up against him, on the overnight flight from New York, tension had built inside him.

So he'd promised himself that he'd tell her at the *end* of their honeymoon, after a week of lovemaking, eating fresh seafood and watching the sun set over the Aegean.

*Appearance is what matters.* How many times had his parents drilled that into him as a child—not just by words, but by example? At twenty-one, he'd thrown himself into the luxury business, determined to do even better than Giannis and Eleni Niarxos had in projecting an aura of perfection. Leonidas had become his brand—global, wealthy, sophisticated, cold.

Except there was this quiet voice inside him, growing steadily harder to repress, that he was more than his brand, so much more. He wasn't the monster his parents had called him; he could be warm and alive. *Like her.*

Daisy licked her delicious pink lips. "What do you mean?" she said haltingly, her voice like music. "I don't know who you are?"

In her arms, pressed against her breasts and belly, she cradled her sketch of him.

It was the sketch which had made him blurt out the words. The man in her drawing looked strong and warm and kind and sure, with humor gleaming from his eyes. Nothing like Leonidas had ever been. Not even as a boy.

But perhaps he could still become that man if—

"Leo?"

"I was never meant to be born," he said. "My very existence is a lie." He gave a grim smile. "You might say I'm a forgery."

"What are you talking about?"

Leonidas took a deep breath. "You think I'm Leonidas Gianakos Niarxos, the son of Giannis Niarxos."

Her lovely face looked bewildered. "Aren't you?"

This was harder than he'd thought. He could not force the words from his lips. His whole body was screaming *Danger!* and telling him to be quiet before it was too late, before he risked everything.

Rising from the chair, he paced the wide terrace. He felt her eyes follow him. He probably looked crazy. Because he was. Keeping this story buried inside him for so long had made him crazy.

Turning, Leonidas gripped the railing of the balustrade, looking out at the sea beneath the hot Greek sun. "My parents married for love." He paused. "That was unusual for wealthy Greek families at the time. And they were young. My father was heir to the Niarxos company, which made luxury leather goods. My mother was the heiress to a shipping fortune. She brought money as her dowry—and a Picasso."

*"Love with Birds,"* Daisy whispered, then cut herself off.

"Yes." He glanced back at her. "From everything I've heard, my parents were crazy about each other." His hands tightened. "But years passed, and they could not have a baby. Society's golden couple was not perfect after all. All of their friends, who'd been secretly jealous of their flaunted passion, taunted them with their smug pity. And when it turned out to be my father's fault that they could not conceive, my mother started complaining about him to her friends. Their love evaporated into rage and blame." He glanced back at her. "I only heard of this years later, you understand."

Daisy's face was pale. "Then you were born…"

"Right." Leonidas gave a crooked smile. "Nine months later, I was born. Their marriage was saved. And that was the end of it."

Setting down her sketchbook carefully on the table, she rose to her feet. Going to him on the edge of the terrace, she said quietly, "What really happened?"

His heart was pounding painfully beneath his ribs. "I'm the only one alive," he whispered, "who knows the full story."

Leonidas looked down at the pounding surf on the white sand beach below.

"From the time I was born, everything I did or said seemed to set my father on edge, making him yell that I was useless and stupid. My mother just avoided me. It was only at fourteen, after my father's funeral, that I learned the reason why."

Standing beside him, Daisy didn't say a word.

"I always had the best clothes, the best education money could buy. *Appearance* was what mattered to them. No one must criticize how they treated their only child." He paused. "If not for Maria, I'm not sure I would have survived."

Reaching out, she put her hand over his on the railing. "Leo…"

Leonidas pulled his hand away. He couldn't bear to be touched. Not now. Not even by her. "I knew something was wrong with me. I could not please them, no matter how I tried. Something about me was so awful that my own father and mother despised me. And though everyone in Greece seemed to think my parents still had this great love affair, at home, they ignored each other—or threw dishes and screamed. Because of me."

"Why would you blame yourself for their marriage problems?"

For a moment, he fell silent. "I heard them sometimes, arguing at night, when I was home during school holidays." He glanced back at the villa. "This is a big house. But sometimes they were loud. One of them always seemed to be threatening divorce. But neither was willing to give up the Picasso. That was the sticking point. Custody of the painting. Not me."

Her stricken eyes met his.

Leonidas paused, then said in a low voice, "When I asked if I could stay at my boarding school year-round, they agreed. Because they could tell other people they'd only done it to make me happy. Appearance was all that mattered to them. My parents stayed together in their glamorous, beautiful lives, pretending to be happy."

"How could they live like that?"

"My father quietly drank himself to death." His lips twisted upward. "When I came home to attend his funeral, I was shocked when my mother hugged me, crying into my arms. I was fourteen, still young enough to be desperate for a mother's love." Leonidas still hated to remember that rainy afternoon, as he'd stared at his father's grave, and his mother, dressed all in black, had embraced him. "I thought maybe she needed me at last. That she…loved me." He gave a bitter smile. "But after the service was over, and her society friends were gone, my mother stopped pretending to be grief stricken. She calmly told me that she was leaving me in the care of trustees until I inherited my father's estate. She was moving to Turkey to be with her lover. She said there was no reason for us to ever see each other again."

"What?" Daisy cried. "She said that? At your father's funeral? How could she?"

He gave a low laugh. "I asked her. *Why, Mamá? Why have you always hated me? What's wrong with me?*" His jaw tightened. "And she finally told me."

Silence fell on the villa's terrace. Leonidas heard the wind through nearby trees, ruffling the pages of his wife's sketchbook on the table.

"My father had been enraged at my mother telling their friends that it was his fault they couldn't conceive, that he wasn't *a real man*. He wanted to shut her up—and go back to being the golden couple of society." He narrowed his eyes. "He had a brother, Dimitris, his identical twin, a few minutes younger. My grandfather had cut off Dimitris without a dime for his scandals, leaving him nothing to buy drugs with. Until my father came to him with an offer—asking him to make love to my mother in the dark and cause her to conceive a child without realizing that the man impregnating her wasn't my father." He paused. "My uncle agreed. And he succeeded."

"What are you saying?"

"My uncle was my real father." Leonidas took a deep breath. "I never knew him. Before I was born, he burned himself out in a blaze of drugs. My father had believed that after I was born, he'd be able to forget he wasn't my real father. After all, biologically I would be, or close enough. But he couldn't forget that his brother had made love to his wife. And he couldn't forgive her for not noticing the difference. Shortly after I was born, when my mother lashed out at him for ignoring their new baby, he exploded, and called her a whore."

Daisy's face was stricken. "Oh, Leo…"

"She forced him to explain. After that, she couldn't forgive what he'd done to her, that she'd made love to her drug-addicted brother-in-law without knowing it. Her own husband had tricked her. Every time she looked at her newborn baby—*me*—she felt dirty and betrayed."

Tears welled in her eyes. "But it wasn't your fault—none of it!"

He took a deep breath, looking up bleakly as plaintive seagulls flew across the stark blue sky. "And yet, it all was."

"No," Daisy whispered.

"Appearance is what matters," he said flatly. "Giannis

wasn't really my father, and my parents despised each other. But to the outside world, they pretended they were in love. They pretended they were happy." He paused. "They pretended to be my parents."

Tears were streaking Daisy's cheeks.

"When my mother said there was no need for us ever to see each other again, right after she'd just been hugging me and crying in my arms, something snapped. And... And..."

"And?"

Leonidas took a deep breath. "I saw her Picasso, sitting nearby, waiting to be wrapped and placed in a crate. Something in my head exploded." He looked away. "I grabbed some scissors from a nearby table. I heard my mother screaming. When I came out of my haze, I'd slashed the entire side of *Love with Birds*, right across its ugly gray heart."

He exhaled. "My mother wrenched the scissors out of my hands, and told me I was a monster, and that I never should have been born." He looked back at Daisy. "Those were her last words to me. A few weeks later, she died in the Turkish earthquake. Her *yali* was smashed into rubble and rock. Her body was found but the painting was lost."

"So that's how you knew the Picasso was a fake," Daisy whispered, then shook her head. "And no wonder you wanted it so badly. No wonder you were so angry when..." She swallowed, looking away.

Looking down, he said thickly, "After I became a man, I thought if I could own the painting, maybe I would understand."

"Understand what?"

"How they could love it so much, and not—"

His throat closed.

"Not you," she whispered.

His knees felt like rubber. He couldn't look at her. Would he see scorn in her eyes? Or worse—pity?

He'd grown up swallowing so much of both. Scorn from

his family. Pity from the servants. He'd spent his whole life making sure he'd never choke down another serving of either one.

But he was about to become a father. His eyes fell to Daisy's belly, and he felt a strange new current of fear.

What did he know about being a parent, with the example he'd had? What about Leonidas—either as a desperate, unloved boy, or an arrogant, coldhearted man—had made him worthy to raise a child?

"Leo," Daisy said in a low voice. With a deep breath, he met her gaze. His wife's eyes were shining with tears. "I can't even imagine what you went through as a kid." She shook her head. "But that's all over. You have a real family now. A baby who will need you. And a wife who…who…" Reaching up, she cupped her hands around his rough jawline and whispered, "A wife who loves you."

Leonidas sucked in his breath, his eyes searching hers. Daisy loved him? After everything he'd just told her?

"You…what?"

"I love you, Leo," she said simply.

His heart looped and twisted, and he couldn't tell if it was the thrill of joy or the nausea of sick terror.

"But—how can you?" he blurted out.

Her lovely face lifted into a warm smile, her green eyes shimmering with tears. "I've always loved you, from the moment we met. Even when I tried not to. Even when I was angry… But I love you. You're wonderful. Wonderful and perfect."

*She loved him.*

Incredulous happiness filled his heart. On the villa's white terrace, covered with pink flowers and overlooking the blue sea, Leonidas pulled her roughly into his arms, and kissed her passionately beneath the hot Greek sun.

Hours later, or maybe just seconds, he took her hand and

led her inside the villa, to the vast master bedroom, with its wide open windows overlooking the Aegean.

Taking her to the enormous bed, he made love to her, as warm sea breezes blew against gauzy white curtains. He kissed her skin, made her gasp, made her cry out her pleasure, again and again.

Much later, when they were both exhausted from lovemaking, they had dinner, seafood fresh from the sea, along with slow-baked lamb marinated in garlic and lemon, artichokes in olive oil, goat's milk cheese, salad with cucumber and tomatoes, and freshly baked bread.

Full and glowing, they changed into swimsuits and walked along the white sand beach at twilight, as the water rolled sensuously against their legs. They stopped to kiss each other, then chased the waves, laughing as they splashed together like children in the turquoise-blue sea, the sunset sky aflame.

Leonidas watched her, the way she smiled up at him, her eyes so warm and bright. Daisy glowed like a star, her wet hair slicked back, the white bathing suit clinging to her pregnant body. His heart was beating fast.

*I love you, Leo.*

The setting sun was still warm on his skin as he came closer in the water. She looked at his intent face, and her smile disappeared. Taking her hand, he led her back to the villa, neither of them speaking.

Once they reached the bedroom's en suite bathroom, he peeled off her swimsuit, then his own. He led her into the shower, wide enough for two, and slowly washed the salt and sand off their bodies.

Drawing her back to the enormous bed, he made love to his wife in the fading twilight, with the dying sun falling to the west, as the soft wind blew off the pounding surf. In that moment, Leonidas thought he might die of happiness.

*I love you.*

For the first time in his life, he felt like he was home, safe, wanted, desired. He and Daisy were connected in a way he'd never known, in a way he'd never imagined possible. Their souls were intertwined, as well as their bodies. *She loved him.* As he held her in the dark bedroom, he knew he'd never be alone again. He could finally let down his guard—

His eyes flew open.

But what if Daisy ever *stopped* loving him?

He felt a sudden vertigo, a sickening whirl as the earth dropped beneath him. He didn't think he could survive.

But how could he make sure her love for him endured, when he had no idea why, or *how*, she could love him? Even his own mother had said Leonidas should never have been born. Whatever Daisy might say, he knew he wasn't good enough for her.

And as for being good enough for their child…

Stop it, Leonidas told himself desperately, trying to get back to the perfect happiness of just a moment before. Squeezing his eyes shut, he held Daisy close. He kissed his wife's sweaty temple, cradling her body with his own.

It was a perfect honeymoon. When they returned to New York a few days later, Leonidas vowed that Daisy would never regret marrying him. If he could not feel love for his wife in his cold, ashy heart, he would at least show her love every day through his actions.

And for the first three months of their marriage, she did seem very happy, as they planned the nursery, went to the theater and even took cooking and baby prep classes together. Leonidas felt like a fool as he burned every type of food from Thai to Tuscan, no matter how hard he tried.

In order to spend his days—and nights—with her, he ignored work, and did not regret it. Even when Leonidas did go in to the office, instead of focusing on sales throughout his global empire, he found himself asking his employees random questions about their lives, as Daisy did. For the first time, he was curious about their families, their goals and what had brought them to work at Liontari.

His vice presidents and board members obviously thought Leonidas was lost in some postnuptial sensual haze. But they forgave him, because the explosive global reaction to his wedding to the daughter of the man he'd sent to prison had caused brand recognition to increase thirty percent. Leonidas and Daisy had had calls for interviews on morning shows, and even four calls from Hollywood, offering to turn their story into a "based on a true story" movie. Daisy had been horrified.

Leonidas had been happy to refuse. He'd discovered to his shock that he was happy working fewer hours. His heavily pregnant wife wanted him at home. She *needed* him at home. How could profit and loss reports compare with that?

But everything changed the day their baby was born.

On that early day in June, when the flowers were blooming outside the modern hospital in New York and the sky was the deepest blue he'd ever seen, Leonidas finally held his sweet tiny sleeping baby in his arms.

The newborn fluttered open her eyes, dark as his own. Her forehead furrowed.

And then, abruptly, she started to scream, as if in physical pain.

"She's just hungry," the nurse said soothingly.

But Leonidas was clammy with sweat. "Here. Take her. Just take her—"

He pushed the shrieking bundle into his wife's welcoming arms. Holding their daughter in the bed, Daisy murmured soft words and let the rooting baby nurse. Within seconds, the hospital suite was filled with blessed silence. Daisy smiled down at her baby, touching her tiny fingers wonderingly. Then she looked up at Leonidas.

"Don't take it personally," she said uncertainly.

"Don't worry," he ground out. But Leonidas knew it was personal. His own daughter couldn't stand to be touched by him. Somehow, the newborn had just known, as his parents had, that Leonidas was not worthy of love. Though Daisy's kind heart had momentarily blinded her to his flaws, her love for him would not last. And it would not save him.

He was on a ticking clock. Any day now, she would realize what their baby already knew.

And by the end of the summer, his prophecy came true. As weeks passed and Leonidas refused to hold the baby again—for her own sake—he watched with despair as his wife's expression changed from bewilderment to heartbreak, and finally cold accusation.

It was the happiest day of Daisy's life when their baby was born in the first week of June.

At least, it should have been.

Labor was hard, but when it was over, she held her little girl for the first time. She looked up at her husband, wanting to share her joy.

But for some reason, his handsome face was pale, as if he'd just seen a ghost.

Their baby was perfect. Little hands, little feet, a scrunched-up beautiful face. They named her Olivia—Livvy—after Daisy's mother, Olivia Bianchi Cassidy. Daisy was nervous, but thrilled to bring her back to the brownstone that had somehow become home to her, to the sweet pink nursery she and Leonidas had lovingly prepared.

It was hard to believe that was two months ago. Now, as Daisy nestled her baby close, nursing her in the rocking chair, she couldn't get over how soft Livvy's skin was, or how plump her cheeks had become in nine weeks. The baby's dark eyelashes fluttered as she slept. Her hair was darker than Daisy's, reflecting her namesake's Italian roots, as well as Leonidas's Greek heritage.

"Come and look at your daughter," she'd said to him more than once. "Doesn't she look like you?"

And every time, Leonidas would give their newborn daughter only the slightest sideways glance. "Yes."

"Won't you hold her?" she would ask.

And with that same furtive glance at his daughter, her husband would always refuse. Even if Daisy asked for help, saying she needed to have her hands free to do something else, like start the baby's bath, even *then* he would refuse, and would loudly call for Mrs. Berry to assist, as he backed away.

Leonidas disappeared from the house, claiming he was urgently needed at work. He started spending sixteen-hour days at the office and sleeping in the guest room when he came home late.

He claimed he did not want to disturb Daisy and the baby, but the end result was that Daisy had barely seen her husband all summer. He'd simply evaporated from their lives, leaving only the slight scent of his exotic masculine cologne.

For weeks, Daisy had felt heartsick about it. Obviously, their daughter wasn't to blame. Livvy was perfect. So it must be something else.

Back in March, during their honeymoon, when he'd told her about his tragic, awful childhood, it had broken Daisy's heart. But it had also given her hope. Some part of Leonidas must love her, for him to be so vulnerable with her.

And so she'd been vulnerable, too. She'd told him she loved him.

For months after that, Leonidas had held her close, made love to her, made her feel cherished and adored. He'd let her draw his portrait in six different sketches, all of them in different light.

Now she felt like those sketches were all she had of him.

Had there been a shadow beneath his gaze, even then? Had he already been starting to pull away?

In the two months since Livvy's birth, Daisy hadn't had the opportunity to do another drawing of Leonidas. But she'd done dozens of sketches of their baby. Looking through them yesterday, she'd been astonished at how much the infant had changed in such a short time.

Mrs. Berry, seeing the sketches, had shyly asked if she could hire Daisy to do her portrait, too, as a gift for her husband's birthday. Daisy had done it gladly one afternoon when the baby was sleeping, without charge. She'd done the drawing with her yellow dog stretched out over her feet, on the floor. Sunny had grown huge, and was always nearby, as if guarding Daisy and the baby from unknown enemies. She was particularly suspicious of squirrels.

Sunny always made her laugh.

Mrs. Berry had loved the drawing. Word of mouth began to spread, from the house's staff, to their families. Friends who came from Brooklyn to see the baby saw the drawings of Livvy, and requested portraits of their own grandchildren, of their spouses, of their pets. Just yesterday, Daisy had gotten five separate requests for portraits. She didn't know what to think.

"Why weren't you doing drawings like this all along?" Her old boss at the diner, Claudia, had demanded earlier that week. "Why were you doing those awful modern scribbles—when all along you could do pictures like this?"

Remembering, Daisy gave a low laugh. Trust her old boss not to be diplomatic.

But still, it made her think.

When she'd done her painting at art school, long ago, she'd been desperate to succeed. Art had always felt stressful, as she'd tried to guess what others would most admire. Each effort had been less authentic than the last, a pastiche of great masterpieces, as Leonidas had said. The painting her husband had bought at the auction for a million dollars was still buried in a closet. In spite of its success that night, she hadn't felt joy creating it. In spite of all her effort, the painting had never connected with her heart.

But these sketches were different. They were of *people*.

It felt easy to simply draw her friends—even new friends she'd just met—and see what was best in them.

Was it possible that Daisy did have some talent? Not for painting—but for *people*?

With a rueful snort, she shook her head. Talent for people? She couldn't even get her own husband to talk to her! Or hold their baby daughter!

Two days ago, heartsick, she'd been thinking of how, as an agonized fourteen-year-old, Leonidas had struck out at the Picasso with scissors. And she'd had a sudden crazy idea.

What if she found the painting for him?

It was a long shot. He'd been looking for it for decades. But maybe he hadn't been doing it the right way. Daisy had a few connections in the art world. If she could give him his heart's desire, would it bring Leonidas back to them?

It was her best chance. A grand gesture Leonidas would never forget. She pictured his joyful face when she presented him with the Picasso. Then he would take her in his arms and tell her he loved her.

Her heart yearned for that moment!

So she called a young art blogger she knew in Brooklyn. Aria Johnson had a huge social media following and a ruthless reputation. The woman was like a bloodhound, searching out stories about priceless art and scandals of the rich and famous. Even Daisy's father had been a little afraid of her.

Picking up the phone, she called her and told Aria haltingly about her husband's history with the lost Picasso.

Daisy didn't explain *everything*, of course. She didn't say a word about the way he'd been conceived. *That* was a secret she'd take to the grave. She just told her that *Love with Birds* had been lost when Leonidas's mother had died in a big Turkish earthquake, some two decades before.

"Yeah. I know the story." The blogger popped her gum impatiently. "People have looked for that Picasso for twenty years. Wild-goose chase. Why else would your father have thought he could forge it?"

"He didn't—"

Aria cut her off. "They only found the woman's body. No painting." Daisy had flinched. *The woman* had been Leonidas's mother. "Other bodies were found, though. Her household staff. A young man who no one came forward to claim."

"Could you look into it?" Daisy said.

"A widow. With money. Hmm… Was she beautiful?"

"I guess so," Daisy replied. What difference did Eleni Niarxos's beauty make?

"Anything else you can tell me?"

She swallowed hard. It felt like breaking a confidence— but how else could she be sure it was the right painting? She said reluctantly, "There's a cut in the canvas. Someone sliced the painting with a pair of scissors."

*"Someone?"*

"Yes. Someone." Quickly changing the subject, Daisy said, "If you could find it, I'd be so grateful. And I'll pay you—"

"You can pay my expenses, that's it. I don't need a finder's fee. I just need to own the *story*. Deal?"

Daisy took a deep breath. It felt like a devil's bargain, but she was desperate. "Deal."

The art blogger paused. "If I find the painting, it might not have provenance."

Meaning, the painting might have been stolen. Which

would make sense. How else could it have simply disappeared during the earthquake?

"I don't care," Daisy said. "As long as the Picasso is genuine. And I want the story of where the person found it."

Aria popped her gum. "Don't worry. I'll get the story."

That had been a few days ago. Now, holding her sleeping baby, Daisy was rocking in the chair in the nursery. It was late August, hot and sweaty summer in New York, but cool and calm inside their West Village mansion. She looked down at Livvy, softly snoring in her arms, in rhythm with the much louder snoring of the large dog snoozing at Daisy's feet.

"Soon," she whispered to her baby. "Aria will find it. And then your father will be home, and he'll realize at last that he's really, truly loved—"

The nursery door was suddenly flung open, hitting the wall with a bang. The dog jumped at her feet. Livvy woke and started wailing, then Sunny started barking.

Looking up at the doorway in shock, Daisy saw her husband, dark as a shadow. He was dressed in a suit, but his handsome face held a savage glower.

For a moment, in spite of her baby's wails, Daisy's heart lifted. Her husband had come home to her at last. Her body yearned for his embrace, for connection, for reassurance. A smile lifted to her lips.

"Leonidas," she breathed. "I'm so glad to see you—"

"Do you really hate me this much, Daisy?" His voice was low and cold. "How could you do it?"

"What?" she cried, bewildered.

"As if you didn't know." Leonidas gave a low, bitter laugh. "I should have known you would betray me. Just like everyone else."

# CHAPTER NINE

THE WELCOMING SMILE on his wife's face fled.

She'd made such a lovely picture, snuggled in the rocking chair beside the nursery's window, holding their sleeping baby, with the floppy golden dog at her feet.

Now Daisy's beautiful face was anguished, the baby was wailing and Sunny was dancing desperately around Leonidas, wagging her tail, trying to get his attention.

He ignored the dog, looking only at his wife.

Turning away, she calmed the baby down, pulling out a breast and tucking her nipple into Livvy's tiny mouth as comfort.

It shouldn't have been erotic, but it was. Probably because he hadn't made love to her in months. Leonidas tried not to look. He couldn't let himself want her. He couldn't.

He forced himself to look away.

She'd hurt him. In a way he'd never thought he'd hurt again.

He never should have told her about his past. Never...

As the baby fell quiet, falling asleep with her tiny hand pressed against his wife's breast, Daisy finally looked up at him. Her green eyes narrowed.

"What do you mean, I betrayed you?"

Ignoring the dog still pressing against his knees, Leonidas glared back, but lowered his voice so as not to wake their child. "You spoke with Aria Johnson."

"Oh, that." She relaxed, then gave a soft smile. "I was

trying to help. I know what the Picasso means to you, and I asked her to find it. I didn't think—"

"No, you *didn't* think, or else you wouldn't have told a muckraking *blogger* that I cut into the painting with a pair of scissors!"

"What?" she gasped. "I never told her it was *you*!"

"Well, she knows. She just called me at the office. And if that weren't enough she's been looking into my mother's past," he said grimly.

Daisy went pale. She whispered, "What did she find?"

"My mother apparently had many lovers, both in Greece and Turkey. She tracked them all down, except for her last one, who apparently died with her in the earthquake." He glared at Daisy. "One of the lovers knew how I was born. My mother must have confessed. So now that blogger knows I'm not really my father's son, but the son of my drug-addicted uncle. She asked me to confirm or deny!"

"What did you say?" Daisy cried.

"I hung up the phone!" Clawing back his hair, Leonidas paced the nursery. Every muscle felt tense. "How could you have told her to look into my past?"

"I didn't! I just told her to find the Picasso!"

He looked down at her, his heart in his throat. "Aria Johnson has a reputation. She can't be bought off. All she cares about is entertaining her army of followers with the most shocking scandal she can find. And she always finds them. This is going to be all over the internet within hours."

Daisy looked up at him miserably, her eyes glistening with unshed tears. "I'm so sorry. I was trying to help."

"Help? Now the whole world is going to learn my deepest, darkest secret, which I've spent a lifetime trying to hide." He clenched his hands at his sides. "I never should have trusted you."

"I'm sorry." She blinked fast, her face anguished. "I didn't mean to hurt you. I was trying to bring you back!"

"What are you talking about?"

"The day Livvy was born, you disappeared!" The baby flinched a little in her arms at the rise in her voice. With a deep breath, Daisy carefully got to her feet, then lifted Livvy into her crib. Gently setting down the sleeping infant, she quietly backed away, motioning for Leonidas to follow, Sunny at his feet. Closing the nursery door silently behind them, Daisy turned to face him in the hallway.

The window at the end of the hallway slanted warm light into the hundred-year-old brownstone, gleaming against the marble floors. The big golden dog stood between them, her tongue lagging, looking hopefully first at one, then the other.

"I need you, Leonidas," Daisy whispered. "Our baby needs you. Why won't you even hold her?"

A tumble of feelings wrenched though him. He couldn't let them burst through his heart, he couldn't. He said stiffly, "I held her."

"Just once, in the hospital. Since then, you've avoided her." Her eyes lifted to his. "You've avoided me."

His wife's stricken expression burned through him like acid. He turned away.

"Work has been busy. You cannot be angry at me for trying to secure our daughter's empire…" Then he remembered that Daisy didn't care about his business empire. It wasn't enough for her. And if that wasn't, how could Leonidas ever be? "I haven't been avoiding you."

The lie was poison in his mouth.

"Please," she said in a low voice. "I need you."

"You don't. You're doing fine. And Livvy is better off with you than with me."

"What is that supposed to mean?"

How could he explain that his baby daughter already knew he was no good? And from the pain and hurt in his wife's eyes, Daisy was rapidly learning the same thing, too. "It doesn't matter."

Reaching out, she put her hand on his arm. "You helped me love art again, after all my hope was lost. Drawing you on our honeymoon, I realized that people are my passion. Not random smudges or colors. *People*." Blinking fast, she tried a smile. "You helped me find my voice."

Daisy had never looked more beautiful to him than she did right now, her green eyes so luminous, her heart fully in her face.

And her love. He saw her love for him shining from her eyes. He didn't deserve it. He couldn't bear it. Because it wouldn't last.

His fate was in her hands, as he waited for Daisy to finally realize he wasn't worthy of her love. *You're wonderful*, she'd told him. *Wonderful and perfect*.

He wasn't. He knew his flaws; he could be cold and arrogant and selfish. But from the moment she'd decided to love him, she had become willfully blind. She had rose-colored glasses and was determined to see only the best of him.

But sooner or later she'd see the real him. Then her love would crumble to dust. To *disgust*.

Just the thought of that ripped him up.

And soon, the whole world would learn about his scandalous birth and not even his wealth or power would protect him. He'd done everything he set out to do. He'd built an empire. He was rich and powerful beyond imagination. But it had changed nothing.

All his worst fears were about to come true. The world would learn that his very birth had been a deceit. His parents had despised him and wished he'd never been born.

Leonidas was unlovable. Unworthy. Empty.

And now he was dragging Daisy into it as well.

"I'm sorry, Leonidas," she said quietly. "I never meant to hurt you. Can you ever forgive me?"

Shaking his head, he looked toward the window at the end of the hallway. If he had any decency, he would let both her and the baby go.

But just the thought of that made his soul howl with grief…

Daisy bit her lip. "Even if Aria publishes everything, why would anyone care? What does the way you were conceived have to do with you?"

He looked at her incredulously. "Everything."

She shook her head. "You had an awful childhood and triumphed in spite of it all. That's the *real* story, whoever your father was."

Leonidas didn't answer.

"Besides. You never know," she tried, "maybe the Picasso will be found…"

"It will never be found." He gave a low, bitter laugh. "It was buried beneath ten tons of rock and fire."

"But you said they never found it—"

"It must have been destroyed." Like so much else.

A long, empty silence fell between them in the hallway.

"Leonidas," she said quietly. "Look at me."

It took him a moment to gather the courage. Then he did. His heart broke just looking at her, so beautiful and brave, as she faced him, her shoulders tight.

"I'm sorry if I've caused you pain," she said quietly. "My desperation made me reckless." Her lovely face was bewildered. "You asked me to marry you. You *insisted* on marriage. You said there was nothing you wanted more than to be Livvy's father. What happened?"

"I don't know."

"If you're never going to hold her, never going to look at me—why are we married? Why am I even here?"

It was clear. He had to let them go. If he didn't, he'd only ending up hurting them so much more.

But how could he let them go, when they were everything?

Hurt them—or hurt himself. There was only one choice to make. But it hurt so much that Leonidas thought he might die. He looked around the hallway wildly, then gasped, "I need some fresh air—"

Turning, he rushed down the stone staircase and stumbled outside, desperate to breathe.

Outside the brownstone mansion, the tree-lined street was strangely quiet. The orange sun, setting to the west, left long shadows in the hot, humid August twilight. He stopped, leaning over, gasping for breath, trying to stop the frantic pounding of his heart.

Daisy came out of the house behind him, to stand in the fading light.

"I love you, Leonidas," she said quietly.

His hands clenched. Finally, he turned to face her.

"You can't."

"The truth is, I've always loved you, from the moment we met at the diner, and I thought you were just Leo, a salesclerk in a shop." Reaching up, she cupped his unshaven cheek. "I fell in love with you. And who you could be. And I only have one question for you." She tilted her head. "Can you ever love me back?"

Trembling beneath the shady trees of summer twilight, Leonidas closed his stinging eyes. He felt like he was spinning out of control, coming undone. But his heart was empty. He'd learned long ago that begging for love only brought scorn. The only way to be safe was to pull back. To not care.

The only way to keep Daisy and Livvy safe from him, to make sure he never hurt or disappointed them, was to let them go.

He had to. No matter how much it killed him. He had to find the strength, for their sakes.

Closing his eyes, he took a deep breath.

Then he opened them.

"No. I'm sorry." He covered her hand gently with his own. "I thought I could do this but I can't."

"Do what?"

He looked down at her.

"Marriage," he said quietly.

Her eyes widened, her face pale. He pushed her hand away.

"No," she choked out. "We can go to counseling. We can—"

"You're in love with some imaginary man, not me. I'm not *wonderful*. I'm not *perfect*. I'm a selfish, cold bastard."

"No, you're not, you're *not*!"

"I am. Why can't you admit it?" he said incredulously. "Whatever you say, I know you've never forgiven me for killing your father."

"I have… I've *tried*." Tears were streaming down her face. "Dad was innocent, but I know now you never meant to cause his death."

"Stop." He looked at her, feeling exhausted. "It's time to face reality."

"The reality is that I love you!"

"You're forcing yourself to overlook my flaws. But I've known from the moment Livvy was born that you'd soon see the truth, as she did from the first time I held her."

"Because she cried? That's crazy! She's a baby!"

"It's not crazy. You both deserve better than me. And I'm tired of feeling it every day, tired of knowing I'm not good enough. I'm not this perfect man you want me to be. Seeing the cold accusation in your eyes—"

"What are you *talking* about?"

"Better to end it now, rather than…" Turning away, he said in a low voice, "You and the baby should go."

"Go?" She gave a wild, humorless laugh. "Go where?"

"Anywhere you want. Your old dream of California."

"You're my dream! You!"

Every part of Leonidas's body hurt. He felt like he was two hundred years old. Why was she fighting him so hard? Why—when everything he said was true? "Or if you want, you can keep this house." He looked up at the place where they'd been so happy, the house with the ballroom where they'd quarreled and the garden where they'd played with the dog in the spring sunshine, where wild things grew in the middle of Manhattan. "I'll go to a hotel." He paused. "Forget what the prenup said. You can have half my fortune—half of everything. Whatever you want."

She looked up at him, tears in her eyes.

"But I want you."

"Someday, you'll thank me," he said hoarsely. It was true. It had to be true. He looked one last time at her beautiful, heartbroken face. "Goodbye, Daisy."

Squaring his shoulders, he turned away, walking fast down the quiet residential lane, filled with the soft rustle of leaves in the warm wind.

But even as he walked away, he felt her tears, her anguished grief, reverberating through his body, down to blood and bone.

*It's better this way*, Leonidas repeated to himself fiercely, wiping his eyes. *Better for everyone.*

So why did he feel like he'd just died?

Daisy watched in shock as her husband disappeared down the quiet lane in the twilight. At the end of the street, she saw him hail a yellow cab.

Then he was gone.

Once, long ago, she'd made Leonidas promise that if she ever wanted to leave, he had to let her go.

She'd never imagined he would be the one to leave.

All her love hadn't been enough to make him stay. He'd turned on her.

Yes, she'd blamed Leonidas once, for her father's unjust imprisonment and death. But she'd forgiven that, even if she hadn't forgotten it. Right?

Well. It didn't matter now.

Tears streamed down her face. Turning unsteadily, she stumbled back up the stoop to enter the house he'd just told her was hers. He'd given up the fifty-million-dollar brownstone easily, as if it meant nothing. Just like Daisy and their daughter.

If he'd cared at all, he never would have abandoned them. He would have tried to make their marriage work. Tried to love her.

But he hadn't.

Daisy closed the door behind her and leaned back against it. Above her, the crystal chandelier chimed discordantly in the puff of air.

The luxury of this mansion mocked her in her grief. This place was a palace. It was heaven. But it felt like an empty hell.

She stared blankly at the sweeping stone staircase where her husband had once carried her up to the bedroom, lost in reckless passion.

Her knees gave out beneath her and she slid back against the wall with a sob, crumpling onto the floor.

Her dog, coming downstairs to investigate, gave a worried whine and pushed her soft furry body against Daisy, offering comfort. She wrapped her arm around the animal and stared dimly at the opposite wall, where she'd framed sketches of her husband and baby.

"Mrs. Niarxos."

She looked up to see Mrs. Berry looking down at her with worried eyes. Swallowing, she whispered, "He left me."

"Oh, my dear." The white-haired housekeeper put her

hand on Daisy's shoulder. Her voice was gentler than she'd ever heard before. "I'm so sorry."

The ache in Daisy's throat sharpened to a razor blade. "I thought, if I loved him enough…" Her image shimmered through a haze of tears. "I thought I could love him enough for both of us."

Mrs. Berry's hand tightened, and she said quietly, "I've known the boy for a long time. He never learned to love anyone. Least of all himself."

"But why wouldn't he? He's amazing. He's wonderful. He…" She heard the echo of his words. *I'm not wonderful. I'm not perfect. I'm a selfish, cold bastard.*

"What can I do, my dear?"

"I…" Shaking, Daisy closed her eyes. Still sitting on the marble floor, she gripped her knees against her broken heart. She couldn't imagine any future. All she saw ahead of her was a bleak wasteland of pain.

Then Sunny put her chin against Daisy's leg, her black eyes looking up mournfully, and Daisy remembered that she couldn't fall apart. She had a baby relying on her.

Five months ago, she'd thought she was ready to raise their baby alone. She'd made plans to go to nursing school, to move to California. She'd been strong in herself. She hadn't needed him.

Where had that strong woman gone?

She'd long since canceled her college registration. Daisy blinked fast, trying to see clearly. She stroked her dog's soft golden fur. She took a deep breath. Strong. She had to be strong.

She looked up at Mrs. Berry. "I need to go."

"Go?"

Daisy slowly got up. She looked around the elegant foyer. "I can't stay here. It reminds me too much of him. And how happy we were…"

The housekeeper gave her a strange look. "Were you really?"

Staring at her, Daisy held in her breath. Had they been happy?

"I thought we were," she choked out. "At least at first. But something happened when our baby was born…"

Across the foyer, Daisy's eyes fell again on the framed sketch she'd done of her husband on their honeymoon. They'd been happy then. Next to that, there was a framed sketch of their baby's smiling face and innocent dark eyes. Just like Leonidas's—and yet nothing at all like them.

With a deep breath, Daisy lifted her chin.

So be it.

Ahead of her, the empty future stretched as wide as a vast ocean.

She could fill that terrifying void with flowers and sea breezes.

"I need to pack," she said aloud, hardly recognizing the sound of her own voice.

By the next morning, Daisy, her baby and her dog were en route to California, in search of a new life, or at least a new place, where she could build new memories. And, she prayed, where she could heal and raise her daughter with love.

"We've found it, Mr. Niarxos."

Leonidas stared at his lawyer.

"No," he said faintly. "Impossible."

Edgar Ross shook his head. "I waited to be sure. We were contacted two weeks ago. It's been authenticated. There can be no doubt."

The two men were standing in his chief lawyer's well-appointed office, with its floor-to-ceiling windows and view of the Empire State Building.

When his lawyer had called him that morning, Leonidas

had assumed that the man must have heard that he'd separated from Daisy. After all, for the last three weeks, Leonidas had been living in a Midtown hotel suite. It wouldn't exactly take a detective to figure out the Niarxos marriage was over.

Even though he'd told his wife to go, part of him still couldn't believe that Daisy and their baby had left New York. He'd returned to the mansion only once since she'd gone, and it had felt unbearably empty.

After that, he'd returned to the hotel suite, where he'd been riding out the scandal ever since the sordid truth about his past had been revealed on Aria Johnson's website, in all its ugly glory. This visit to his lawyer's office, on the thirty-fourth floor of a Midtown skyrise, was his first public outing in days. At least the scandal was starting to abate. Only two paparazzi had followed him here, which he took as a victory.

Misinterpreting his silence, his lawyer gave Leonidas a broad smile. "I don't blame you for being skeptical. But we really have found the Picasso."

"How can you be sure?" Leonidas's voice was low. "I don't want my hopes raised, only to have them crushed. I'd prefer to have no hope at all."

Just like his marriage.

He could still see Daisy's beautiful face in the warm Greek sun, surrounded by flowers on the terrace of his villa. *I love you,* she'd said dreamily. *You're wonderful. Wonderful and perfect.*

So different from her agonized, heartbroken face when, on the street outside their New York home, he'd told her he was leaving her.

Leonidas couldn't get those two images out of his mind. For the last three weeks, he'd been haunted by memories, day and night, even when he was pretending to work. Even when he was pretending to sleep.

"Would you like to see your Picasso, Mr. Niarxos?"

Leonidas focused on the lawyer. He took a deep breath, forcibly relaxing his shoulders as they stood in the sleek private office with its view of the steel-and-glass city, reflecting the merciless noonday sun. "Why not."

With a big smile, the lawyer turned. Crossing the private office, he reached up and, with an obvious sense of drama, drew back a curtain.

There, on the wall, lit by unflattering overhead light, was the Picasso. There could be no doubt. *Love with Birds*.

Coming forward, Leonidas's eyes traced the blocky swirls of beige and gray paint. His fingers reached out toward a jagged line in the upper left corner, where the image was slightly off kilter, clumsily stitched back together. In the same place where he'd stabbed it with scissors, as a heartsick, abandoned fourteen-year-old.

"How did you find it?" he whispered.

"That art blogger found it. Aria Johnson. She found a relative of your mother's…er…last lover." He coughed discreetly. "A twenty-two-year-old college student in Ankara. He'd taken the painting to his aunt's house the day before he disappeared in the earthquake."

"Took it? Stole it, you mean."

"Apparently not. The young man told his aunt the painting was a gift from some rich new girlfriend. She never learned who the girlfriend was, and she had no idea the painting was worth anything. She only kept it because she loved her nephew."

Leonidas stared at him, barely comprehending.

After years of fighting tooth and claw to keep her husband from taking the painting from her, Eleni had simply *given it away*? To a young lover she barely knew? How? Why?

And then he knew.

His mother had been broken, too. Betrayed, heartsick, desperate for love.

The thought was overwhelming to him. So it wasn't just Leonidas who felt that way. His mother had taken young lovers and given away her biggest treasure. His father had quietly drunk himself to death. Did everyone in the world feel broken? Feel like they were desperate for love they feared they'd never find?

He looked at the jagged tear across the priceless masterpiece. Ross followed his gaze.

"Er…yes. The aunt tried to repair the cut with a needle and thread, out of respect for her nephew's memory." His lawyer flinched. "You see the result."

It took Leonidas a moment to even find his voice. "Yes."

"She nearly had a heart attack when Aria Johnson told her she'd been keeping a Picasso in her gardening shed for the last twenty years."

"How much does she want for it?"

"The art blogger told her she'd be a fool to take less than ten million. That seemed a reasonable price to me, since she could potentially have gotten even more at auction. So as soon as it was authenticated, I paid her."

"You're saying the painting's mine?"

"Yes, Mr. Niarxos."

Leonidas took another step toward the painting. With his parents now dead, there was no longer anyone to scream at him for trying to touch it. Reaching up, he gently stroked the roughly stitched edge where he'd once hacked into it.

"We will of course send it to be properly restored—"

"No. I'll keep it as it is." Drawing back his hand, Leonidas looked at the treasure he'd chased all his life. *Love with Birds*. Looking at the gray and beige boxy swirls, he waited for joy and love to fill his heart.

Nothing happened.

"I thought you might wish to arrange something with

Liontari's PR department," the lawyer said behind him. "Let them do outreach on social media. This will make a nice end to the soap opera story currently making the rounds about your, *er*, origins. If there's one thing the public likes more than a scandal, it's a happy ending."

Barely listening, Leonidas narrowed his eyes, tilting his head right and left to get a better angle as he looked at the painting, waiting for happiness and triumph to fill his heart.

All his life, he'd chased fame and fortune, luxury and beauty. He'd chased this masterpiece most of all.

Why didn't he feel like he'd thought he would feel? This was the possession that was supposed to make him feel *whole*. This painting was supposed to be love itself.

But Leonidas felt nothing.

Looking at it, he saw neither love nor birds. He saw meaningless swirls and boxes of gray and beige paint.

He felt cheated. Betrayed. His hands tightened at his sides. This painting meant *nothing*.

"Sir?" His lawyer sounded concerned. "Is there a problem?"

Leonidas looked away. "Thank you for arranging the acquisition." The sharp light from the skyscrapers of the merciless city burned his eyelids. His throat was tight. "You will, of course, receive your finder's fee and commission."

"Thank you, sir," Ross said happily. When Leonidas didn't move, he said in a different tone, "Uh…is there something else you wish to discuss, Mr. Niarxos?"

This was the moment to ask for his divorce to be set in motion. Leonidas had already been dragging his feet for too long. Just last week, when he'd stopped by his old house, hoping for a glimpse of his family, Mrs. Berry had told him Daisy had rented a cottage in California, three thousand miles away.

"Rented…a cottage?" he'd asked, bewildered. "I gave her this house!"

"She didn't want it without you," his housekeeper said quietly. "I'm sorry, sir. I'm so sorry."

He'd felt oddly vulnerable. "I'm the one who ended it."

"I know." The white-haired woman had given him a sad smile. "You hated for her to love you. How could she, when you can't love yourself?"

Hearing those awful, true words, Leonidas had fled.

He could never go back to that house or see Mrs. Berry again. Never, ever. He'd pay her off, put the house on the market—

"Ah. I was afraid of this," the lawyer said with a sudden sigh. Turning, he sat down behind his huge desk, and indicated the opposite chair. "Don't worry, Mr. Niarxos. We can soon get you free."

Still standing, Leonidas frowned at him. "Free?"

Edgar Ross said gently, "It's all over town you've been living in a suite at the Four Seasons. But don't worry." He shook his head. "We have your prenup. Divorce won't be hard, as long as Mrs. Niarxos doesn't intend to fight it."

No, he thought dully. Daisy had already fought as hard as she could for their marriage. She would not fight anymore. Not now he'd made it clear there was no hope.

He'd lost her. Lost? He'd pushed her out of his life. Forever.

He looked up dully. In place of a loving, beautiful, kindhearted wife, he had a painting. *Love with Birds*.

"Sir?" Ross again indicated the leather chair.

Leonidas stared at it. All he had to do was sit, and he'd soon get his divorce. His marriage would be declared officially dead. He'd lose Daisy forever, and their child, too. Just as he'd wanted.

He could take the painting to join the rest of his expensive possessions, back at his empty house in the West Village, or any of his other empty houses around the world. Instead of love and legacy, instead of a family, he'd have the painting.

*You hated for her to love you. How could she, when you can't love yourself?*

Leonidas had never been worthy of Daisy's love. She'd called him wonderful. She'd called him perfect. He was neither of those things. No wonder he was scared to love her. Because the moment he did—

The moment he did, she'd see the truth, and he would lose her.

*But he'd lost her anyway.*

The thought made his eyes go wide. He'd sent her away because he was terrified of ever feeling that hollowness again in his heart, of wanting someone's love and not getting it.

But he loved Daisy anyway.

With a gasp, Leonidas stared out the window. A reflected beam from another skyscraper's windows blinded him with sharp light.

*He loved her.*

He was totally and completely in love with his wife. And he had been, from the moment he'd married her. No, before. From the moment he'd kissed her. From the moment she'd first smiled at him in the diner, her face so warm and kind, so beautiful and real in her waitress uniform—

*Nice suit. Headed to court? Unpaid parking tickets? You poor guy. Coffee's on me.*

Daisy always saw the best in everyone. Including him.

Leonidas looked again at the Picasso. The painting was not love. It could never fill his heart.

Only he could do that.

All these years, he'd blamed his parents for his inability to love anyone, including himself. And maybe it was true.

But sooner or later, a man had to choose. Would he bury himself in grief and blame, and die choking on the dirt? Or would he reach up his hands, struggle to pull himself up and out of the early grave, to breathe sunlight and fresh air?

Leonidas chose life.

*He chose her.*

"I have to go," he said suddenly.

"What?" His lawyer looked bewildered, holding a stack of official-looking papers on his desk. "Where?"

"California." Leonidas turned away. He had to see Daisy. He had to tell her everything, to fall at her feet and beg her to forgive him. To take him back. Before he'd even reached the door, he broke into a run.

Because what if he was already too late?

# CHAPTER TEN

THE BOUGAINVILLEA WAS in bloom, the flowers pink and bright, climbing against the snug white cottage overlooking the sea.

After three weeks of living there, Daisy still couldn't get over the beauty of the quiet neighborhood near Santa Barbara. From the small garden behind her cottage, filled with roses and orange trees, she could see the wide blue vista of the Pacific. Looking straight down from the edge of the bluff, she could see the coastal highway far below, but the noise of the traffic was lost against the sea breezes waving the branches of cypress trees.

Looking out at the blue ocean and pink flowers, Daisy couldn't stop herself from remembering her honeymoon, when Leonidas had kissed her passionately, on the terrace of a Greek villa covered with flowers, overlooking the Aegean. Even now, the backs of her eyelids burned at the memory.

When would she get over him? How long would it take for her to feel whole again?

"So? Did you decide?"

Hearing Franck Bain's voice behind her, she turned with a polite smile. "No, not yet. I'm not even sure how long I'm going to stay in California, much less whether I'll open my portrait business here."

"Of course." The middle-aged artist's words were friendly, but his gaze roamed over her, from her white peasant blouse and denim capri pants to her flat sandals. The echo of her old boss's words floated back to her. *You know he's in love with you.*

No, Daisy thought with dismay. Franck was her father's old friend. He couldn't actually be in love with her.

Could he?

Franck had called her from his home in Los Angeles that morning, saying he'd heard she'd moved to Santa Barbara, just an hour to the north. He'd offered to drive up for a visit. Remembering how he'd burst in at her wedding, she'd been a little uneasy. But he'd explained smoothly, "My dear, I was just trying to keep you from making a big mistake. If you'd listened to me, you wouldn't be going through a divorce now."

Which was true.

Daisy *did* want to get to know Santa Barbara, and look at possible locations for a portrait studio. Living in New York, she'd never learned to drive. When Franck offered to drive her wherever she wanted, even putting a baby seat in the back of his car, how could she refuse? Didn't a person going through a divorce need all the friends she could get?

*Divorce.* Such an ugly word. Every day for the last three weeks, since she'd rented the snug cottage, she'd waited in dread for the legal papers to arrive.

But there was no point putting it off. Leonidas didn't want her. He didn't want Livvy. He was done with them. He didn't care how much he'd hurt them.

Maybe Franck had been right when he'd shouted out at her wedding that Leonidas was a liar who'd killed her father.

Because there was no mercy in her husband's soul. He'd had her father sent to prison for an innocent mistake. For Daisy's own innocent mistake of trying to help him find the Picasso, Leonidas had cut her and their baby out of his life—forever.

With a lump in her throat, Daisy looked at their sweet,

plump-cheeked baby in the sunlight of the California garden. Three-month-old Livvy had fallen asleep in the car and was still tucked snugly into her baby carrier outside.

"Thanks for showing me some of your drawings," Franck said, smiling at her. He considered her thoughtfully. "You're very good at portraits."

"Thanks." She hoped he wasn't about to suggest that she do a drawing of *him*. She felt weary of his company, and a little uncomfortable, too.

The way Franck had looked at her all afternoon was definitely more than *friendly*. Ten minutes before, on their way back to her cottage, he'd invited her to dinner, "to discuss your business options." Yeah, right. She'd been relieved to say no. Thank goodness she had a dog waiting at the cottage who needed to be let out into the garden!

Now Sunny bounded around them happily, sniffing everything from the vibrant rose bushes to the cluster of orange trees, checking on baby Livvy like a mother hen, then running a circle around the perimeter of white picket fence.

The only thing the large golden dog didn't seem to like was Franck.

The dog had growled at him at first sight, when he'd arrived to pick them up in his car. Daisy had chastised her pet, and so Sunny had grudgingly flopped by the stone fireplace to mope. But even now, the normally happy dog kept her distance, giving him the suspicious glare she normally reserved for squirrels.

"Yes," Franck said, stroking his chin as he looked at Daisy. "You have talent. More than I realized. I wonder if…"

Oh, heavens, was he about to proposition her? "If what?"

"I've moved my business to California." His thin face darkened. "Your husband ran me out of New York."

That was news to her. "Leonidas? Why?"

He shook his head. "It doesn't matter. He'll soon be

your ex." Franck smacked his lips—she could swear he did. "Your divorce will make you very wealthy."

The last thing Daisy wanted to do was discuss the financial details of her divorce with Franck Bain. She looked at his sedan parked on the other side of the picket fence, wishing he would leave already. "Um…"

"So obviously you won't need an income. But I wonder," his gaze swept over her, "if you might be interested in doing something with me. For pleasure."

Ugh. The way he said *pleasure* made her cringe. She responded coldly, "What are you talking about?"

He lifted a sparse eyebrow. "You could be part of something big."

"I'm sure you are involved in many big things. Don't let me keep you from them."

"There's a good market in lost masterpieces." He tilted his head slyly. "Especially old portraits."

Daisy stared at him. Unease trickled down her spine. Could he possibly mean…? "What market?"

"Don't pretend you don't understand." He grinned. "How do you think I got so rich? I help clients find the paintings they most desire."

Time seemed to stop beneath the warm California sunshine. "You mean…by creating them?"

Franck shrugged.

"It was you," she whispered. "All this time you said my father was innocent. But you knew he was guilty. You were his accomplice."

Franck shook his head scornfully. "How else do you think Patrick was able to stay home and take care of you after your mother died? *She* brought in the income. His gallery barely made a penny."

She said hoarsely, "I can't believe it…"

"Patrick refused my offer for years. Then he suddenly had to take care of a little kid by himself. He came to me, desperate. We agreed that I would paint, and he'd use his connections to sell the art. We did very well. For years." Franck's reptilian eyes narrowed. "Until he wanted to go for the big score, selling a Picasso. We never should have tried it."

"Why did you, then?" she said in a small voice.

He shrugged. "Your father was worried about you. You'd just flamed out as an artist. And he was sick of selling forgeries to the nouveaux riches. He wanted to leave New York. Move somewhere and start over."

Memory flashed through her, of the night she'd been crying over her failure to sell a single painting.

*We could start over*, her father had told her suddenly. *Move to Santa Barbara.*

*What about your gallery, Dad?*

*Maybe I'd like a change, too. Just one more deal to close, and then...*

Could he have possibly taken such a risk—done something so criminal—just because he couldn't bear to see his daughter cry? Guilt flashed through her.

She glared at Franck. "You sat through his trial every day and never admitted you were his accomplice. You let him go to prison alone!"

He rolled his eyes. "The Picasso was your father's idea. I was happy selling cheap masterpieces to suckers. Selling a Picasso to a billionaire? I never liked the risk." He scowled. "And then your husband ruined everything. I'd done a perfect copy of the Picasso. But I heard last week that Niarxos had chopped it up with a pair of scissors as a kid?" He glowered. "How was I supposed to know? Who *does* that?"

"Someone who's hurting," Daisy whispered over the lump in her throat. Her heart was pounding. The foundation of what she'd thought was true in her life was dissolving beneath her feet.

*I didn't do it, baby*, her father had pleaded. *I swear it on my life. On my love for you.*

Her father had lied. He'd told her what she wanted to hear. What he'd desperately wanted her to believe.

But why had Daisy let herself believe it?

When her mother got so sick, her father had stopped spending time at the gallery, spending it instead at home with his beloved wife, and their young daughter. Yet somehow, his gallery had done better than ever. He'd hired more people. Instead of their family having less money, they'd had *more.*

Why hadn't Daisy ever let herself see the truth?

Because she hadn't wanted to see. Because she'd wanted to believe the best of her father. Because she'd loved him.

And she still loved him. She would have forgiven everything, if he'd just given her the chance...

"Why didn't Dad tell me?" she said brokenly.

Franck shook his head. "He said you had to believe the best of him, or he was afraid that you wouldn't survive."

"That *I* wouldn't survive?" she said slowly. She frowned. "That doesn't make sense. It..."

She had a sudden memory of her father trying to talk to her, the day he'd been questioned by the police.

*Daisy, I've been arrested...* He'd paused. *You should know I'm not perfect—*

*Of course you are, Dad*, she'd rushed to say. *You're perfect. The best man in the world. Don't try to tell me anything different.*

Would he have told her then? If she hadn't made it clear she didn't want to know about his mistakes?

And Leonidas. It was true that she'd never totally forgiven him for what he'd done to her father. She'd tried to forget. She'd told him he was perfect. Because she loved him.

The men she loved had to be perfect.

*I'm not wonderful. I'm not perfect. I'm a selfish, cold bastard,* he'd told her. And she'd insisted he was wrong.

But he wasn't. Leonidas could be selfish. He could be cold. Why couldn't she admit that, and say she loved him anyway?

Rose-colored glasses were a double-edged sword. She'd believed in her father, believed in her husband. She'd boxed them in, pressuring them to live up to that image of perfection, an image no one could live up to for long.

No wonder Leonidas had fled.

She'd insisted on his perfection, as if he were a shining knight on a white charger. And when he'd finally shown his weaknesses, she'd betrayed him, by telling his secrets to some reporter.

The fact that the lost Picasso had been finally found, as she'd heard that morning in the news, did not absolve her. Her cheeks went hot with shame.

Leonidas had been right. She'd betrayed him.

"We could be partners, you and I." Speaking softly in the sunlit garden, Franck moved closer to her. "My hands aren't what they used to be, but I have connections now. Even if you don't need the money after your divorce, you could do the paintings just for fun." He cackled. "Old masters for suckers. Much more satisfying than sketching fat babies and dogs!"

Daisy jerked back, glaring at him. "I *like* fat babies and dogs!"

His forehead furrowed. Seeing rejection in her set jaw, he stiffened, scowling. "Fine." Then his pale blue eyes gleamed. "But you owe me. For all those months I took care of you." He gave an oily smile. "If you won't paint for me, I'll take payment in other ways—"

He grabbed her roughly. She tried to pull away. "What are you doing—don't!"

"Don't you think I deserve a little kindness," he panted,

his long fingers digging into her shoulders, "for all those months I took care of you—"

She struggled desperately as he lowered his head. Before he could force a kiss on her, she screamed—

Then everything happened at once.

Her baby woke and started wailing in the baby carrier...

Her dog rushed toward Franck, showing her teeth with a growl...

Daisy lifted her knee up, hard and sharp, against Franck's groin, causing him to give a choked grunt, and release her...

And—

"Get the hell away from her!"

Leonidas's enraged, deep voice boomed behind her. As Franck was stumbling back from her blow, her husband was suddenly there, vengeful in his black shirt and trousers, his powerful body stepping in front of her. Daisy's mouth parted in shock as Leonidas punched the other man hard in the jaw, knocking him to the ground.

"Don't you dare touch her!"

"Leo," she whispered, wondering if she was dreaming.

His tall, muscular form turned anxiously. "Are you all right, *agape mou*? He did not hurt you?"

Rubbing her shoulders a little, she shook her head, her eyes wide. "I'm all right."

Leonidas exhaled with relief. He scooped up their crying baby, who immediately quieted, comforted in her father's arms. Then he drew Daisy close, searching her gaze intently with his own.

"I'm so sorry," he said in a low voice. "Can you ever forgive me?"

Daisy stared up at Leonidas's handsome face. His jaw was dark with five o'clock shadow, as if he hadn't had time to shave. His usually immaculate clothes were rumpled, as if he'd rushed straight from the airport. His black eyes were vulnerable, stricken.

"Can *I* forgive *you*?" she repeated, bewildered.

"Very touching," Franck snarled at them from the grass.

"Shut up," Daisy told him, at the same moment Leonidas said pleasantly, without looking at the man, "Another word, and I'll set the dog on you."

Their normally goofy, people-loving dog was, indeed, growling at the man threateningly.

As Sunny approached, Franck Bain scrambled back, flinging himself over the white picket fence into a tangle of rose bushes. Daisy heard his sharp yelp followed by swift footsteps. His car engine started with a roar, then he peeled off down the road.

"Sunny!" Daisy's blood was still up as she called her pet back into the middle of the garden. Kneeling into the soft grass, she petted her dog again and again, crooning, "Good girl!" as the dog's tail wagged happily.

"I couldn't understand why you got involved." Behind her, Leonidas's voice was low. "The first time you heard crying in an alley, I didn't know why you insisted on going to see what it was. It seemed better to ignore it."

Still kneeling beside her dog, Daisy turned her head. Her husband stood behind her, tall and broad shouldered. His handsome face was full of emotion.

"You insisted on taking care of the puppy, when you barely had enough money to take care of yourself. It was foolish." He took a deep breath, his dark hair gleaming in the sun. "Why try to save something abandoned? Something so unloved and broken?"

She saw sudden tears in his black eyes.

"Now I understand," he whispered. "Because you did the same with me."

Daisy's lips parted. Rising to her feet, she reached for him. He pulled her into his powerful arms.

"Oh, my darling," Leonidas breathed into her hair, holding her close against his hard-muscled chest. "How can you ever forgive me for leaving you? I thought I could never be the man you needed me to be, and I couldn't bear to let you down. But I never should have run away like a coward..."

"Stop." Daisy put her hand on his rough cheek. "I was wrong about so much. All that time I blamed you for putting an innocent man in prison... Franck admitted that my father was guilty, all along. And I refused to see it. Because I needed my dad to be perfect." She lifted her gaze to his. "Just like I needed my husband to be perfect. I'm so sorry."

"I would give anything to be perfect for you." Holding their precious baby in the crook of one arm, he looked intently into her eyes. "You deserve it, Daisy. But I knew I could never be. I could never be good enough to deserve your love."

She clung to him in her cottage's flower-filled garden, overlooking the wide blue Pacific. "But you can—you *are*—"

"I convinced myself that you and Livvy would be better off without me. But after you left, my soul was empty. Nothing mattered. Even when I finally acquired the Picasso—thanks to you—"

"I heard about that. Was it everything you dreamed of?"

Leonidas looked down at her. "I finally had it, this thing I'd been searching for half my life, and I felt *nothing*. It was just swirls of paint. And I realized that everything I'd ever feared had come true. I'd lost the love of my life, by being too proud and stupid when you tried to save me, by not being brave enough to risk my heart. Now the only thing I fear," he said quietly, "is that I've lost you forever."

Her lips parted. "What did you say? The love of your life?"

"I love you, Daisy." Leonidas looked from her to the small, drowsy baby still cuddled against his hard-muscled arm. "You and Livvy are my life." He took a deep breath. "And I'll spend the rest of that life trying to be perfect for you, trying to be whatever you need me to be—"

"No," she cut him off. His handsome face looked stricken. Reaching her hand up to his rough, unshaven cheek, Daisy said, "You don't need to be perfect, Leo. You don't need to do anything or change anything. I love you. Just as you are."

His dark eyes shone with unshed tears. Taking her hand in his own, he lifted it to his lips and kissed it passionately. *"Agape mou—"*

Sooner or later, we all learn the truth, Daisy thought later. The truth about others, the truth about ourselves. If you could be brave enough to face it. Brave enough to understand, and forgive, and love in spite of everything.

As her husband pulled her against his chest, into the circle of his arms, with their tiny baby tucked tenderly between them, and their dog leaping joyfully around their feet, he lowered his head and kissed her with lips like fire.

And Daisy really knew, at last, what love was.

It wasn't about rose-colored glasses or knights on white horses. It wasn't about being perfect. It was about seeing each other, flaws and all. Loving everything, the sunshine and shadow inside every soul. And not being afraid.

As Leo kissed her beneath the orange trees, with their feet in the grass and dirt, it was better than perfect.

It was real.

Leonidas looked out of the back window of their West Village mansion with dismay. Amid a snowy January in New York City, another foot of snow had fallen the night before.

In their yard, Sunny was leaping back and forth through the blanket of white, chasing a terrified-looking squirrel. Snow clung to their dog's golden fur, including her ears and eyelashes.

"This is a disaster," Leonidas groaned to his wife, who was watching from the breakfast nook.

She looked up at him tranquilly, turning a page of her book. "How so?"

"If we let her inside again, Mrs. Berry will kill us." He sighed. "Sunny will just have to live in the yard from now on. I'll build her a dog house."

"*You* will?"

"I'll hire someone," he conceded. "Because Sunny can never come back inside. She'd track snow and dirt all over the floors and make the whole house smell of dog."

"No, she won't," his wife said serenely, turning another page. "You're going to give her a bath."

He looked back with alarm. "Me?"

Daisy smiled. "Who better?"

Leonidas's eyes lingered on her. Even after a full night of lovemaking, his wife looked more desirable than ever, sitting at their breakfast table in a lush silk nightgown and robe, sipping black tea and reading a book, as baby Livvy, now seven months old, batted toys in a baby play gym on the floor.

Leonidas said with mock severity, "Do you really think you can give me orders and I'll just obey? Like a pet?"

She looked up from her book, her pale green eyes limpid and wide, fringed with dark lashes. Tilting her head, she bit her pink lower lip. Her shoulders moved slightly, causing the neckline of her robe to gape, hinting at the cleavage of her full breasts beneath the silk. His heartbeat quickened.

"Fine," he said. "I'll give the dog a bath. Not because you asked me. Because I want to."

Her smile widened, and she turned back to her book, calmly taking another sip of tea. He watched her lips press enticingly against the edge of the china cup, edged with twenty-four-carat gold.

"Maybe we can have a little quality time later," he suggested.

Daisy looked at him sideways beneath her lashes. "Maybe."

Glancing at their innocent baby, who seemed to be staring at them with big brown eyes, drool coming from her mouth as she'd just gotten her first tooth, Leonidas sat down next to his wife at the table. "Maybe we can have a *lot* of quality time later."

Smiling, she put her hand on his cheek. "Maybe."

They'd been married for nearly a year, but for Leonidas, it felt like they'd just met. Every day, he felt a greater rush, a greater thrill, at the joy of being with her.

But at the same time, he felt safe. He felt adored. He felt…home.

In the four months since they'd returned to New York, many things had changed. Daisy had become the most in-demand portrait artist in the city, all the more celebrated because she took so few clients. "I'm already so busy with our baby, and you," she'd said. "I simply don't have time for more right now."

Who was Leonidas to argue? Whenever she was ready to become a full-time artist, he suspected Daisy would take over the world. He felt so proud to be her man. Especially since, as she often told him, he was the one who'd given her the courage, and inspiration, to draw again.

He was home more now, too. His company was in the process of hiring a new CEO, as Leonidas had decided to step back and merely be the largest shareholder. "I don't have time for more," he'd told his wife tenderly. "I'm already so busy with the baby. And you."

He was glad to be leaving the company in good shape. The shocking scandal of his birth, building on the soap-opera-like quality of his wedding and fatherhood—which had already gone viral on social media— had created so much outrageous publicity that Liontari's brands had all gone up an average of six percent, causing a huge leap in shareholder value. Even the story that, as a rebellious, heartsick teenager, Leonidas had chopped up his mother's Picasso with scissors when she abandoned him, somehow had added a darker, sexier edge to some of his more traditional brands. Even the most elite, art-loving clientele had forgiven Leonidas for it, after he'd donated the Picasso to a museum last month.

He'd once believed that if people ever learned the truth about him, they would destroy him with pitchforks and scorn. Instead, he'd become some sort of folk hero. He'd heard rumors of a telenovela in development, based on his life.

People were complicated, he thought. Success could be fleeting. All you had to do was look at Franck Bain, once so successful, to see that. A week after the man had fled Daisy's rented cottage in California, he'd been arrested in Japan for trying to pass off a supposedly lost Van Gogh.

Leonidas shook his head. He couldn't pretend he regretted the man's imprisonment. He deserved it. Though Leonidas liked to believe he was a changed man, an understanding, loving person who would never think of taking vengeance on others, he was glad he didn't have to prove it with Bain.

And it left Leonidas free to move on with his life, to more important things, like spending time with his wife, his child and his friends. They were all that mattered. The people who loved him. He loved them, too. Daisy and Livvy most of all.

He looked down at his wife now as she sat at the kitchen table. She gave him a mysterious smile. He was intrigued.

"Are you hiding something from me?"

"Wouldn't you like to know."

"Yes," he whispered, leaning forward. Drawing his hand

down her long dark hair, he moved his lips against her ear, soft as breath. "And you're going to tell me."

He felt her shiver beneath his touch. He ran his hands over the blush-colored silk, softly over her shoulders, to her back, to her full breasts...

Her *very* full breasts.

He blinked, then pulled back, his eyes wide as he searched his wife's gaze. "Are you... You're not..."

"Not pregnant? I'm not."

He exhaled, shocked by his own disappointment. He hadn't even been thinking about trying for another baby, not yet. After all, Livvy was only seven months old. Was he really ready for another baby in the house?

More mayhem. More chaos. More love.

Yes, Leonidas realized. Yes, he was. He wanted another baby. Or six. A large family, big enough for a football team—that sounded perfect.

But there was no rush. He'd just keep putting in the practice, intensely and passionately, every night in bed. A smile traced the edges of his lips. It was a tough job, but someone had to do it.

"It's all right," he said huskily, lowering his head toward hers. "We'll keep trying..."

Daisy put her hand on his chest, stopping him before he could kiss her.

"I'm not," her green eyes twinkled, "*not* pregnant."

His forehead furrowed as he searched her gaze. Then he sucked in his breath. "Not *not* pregnant?"

Daisy ducked her head, her smile suddenly shy. "It must have happened at Christmas. Maybe Christmas Eve. That time under the tree..."

"*Agape mou,*" he said, dazzled with joy. Taking her in his arms, he kissed his wife passionately at the kitchen table. As he held her, he wondered what he'd done to deserve such happiness.

Then the dog door thudded loudly, and suddenly there was a large wet hairy dog between them, shaking water and snow all over the room, and their baby girl gurgled with laughter. As Daisy pulled back from her husband's embrace, her eyes danced as she laughed, too.

And Leonidas knew their joy would last forever. Their lives wouldn't be all laughter, for sure. But they'd build their future together, day by day, through snow and sun, rain and roses.

It would never be perfect. But it would be happy.

Just like him. Once, he'd been lost. He'd been broken. But Daisy had loved him anyway. He'd learned the meaning of love from the woman who, in spite of his flaws, had given him her precious heart.

\* \* \* \* \*

# COMING SOON!

We really hope you enjoyed reading this book.
If you're looking for more romance
be sure to head to the shops when
new books are available on

## Thursday 17th
## July

To see which titles are coming soon, please visit
**millsandboon.co.uk/nextmonth**

# MILLS & BOON

# LET'S TALK
# *Romance*

For exclusive extracts, competitions and special offers, find us online: